H█████ ███ ███ █████ ██ ██████ Scotland
lo██ ██ ███y█████ ██e else, hav███ ███ to ████ ███ ople and
the country (despite nine months of rain and three months of
bad weather). Of Polish descent, her father was stationed in St
Andrews during the war, and spoke so fondly of the town that
she applied to study at the university, and was awarded a place.

She has worked as a researcher, a mathematics teacher, an IT
officer and finally in senior management, a post she left to write
full time. She is the author of the Von Valenti novels and now lives
in a fishing village in Fife.

Also by Hania Allen

The Polish Detective
Clearing the Dark
The Family Business

THE
ICE HOTEL

Hania Allen

CONSTABLE

CONSTABLE

First published in Great Britain in 2021 by Constable

This edition published in 2021 by Constable

1 3 5 7 9 10 8 6 4 2

A CIP catalogue record for this book
is available from the British Library.

ISBN: 978-1-47213-525-4

Typeset in Bembo by Photoprint, Torquay
Printed and bound in Great Britain by Clays Ltd, Elcograf S.p.A.

Papers used by Constable are from well-managed forests and other
responsible sources.

MIX
Paper from
responsible sources
FSC
www.fsc.org   FSC® C104740

Constable
An imprint of
Little, Brown Book Group
Carmelite House
50 Victoria Embankment
London EC4Y 0DZ

An Hachette UK Company
www.hachette.co.uk

www.littlebrown.co.uk

To Shelagh Graham, whom I wish I had known better

CHAPTER 1

'It's happened again, hasn't it, Maggie?' Dr Langley was watching me, her face a mask. 'Tell me about it.'

'I've told you before. It's always the same.'

'Tell me again.'

Again? Why did she want to hear what she'd heard so many times before? But she was the doctor.

'It's night,' I began. 'I'm in a dark room, with windows from floor to ceiling. The windows have shutters.'

'Are they open?'

I made a point of not answering directly whenever she interrupted. 'The moonlight makes patterns of light on the floor. But I don't linger because I've seen the door in the far wall. I skirt the furniture, which is covered with dustsheets. As I reach the door, something makes me look back. The furniture is gliding across the floor, the pieces zigzagging past each other. I hurry into the next room, and the rooms after that. Then I'm there.' My heart began to pound as the memory returned. 'The bathroom is large, with no windows. It's flooded with a harsh light.'

'Where's the light coming from if there are no windows?'

She hadn't asked this question before. 'I don't know,' I said. 'Is it important?'

'Everything you say is important.' She smiled. 'Please go on.'

1

'The bathroom is tiled in white – the walls, the ceiling, the floor. The bath is in the middle of the room, sunk into the ground like a swimming pool. The water is level with the floor, and the surface is still.'

I hesitated, as I always did at this point, because I felt a constriction in my chest. 'I look into the bath but it's too murky to see. Yet I know something lies hidden under the water. I stretch a hand towards the taps and try to pull out the plug. But I can't shift it. The chain is lying along the bottom and something heavy is weighing it down. I grip it with both hands and tug sharply. The thing at the bottom stirs, as though it's wakening. Then I know I'll have to do what I've dreaded since entering the house. I plunge my hands into the water and slide them down the chain. They're so numb I can barely feel them. Icy water spills over the edge and soaks into my feet.' I squeezed my eyes shut in an effort to blot out the image. 'I pull hard, straining against the weight, and the thing shifts and starts to rise. The water thickens, changing colour from brown to dark red.' My eyes flew open.

'Breathe deeply. You're nearly there.'

'I try to loosen my grip, but I can't. I hear something behind me. I turn round. The room's empty. The door's disappeared. It's tiled over, become part of the wall. I pull and pull, and the thing in the bath reaches the top and breaks the surface.' The last words came out in a rush.

'And you wake up.'

I nodded, seized by a sudden fear. It was as though tentacles were coiling round my throat. I opened my mouth wide, panting, and struggled for control until my breathing grew regular.

'How does waking feel?' Dr Langley said gently.

I ran a hand over my face. 'I'm in a sweat and out of breath. I think I must have cried out. The woman in the flat above gave me a strange look when I passed her on the stairs.'

Dr Langley placed her palms together as though in prayer. For a second, I imagined her mumbling in Latin. 'What do you think is in the bath, Maggie?'

Another question she hadn't asked before. I wondered whether she was trying to trick me but I dismissed the thought. She was my doctor. 'I've no idea,' I said. 'But there was one thing that was different. The smell.'

'Describe it.'

'It was dank, like a pond. Or a river.'

And laced with something impossible to describe, something I'd smelt in the chapel at the Ice Hotel. Oh, God, that chapel. My stomach lurched. I swallowed hard, trying to stop the retching.

Dr Langley rose quickly and walked to the sideboard, her shoes squeaking on the polished parquet. She poured noisily from a crystal decanter. I slumped back, listening to the tone change as the glass filled with water.

The doctor's office was like none I'd seen. And I'd seen a few. The sideboard was antique. I'd asked about it at our first session, more to keep the conversation going than from genuine interest. Above it, a gilt-framed mirror hung from the picture rail. There was a time when I'd have leant forward to admire my reflection. Not any more.

'Drink this,' she said, handing me the glass.

I wrapped myself in the powdery scent of her perfume, and listened to the room's sounds. They seemed strangely magnified: the ticking of the grandfather clock, the distant traffic through the partly shuttered windows. I drained the glass, holding on to these sounds as though sanity depended on it.

She returned to the desk.

'I know I'm not supposed to smoke in here,' I said, 'but would you mind if I did?'

It was the first time I'd asked this question. The expression in her eyes changed. So, after all these sessions, I could still surprise her. The thought gave me a cat-got-the-cream sense of satisfaction.

'I didn't know you smoked,' she said.

'I started yesterday,' I lied.

'I'm afraid smoking is no longer allowed.'

'Oh, well, no harm in trying.'

She smiled then, a wide smile that showed her perfect teeth. A Julia Roberts smile. She was older than Julia Roberts, her hands one of the giveaways, putting her in her early fifties. She was slim for her age, without the leanness of women on permanent diets. Her sharp trouser suit and silk blouse, ruffled at the neck and cuffs, would have been purchased on one of her trips to Edinburgh. Dundee didn't sell clothes like that. She wore only a trace of make-up over skin that was largely unlined. But she'd let her hair go grey, even though the cut was modern. If she'd dyed it, it would have taken ten years off her age. Her most remarkable features, however, were her eyes. They were large and doe-like. And they saw everything. *If anyone can help you, Maggie, she can.* My GP's words.

From somewhere within the building a door slammed, shredding my nerves. 'Why am I having this dream?' I said, trying to keep my voice steady.

She studied her finely manicured hands. The nails were varnished in the palest rose. I thought of my own, ragged, bitten to the quick, and slid my hands under my knees.

'You need to bear in mind, Maggie, that there's rarely a simple explanation for a dream.' She was in teacher mode now. 'Dreams consist of elements, which have to be disentangled. That's not always easy. In yours, some associations are clear. The smell of river water, for example.' She leant forward. 'But the thing you can't see, the thing that's under the water – that holds the key. It's something you want to discover, which is why you can't release

4

the chain and the door disappears, trapping you in the bathroom and forcing you to make the discovery. But it's also something you dread discovering, so your brain wakes you before the thing reaches the surface.'

'And the water turning to blood?'

'That's not so surprising, given what happened at the Ice Hotel. But the white tiles.' She made an arch with her fingers. 'Your subconscious is drawing your attention to them. My suspicion is you've seen them somewhere. Can you remember?'

'I can't remember what day it is, let alone where I've seen white tiles,' I said, hoping she wouldn't realise I was lying.

'Then that's something we'll keep working on.'

'And when I find out what's under the water, I'll stop having the dream?'

'It's equally likely you'll stop having it before you find out.'

I rested my head against the back of the chair and stared at the ceiling. I hadn't always had dreams. My childhood and early teens had passed without them. Dreams had appeared at the onset of adulthood and, with it, responsibility. But the dream that had reduced me to a fraction of my former self was recent, brought on by the terrible events earlier in the year. Weeks would pass without it, then, for no apparent reason, three would come consecutively, like buses. I wondered whether the others who'd been at the Ice Hotel had dreams. Liz might, although I doubted Mike would. But not Harry. Not now.

Dr Langley's voice broke into my thoughts. 'You're making progress.' She was writing, adding today's observations to her case notes. 'Don't you feel it?'

'I feel as if I'm living someone else's life.'

She replaced the cap on her fountain pen, then blotted and closed the file. She always did it in that order. I was fascinated both by this little ritual and by the medical profession's apparent disregard for the ballpoint.

'We went a little further today,' she said. 'I see evidence of improvement each time we meet.'

'The men in white coats aren't coming for me, then?'

'When you can recall your experiences without reliving them, you'll be through the worst.' She searched my face. 'But there's something you're holding back. Something you're not telling me.'

I kept my expression blank. It was a look I'd perfected in recent weeks.

'I'm not saying you're doing it deliberately.' She hesitated. 'But you've still to tell me what happened at the Ice Hotel.'

What did she want to know? It had been in all the newspapers.

'You're back at work in the New Year.' She had the file open again and was scanning the pages. 'A pharmaceutical company, isn't it?'

She played these little games. She knew the name, but wanted to see if I remembered it. She knew everything about my life: my childhood, my time at university, my first job in Newcastle. And the move to Dundee.

'It's Bayne Pharmaceuticals, Dr Langley,' I said, my voice level. 'They've given me six months' leave of absence. My boss has been brilliant about everything.'

'And how are you sleeping? On the nights you don't have the dream,' she added.

'Having a drink before bed helps.'

I wondered if she'd guessed I needed to drink myself into oblivion. Even then, I rarely slept through. The worst hour was three in the morning: I'd wake and, unable to sleep, would chain-smoke in bed. But she knew I drank before our sessions. She couldn't fail to notice the odour on my breath. I rarely went to see her without at least two drinks inside me. The first gave my brain cells a wake-up call, but a second was needed to make them fully functioning.

She was watching me. 'You *will* get over this, Maggie. But you've got to give yourself a chance.'

I looked into her eyes, wondering why, after all these months, she still believed it. Probably because she didn't know the whole story. Nor did I, come to that. Yet until I did, there'd be no recovery and the dream would overwhelm me. All it needed was a single sharp tug at the thread of my fraying sanity, and it would unravel completely.

'It isn't just about what happened there,' she said, 'although those events were terrible enough. Something else is behind this dream.' She paused. 'And you've come to the same conclusion.'

After a silence, I said, 'The police got it wrong. They got it all wrong. I need to know what really happened.'

'And what's stopping you?'

'I might discover something that . . .' I tailed off, unable to find the words.

'Something you want to discover, yet something you dread discovering?' she said softly. 'The thing in the bath?'

'If I discover it, will it release me from this . . .' I gave my head a small shake '. . . from this hell?'

'Nothing else will. And I think you know that. But we can make the journey together.' Her gaze held mine. 'Will you tell me what happened?'

I nodded slowly.

'Start at the beginning, then. Start with how you came to be at the Ice Hotel.'

So, as the wind seized the windows and rattled them, wailing to be let in, I told Dr Langley everything.

CHAPTER 2

It was Harry who'd raised the idea.

We were in Liz's back garden. Summer was slipping away, making a last desperate attempt to survive with a spell of balmy weather. Although the time for shorts and T-shirts had passed, there was enough heat in the pale September sun to warm our upturned faces.

I was watching Liz's children, Annie and Lucy. They were running round the plum tree, playing a chasing game I recognised from childhood, their shrieking laughter eclipsing the droning of the wasps that were drunk on the rotting plums. The girls had inherited their mother's looks – creamy skin, blonde hair and blue eyes – but their hair wasn't straight like hers, hanging instead in short heavy ringlets, which bounced as they moved. The curls were held back with hair slides and, as Annie and Lucy were identical twins, the colour of the slides was the only way to tell them apart.

Liz Hallam was the sister I'd never had, my closest friend with whom I'd passed a blissful childhood and teens. We lost touch, then after her divorce she'd moved from London to Dundee to start a new life with her children. I'd run into her two years earlier, and we'd taken up our friendship as though we'd never put it down. It was she who'd introduced me to Harry Auchinleck, 'a gay gentleman in his fifties' and a professor at the University of Dundee. An accredited Cordon Bleu cook, he shared Liz's love of entertaining, and most of our Sundays were spent at his legendary buffet lunches. Harry and I hit it off immediately, and it wasn't long before the three of us became inseparable.

Liz was picking over the last of the strawberries, examining each one before popping it into her mouth. As she chewed, the velvety mole on her cheek jiggled up and down. I'd once tried to give myself a beauty spot with an eyebrow pencil, but had smudged it without realising, and spent the entire evening at a party looking as though I had a tadpole on my face.

Harry had just mooted the idea of the holiday. He was sitting under the parasol, wearing his battered Panama hat. He'd exchanged his spectacles for an ancient pair of sunglasses that were held together with sticky tape. 'So we're agreed, then,' he said, pushing them further up his nose. 'And you're sure next spring will work for you, Liz?'

'Absolutely,' she said, running a hand over her ponytail. 'I can leave the girls with their grandparents, or there's a friend at work, Siobhan. She's awfully fond of the children and has helped out in the past. But let me get my phone so I can check the dates.'

As she passed me, moving with the idle grace that comes naturally to some women, I caught a trace of her signature perfume, Paris, by Yves Saint Laurent.

'It was too easy, Harry,' I said. 'I was certain that prising Liz from her children would be much more difficult.' I leant back, drenching myself in the heady scent of jasmine.

'My dear, gift horses and mouths spring to mind. If only persuasion were as easy with my head of department.'

I smiled, my eyes still closed. 'I thought those travel brochures you brought might be tempting Fate.'

'The important thing is that she's agreed to take a holiday. She's run ragged half the time, and it's healthy to loosen the umbilical cord a bit.' He lowered his voice unnecessarily. 'I'm delighted you're able to come. It would have been improper for me to take her away, even though I'm a crusty professor, old enough to be her father, and everyone knows I bat for the other side.'

'Harry, no one bothers about that sort of thing these days.'

At that point, Liz returned with her phone. She scanned the screen. 'March, you said? How about the first week?'

'Has to be second week, my dear.'

I glanced at him, surprised at the firmness in his voice. 'I thought you had that conference in Rome. Aren't you the chairman or something?'

'I've decided to cancel.' His tone discouraged further questions. 'Now, children, I know we discussed a beach holiday, but I've rather set my mind on skiing.'

'Fine by me,' Liz said. 'France or Switzerland?'

He poured himself another Pimm's. 'Sweden.'

'I didn't know there was skiing in Sweden,' I said. 'Seems an odd choice.'

'I was there briefly last year, and I'd really like to see the place properly.'

'Okay, where are the brochures?' I said, watching the twins.

They'd stripped to their knickers and were running under the arcing jets from Liz's garden-watering contraption. Thoroughly soaked, they charged at Harry and banged into the table, upsetting the jug of Pimm's. They pressed against him, leaving wet marks on his trousers.

Annie, the older of the twins by five minutes, spoke with the authority conveyed by her status. 'Do the trick with the flower, Harry.'

His round face broke into creases, happiness making him

10

instantly younger. He removed the red carnation pinned to his cricket whites and, with an impressive sleight of hand, made it disappear. He held up both hands, palms outwards, for the girls to inspect, then reached over and pulled the carnation from behind Lucy's ear. The girls squealed with delight.

Lucy jumped up and down. 'Do it again, Harry. Do it again.'

So Harry did it again. I'd seen this trick many times, as had the girls, but we never tired of it. Fortunately, neither did Harry.

Liz shooed the twins away, and they skipped off happily. 'There's skiing near the border with Norway,' she said, poring over a catalogue.

'Nothing further south?' he said, disappointment in his voice.

'That's not where the mountains are, I'm afraid.' She turned the pages, frowning in concentration, then sat up so quickly she spilt her drink over her jeans. 'Oh, wow, forget skiing. This is it. This is the one.' She read from the brochure:

'*For a winter holiday with a difference, why not spend a week discovering the spectacular scenery of Lapland, the land of the Northern Lights? The highlight of this unforgettable experience is a stay in the unique Ice Hotel.*'

'Ice Hotel?' Harry said.

She read on: '*Set near the town of Kiruna, the Ice Hotel is built entirely of ice and snow − a staggering 30,000 tons of snow and 10,000 tons of ice are used in its construction. Each spring the Ice Hotel melts and each winter it is rebuilt to a different design.*'

'A building made of *ice*? Not sure the old constitution will stand it.'

'We're not in the Ice Hotel the whole week, sweetheart. Four nights in a nearby hotel.' She looked up, her expression anxious. 'Please, Harry, let's go. We can do skiing some other time.'

He smiled faintly. 'Of course, my dear, if that's what you've set your heart on. But where exactly is Kiruna?'

'North of the Arctic Circle. There's an airport, so it's not exactly in the sticks.'

'The Arctic Circle.' He spoke quietly, almost to himself. 'A fair distance from Stockholm, then, but if there's an airport I could fly there.'

I tried to catch his eye. Was it my imagination, or was he deliberately not looking at me? First he'd cancelled attendance at the Rome conference, which he'd spent months organising, and now he was muttering about flying to Stockholm. Something wasn't right.

'You're awfully quiet, Mags,' Liz said. She handed me the brochure. 'Here, take a look.'

I studied the photograph. I was mildly disappointed: I'd expected a tall, tiered building, white and heavily decorated like a wedding cake. But the Ice Hotel was an elongated igloo with low rectangular structures on either side. It squatted against the darkening sky like a monstrous pale toad. And it wasn't white. It was blue – faintly, but distinctly, blue.

There was one other photograph. The caption read: *A guest in one of the Ice Hotel's bedrooms*. A girl wearing ski-suit, fur hat and gloves was sitting on a bed covered with animal skins. Frosted snakes curled behind her head, like an anaemic Medusa's, but she seemed oblivious, leaning back, smiling radiantly. With a shock of recognition, I saw that she was leaning against a headboard made of ice, and the snakes were the curved patterns.

I ran a finger over the outline of the building. An uneven glow radiated from its depths, as though the bloated toad had swallowed fire. It was surreal, scary and magnificent. And then I knew that I had to see it.

Liz took my silence for hesitation. 'Come on, Mags, it'll be a hoot and a half.'

I looked up. 'Oh, yes,' I said softly. 'Let's do it.'

She laughed, a light ringing sound, like a bell, and pushed Harry playfully. He pretended to fall off the chair, scattering the brochures.

He nudged his sunglasses on to the bridge of his nose, and peered at the catalogue. 'My God, but look at the cost. I can't afford this. I'm on the edge of ruin, as it is.'

'There's a special offer, sweetheart. If we book within seven days, it's half-price. We really need to do this tomorrow at the very latest.'

'Only seven days? How very awkward. Even with the discount, it's a bit steep. What sort of people can afford this sort of holiday? I'm a humble academic, remember.'

'Ah, but it'll be fantastic,' she said, squeezing his arm. 'The holiday of a lifetime. You can mortgage the Rubens.'

'Nice if I had one to mortgage. There's nothing for it. I'll have to write another book.'

'You do know you won't be able to wear carnations in the Ice Hotel, don't you? They'll shrivel at those temperatures.'

'Ha, that's not the only thing that'll shrivel, dear girl.'

I listened as they made plans.

'Look, there's a website,' Liz was saying. 'We can book online. Shall we use my laptop?'

I lay back, warmed by the sun, trying to imagine a night in a building made of ice. I closed my eyes and pictured the gleaming igloo. But something had changed. The light was dwindling, fading slowly at first, then more quickly until, with a bright flicker, like the sudden rekindling of dying embers, it vanished. The Ice Hotel darkened, growing menacing against the livid sky.

I opened my eyes, touched by a strange fear.

Liz was on her feet. Her eyes were shining. 'Come on, if you're coming, Mags.'

The feeling passed. My excitement returned and I followed them indoors. In her office, Liz made the booking. With a few clicks, our fate was sealed.

It was March of the following year, and the plane was approaching the runway at Stockholm airport. Harry was wedged between us, squeezing our hands tightly. He'd developed a fear of flying years before after his plane had landed badly at Charles de Gaulle airport. Sweat had broken out on his forehead and his eyelids were fluttering. Although he'd taken enough temazepam to knock out a horse, it had done nothing to reduce his strength, and I winced as he crushed my fingers.

I glanced across at Liz. 'You okay? You look a bit preoccupied.'

'I'll be fine once we've landed and I can call the twins.' She looked away. 'I'm just awfully worried they'll be suffering from separation anxiety.'

'The twins, Liz? Or you?'

She threw me a lopsided smile. It was clear she was finding it difficult away from her children. I disentangled myself from Harry and squeezed her fingers. Her hands were cold.

I wondered whether Harry had caught the conversation. His eyes were closed, his breathing shallow. I thought he was asleep but I felt his body stiffen as the wheels touched the tarmac.

An hour later, in the main airport café, we were waiting for our flight to Kiruna to be called. Harry looked queasy, Liz was drinking espresso, and I was demolishing a second breakfast.

Liz glanced at the smorgasbord. 'Keep eating like that, Mags, and you can kiss goodbye to that hour-and-a-half-glass figure.'

I pushed the plate away, smiling. My metabolism allowed me to eat as much as I liked. But my smile faded as I saw Harry's complexion. How would he manage in a twenty-seater plane?

14

As if reading my thoughts, he said, 'Could one of you children please remind me to take my pills before we board? Otherwise you'll have to scrape me off the ceiling.'

'Shush a minute, listen to this,' Liz was saying. Her eyes were glued to the large TV screen. 'It's a news clip about a murder. There's a picture of a hotel. I can't understand very much – it's in Swedish.'

The hotel was a six-storey, stone-faced building. A blue-and-yellow flag fluttered wildly over the canopied entrance.

'I think I know what this is,' Harry said, nodding at the screen. 'The Stockholm hotel murders. But I don't understand – it was over and done with some time ago. Why has it reared its ugly head now?'

An English translation appeared, ticker-tape style, across the screen.

He leant forward, squinting. 'A year on, they still haven't caught the perpetrator, although the police say the net is closing. That's something at least.'

'You know about this?' I said, surprised.

He nodded slowly. 'Last year, there was a series of gruesome murders in a large Stockholm hotel. In more than one hotel, now that I remember. All very Grand Guignol. The victims were dispatched in particularly grisly ways.' He lowered his voice. 'One of the murders was so terrible that the details were kept from the press.'

Liz was staring at him. 'How do you know so much about it, Harry?'

'I was at a conference in Uppsala when it happened. We got a daily blow-by-blow account, so to speak. Uppsala is not far from Stockholm so, as you can imagine, we were all rather alarmed. I think everyone who stayed in a Swedish hotel at the time was. But then it all stopped suddenly.' He hesitated. 'There can be only

15

one reason why this has surfaced now. There must have been another death.' He turned to the screen but the news had finished and, in place of the hotel, there was a weather map.

Liz frowned. 'Perhaps Sweden wasn't such a good choice of location, Mags.'

'Oh, come on, show me a country that doesn't have murders. Anyway, we won't be anywhere near Stockholm.'

'I told you we should have gone for a beach holiday.'

'You did not, you little fibber,' I said, grinning.

I turned to Harry, hoping to engage him as my ally, but he was staring at a point behind me. His eyes were wide with excitement. I turned round.

Two men had entered.

Both were tall, six foot or more, and well built. The older was dressed impeccably, the cut of his clothes hinting that they'd been tailor-made. His green Harris Tweed jacket was buttoned over a cream roll-neck sweater, which he was fingering at the throat as though it was too tight. His trousers, which lacked the usual faded look of brown corduroy, were sharply creased, the creases saying more about him than anything else.

He held his head confidently, studying the room with an air of boredom, like a well-fed lion surveying his territory. As he moved his head, our eyes locked for a second, but he looked past me immediately, not interested in what he'd seen. He had the pale, unlined skin of someone who stays out of the sun, and a thin mouth set in a sneer as though nothing was up to his usual standard. His hair, styled to disguise that it was receding, was the same salt-and-pepper colour as Harry's. There was an unmistakable aura about him. It took me only a second to recognise it. It was power. And he reeked of it.

His companion, casually dressed in sports clothes, had the same hooked nose and brown eyes, but darker hair. He seemed nervous and fumbled in his carry-on bag, dropping his mobile phone with a clatter.

'He's here,' Harry said, reverence in his voice. 'He's actually here. I'm in the same room as Wilson Bibby.'

'Wilson who?' I said.

'Wilson Bibby the Third.' His eyes were riveted on the men. 'Of the Bibby Foundation.'

'I've never heard of it,' I said, my curiosity rising. 'Is it a charity?'

'I prefer to call it a charitable foundation,' he said stiffly. He seemed unsure whether to continue. 'Years ago, I applied to the Foundation for a grant. They looked kindly on my application, and have been funding my research ever since.'

'I take it you're talking about the older man,' Liz said. 'He looks terribly serious. Have you met him?'

'Good heavens, one simply doesn't meet a man like Wilson Bibby. He's far too important.'

'If he's that important, why is he in an airport café like everyone else?' I said.

'I think, my dear, it's because he's travelling incognito. He's been the victim of several failed kidnap attempts. And there was a well-publicised stalking case a couple of years ago.'

I studied Wilson Bibby with growing interest. He wasn't acting like a man afraid of being kidnapped. 'What else does he do, apart from giving money to deserving academics?'

'He's a benefactor in other ways. He's used some of his billions to establish a charity for poor children in South Carolina.'

'Why South Carolina?'

'His family hails from Charleston. They go back several generations. I think one of them fought at Gettysburg. At least, that's what Bibby claims. But, then, every American I've met from the south has an ancestor who fought at Gettysburg.'

Wilson was speaking into a mobile phone. His call finished, he handed the phone to the younger man, who snapped it shut.

'His manners are said to be impeccable.' Harry smiled knowingly. 'Forget truth and justice, my dear. Charm is definitely the American Way. He's a real southern gentleman. And he keeps a stable of mistresses. But you'd expect that of a real southern gentleman.'

The men made for a nearby table, Wilson in the lead, his companion shouldering both sets of carry-on luggage.

'Who's the other one?' Liz said.

'His son, Marcellus.' The admiration was gone from Harry's voice. 'He used to be part of the New York set, an *enfant terrible*. It's widely known that his father threatened to disinherit him unless he mended his ways and settled down to something meaningful. Now he helps run the Foundation – he's the one I correspond with when it's time to renew my grant. He seems well disposed towards academics but, by all accounts, Wilson keeps him on a tight leash.'

'How do you know so much about them?' I said.

'My dear, when you depend on external funding for your research, it's politic to find out what you can about those who provide it. I follow the fortunes of the Bibbys with great interest. Take Marcellus, for example. I see the name doesn't ring a bell. You don't remember that brouhaha in the media about him? It would have been a year ago.'

I shook my head.

'A New York socialite was found dead of an overdose in her Manhattan apartment. The police claimed Marcellus had been with her on the night she died, but there was nothing conclusive in the way of evidence. His fingerprints were all over the place, of course, but that's hardly surprising as they were seeing each other at the time.'

'I take it that, as he's here, he wasn't charged.'

'Word was that his father pulled a few strings.' Harry smiled grimly. 'Marcellus may have had something to do with the incident, but his father has the clout to have things hushed up. It was after that that we heard less about Marcellus's wild ways, and more about his work with the Foundation.'

The men were sitting not far from us. Wilson ignored the No Smoking signs and lit a cigar, puffing vigorously. A cloud of smoke drifted to our table, carrying with it the rich aroma of expensive tobacco. He murmured something to his son, who rose quickly and made his way towards the self-service counter. As he passed our table, he stared at me and continued to stare until he collided with a woman holding a tray of food. I turned away, in time to catch the smile on Liz's face.

Harry was fidgeting, apparently trying to make up his mind about something. With a decisive movement, he scraped his chair back. Wilson turned at the sound, frowning as he saw Harry bearing down on him. His mouth twisted into a *moue* of distaste, and he scanned the room rapidly.

Harry was all politeness. 'Mr Bibby, my name is Henry Auchinleck. I'm a professor at the University of Dundee.'

Bibby gaped, his cigar halfway to his mouth.

'In Scotland,' Harry said, as though Bibby might not know where Dundee was. 'My research into modern defence strategies has been funded for many years by your Foundation. I want to take this opportunity to thank you for making it possible. You see, our British funding councils are not predisposed to supporting my area of research, but your Foundation has had the foresight so to do.'

I could almost smell Harry's obsequiousness. I didn't know whether to be amused or appalled. Liz was gazing at him with a look of anguish.

Bibby nodded briefly. Then, drawing on his cigar, he turned away.

For a second Harry stood, unsure of what to do. He returned slowly to our table. 'He might at least have said something,' he muttered, sitting down.

Liz stroked his arm. 'Don't take it personally, sweetheart. I should imagine he has grateful people approaching him all the time. He must get rather fed up with it.' She shot Bibby a look. 'But ignoring you like that was dreadfully rude.' She didn't lower her voice. 'What a bastard.'

I glanced around. 'Once again, Liz, but this time say it a bit louder. I don't think everyone in the room quite caught that.'

Marcellus had returned. He placed the tray in front of his father, and arranged the coffee so it was within easy reach. A waiter approached and, pointing to the No Smoking sign, said something I couldn't catch. Wilson shrugged and, with a bored expression, stubbed the remains of the cigar on the underside of the table.

'I've got it,' Liz said suddenly. 'It was Marcia. The woman who died of an overdose. Her name was Marcia Vandenberg. It was last year, wasn't it, Harry?'

'Well remembered, my dear.'

'A bit of a bitch, apparently. She had affairs with half the men on Wall Street. She made enemies, mostly among their wives. Really silly of her to do that. Anyway, there was a feature about the overdose in *Hello!* magazine, but Marcellus wasn't mentioned – I would have remembered a name like his.'

'Then it looks as if Wilson did indeed hush things up,' I said.

Intrigued, I leant forward and studied Marcellus. He was lighting another cigar for his father, waiting patiently while Wilson puffed, taking his time. Neither man seemed to notice the irate waiter bearing down on them.

★ ★ ★

We were boarding the flight to Kiruna. The plane was so small that the concept of first and second class didn't apply. We weren't given boarding cards, but told to fill the plane from the rear.

I found myself next to Wilson Bibby. I'd expected him to ignore me as he had Harry so I was surprised to hear him say in a soft southern accent, 'What takes you to Kiruna, ma'am?' He was smiling, his eyes full of warmth.

'I'm on holiday,' I said warily. 'We're going to the Ice Hotel.'

My carry-on bag was still in my lap. He glanced at the label, then pointed to an identical label on his own. 'Then we're on the same tour. My name's Wilson, by the way.' He indicated Marcellus across the aisle, two rows in front. 'I'm here with my son.'

He held out his hand. The skin was smooth, the nails expertly manicured. I hesitated, then put my hand in his, feeling my knuckles crack as he squeezed.

'Maggie Stewart.' I massaged my fingers, wondering why he hadn't given me his full name. Whatever the reason, I decided to play along. 'What made you come on this tour, Wilson?'

He smiled broadly, showing perfect teeth polished to such a high shine he could have been in a toothpaste advert. 'It's the snow. I love it. I can't get enough of it. Whenever I can, I travel to cold climates. The best, of course, is Antarctica.'

'Lapland should be just the place, then,' I said brightly. 'And have you had a chance to look round Stockholm?'

'I've been here for a few days on business. I'd always wanted to visit the Ice Hotel so I've postponed some of my meetings to make the trip north.'

'If you love the snow so much, why do you live in the southern part of the USA?'

He turned his gaze on me. 'How do you know where I live, ma'am?' His voice had a steel edge.

I thought quickly. Appealing to a man's vanity usually worked in sticky situations. 'I can tell from your accent that you're a southern gentleman.' It made me cringe, but I said it anyway. 'You sound just like Rhett Butler.'

I could tell he was delighted with my answer. His gravelly laughter echoed round the small plane.

'So what do you do for a living, Wilson?'

'I have a variety of interests as a businessman,' he said smoothly. 'You?'

'I work in finance. A pharmaceutical company in Dundee.'

He drew his brows together and, for a second, I thought he'd made the connection with Harry. 'Scotland?' he said. 'My family came from there, originally.'

He ordered a whisky, then proceeded to give me an unabridged version of his family history, his narrative rolling along sluggishly like the Mississippi. I listened politely, noticing how careful he was not to mention the name Bibby.

He fumbled in his bag, and produced what looked like a large diary. It was bound in heavy-duty canvas cloth in a red-and-blue tartan. 'My organiser. You'll recognise the tartan, of course.'

When I said nothing, he added, 'It's MacGregor. As I told you, I'm a MacGregor on my mother's side. I have these made every year.'

He opened the book at the back. The pages were edged in gilt and imprinted with an elaborate watermark. The lettering was a fine black copperplate.

'It's essentially a diary – see the month and date at the top? – but I can also use the pages for memorandum notes.' He flattened the book on his lap. 'You can see the perforations if I open it out.'

There were two pages for each day. Each had space at the bottom for Wilson's signature, and the signature of a witness.

What added to the book's thickness were the carbons attached to the pages.

'I've never seen one like it,' I said, fascinated.

He seemed pleased. 'My own design. I've learnt the hard way that verbal instructions have their weaknesses. This enables me to keep track of my decisions on the move.'

I thought of the instructions I gave my own staff in texts, emails and scribbled Post-it notes. Wilson's modus operandi was that of a man not used to relinquishing control lightly. Pandemonium would ensue if he lost his diary. Perhaps he slept with it under his pillow.

'A pretty tartan, don't you think?' he said. 'I'm having a kilt made.' He returned the diary to his carry-on bag and delved about inside, producing a bottle of pills.

I glanced quickly across the aisle. Harry was gripping the arms of his seat, staring straight ahead, the veins in his neck swollen. I felt a pang of guilt. Neither Liz nor I had reminded him to take his medication.

Wilson threw his head back sharply and swallowed several pills in one gulp.

'Do you have a fear of flying?' I said.

'Health is a real pain in the ass, Maggie,' he replied, sidestepping my question. He replaced the bottle in his carry-on, but not before I'd had a good look at the label. 'My doctors have instructed me to watch everything I do,' he continued. 'I'm not supposed to exert myself, I've been put on a special diet and I've been told to cut down on drinking and smoking.'

I watched him swallow his Scotch, remembering the fat cigar at the airport.

He caught me looking. 'Cut down, but not cut out.' He smiled disarmingly. 'If the bastards had said cut out, I'd be searching for better doctors.'

He was so sure of himself I decided to end the pretence. 'Mr Bibby, you may not be aware you upset my friend at the airport,' I said, as politely as I could. 'I can understand it must be annoying to be constantly approached, but Harry was hurt. He was trying to thank you for funding his research.'

Wilson stiffened. The smile vanished and a glittery look came into his eyes. He was like a snake, sizing up its victim, waiting for the moment to strike. The heavy-lidded reptile eyes moved across my face. My breathing quickened. This was not a man to cross.

'He was your friend?' He smiled thinly. 'Well, he should know better than to creep up on people.'

I was disappointed he'd mistaken my tone. 'That's still no reason to behave the way you did,' I said hotly. I knew how it would sound, but I couldn't stop myself. 'What happened to the manners the south is so famous for?'

I'd touched a nerve. The snake's eyes vanished and, for an instant, he looked bewildered.

But he recovered his composure quickly. 'I admit I may have been rude to your friend. But there's something I'm sure you'll appreciate, young lady.' He brought his face closer to mine. 'A man like myself will always be on the defensive when approached by strangers, even in public places.'

'You're not travelling with a bodyguard.' It was a stupid remark, I realised, after I'd said it.

His reply stunned me with its candour. 'Back home, I have several. On vacation, my son Marcellus acts as my bodyguard. He's a martial-arts expert.' He said it with a comfortable insolence, as though this single fact was a guarantee of his safety.

I glanced across the aisle. Marcellus had removed his sweatshirt, revealing an army-green singlet stretched tightly across his chest. His arms were like tree trunks, the veins bulging.

'I understand your son works for your Foundation,' I said.

Wilson seemed unsurprised by the remark. 'He manages our New York office. Of course, I see less of him than I'd like, but we take our vacations together. We travel incognito, even though it means we have to drop our standards now and again.'

I studied Marcellus's clothes. They were more suited to a holiday in the Bahamas.

Wilson must have read my expression. 'The main problem is agreeing the location. You see, unlike myself, Marcellus is a sun-worshipper. He can't stand the cold.'

As we started our descent into Kiruna, Wilson's last words rang in my head. The holiday couldn't have been Marcellus's idea. The Ice Hotel was a strange choice of location if you couldn't stand the cold.

CHAPTER 3

Kiruna airport was packed. All flights that day seemed to have arrived at once.

We pushed our way into the tiny arrivals lounge, searching for our tour guide. I spotted a young man holding a company placard and scanning the crowd anxiously.

Harry was the first to reach him. 'I'm Harry Auchinleck,' he said, beaming. 'I believe we're on your tour.'

'The Dundee group? Great. I'm Leonard Tullis. Call me Leo.' He smiled broadly, showing uneven teeth. His fair hair was a tangle of curls, as though he was just out of bed. He seemed too young and, anywhere else, I'd have taken him for a sixth-former. 'First things first,' he said. 'I'll need your names.'

The Bibbys came forward. Wilson stood aside while Marcellus took care of business. Leo made a mark on his sheet but, if he recognised the name, he gave no indication.

A girl with fiercely permed red hair was next. She watched anxiously as Leo ran a finger down the list. He found her name, and she relaxed visibly, flashing him a smile that illuminated her face. She seemed to have limitless energy, like a puppy, and was unable to stay still for long. Her porcelain skin, vacant blue eyes and Cupid's-bow lips reminded me of a Dresden china doll. Leo

26

glanced at her from time to time, interest on his face, and I wondered whether, like a china doll, she could be damaged easily.

The last names on the list were Jim and Robyn Ellis. Robyn was a small woman, marginally bigger than her enormous rucksack. She had to lean forward to keep her centre of gravity from toppling her backwards. Her husband was remarkably the same – they could have been brother and sister – although he was taller. Both were wiry with short, greying hair that stood straight up, like brush bristles. Their physique was that of hill-walkers, which they probably were given the condition of their boots. They made a beeline for the wall and peered with bloodshot eyes at the map of the local terrain. Robyn made notes. I turned away, smiling. I knew the type – they meant business.

Leo called us to attention. 'Okay, folks, time to rock and roll.'

He pulled up the hood of his black ski-suit and fastened it firmly at the neck. I watched his deliberate movements impatiently, hungry for my first glimpse of Lapland. When he drew on his gloves and worked them over his hands, pressing firmly between the fingers, I could wait no longer. I pushed open the swing doors and stepped outside.

My initial reaction was one of shock, laced with disbelief.

The freezing air crisped my face and hands, the cold seeping through my clothes and into my body. I gasped, drawing in air that seared my throat, reminding me of my first clandestine iced vodka. A second later, I was shuddering. And it was still only midday.

Leo had brought the others outside. He watched me with amusement in his eyes. 'You think this is cold?' The corners of his mouth lifted. 'The temperature starts dropping about now.' He led the way to the coach.

Once we were on the road, he explained he'd be posting daily notices in the Excelsior Hotel's foyer, even on those days we'd be sleeping in the Ice Hotel. Preliminaries over, he described the excursions. But at that point I only half listened. I'd read the brochure several times.

The road to the Ice Hotel wound through the suburbs of Kiruna. I glimpsed a steepled church, colourful buildings with vertiginously sloping roofs, and a park where children shrieked in the snow. The houses yielded to dense forests of conifers, broken by snow-covered tundra and frozen lakes. In the far distance, the mountains thrust their peaks to the sky, the white crowns bright in the sunlight.

Harry's colour had returned and he was chatting happily to Liz. Leo was sitting with the red-haired porcelain doll, mounting a charm offensive. The Bibbys were at the front. The heat in the coach seemed insufficient for Marcellus, who kept his thick parka tightly buttoned. His hair, released from its ponytail, hung untidily over his shoulders. He'd clamped his mobile to his head and was talking into it, rarely pausing to listen. Wilson was dozing, the snake eyes starting to close, his head lolling forward and jerking him awake. I smiled to myself. The early start – and the whisky – had finally caught up with him.

Leo's voice cut into my thoughts. He was standing at the front of the bus. 'Ladies and gentlemen, we'll soon be arriving at the Excelsior. We're going to be joined by the final member of our party, who's making his own way there. His name is . . .' he peered at the sheet '. . . Mike Molloy. I've got one more item of house-keeping, which is to read out your room numbers. They'll be posted on the noticeboard in the foyer. Remember that your room number is the same in both the Excelsior and the Ice Hotel.'

The coach juddered to a halt. I followed the others out, bracing myself for the sudden stab of cold. The snow was soft and clean after a recent fall and I sank up to my knees in the drift.

I floundered helplessly, my breath forming warm clouds in front of my face.

The Excelsior stood at the top of a short incline, its red plaster façade and crisscross of wooden beams reminiscent of the buildings in Kiruna. A thick mantle of snow clung to the steep roof in a victory of friction over gravity. Without warning, a huge clump fell to the ground with a soft whooshing sound, sending up a shower of white powder. On the wide slope, conifers had been planted at regular intervals. They stood to attention, like a parade of alpine soldiers, the ice-coated arms of their dark branches bent to snapping point.

We'd arrived early. The path was still being cleared, and the workmen were throwing us anxious glances.

But we'd lost interest in the Excelsior. Flanking the path, forming a welcoming party, was a group of life-sized ice statues.

They were circus characters. The largest and most striking was the clown. Tufts of ice hair, glinting in the sunshine, had escaped from beneath the rim of the bowler hat he wore back off his forehead. His face had been roughened to simulate a clown's paint, the markings adding the finishing touches to the coarse clown's lips and Charlie Cairoli nose. Ice tears trickled down his cheeks as his wistful gaze implored you to ignore the clown's trappings – frilly shirt, baggy pantaloons and oversized shoes – and see the man beneath. A small drum hung from his neck. He stood, shoulders back, arms raised high, drumsticks poised and ready to strike.

A ballerina stood opposite, gazing dreamily at the clown. Her hair was swept up into a chignon and held in place with a single ice flower. A garland of the same flowers curved across the bodice of her impossibly frilled tutu. She stood *en pointe*, arms above her head, fingers touching lightly. Her head was tilted to the side, a seductive smile on her lips as she watched the clown begin his drumroll. Beside her, a juggler was leaning forward, on the point of throwing his skittles into the air. He was distracted by the ballerina and was turning his head towards her, a look of anguish in his eyes. Opposite him, a barrel-chested strongman, sporting a magnificent handlebar moustache, was flexing his arm muscles theatrically. The ice had been so well polished that his hair, parted down the middle, seemed silky with oil.

A group of ice penguins had gathered at the Excelsior's entrance. They stared sightlessly up at us, their bow ties and tuxedos a fond indulgence on the part of the sculptor. Next to them was a lion-tamer in military-style trousers and boots, an animal skin across his chest. He was holding a whip the way a conductor holds a baton. Below him crouched a maned lion, ready to spring into the air.

The recent fall had covered the statues only lightly, and patches of blue ice, like the skin of moulting animals, were visible through the snow. I ran my fingers over the lion's head, feeling the finely chiselled grooves in the ice fur. As I rubbed his muzzle, I thought I saw the expression in his eyes change.

Leo broke the spell. 'Lunch is about to be served, so please do come inside. And don't forget today's tour of the Ice Hotel. We meet in the Activities Room at three o'clock.'

The Ice Hotel. I spun round and peered down the path, past the coach and beyond.

Its shape was instantly recognisable from the brochure. Shafts of light radiated from the curved surface and, for an instant, I was dazzled. Then a cloud slid across the sun and I saw it clearly – the long blue igloo and the flat structures. Something dark hung over the entrance, as though the bloated toad was yawning.

I felt a strange sense of unease. Liz was tugging at my arm, urging me into the Excelsior. But I was unable to move. A chill was creeping through my body, a chill that had nothing to do with the plummeting temperature.

Lunch was over, and we had an hour to kill before our tour. We decided to have a drink in the lounge.

I'd peeked into the room on the way to the restaurant. One end was elegantly furnished with coffee-tables, maroon sofas, and a baby grand. Cream curtains, held back with sashes, framed the large bay windows. At the other end was the bar, with taller tables, wooden chairs, and recesses in the wall that gave drinkers a measure of privacy. As this was Monday, the room was spotless and the dark red carpet smelt of shampoo. I wondered idly what it would smell like by Friday.

Harry, who never wasted time when someone mentioned a drink, marched into the room.

'My God.' He stopped dead. 'Who is that Adonis?'

Liz was peering over his shoulder. 'Ooh, Harry, he *is* rather gorgeous,' she murmured.

There was only one person in the lounge. He lay sprawled in a chair. His arm was slung lazily over the back, pulling his jacket open and straining the shirt across his chest. His legs stretched endlessly, his ankles crossed in such a way it was impossible not to see the Bart Simpson socks. His silk suit was superbly tailored, possibly even handmade, and gave him the air of a Chicago gang-ster. Apart from the socks, his other concession to individuality was the bubblegum-pink tie, which he fingered softly as though needing to check the quality. His hair was expertly cut and, I suspected, deliberately tousled. Despite his relaxed features, there was something disturbing about him, something I couldn't put my finger on.

He got to his feet.

I was conscious we were staring. I walked over, smiling awkwardly. 'I'm Maggie Stewart.'

There was a pause as he took his gaze off my hair. 'Mike Molloy,' he said, in a strong Irish accent. 'At your service.' He smiled easily, as if to say, 'Any time, and as often as you like.'

Liz and Harry seemed to have lost the power of speech, so I made the introductions.

'Delighted.' Harry beamed, having finally found his voice. He hurried forward, hand extended, and pumped Mike's arm. 'May we join you?'

'Of course,' Mike said warmly.

We took our seats.

'You people with a group?' he said, looking at no one in particular.

'We're with Leo Tullis,' I said. 'He told us there'd be another member of his group here. That would be you?'

'That's right,' he said softly.

'So where have you flown in from?'

'I was in Stockholm all last week. It made sense to stay over the weekend and fly to Kiruna this morning.'

I glanced at his clothes, wondering why, north of the Arctic Circle, he was dressed like a banker.

He caught me looking and smiled ruefully. 'These are my work clothes.'

I smiled back. 'I'd gathered that.' I hesitated. 'Is it a Swedish company you work for?'

'Mane Drew.' There was a hint of pride in his voice.

'The name's familiar. IT consultancy?'

'They're one of the bigger Scottish companies. They service most of the south of Scotland, with branches in the major cities.'

'But you're working in Stockholm?'

'I helped Mane Drew set up a branch there last spring. The

irony is that, although I work out of the Dundee office, I'm hardly ever there.'

'Your accent's not Scottish, though,' Liz said. 'You're Irish, aren't you?' She was gazing at Mike, her expression deliberately softened.

I rubbed my mouth so he didn't see the smile. When Liz dangled her charms, it worked with most men, but I was curious to see how this one would react.

He flicked a speck of fluff off his lapel. 'Well now, I was transferred to Dundee eighteen months ago from our Dublin branch . . .' he looked up at Liz '. . . to inject a little Irish talent into Scotland.'

'Indeed,' Harry said, under his breath.

'I flew here after my morning meetings.' Mike glanced down at his pinstripe. 'Some eejit sent my luggage somewhere else, which is why I'm dressed like this. I need to get some ski clothes. It's cold enough here to freeze the brass ones.' He settled back, crossing his legs. 'This holiday was a last-minute decision. I'm wondering what I've let myself in for.'

'You had to work this morning?' Liz said, pouting. 'Poor you. On the first day of your holiday, as well.'

'It wasn't that bad. Mainly presentations. I slept through most of them.' A mischievous look came into his eyes. 'The last speaker was some woman, an A-type female. She'd pinned her hair up, twisted in this funny way, it was. Well, in the middle of her talk, the pins came loose and it began to unwind. You should have seen the faces, especially on the women.'

Harry was hanging on Mike's every word, his eyes glazed.

'So the hairpins came out, one by one, and her hair fell over her shoulders. It was a good trick, and no mistake. Certainly got everyone's attention.'

'You thought it was deliberate?' I said coldly, suddenly sympathetic towards a woman I'd never met.

He laughed then, a deep resonant sound. 'Come on now, all women do it. I know one who undoes another button before a talk. She never gets asked any questions, because no one's paid any attention to what she's said.'

'Sounds like you don't believe in equality of the sexes,' Harry said, in a tone of playful admonishment.

The corners of Mike's mouth lifted, dimpling his cheeks, making him look like a boy. 'Not only do I believe in it, I'm fighting to get it back.'

It was impossible not to stare into his eyes. The brown irises were flecked with amber, the effect both fascinating and disconcerting. When he smiled, which was often, his eyes glowed with a warm confidence: Mike Molloy wasn't a man whose ego needed constant massaging.

He was watching me, apparently waiting for my reaction. 'So how do you all come to know each other?' he said, when no reaction was forthcoming.

'Mags and I were best friends at school. We lost touch and then met up . . .' Liz turned to me. 'When was it now? I can't quite remember.'

'A couple of years ago,' I said, looking at Mike.

'That's it. We literally ran into each other in Debenhams, at the January sales.'

Mike continued to watch me. The expression in his eyes was unnerving. 'So what's it like living in Sweden?' I said, for something to say.

He shrugged. 'On the plus side, no one cares if you're a Catholic or a Prot.'

'And on the minus?'

'Swedes don't know how to party – I've been at better wakes, to tell the truth – so you have to make your own fun.' He grinned. 'Last Saturday, I hooked up with a group of Yanks. We spent the evening drinking in hotels. It was a blast. I spent most of Sunday sleeping it off.'

Harry had been waiting for an opportunity to join the conversation. 'Talking of drink, there's time for a quickie before our tour. What do you say to a little Bollinger? My treat, of course.' He got to his feet. 'Let me see if I can find the barman.'

Mike nodded at Harry's retreating back. 'That feller's face looks familiar.'

'You'll have seen it on television,' Liz said. 'He's written a bestseller, *The Modern Terrorist: Nature or Nurture?* You must have heard of it.'

From Mike's expression, I guessed he hadn't. But I hadn't heard of Harry before Liz had introduced us.

'*Nature or Nurture?*' He pulled a face. 'Sounds far too theoretical. I once went to a talk called something like that. It was given by this university boffin. Had a face as long as a week. The talk was totally incomprehensible. I'm not even sure he had his teeth in at the time.'

Liz laughed. 'Ah, but Harry's books are different. I took a module on terrorism when I was at college, and the books on the reading list were all by him. Jolly good they were, too. And his talks can be hysterically funny.'

'You must have heard him on the radio,' I said. 'Professor Henry Auchinleck? The expert who advises governments on terrorism?'

Liz was watching Mike. 'Not just governments, NATO, the EU, the UN – you name the initials. He's a brilliant academic. Got more medals than Montgomery.'

'Can't say I recognise the name. But an academic, you said?' He rubbed his chin. 'Hardly the fast lane. It's down there with lawyers and financiers.'

'Careful,' Liz said, before I could reply. 'Maggie's an accountant.'

He studied me. 'I took an accountancy course once. Not exactly rocket science, is it? Just figures on a spreadsheet.'

I couldn't let this go. 'Yes, sweetie,' I said, forcing a smile, 'but I can do it backwards and in high heels.'

'Well, that's lovely now, Maggie.' His lips twitched. 'So where do you do your sums?'

'*Sums?*'

'We work for the same company,' Liz said quickly. 'Bayne Pharmaceuticals.'

He straightened his tie. 'The Dundee drug company? We did some consultancy for them a couple of months ago, I believe.'

'You believe correctly,' I said, my smile coming easily now. 'Our servers haven't been the same since.'

'A sense of humour. I like that in a woman.'

'Mags is deputy finance director. She practically runs Bayne's.'

'No, I don't,' I said, annoyed that Liz was embarrassing me in front of a stranger. I frowned at her, trying to signal that I wanted to bring the topic to a close. 'Don't believe everything Liz tells you, Mike. I'm just a pawn in a giant game of chess.'

'Have you found the job difficult? The finance people at Mane Drew are permanently on the verge of nervous breakdowns.'

I hesitated. 'The first six months were hell.'

'I'm betting the men in your department didn't make it easy.'

I was surprised by this comment, coming from a man. 'I've learnt to expect that, especially as my boss told me I beat off some stiff internal competition.'

'That won't have made you popular.'

'It didn't.' I kept my voice level. 'But I'm no longer prepared to stroke young male egos.'

He grinned. 'I have to do that all the time.'

Harry returned with a bottle of champagne. He removed the cap and popped the cork with expertise born of practice.

I sipped, watching Mike over the rim of the glass. He was joking with Harry, encouraging him to drink up, glancing at me now and then as though seeking my approval. Liz was laughing, turning from one to the other. The scene seemed innocent enough. So why did I feel a prickle of anxiety?

CHAPTER 4

The Activities Room was at the end of the long corridor leading from the foyer. It was 3 p.m. and a group was gathering. Mike, still in his pinstripe, arrived with Harry. They were deep in conversation.

'So what about it, Mags?' Liz said, watching them. 'You up for a holiday romance?'

'I think not. I haven't had any luck with men recently.'

'Yes, well, you do total most of your relationships. But I rather think this one would help take your mind off the last. He was a disaster and a half.'

I glared at her. Yet she was right. It hadn't taken me long to grasp that my last boyfriend didn't want a girlfriend. He wanted a nanny. 'I'm over him, Liz. And from now on, I'm not lowering my guard.'

'Really? No more romantic attachments?'

'That was the old Maggie. The new Maggie is done with meaningful relationships.' I smiled wearily. 'Nothing but casual affairs from now on.'

'Then I'd say Mike Molloy would be just the ticket.'

'He's not my type. He's got a huge opinion of himself and he's not afraid to show it in public.'

But it was simpler than that: my instincts told me to steer clear of him. Unfortunately, that was becoming increasingly unlikely. He and Harry seemed to be hitting it off.

'That's right, dear boy,' Harry was saying. 'Cooking is one of my hobbies. When I'm not slaving in a hot lecture theatre, I'm slaving over a hot stove. Look, next time you're in Dundee, you must come to one of my Sunday buffets.' He smiled indulgently. 'From what you've told me, I'd hazard a guess that you're a bit of a domestic god yourself.'

'That I am. I love cooking Thai.'

'With me, it's French. I like my food saucy.'

Mike winked. 'A bit like yourself, Harry.'

'Oh, do you think so?' Harry simpered, blushing to the roots.

I listened with curiosity. For all Mike's macho image, he was comfortable enough with his masculinity to banter like this with a gay man. And Harry loved innuendo, whether from a man or a woman. He was so obviously happy that I couldn't help but be grateful Mike was showing such an interest in him.

There were a dozen of us waiting for the guide. The redhead, who was wearing a fur-trimmed hat and huge quilted jacket, its burgundy colour matching her hair, had told us at lunch that her name was Jane Galloway. The Ellises arrived late, looking as though they'd just had a row. Robyn was red in the face and hissing at her husband, who was trying to ignore her. I turned away to hide a smile. The Ellises were going to be fun.

The Bibbys were absent. I wondered why, given Wilson's comment about wanting to visit the Ice Hotel. Perhaps they were getting a personal tour later. The things money can buy.

Leo Tullis appeared, clutching his clipboard.

'Are you conducting the tour, Leo?' I said.

'I could do, I've been on it so many times. No, it's one of the hotel staff.'

Right on cue, a young woman marched down the corridor.

'Good afternoon,' she said. 'My name is Marita and today I will be your guide.' She spoke in a calm businesslike manner, as though she was reading the news.

Unlike most Swedes, Marita was short. Her blonde plaits, threaded with red ribbons, were wrapped round her head in a style more Germanic than Scandinavian. The patterned jacket, threatening to burst open, and the black skintight trousers, did nothing but emphasise the heaviness of her figure. What endeared her to me was that she seemed entirely unconcerned by it.

She surveyed the group, her gaze lingering on Mike's suit. I could guess what she was thinking: only a complete idiot would dress like that. Mike smiled at her, apparently oblivious to the effect his clothes were having.

When Marita had everyone's attention, she took a deep breath, pushed her bust out further, and launched into her speech. 'Welcome to the Ice Hotel. As we are two hundred kilometres north of the Arctic Circle, the outdoor temperature can drop to as low as minus thirty degrees Celsius. So before we take our tour you will need to dress appropriately.' She paused for emphasis, making a point of glancing again at Mike's suit. 'Everything you need can be borrowed from the Activities Room. Now, please follow me.'

Her command of English was excellent, although the words were thickly accented and the delivery more sung than spoken. Harry, always unforgiving of foreigners, nudged me and pulled a face.

The Activities Room was the size of a small warehouse: coloured snow-suits hung in rows that occupied much of the room. There was little else apart from the cupboards and slatted wooden benches lining the walls. Robyn marched to the nearest rack and squeezed a snow-suit with both hands. She released it quickly and inspected the material as though checking the quality.

'We have snow-suits of different sizes and thicknesses,' Marita said, motioning to the racks. 'On the trays above the suits, you will find gloves, hats and ski masks. Outdoor boots are at the back. The cupboards contain sports items – snowshoes, skis and ice-climbing equipment.' She spoke quickly and confidently, in what was evidently a highly practised routine. 'Now let's get our suits on, as I'm sure you are impatient to see the Ice Hotel.'

She picked out a suit from the middle rack and dressed quickly. I took the first medium-sized snow-suit I could find and clambered into it. It was one of the thicker suits, and I was sweating by the time I'd zipped it up over my clothes.

At the back of the room, I found a pair of knee-high boots. I sat down next to the fire door and struggled with the stiff straps.

Liz was examining the door. 'Where do you think this leads to, Mags?'

'The outside. It's a fire door, I think.'

'A fire door, here? Really? In all this snow?'

'I'm sure they have fires, even in Lapland.' Sweat was dripping from my brow. 'What size is your snow-suit, Liz?'

'Small, and extra long.' She studied me, looking slim and elegant in her white suit. 'What on earth are you wearing? I'm sorry to have to say this but you look just like the Michelin Man.'

'Thanks.' I was sweating heavily now, my clothes sticking to my back. 'So where's Harry?'

'He's helping Mike with his inside leg measurement,' she said meaningfully. 'Can you stand up in that thing?'

Ignoring her, I heaved myself off the bench and waddled out of the room.

We left the Excelsior and followed Marita down the slope to the Ice Hotel. Leo hadn't been exaggerating: the temperature was plunging.

Marita gestured to the low wooden building on our right. 'That is the Locker Room where you will change before you sleep in the Ice Hotel.'

'About that,' Jim Ellis said hesitantly. He peered at Marita, his eyes huge behind his spectacles. 'I've been meaning to ask. What should we wear?' Robyn glowered at him, as though he'd made a social gaffe.

'Only a sleep-suit. No other clothes.' Marita smiled encouragingly. 'Put your things in a locker, making sure to use the one with your room number, as it is reserved for you. At the back of the washroom, there's a door that takes you outside, then to the Ice Hotel's side door.'

A murmur passed through the group. Jane Galloway gave me a look that said, 'This can't be right.'

'You mean we go outside after we change?' Jim said.

'That is correct.'

'What happens if we get cold at night? I mean so cold we can't sleep.' He tried not to look at his wife.

Marita smiled indulgently. 'It's a psychological thing. You might think you'll be cold but you'll be surprised how quickly you warm up. There is hot lingonberry juice in the Locker Room, and in the morning my colleague Karin and I will bring some to your room.'

I felt sorry for Jim. The holiday must have been his wife's idea. But others seemed to be having their doubts. Liz was speaking earnestly with Mike and Harry, and Jane was frowning as she listened to the Danes I'd seen taking over the restaurant at lunch. It was too late to worry about the cold. We were here now.

Marita stopped outside the Ice Hotel's entrance, an arch-shaped opening carved into the ice. The double doors, also of ice, were hung with reindeer skins, the interweaving of brown and cream in the coarse hair making them look dark from a distance. Ice columns, so smooth they might have been carved from a single block, stood on either side.

Marita was in full flow again. 'The Ice Hotel is not only a hotel, but also an art gallery. The rooms house ice sculptures of the highest quality. Between the hours of ten a.m. and five p.m., it is open to visitors, but for the rest of the time it is a hotel.' She smiled dreamily. 'But an unusual, in fact a unique, hotel.'

She gripped the antler handles and pulled. The doors opened smoothly and silently. We followed her inside, pushing each other in our hurry.

'This is the foyer,' she said, with pride in her voice.

There were gasps of amazement from those in the front. I looked past them.

Two rows of fluted ice columns stood on either side of the foyer, directing our gaze to the ice chandelier hanging from the vaulted ceiling. It was suspended by an impossibly thin cord, its cream candles protruding at all angles, like crooked teeth. Through the far wall where the ice was thinner, shafts of blue light streamed in, stamping their colour on the room. Emptiness, reminiscent of an ancient cathedral, lay on the place. Yet despite the stillness, the air shimmered like a veil that was about to be drawn back by an unseen hand.

'Would you look at this place?' Mike said, breaking the silence. 'Are the candles ever lit?'

'They are at night,' Marita said.

'Won't they melt the chandelier?'

'They are special candles that give out little heat. Look closely. They are arranged so their flames point away from the ice.'

Liz was crouching, examining the floor. 'I don't believe this. There's snow everywhere.' She glanced up. 'It'll turn to slush, won't it?'

Marita removed a glove and scooped up a handful of snow. 'The atmosphere in the Ice Hotel is too dry for condensation to form. The snow therefore doesn't get wet. It is more like sand.' She let it fall, and turned her hand to show us her dry palm. 'It's the same everywhere in the Ice Hotel. The exception is the bar where the heat and perspiration from many bodies can raise the humidity level.'

'And what happens then?' Harry said.

She kept her expression blank. 'The ice on the ceiling melts and drips into your drink.'

I smirked. Harry seemed less than amused.

Marita indicated that we should look around. We wandered among the columns. Jim poked a suspicious finger into the snow. Robyn, who'd been watching, yapped so loudly that heads turned. She stomped away. He straightened and followed her, like an obedient puppy.

Liz was turning in a slow circle, a frown of concentration on her face.

'You'll get dizzy doing that,' I said.

'This place is like a rabbit warren. If I need a pee in the middle of the night, I just know I'm going to crash into these enormous columns.'

'The lights in the chandelier will be on, didn't Marita say?'

'You think they won't burn out?' She gazed at the candles doubtfully. 'If you run into one of these columns face on, it's goodbye, Vienna.'

'Good point. I'm staying in my sleeping bag and crossing my legs.' After a quick glance around, I said in a low voice, 'Liz, you know things about drugs. What's Coumarinose used for?'

She seemed surprised by this sudden shift in the conversation. 'It's an anticoagulant. Why do you ask?'

'Wilson Bibby swallowed some on the plane. Why would he need an anticoagulant? To prevent deep-vein thrombosis while flying?'

'Anticoagulants are prescribed for people who have abnormal heart rhythms. They either reduce the risk of strokes, or of heart attacks. Or perhaps both,' she added vaguely. 'But don't quote me, I'm not a doctor.'

'You're saying Wilson might have a heart problem?'

'And if he's taking Coumarinose, he really shouldn't be drinking or smoking.'

'Why do you think he appears to care so little about his health?'

'Because the rich believe they're immortal.' She shrugged. 'Anyway, why are we talking about him? Let's explore.'

We moved deeper into the foyer, following the tinkling sound of running water. A circular ice fountain, decorated with leafy ice grapes, stood beneath the chandelier. The plump bunches curled round the stand, climbing to the rim of the basin where they spread thickly. The water was pumped through an arrangement of ice lilies. It flowed out through the stamens, swirled round the basin, and drained away.

Jane Galloway held a finger under the stamens. 'Why doesn't the water freeze?'

Marita's lips twitched. 'Partly because it is constantly moving, and partly because it is almost one hundred per cent industrial-strength antifreeze.'

'Yikes.' Jane pulled her hand back as though she'd been stung. Mike nudged her and smirked. She nudged him back harder.

Marita was in tour-guide mode again. 'The Ice Hotel is built from ice harvested from the nearby river, which is frozen at this time of year, of course. When you're on the river, you'll see workmen removing next year's blocks for storage.' She paused for effect. 'That means there are areas of the river which will not be frozen over. You must take great care on the ice. If you fall in, even with a snow-suit, at these temperatures your chance of survival cannot be guaranteed.'

'I read that the river Torne is particularly fast-flowing,' Jane said.

'Not at the moment. It is . . .' she frowned, trying to remember the word '. . . sluggish. However, when the snows melt in spring, the current is strong. Objects in the river, including those on the bed, are swept into the Gulf of Bothnia.'

She waited for this message to sink in. We looked suitably impressed. Even Harry managed to keep a straight face.

'You may have noticed the absence of windows in the foyer. When the Ice Hotel is constructed, low-voltage cables are buried in the ice, and tiny lamps are fixed to the walls to provide illumination. A few rooms have a glass ceiling window, and light comes in that way also, although the ceiling windows are intended primarily for viewing the aurora borealis from the comfort of your room.'

'Are we likely to see the aurora?' I asked eagerly.

She fixed me with her gaze. 'We are in a period of maximum solar activity, so there is a high probability of seeing the aurora this week.'

'Where's the best place for viewing?'

'The easiest to reach is probably the river.' She hesitated. 'But there is another place, a viewing platform at the top of the church tower. You have to climb the steps as there is no elevator. I haven't been up there myself, but I am told that it is worth the effort.'

'The rooms aren't identical, then?' Jim said. His good spirits had returned. His wife was busy examining the ice lilies.

Marita smiled appreciatively, evidently pleased that this question had been asked. 'The rooms are unique. You will see in what way shortly. Let us continue.'

Behind the fountain, a low ice table and chairs stood casually, like a group of old friends. Marita motioned to the chairs but, although reindeer skins covered the seats, no one seemed prepared to sit down. There was a single object on the table: an ice vase with ice roses, some in bloom, others in bud. Snow, pressed on to the ice, frosted the roses like sugared fruit.

'Now, it is time to visit the bar,' she said.

Harry, who'd been stroking the reindeer skins, perked up. 'Excellent. May we have a drink now?'

'If you must,' she said brusquely, 'but we are not staying there long.'

She turned sharp right. We bustled through a bottle-shaped entrance into a high-vaulted room.

The bar was open for business. The guests stood at tall ice tables, drinking from chunky-looking glasses. Low tables and reindeer-covered chairs like those in the foyer were dotted around the room. A mock fireplace, complete with mantelpiece, fender and leaping flames, was set into the wall. Behind the icy flames, a flickering reddish-orange light was designed to give the impression the fire was lit. Although it was impossible to be fooled, the flames threw their false warmth at us, lifting the chill in the room.

'Tomorrow, your first night at the Ice Hotel, the management will be holding a reception here. Karin and I are the hosts. We will be giving you a Purple Kiss.'

'A kiss?' Mike flashed Marita a smile that showed his even white teeth. 'I'll be first in the queue.'

She eyed him coldly. 'Purple Kiss is a cocktail. You would know that if you had read your dossier.'

A faint titter ran through the group.

I whispered into Liz's ear, 'There's always one.'

She pretended she hadn't heard and smiled prettily at Mike, keen to show she'd appreciated his remark.

'You're such a tart, Liz,' I murmured, smiling.

Back in the foyer, Marita ran a hand across one of the red velvet curtains hanging against the walls. 'These lead to the sleeping areas.' She pushed the curtain aside and disappeared.

We followed, nearly running to keep up. After the vaulted spaces of the bar and foyer, the ceiling seemed too low. And it was darker here.

Marita stopped abruptly, causing a minor pile-up. She motioned to a ceramic plaque embedded in the wall. 'Please look closely. This is the room number.'

Harry, a giant baby in his powder-blue suit, brought up the rear. I hung back to walk with him, and slipped a hand through his arm. He was like a boy on a school trip, his face shining with excitement.

'I love her to bits, don't you, Maggie? When she's not a tour guide she must be a Rhine maiden. Do you think she sings Wagner?' He put on his glasses and peered at the nearest wall plaque. 'This might be my corridor. Yes, I'm in room fifteen, further along.'

'Then it's my corridor too. I'm in room sixteen.' I tugged at his arm. 'Come on, or we'll get lost.'

Marita had stopped outside room twenty. 'We have time to see only two or three rooms, but this is one of the more interesting. We call it the Chess Room.' She drew back the curtain.

Behind it was an arch-shaped entrance.

It was Robyn who voiced my thoughts. 'But there's no door,' she said shrilly. 'It's just a curtain.'

Marita was ready with the reassurances. 'Please don't be alarmed. Your valuables will be safe in the lockers.' She stepped into the room and, holding back the curtain, ushered us through.

Robyn had opened her mouth to speak but thought better of it. She followed the others inside, looking slightly outraged.

Harry held back, signalling to me to stop. 'I bet she and her husband were planning a night of passion,' he whispered. 'But not now they know anyone could burst in on them.'

I tried to picture the Ellises writhing under the reindeer skins, and failed. Harry, shaking with laughter, took my elbow and guided me into the now-crowded Chess Room.

Miniature lights hung high across the walls, winking rhythmically and throwing faint splashes of colour on to the ice. In the centre of the room lay the double bed, a block of ice buried under reindeer skins. I fingered them carefully, remembering Jim's doubts, and wondered how effective skins were as insulation.

It was then that I saw the ice statues: huge chess pieces, a king, queen and knight standing proudly around the room. Carved into the pressed snow on one of the walls was a chessboard. The Danes crowded in front of it, arguing loudly.

Marita was watching, curiosity in her eyes. 'Can you see who will win? And in how many moves? Each day we carve a different puzzle on to the wall and invite our guests to solve it.' She paused. 'It is black's turn.'

The Danes moved away, still arguing. I studied the board, biting my lip in concentration. It was an unusual play but, after a minute, I had it. 'It's now impossible for white to win. Black will win in three moves, but only if he sacrifices his queen.' I moved my finger to show Marita. 'But if black keeps the queen, he'll take a minimum of two – no, three – further moves to win.'

She gawped. 'That is absolutely correct.'

A murmur ran through the group. Mike was smiling, clapping soundlessly. Jane, beaming, gave me a thumbs-up.

'You solved it very quickly,' Marita said.

I shrugged, puzzled by her remark. 'It was obvious.'

'I didn't know you played chess, Mags,' Liz said.

'My father taught me when I was a child.' I grinned. 'I used to bunk off sports to play in the chess club. I was school champion. Don't you remember?'

'You bunked off sports?' Mike said, in amazement. 'To play *chess*?'

'We have a chess set in the Excelsior,' Marita was saying, 'although we find that our guests prefer outside activities.' She turned to the group. 'There is time to visit one more corridor. Please stay close or we will become separated.'

We filed out through the curtain and followed her back the way we'd come. Jim Ellis mouthed a hurried 'Well done', as he overtook me to join his wife.

As Marita passed room 15, Harry stopped and said, 'Oh, wait, please. Can we go in here? It's my room.'

She hesitated. It was clear she wanted to avoid this room. But Harry pushed back the curtain, and we trooped in.

'Aha,' he said triumphantly, 'I've got a ceiling window.'

The room was plainer, if brighter, than the Chess Room. The double bed lay in the centre, but there was nothing else. I wasn't surprised Marita didn't want to waste time here.

'Holy Mother o' God.' It was Mike.

I wheeled round. Behind us, set into a deep alcove, was a huge ice statue of the god Pan.

His conical horns grew through shaggy hair, which curled thickly over his head and fell in ringlets below his lightly pointed ears. Hair sprouting from his cheeks tangled into a beard, ending in two strands like a goat's. His eyebrows arched like pointed moustaches and, below his flared nostrils, his lips were drawn back into a demonic grin that I found disturbing. He was holding a set of pipes to his mouth, his fingers so long they touched above the reeds. Matted hair covered his neck and chest.

I looked down his body, expecting a goat's legs and hoofs, and then saw what had shocked Mike. The sculptor had given Pan an erection. But this was no ordinary erection. The enormous penis wasn't human, it was an animal's, buried in the belly hair. It ran along the abdomen and halfway up the chest.

'Good heavens!' Harry said, breaking the silence. He pushed his glasses further up his nose and openly scrutinised the penis. 'Now we know why he was called the Great God Pan.'

The tension was broken, and peals of laughter echoed through the room. We crowded round the statue, examining it, marvelling at the detail. I touched the penis. It was so lifelike that I half expected it to throb under my hand. As I turned away, I saw Mike watching me, his gaze steady.

Harry drew me to one side. 'Maggie, I'm not sure I'll be able to sleep with that thing grinning at me. There's a lamp behind it. Do you think I'll be able to switch it off?'

I peered into the alcove. Light was filtering through the statue from a lamp high in the wall, but I could see no way of turning it off. 'Marita, is that light on all night?' I said.

She seemed grateful for the change of subject. 'In the early hours of the morning, all the Ice Hotel lamps are turned off from the master switch in the Excelsior.'

'There you are,' I said to Harry. 'It'll be too dark to see him. That means he won't see you, either.'

'I suppose I could get used to it,' he said, eyeing the erection.

Mike clapped him on the back. 'Now you know where you can hang your clothes, Harry.'

Jane, standing with the Danes, sniggered loudly. Robyn, tutting softly, threw Mike a look of disapproval. Jim had his back to her, probably so she couldn't see the expression on his face.

We visited one more room. In the Scottish Room, we found Macbeth seated on a crude ice throne. Stretched across his lap was the dead king, Duncan, staring sightlessly at his murderer.

Macbeth's left arm was under the corpse, cradling it as a mother would a child. His right hand was removing the crown from Duncan's head. Scratched into the snow-covered wall, three witches danced in a frenzy round a bubbling cauldron, their arms flung back, beards billowing about their faces. Behind them, Birnam Wood marched to Dunsinane.

'This brings our tour of the Ice Hotel to an end,' Marita said, in her sing-song voice. 'I should mention two further buildings that may interest you. Adjacent to the Ice Hotel is the Ice Chapel, where we hold services, including christenings and weddings. And behind the Ice Hotel, on the riverbank, there is an Ice Theatre, a replica of London's Globe Theatre. I should remind you that every Sunday there is a performance in the Sami language of one of Shakespeare's plays. This Sunday, it will be *Macbeth*.'

'Are we going to get anything out of it?' Mike said, scratching his face. 'I hear Sami's a weird language, and no mistake.'

'That should not deter you from seeing the play. Few Swedes understand Sami, but we still go.' She looked directly at him. 'Anyway, you will be familiar with *Macbeth*. I can tell from your accent that you are Scottish.' She beamed, delighted with herself.

I glanced at Mike. The look on his face was priceless.

'And now I must leave you,' she said. 'I hope you have enjoyed the tour. It has been a great pleasure for me also.'

She inclined her head, acknowledging our applause. We watched her sashay down the corridor, her heavy buttocks rolling as she walked.

CHAPTER 5

The group dispersed. The Ellises marched out first, Robyn in the lead, then Jane left with the Danes, who were still arguing about chess. Harry announced he was going to unpack (and it would take him ages), and Liz said she needed to call the twins before her nap. Mike left for a long workout after accepting with alacrity Harry's invitation to meet later in the bar.

I wandered around the Ice Hotel, getting hopelessly lost until I eventually stumbled upon the corridor that led to the suites. I chose one at random. It was larger than the regular rooms, the main feature being a giant ice peacock. He was spreading his tail feathers to create a fan-shaped headboard for the double bed nestling inside his body. Ice trees grew in the corners of the room, their gnarled branches creeping across the ceiling and intertwining to form a dense canopy. Myriad tiny white lights, glowing hypnotically, hung like raindrops from the branches.

It would soon be the hour when the Ice Hotel ceased to be a gallery and became a hotel. I found the signs to the foyer and left by the main entrance.

The Ice Chapel stood separated from the Ice Hotel by a narrow path that led to the river. From its door, I could see the expanse of frozen water and the snowcapped forest on the far side. The sun had not yet set but the temperature had dropped, and a chill gripped my body. Promising myself only a few minutes outside, I started towards the bank.

Workmen were warming their hands at a smoking brazier. They watched silently as I passed, making no attempt to detain me. A JCB was still out, its faint angular shadow stretching long arms as it lifted the ice blocks and laid them in neat piles. I walked on to the river and peered down. The water, black in the failing light, slid silently past, carrying fragments of blue ice. The man at the controls shouted what could have been a warning, signalling to me to move away. I stepped back and watched the cutting of the ice until a combination of boredom and cold prompted me to leave. As I turned away, I caught a glimpse of the church tower in the distance. The tower with the viewing platform. Perhaps the aurora would be visible tonight.

I retraced my steps to the chapel, and pulled at the antler handles.

The interior was larger than I'd expected. A dozen ice pews covered with skins lined the nave, although there was room for easily twice that number. At the far end, a bare ice altar, striking in its simplicity, stood on a platform. It was overshadowed by the rose window carved high into the wall, its tracery as intricate as anything in a stone-built church. But there was no glass. The chapel was open to the elements. Glass would serve little purpose, I remembered then, as the daytime air temperature would be the same inside and out.

The pulpit was located at the side, its curving sweep of steps sprinkled liberally with snow. Unlike the Ice Hotel's columns, it was crudely assembled from small slabs of ice with snow pressed into the joins to mask them. There was nothing else in the chapel other than the broad columns at the ends of the pews.

Something at the pulpit's base caught my eye: symbols, carved into the snow. They jumbled around each other as though the sculptor had overreached himself and run out of space. I removed a glove and traced the outline of a shape with my fingers. It was a mythical beast, the long arrowed tail curling back under the belly to protrude obscenely between the front legs. Lettering, too faint to be legible, was scratched into the pedestal.

I was trying to decipher the letters when my legs buckled. I staggered and fell to my knees. The back of my throat tightened, and I realised with dismay that I was going to be sick. I swallowed repeatedly, trying to control the convulsions, and braced myself for the ultimate indignity of vomiting my lunch in a church. In desperation, I hugged the pulpit, pressing my face into the gritty coldness, praying for the nausea to subside.

I lifted my head and gazed at the figures. And then I saw something that sent a ripple of fear through my body. The mythical beasts had vanished. In their place, a half-formed vision appeared.

It took shape slowly, like a developing photograph, faint to begin with, then taking on recognisable form. It was a body lying on the ground, blood pumping from it, like wine from an over-turned bottle. Snow fell, shrouding the figure, melting in the red warmth.

I squeezed my eyes shut and, shaking uncontrollably, willed the image to disappear. After what seemed like an eternity, I opened my eyes. The figure had vanished, and the beasts were back, leaping into the air, tumbling, vying for space. I struggled to my feet, leaning against the pulpit, but my legs failed and I slid to the ground. On all fours, I crawled to the nearest pew and hauled myself up. Hunched over, elbows on knees, I pressed the heels of my palms into my eyes and sat, trembling, as the warmth drained out of me and my limbs became stiff.

The wind grew, gusting past the chapel, raking the walls with its fingers. I counted to a hundred, then dragged myself up and limped towards the door.

I was pushing against the handles when I heard the sound. It came from the pulpit, as though one of the mythical beasts were coming to life, whining to be released from his icy prison. I listened, my heart thumping painfully. It was more of a sob than a whine and, for one terrifying moment, I thought it was human. But it would be foolish to turn round. The chapel was deserted. It would be the wind moaning through the rose window.

I was alone in the sauna. The fragrant steam warmed my body, suffusing my nostrils with the tang of sandalwood.

There'd been no reply to my hesitant knock at Liz's door. I'd snatched a coffee and cake in the lounge and made my way to the spa. As I passed the gym, I peered through the glass door. Mike was lifting weights, the Danes watching. He said something that made them laugh, and a big fair-haired man, whom I hadn't seen on the tour, punched him on the shoulder.

Now, in the sauna, I sat wrapped in a towel, trying to make sense of what had happened in the chapel. I'd seen things like that before, although not since my teens. My mother had looked at me strangely when I first described them. She reassured me they were nothing to fear, the product of an overactive imagination and she, too, had had them as a child. They were rarely explicit, more a collage of unconnected images with a dreamlike quality where everything was blurred at the edges. Like dreams, I forgot them quickly. But there was one I hadn't forgotten, one I couldn't forget, of the prostrate body of my neighbour's son. Two days afterwards, he'd been struck by a car and died silently on the pavement, eyes staring sightlessly into the clouds.

I sank back against the wall, gripping the towel, remembering what I'd seen in the chapel: the bloodstained body, a sharp bright image, not blurred at the edges.

The steam swirled around the chamber, its heat soaking into my skin and banishing my anxiety. I must have dozed off because, when I opened my eyes, the sauna was a crush of people staring because my towel had slipped. I showered and left, my limbs feeling heavy but relaxed, as though my body belonged to someone else.

The lounge was empty. I ordered a glass of white wine and carried it to the table by the window. The sun had dropped below the horizon, and the sky was turning purple. Strips of cloud, like shredded paper, hung over the unbroken field of snow.

'May I join you, ma'am?'

I looked round, startled. 'Mr Bibby.'

His voice was like his father's, a deep southern drawl. 'Please call me Marcellus.'

He was so large that he eclipsed the light in the room. I smiled awkwardly, motioning to the chair opposite.

He set down his beer and, lifting the wooden chair as though it were a toy, positioned it so he was facing me. As he eased his bulk into it, the seat bent slightly under his weight.

I saw his features clearly now. His skin was coarse and pitted around the nose, and he had the sunken eyes and premature facial lines that are the hallmark of a life of dissipation. But I'd been wrong about one thing: his eyes weren't brown. They were black pools, like viscous oil. He smiled then, and the creases round his eyes deepened.

'I'm Maggie,' I said warmly. 'Maggie Stewart.'

'A pleasure.' He held out his hand.

I hesitated, remembering his father's bone-crunching grip. But it would have been bad manners to refuse. I put my hand into his, tensing as his fingers curled round mine, then astonished at the gentleness with which he squeezed.

'Did you make the tour of the Ice Hotel?' he said. 'I was sorry I missed it.'

'Yes, I noticed you weren't there.'

'You did?' he said quickly. The expression in his eyes softened. Slightly embarrassed, I reached for my glass. 'All the information is in your dossier,' I said, wanting to move the conversation on. 'And you can wander around the place during the day.'

He was watching me, a half-smile on his face. He leant back. The chair groaned ominously.

'Your father told me you're from Charleston.' I wondered whether Wilson had relayed our conversation, especially my outburst. I decided he hadn't. He would have forgotten our chat the moment he stepped off the plane.

'My father still lives there. But I've moved to New York.'

'It must be quite a shock coming this far north. I can't remember when I've been so cold. And I live in Scotland.'

'I've had time to acclimatise. I've been in Stockholm for a few days.'

'You've got over jet-lag, then.'

'I wish,' he said, with feeling. 'No, I find it impossible when I travel east. It takes days. I find myself nodding off over dinner and then I'm wide awake at one in the morning.' He smiled broadly. 'You don't happen to know of a cure?'

'For jet-lag? There's only one cure. Drink heavily.'

He threw back his head and laughed. 'Ma'am, if there's one thing I've learnt, it's when to take advice. What do you say to another glass of wine?'

I was warming to him. 'Well, why not? Dinner isn't for ages.' I settled back, stretching my legs.

He signalled to the waiter for more wine and another beer.

The lounge was filling. The Danes appeared, Jane Galloway with them, and their laughter soon reached us from the bar. But there was no sign of Liz or Harry. Or Mike.

Our drinks arrived.

I lifted my glass in acknowledgement. 'Thank you.'

'Don't mention it, ma'am.'

'It's Maggie.'

He hesitated. 'Maggie.'

I sipped slowly. 'Your father tells me you run the Bibby Foundation.'

'I'd hardly call it "run". My father is the director. I do the day-to-day.'

'What does that entail exactly?'

He crossed his legs. The chair creaked, but it held. 'We get applications from all over the world. For funds – the Foundation is essentially a charity. My father decides how the funds are to be awarded. It's his money, after all.' There was a note of sourness in Marcellus's voice. 'My job is to ensure that the money gets to the successful applicants. And that they spend it the way they say they will.'

'What kinds of applications do you get?'

'There are different categories, and they change from year to year. We're in Stockholm because my father is setting up something with Sweden. It's totally new.' He took a gulp of beer. 'I can tell you, it's no secret. We receive applications from schools in the southern states of the US. As well as giving them aid in the form of grants, my father is organising a programme of exchange visits to schools in Sweden.'

'So Swedish children visit South Carolina, and vice versa?'

'Not just South Carolina. The programme will eventually extend to all the states in the US. The Swedes won't have to pay a penny. My father is funding it entirely, capital costs, running costs. The whole nine yards.'

'Why Sweden?' I said, curious.

He gazed at me with his sloe-black eyes. 'My father's intention is to do this all over the world. Sweden just happens to be the first country that's responded to his invitation.'

'And the Foundation is funding all of this?'

There was more than a trace of irritation in his voice now. 'All of it.'

I did a rapid calculation. The scheme would cost millions, billions even. It would make a serious dent in Wilson's coffers, if not empty them entirely.

'It's going to mean a lot of extra work for the Foundation,' I said cautiously.

'The work's not the problem.'

I was tempted to ask what was, but the finality of his tone stopped me.

After a pause, I said, 'Marcellus, you may already know this but one of my friends, Henry Auchinleck, is an academic who's been receiving grants from the Bibby Foundation.'

'An academic?' He shook his head. 'Then advise him to look elsewhere for his money.'

I felt my mouth go dry. 'Why?'

Marcellus's mobile rang. He reached into his pocket. 'Because his source of funding is about to come to an end.' He glanced at the phone. 'I'm sorry. I need to take this.' He got to his feet. The chair came with him. He pulled it away and set it on the floor.

I gripped his arm. 'Wait. Please. What do you mean, his source of funding is about to come to an end?'

'As of next year, my father is scaling down the Foundation's range of supported activities. He's decided scholarly research is to be the first casualty.'

'Funding for research is coming to an end? That's definite?'

'He still has to run it past the board of governors.'

'And what are they likely to do?'

He laughed bitterly. 'Nothing. They'll do absolutely nothing. They never do. They probably won't like it, but my father always gets his way.' He hesitated. 'As I said, it's his money. Now you really must excuse me.' He clamped the phone to his ear and left the room.

I thought about the resentment in Marcellus's eyes as he'd said it. And he'd said it twice: *It's his money.*

Money that Wilson was spending like water.

CHAPTER 6

I was still grappling with the implications of what Marcellus had said when Mike arrived. Flushed after his workout and breathing heavily, he looked ready for a drink.

'I wouldn't sit in that chair,' I said lightly. 'It's liable to break.'

He stared at the array of glasses. 'You been here long?'

'I'm a fast drinker.'

He set down his beer. 'So, Maggie, before she comes in, tell me about Liz. I'd like to get to know her better, but I don't want to make a fool of myself right and left.'

'She's not married.' I kept my gaze steady. 'I'm guessing that's what you want to know.'

He laughed. 'Just like a woman. Straight for the jugular.'

'You should look her up when we're back in Dundee. You can meet her children,' I added mischievously.

He didn't rise to the bait. 'What sort of a person is she?'

'Easy to talk to. Personality-wise, she's just like me – warm and wonderful, and she laughs a lot.'

'A merry widow?' A smile crept on to his lips. 'Even better.'

'Actually, she's divorced.'

'And is she with someone at the moment?'

It was my turn to laugh. 'Now who's going for the jugular?'

'It's a straightforward question, so it is.'

'Well, here's a straightforward answer. It's none of your business.'

He shook his head in mock exasperation. 'And here I am thinking I might enlist your help.'

'I'd think again, pal,' I said good-naturedly. 'Oh, did I mention she's into karate and judo? You wouldn't think it to look at her, but she's incredibly strong. She can floor a man twice her size,' I added, making a point of looking at Mike's body.

He said nothing, but his smile widened.

'What about you?' I said, after a brief silence. 'What are you all about?'

If he was surprised by the directness of my question, he didn't show it. 'I work hard and I play hard.'

'And what form does playing hard take?'

'I'm like everyone else. I drink, I socialise, I . . .' He moistened his upper lip with his tongue.

'Womanise?'

'Who doesn't? I'm a red-blooded male. It's not a cause of confession.'

'Yet something tells me there's a side to you you're trying not to reveal,' I said playfully. 'What really lights your fire?'

He opened his arms in an expression of surrender. 'You got me. I like to gamble.'

'I'm guessing cards. Poker?'

'Spot on.'

'What kind?'

'The kind with high stakes.'

'In Dundee? Where? That place on West Marketgait?'

'It's not a part of Dundee you're acquainted with. These are private games.'

I studied him. 'You know, Mike, I've never seen the attraction in risking hard-earned money.'

'It's the possibility of relieving someone else of theirs that's the attraction.' He lifted his glass. 'Eight players. Minimum stakes, a thousand apiece.'

'Pounds?' I said, appalled.

'I'm not talking pence.' He wiped his mouth with the back of his hand. 'Are you shocked?'

'How did you get into it?'

'When I was young, we all did it. There are plenty of places in Dublin.'

'And you say these sorts of games go on in Dundee?'

'It's not in Yellow Pages. Only the cognoscenti know where to go. I'd offer to take you when we're back, but somehow I think you're not a player.'

I stared at him, aghast.

'That's what I thought.'

'Do you ever lose?'

'Mostly I break even, though there are times when I come out with my pockets crammed. Ah, but it's a grand feeling when that happens.'

I was seeing him in a new light. Yet I thought he'd been a little too quick in his reply about gambling. There was another dimension to him, a dimension he was being careful not to reveal.

After a silence, I said, 'Have you heard of the Bibby Foundation?'

His expression changed, and he set down his glass.

'I'll take that as a yes.'

'It's impossible not to have heard of them. Wilson Bibby has just unveiled his big new schools initiative.'

'You know about that?' I said, surprised.

'The Swedish papers are full of it. And, I expect, so are the papers everywhere else.' He rolled the glass between his palms. 'The Bibbys were in Stockholm last week, meeting members of the Swedish government.'

'And this week they're at the Ice Hotel.'

He glanced up. 'Yes, I heard they'd be coming here.'

Surely Bibby, a man who travelled incognito, wouldn't broadcast his holiday location to the world. 'How on earth did you know that?' I said.

'One of the Yanks I was drinking with is working with Bibby. He told me. So what's the big interest in the Bibby Foundation?'

'I've just been speaking to Marcellus Bibby, and—'

'You've been speaking to him?' A look of horror crossed Mike's face. 'Listen, Maggie, it's not often I give women advice, but I'm telling you now to steer clear of him. Of both of them.'

'That's not going to be possible. We're in the same hotel.'

He ran a hand through his hair, sighing in irritation.

'Why should I steer clear of them?' I said defensively.

A pulse was beating in his temple.

'I'm concerned, Mike, because Harry relies on the Bibby Foundation for his research funding.'

'He accepts money from them? Holy Mother o' God. This just gets better and better.' His jaw muscles clenched. 'Sounds like Harry's moral compass has led him to places it shouldn't. Take it from me, you need a long spoon to sup with the Bibbys.'

'You're exaggerating,' I said, looking away.

His voice was laced with sarcasm. 'Is this why you're all here, then? To see the great grand man? Like flies to shit.'

'We had no idea Wilson Bibby would be at the Ice Hotel,' I said hotly.

But Mike had known. He'd known, and he'd chosen the Ice Hotel for a last-minute holiday. I wondered then just how last-minute it had been. He'd been drinking with the Americans on Saturday. Had he made a snap decision when he'd learnt about Bibby's Ice Hotel vacation? Perhaps it was Mike who'd wanted to see the great man. But, given his strong feelings about Bibby, I couldn't help but wonder why.

'What do you have against Wilson Bibby?' I said. 'Come clean, Mike.'

'The man's a gobshite. A streak of piss.'

'Once again, please. This time with feeling.'

He shot me a look of venom. 'Let's just change the subject.'

'If you like,' I said, shrugging.

'Tell me to mind my own business,' he said, after a pause, 'but is Harry gay?'

'If he were, would you have a problem with that?'

'Of course not. I don't give a fiddler's fart one way or the other. My young brother is gay. No, it's just that I like to know the lie of the land.' His lips twitched. 'I love his voice. It's a male version of Maggie Smith's in *The Prime of Miss Jean Brodie*.' He swirled his beer. 'He strikes me as a pathological optimist.'

'He has to be. He's an academic.'

'How did you meet him?'

'Liz introduced us a couple of years ago.' I smiled, remembering. 'She took me to one of his lectures.'

'Not *Nature or Nurture*?'

'I have to confess I haven't read his book but, yes, I think it was. He told us about the international terrorists he's interviewed.'

There was admiration in Mike's voice. 'He's interviewed terrorists?'

'Some were serving prison sentences. He was deliberately vague about the whereabouts of the others. But I must tell you, you'll laugh at this, he was recounting the story of how he'd lost his passport somewhere in the Middle East, and was being held overnight in this hole of a prison. You know he has this cowlick in his hair? Well, he reached up to push it back, and his glasses went flying into the front row. Some bloke leapt out of his seat and caught them, and Harry asked him if he wanted to join the university cricket team. Then he carried on with his talk as though nothing had happened.'

Mike grinned. 'Got to admit it, he has flair.'

Right on cue, Harry arrived. His clothes were usually the stuff of television makeovers, but he was dressed more soberly in a navy suit that was so old the style was coming back. He was wearing a blue-and-white-spotted bow tie, the type my father called a 'proper bow tie' and not one of those 'modern elasticated contraptions'. Expertly knotted, it said everything about him.

'Ah, you're here, children,' he said. 'Let me get myself a drink.' He caught the waiter's eye.

I wondered whether I should broach the subject of Bibby and his funding, but this was not the time. Better to wait until we were alone.

'Tell me now, Harry, what's it like being an academic?' Mike said. 'Is it really all croquet and cucumber sandwiches?'

'Good Lord, no. But it is wonderful, a life of great variety. There's teaching, which I love — all those fresh young minds. And then there's research. I would have to be honest, however, and say it's research that keeps me in academia.'

'So what's the attraction?'

He polished his spectacles. 'It enables me to travel and meet people, not just academics but from all walks of life. I've met terrorists, and been in a couple of tight spots. Occasionally, I'm asked to do the odd bit of research for the police, and sometimes I have to testify in court. And then there are the book deals.' He tapped the side of his nose. 'Unbelievably lucrative.'

Mike laughed. 'Haven't you ever had a proper job?'

I closed my eyes, embarrassed at his gaucheness.

'Like what, dear boy?' Harry said quietly.

'Doing what Maggie does, for example.'

I threw Mike a look, annoyed he'd dragged me and my job into the conversation.

'Ah, the money.' Harry eyed me appreciatively. 'Never understood it. It's outwith the orbit of an academic, I'm afraid.' Harry's views on how the rest of the world made a living were well known to Liz and me, but he never missed an opportunity to articulate them to others. 'If you want to know what God thinks about money, look at the sort of people he's given it to.'

Mike grinned. 'Game, set, and match.'

I glanced at my watch. 'Does anyone know where Liz is?'

'She's talking to the twins,' Harry said. 'She's going to meet us in the restaurant.'

'That's a long time to be on the phone.'

'She's in the computer room, my dear. Some whizzo internet trickery that allows her to see the twins as she speaks.'

'I didn't know they had computers,' Mike said. 'There's just time to check my email before dinner. See you all later.' He rose hurriedly and left the room.

I caught Harry's eye.

'Yes,' he said, smiling, 'he could have checked his email on his phone. I suspect the attraction is not the computers, but the lovely Liz.' The smile faded. 'But if he breaks her heart, I'll kill him.'

I put a hand on Harry's arm. 'There's something I need to talk to you about.' This was going to be difficult. 'I've been speaking with Marcellus Bibby.'

He looked startled. 'Have you indeed?' he said faintly.

'He and Wilson were in Stockholm last week, promoting some new initiative.'

'I know about that.'

'You do?'

'The Bibby Foundation keeps us abreast of new enterprises. They're good that way. There was a big write-up in the autumn newsletter about this Stockholm event.' He smiled sheepishly. 'I must admit, I rather dragooned you and Liz into choosing this week for the holiday. You see, I had intended to pop over to Stockholm and arrange a meeting with Wilson Bibby.'

So that was why he'd cancelled Rome. My breath came out in a rush. 'A meeting? But why?'

'I need to persuade him to continue funding my research. I thought that a face-to-face, where I could thrall him with the force of my argument, would clinch it. I was going to give him a signed copy of my book.' A look of sadness crossed his face. 'As you saw at the airport, I rather blew it. I was caught on the hop – I simply didn't expect to see him there. But I had to speak to him because I thought it might be my only chance. He could have been jetting off to anywhere.' He patted my hand. 'Still, not to worry. I'm sure no irreparable harm was done.'

'Oh, Harry,' I moaned, 'I don't know how to tell you this.'

He smiled kindly. 'Tell me what, my dear?'

I scrolled through the phrases I could use, but there was going to be no easy way. 'Wilson is reorganising the Bibby Foundation. He intends to drop some of the things the Foundation supports. Research will be one of them. Marcellus said that—' I stopped, seeing the look on Harry's face.

He was leaning forward, staring into my eyes. 'He's cutting support for research? Are you sure that's what he said? You couldn't have misunderstood?'

'Marcellus was quite clear.' I clutched Harry's arm, alarmed at his despair. 'But it's not definite. Wilson still has to get his board's approval, and they won't like it, according to Marcellus.'

'I'm not surprised. There are leading academics on the governing body, some of whom I know personally. But I wonder why I haven't heard about this. There was nothing in the newsletter.'

'I had the impression Wilson's told no one yet. Marcellus said that, if it happens, it won't be until next year. It isn't the end of the world. It leaves you time to find another source of funding, doesn't it?'

He was struggling to keep himself under control. 'I very much doubt it. I try every year, and the Bibby Foundation is the only organisation that gives me a grant.'

'What about applying for government funding? I would have thought, with all the terrorism—'

'I've tried that avenue, but there's simply too much competition. No, there's no point applying elsewhere. I'll have to start a completely new line of research, which won't be easy at my age. And, whatever my colleagues say, I'm not ready for a pipe-and-slippers life just yet,' he added defiantly.

'Oh, no,' I murmured.

He dropped his head. 'I must admit this is a body blow I hadn't expected.'

I squeezed his hand, anguished, unable to think of anything to say.

He sat slumped, face slack, mouth half open, probably wondering which sleight of hand could make all this disappear, like one of his carnations.

'Come on, Harry.' I guided him gently to his feet. 'Time for dinner.'

The restaurant was on the first floor. A large, warm room, it was decorated in the same cream and maroon as the rest of the Excelsior. The single picture window was framed with silk curtains that pooled on the floor in a swirl of cream. Nothing could be seen through the glass except the Ice Hotel, a ghostly imprint against the dark sky.

Our group was seated at the long table that ran the length of the room. We were all present. All except the Bibbys. They had a private table at the window, and were conversing across a couple of bottles of wine. Wilson seemed to be doing all the talking. And all the drinking. He looked relaxed in a brown sweater and tan slacks. Marcellus was wearing designer army camouflage clothes.

Harry was seated opposite me, with Liz beside him and Mike on her other side. He let out another button of his waistcoat. 'I'd never appreciated the taste of reindeer before, but that casserole was delicious.'

Good food was guaranteed to lift Harry's spirits. I was now bitterly regretting having told him about Wilson's funding decision. It would have been better to leave him in a state of happy delusion, and wait until our return before bursting his bubble. Poor Harry. That he was so dependent on charity for his research explained his ingratiating behaviour at the airport. But what had taken me completely by surprise was his throwaway comment about his plan to visit Wilson. Yet the Ice Hotel had been Liz's choice of venue. Had Harry conspired with her to ensure that we chose to come to Sweden? Could he have been so manipulative? No, I was sure Liz would have told me. Harry had just seen an opportunity and taken it. And it had come to nothing.

Dessert arrived, a concoction of loganberries and ice cream served in individual ice dishes.

'You have to eat it quickly,' said an unfamiliar voice, 'or the ice will melt.'

The voice came from my immediate right. It was the fair-haired man I'd seen in the gym with Mike. His hair, which on closer inspection was a red shade of blond, was long and thinning on top.

He smiled broadly. 'My name is Jonas,' he said, pronouncing it Yonas. 'Jonas Madsen,' he added.

'Maggie Stewart.'

He held the dish to his chin and spooned the food into his mouth. His hands were as big as plates, with bristly hairs standing on his fingers. His face was so fleshy that, seen from the side, his eyes disappeared into his head.

'Is this your first time at the Ice Hotel?' he said. His words were slightly slurred. Empty beer bottles littered the table in front of him.

'Yes, I'm here with friends.' I dipped my spoon into the loganberries. 'But you said "first time". Have you slept in the Ice Hotel before?'

'When you've done it once, you want to do it again. A bit like sex.' He smiled directly at me. 'In fact, a lot like sex.' He glanced at my breasts. His eyes glazed over and he began to sway. For a second, I thought he was going to fall on to the table, but he blinked hard a few times and kept himself upright.

'Jonas,' I said, when the silence had gone on too long. 'Is that a Swedish name?'

He attacked his dessert, scooping up the remains of the berries. 'I'm Danish.' He motioned to his friends. 'We are all from Copenhagen. Do you know it?'

'I've never been.'

'You should visit. It's a beautiful country.'

'What's it like living there?'

'I don't live in Copenhagen. My home is in Göteborg now.'

Geography was never my strong point. 'In Denmark?'

'Sweden. I work for a Swedish company.' He set down the ice dish. 'Göteborg is a wonderful city. It's a pity my company is always sending me to Stockholm.'

I was having difficulty keeping up. 'Why don't you live in Stockholm, then?'

'I have a woman in Göteborg.' He glanced at my breasts again.

'Anyway, it's no skin off my face. The company pays for the hotels. I've been to Stockholm so many times I must have stayed in all of them.'

'Don't you get bored with hotels?' I said, bringing the napkin to my lips. 'All that powdered coffee and tiny soap?'

'It depends on the hotel. My favourite was the Maximilian.' He smiled lazily. 'It was the best. Not too large, but not small either. And the finest wine cellar in Europe. The company kept a suite there. But the hotel closed down last year because—'

There was a sudden shout as the Dane next to Jonas knocked over a bottle. Beer spilt on to the table, spreading in all directions. Jonas jumped up as though touched with a cattle prod. He grabbed his napkin and mopped at his crotch, cursing in Danish as his friends bellowed with laughter and slapped the table. He hissed, wiping himself down, then resumed his seat and called to the waiter for more beer. When the man reappeared, he thanked him, took the bottle and drank deeply.

'You must excuse my friends. They have no manners.' He smiled suddenly. 'So did you go on the tour of the Ice Hotel?'

'Absolutely. It was simply marvellous.'

'Then you know that the Ice Hotel is different every year. It's why I always make time to look around it.'

'I didn't see you on the tour.'

'Sometimes I take the tour.' He pulled a face. 'But not if Marita is the guide.'

'I thought she was excellent,' I said, leaping to her defence.

'I don't know how to say it in English, but she's—' He stopped and conversed quickly with one of his companions. 'Tight-arsed,' he said loudly, his face serious. 'But occasionally Karin gives the tour. She is much more . . .' he paused for a second '. . . loose-arsed.'

73

I nodded, making a supreme effort to keep my face straight. Most of the conversation in the room had stopped.

Jonas gazed across at the Bibbys. He motioned with the bottle. 'Who are those two sitting on their own?'

'Wilson Bibby and his son, Marcellus. Have you heard of the Bibby Foundation?'

'What is it? A type of cosmetic?'

'A charity.'

He spoke slowly, his words distorted. 'Why don't they sit with us? Are they tight-arsed too?'

Harry, who'd been listening to Jonas, drew himself up. 'The father is certainly not very sociable. In fact, he's downright rude. He ignored me in Stockholm when I tried to speak to him.'

Jonas's words were now so slurred I could hardly make them out. 'That is not very nice. He should come here and apologise.' He aimed at the word several times and still missed. Hunching his shoulders, he planted his hands on the table and scraped his chair back. The room was now completely silent. He staggered to his feet, overturning the chair. Then, swaying alarmingly, he thrust his head forward and lurched across the room. I knew this type of drunk: soaked enough to lose the use of his legs but not enough to lose the contents of his stomach.

Marcellus sprang to his feet and put himself between Jonas and his father. 'I suggest you return to your table, sir,' he said.

Jonas tried to stand straight. 'And if I don't?'

'I might forget my manners,' came the soft reply.

A murmur rippled through the room. One of the waiters stepped forward, but his companion caught him by the arm and shook his head.

Marcellus and Jonas were large and evenly matched. But Marcellus was a martial-arts expert, and Jonas was drunk. His friends leapt out of their seats and pulled him away. He grumbled loudly, trying to shake them off, but he was outnumbered. They dragged him unceremoniously from the room, still protesting, and his shouts grew weaker as they stumbled down the stairs.

Marcellus resumed his seat and he and Wilson continued their conversation as though nothing had happened. I watched him pour wine for his father, a faint smile on his lips, and wondered idly how often he had to deal with the Jonases of this world. He caught my eye, and nodded briefly. I smiled back.

Mike's voice cut into my thoughts. 'Pity about that.' He sounded genuinely disappointed. 'I was keen to see how it was going to end. I'd have put money on Marcellus, given the condition the other feller was in.'

Harry was subdued, but his expression said it all: he, too, seemed disappointed that Jonas's attempt at a confrontation had been thwarted. Liz slipped her hand into his and leant into him, smiling, saying something I couldn't hear.

The waiter brought coffee, and reloaded the tray with the empty bottles, muttering under his breath. I was relieved that Jonas's half-hearted challenge had come to nothing. But as I sipped slowly, I couldn't dispel the image of Marcellus, chest puffed out like a cock pigeon, balling his fists, ready to smash them into Jonas's face.

CHAPTER 7

It was Tuesday, the day of the snowmobile safari, and we were boarding the coach. The sun was a pale yellow ball grazing the horizon.

As Leo Tullis conducted the name check, I scanned the seats. Liz and Harry were at the back, chatting with Mike. The Ellises, dressed as though leading an expedition to the Pole, were sitting behind the driver.

Wilson's voice boomed out from a few rows behind. 'Have you been on a snowmobile before, ma'am?'

I craned my neck. He was sitting with Jane Galloway.

She smiled shyly. 'Never.'

'The first time I rode on one of these contraptions was when I visited Greenland. It was quite an experience, I can tell you.' He launched into a rambling monologue about the pros and cons of snowmobiles versus husky-drawn sledges, leaning in so close that she was forced to draw her head back.

Marcellus was missing. I noticed he'd skipped breakfast. Perhaps the cold had defeated him. But, as the driver started the ignition, he climbed into the coach.

He lowered himself into the seat beside me. 'Good morning, ma'am,' he said softly. He unfastened his parka, snapping the poppers one by one, his hand moving slowly down the jacket. He opened it out, but kept it on. 'I'm sorry about that little spat last night. I hope it didn't spoil your dinner.'

'Do you have to deal with that sort of thing often?' I said quietly.

'Someone wanting to take a swipe at my father?'

'That's one way of putting it.'

He looked away. 'It happens.'

'You must be constantly on your guard.' I glanced at his chest. It was the sort you could hang forty medals on. 'What brand of martial arts do you practise?'

'Shotokan.' I must have looked blank because he added, 'It's the no-nonsense brand.'

'Your father told me he was nearly kidnapped once.'

Marcellus swung round, his neck jerking so sharply that the bones cracked.

God, he must have thought I was criticising him. 'Although I'm sure he can rest easy with a martial-arts expert around,' I added quickly.

'I like to think so.' He smiled faintly, a movement at the corner of his mouth that had more to do with politeness than friendliness.

I turned away. We journeyed in silence.

A familiar voice rose above the general hum of conversation. Jonas Madsen, sitting in front of Marcellus, had turned to call to someone at the back. His face was mottled, his red-rimmed eyes were bloodshot and he stank of beer.

'Olof!' The rest was in Danish.

Olof shouted something back, which ended the conversation. Jonas, turning away, caught sight of Marcellus. His eyes narrowed, and his lips curled into an expression of distaste. For one electrifying moment, I thought he was going to take a swing at him, but good sense prevailed and he settled down in his seat. Marcellus gazed calmly at the back of Jonas's head. The look on his face was unreadable.

We were approaching the snowmobile depot. Leo Tullis stood up next to the driver and gave us some brief information about the trip for the benefit, he said, in a mocking but good-natured way, of those who hadn't bothered to read his notice. The part I assimilated was that lunch would be at the top of the mountain.

The depot was a slatted wooden building hulking inside a wire-fenced enclosure. A line of snowmobiles stood outside. I did a quick head count. We were sixteen, so we could have a machine each.

We assembled in the waiting room, chattering excitedly. It smelt strongly of tar, and the furnishings consisted of half a dozen rickety chairs and a foam sofa. Leo disappeared and returned shortly with a burly man in snow-suit and boots.

Leo lifted his arms to get our attention. 'This is our guide. His name's Sven. I can't pronounce his surname,' he added, with a grin.

Sven laughed and clapped Leo on the back, sending him sprawling. 'Snow-suits are in the changing room.' His voice was guttural, the accent thick. 'Then we'll start the machines. You can ride on your own, or with a partner.' He caught my eye and winked.

In the changing room, a smaller version of the Activities Room, Harry sidled up to me. 'Maggie, can I ride pillion with you? I'm a bit nervous about going on one of these contraptions on my own.'

'Of course, but you'll have to hang on. I'm a bit of a speed demon.'

'My dear, how fast can you go in that old banger of yours? Forty? And I should imagine that's downhill with a following wind.'

Liz was clambering into a white suit. 'Are you coming with me, Mike?' She buttoned her hood.

'Sure,' he said, after a moment.

His expression suggested he'd have preferred to ride on his own. I smiled to myself. Whatever Liz had intended, she might have miscalculated.

We lined up behind the snowmobiles and watched Sven demonstrate the controls.

'It sounds deceptively simple, Maggie,' Harry said nervously.

'It has to be. Most of the people using these are tourists.'

Sven finished the demonstration. 'Remember that once you get going it will be noisy. If you are in pairs, you won't hear each other speak, so don't try. And I would keep your hood up and your gloves on because, although the handles are heated, there is a strong wind chill. I will be at the front and Leo at the back, so there's no danger of anyone getting lost.' He stroked his cheek thoughtfully. 'Although you would be surprised how people still manage it. I lost three machines last season.'

I switched my gaze to Harry. I could tell this was something he hadn't wanted to hear.

Sven climbed on to the front snowmobile. At Harry's insistence, we took the next machine in line.

'I want the guide in my sights the whole time,' he said, eyeing Sven. 'Not just because he's a magnificent specimen, but because I don't fancy my chances with the polar bears.'

'Harry, there are no polar bears here.'

He looked at me over the rim of his reading glasses. 'We're north of the Arctic Circle, dear girl, which means that polar bears are a distinct possibility. And where there are polar bears, man is not top of the food chain.'

I removed his glasses gently and tucked them into his pocket before climbing into the front seat. Harry pulled up his hood and clambered on behind me. I started the ignition, revving the engine experimentally. The snowmobile jerked forward, and Harry flung his arms round my waist, clinging on as though his life depended on it. Sven moved away and we followed in an orderly line.

We went slowly at first, gathering speed as our confidence grew. Once through the double gates that marked the depot boundary, we were in wilderness. The terrain was varied. We travelled mostly on paths snaking through the tundra, although on one occasion we crossed a main road. Every so often Sven stopped us, using a prearranged signal, then he and Leo did a quick count. The first time we pulled up, I asked Harry if he wanted to try the controls, but he stared at me as though I'd grown horns.

'You must be joking, my dear. If you let me drive, I'll inflict grievous bodily harm on this machine, and we'll find ourselves in a ditch. No, you're doing so well. But you might think about slowing down. If we go any faster, we'll travel back in time.'

'I'm keeping up with Sven,' I said, in mild irritation. 'That's hardly fast.'

At the next stop, which was longer and gave us an opportunity to stretch our legs, I left Harry and went to find Liz.

She was rubbing her backside, Mike watching her. 'I'm saddle-sore already, Mags, even through this thick suit.'

'You're too skinny.' I grinned. 'You need a derrière like mine.'

'How's Harry managing?' Mike said.

'He thinks we're going to be eaten by polar bears.'

The Bibbys were with their snowmobile near the back of the line. They were deep in conversation, Marcellus holding his mobile to his ear. 'Don't even think about dicking me around, pal,' I heard him say into the phone, his voice measured.

There was a sudden shout. Jonas was ambling towards them, bellowing and gesticulating.

Marcellus lowered the phone. 'Pardon me?'

Jonas pushed him hard in the chest with both hands. Marcellus fell back, dropping the phone, and would have lost his footing had his father not grabbed his shoulders and steadied him.

'What's your problem, asshole?' Marcellus hissed, squaring up to Jonas. 'You want to take a pop at me? Okay, then. So come on.'

I stared, appalled. 'There's going to be a fight,' I murmured.

Jonas lunged, taking a wide swipe, but Marcellus sidestepped the blow neatly and, with a simple but effective martial-arts manoeuvre, forced Jonas to the ground. A circle of people formed. Jane stood beside me, white-faced, a spray of red hair escaping from her hood.

Leo reached the scene ahead of Sven. 'What the hell's going on?'

Marcellus was bending over Jonas, holding his wrist in an excruciatingly painful grip.

'You,' Leo shouted to Marcellus. 'Let him go.'

Marcellus released his grip and Jonas fell backwards.

'Now tell me what happened,' Leo said, running a hand over his face.

Marcellus spoke quietly. 'I was talking on my cell when this lunatic lunged at me, sir.'

'He's telling the truth,' Robyn Ellis said, jabbing an indignant finger at Jonas. 'That man is drunk. He shouldn't be on our trip.'

A murmur ran through the group.

Wilson was standing well back, watching the scene with cold amusement.

Leo raised his voice so we could all hear. 'Right then, if there's any more trouble, the trip's off and we all go back. Do you understand?' He looked at Jonas who was brushing snow from his suit. 'Do you understand?' he shouted.

Jonas hesitated. '*Ja, ja*,' he said quietly. With a murderous glance at Marcellus, he loped back to his friends, who crowded round him, yelling in Danish.

Sven jerked his head towards the snowmobiles. 'Time to go, everyone.'

Harry had joined us, and was watching the scene, quivering with excitement.

'Really, Harry,' Liz said disapprovingly, 'all this testosterone.'

'Yes, absolutely splendid.'

'That was stupid of Jonas,' I said. 'Ballsy, but stupid.'

Mike stopped Leo as he trudged past. 'I thought you handled that brilliantly.'

Leo shrugged wearily. 'I've been on the course. Dealing With Difficult People.'

'I'm sure it's nothing to be concerned about,' I said. I felt my lips twitch. 'Just alpha males, marking their territory.'

The men glared at me.

We set off on the final leg. After crossing a frozen lake, we approached the last hurdle: the ascent of the mountain. Sven took a circular route, not the fastest way, but the easiest. It was heavy going and made me even more determined that Harry should drive on the way back.

I glanced at the sky. A faint band of grey cloud smeared the horizon. I felt my spirits lift: the chances of seeing the aurora tonight were good.

The woodland grew denser, and the incline steeper, but the path was wide and the machines had little difficulty with the final climb. We emerged from the forest into a steep clearing, crowned with a brightly painted chalet. To our left was an iron railing. A flight of wooden steps, swept free of snow, led to the summit.

Sven gave the signal to stop, and waited until we'd cut the engines. He motioned towards the slope. 'It is too steep to go further. We will park the snowmobiles beside the steps, one in front of the other. We must make sure the machines are secure. I will check the brakes.'

'That was a magnificent trip,' Harry was saying. 'I must say it's made me feel quite peckish. See you at the top.' He grasped the railing and moved stiffly up the steps, walking like John Wayne.

I watched as Sven double-checked my brakes.

'This is how you lock.' He pulled the lever. 'I have to make sure everyone understands how to do it. The lever should not be stiff. Now you try it.'

I fumbled under the handle.

'Better if you remove your mitten. Yes, good. Now, to unlock the brakes, move the lever in the other direction.'

I pushed the lever, surprised at the smoothness of the mechanism. I pulled the lever and relocked the brakes.

Sven nodded, then moved on to the next machine. 'No need to stay,' he said, seeing my hesitation. 'I would go to the chalet before the food disappears. How do you say it? First arrived, first served.' He motioned down the slope. 'But after lunch, you should take a walk.'

'What's down there?'

'A magnificent view. The best in these parts. It is one of the reasons we bring visitors here. Mind your step, though. There is a ledge you have to climb over – see there where the ground flattens – but then the path takes you through the trees straight to the vista point. You can't miss it.'

'Thank you.' I tramped up the slope towards the chalet, my boots sinking in the soft snow.

Lunch was a ragoût of reindeer meat, followed by sticky berry cake. I left the others, and took my plate outside to one of the trestle tables bolted to the ground. It was warm out of the shade, and I turned my face to the sun.

'You should be careful. The air is thinner here.' Jonas was plastering his skin with a white powdery cream, his blunt fingers moving over his face in rapid strokes. His eyes were still blood-shot and he looked as though he was nursing a hangover.

'How are you feeling today?' I said coldly.

'I shouldn't have had so much to drink last night.' He paused. 'Did I behave badly?'

'Can't you remember?'

'It is a blur, I'm afraid.'

He must have taken my hesitation for censure, because he continued in a shamed voice, 'I am trying to drink less, but it is difficult. You see, I am from Copenhagen,' he added, as though that explained everything. 'If I have offended you, I cannot apologise enough.'

I wasn't the one needing the apology, I thought, remembering his recent treatment of Marcellus. Jonas seemed more concerned about his heavy drinking than about throwing a punch at some-one. But I said nothing.

He turned away and walked down the incline, shoulders hunched.

'Look, Liz,' I heard Harry say, 'I am not driving one of those things. Maggie is perfectly proficient and I'd be a poor second at it. Maggie, will you make Liz see reason? She thinks I need excitement in my life.' He sat down heavily. 'She wouldn't say that if she witnessed the Punch and Judy of Faculty Council meetings.'

Mike had followed them out. He stretched, yawning. 'I'm taking a look around. Fancy a walk to that vista point, Liz?'

She glanced at Harry, then at me. 'You go, Mike,' she said. 'I'll catch you later.'

He shrugged, then took his beer to where Jonas was standing near the snowmobiles. He thumped him on the arm to get his attention. A minute later, their raucous laughter reached us.

I was amused at Liz's show of loyalty. 'Don't worry about us,' I said. 'Go and join him.' I leant my head against the wall. 'I'm going to take a little snooze.'

She hesitated for only a second, then left, making her way slowly down the steps.

I was nodding off when I felt a sharp tap on my arm. Harry was staring straight ahead.

A family of reindeer had appeared from behind the chalet. They skittered about nervously, the big male pawing the ground with a scarred hoof. They stopped not far from the table, and gazed at us for several seconds, their liquid eyes wide with curiosity. Then, just as suddenly, they lost interest and moved away, nuzzling the ground.

'These are the first we've seen,' I whispered, tugging at Harry's sleeve. 'Come on. Let's get some photos.'

I rose too quickly, and the reindeer jumped away. Harry took my arm, and we followed the animals down the clearing.

He was having difficulty in the snow. 'Take care, my dear. It's treacherous underfoot.'

The ground levelled off, and the walking became easier. I looked around for Liz. She'd left the steps and was making her way towards Mike and Jonas, who were near the ledge, drinking silently now.

The reindeer had stopped a few feet from her.

'Liz,' I hissed.

She turned and, seeing the animals, pulled a camera out of her pocket. She held it out, gesturing to me to take a photo.

'Go on, Harry,' I said. 'You be in the picture. The twins will want to see you, too.'

85

He seemed pleased. 'Do you think so?' He waded over to Liz.

But the reindeer wouldn't stay still. No sooner had they stopped, and Liz and Harry had crept over, than one sprang away and the others followed. Eventually, they trotted over the ledge and disappeared.

'Hold on to me, sweetheart,' Liz said. 'We're climbing over.' She put an arm round Harry, and he clambered down by sitting on the edge and swinging his legs.

I peered over. The broad ledge was five feet high. The reindeer had taken up position to the right where the foraging was better. Ignoring Liz and Harry, they tugged at the moss growing between the trees, grazing the bark with their velvet antlers.

Liz tiptoed across. Careful not to spook the animals, she motioned to Harry to join her, then signalled frantically at me to take a picture. She smoothed down her ponytail, pushing stray wisps of hair behind her ears.

I was fumbling with the lens cap when I heard the sound.

I spun round. The line of snowmobiles was slipping down the incline. They went slowly at first, but gathered momentum frighteningly quickly, toppling their neighbours like giant dominoes. Their metallic screeching grew so loud it was painful to hear. I watched, transfixed, as the machines slid heavily towards the overhang. Only then did I remember Liz and Harry.

Harry was gazing up with a puzzled expression. Liz looked terrified. I waved my arms like a person demented, screaming at them to get out of the way. As the first of the snowmobiles pounded over the edge, Liz sprang towards the safety of the trees. The machines thundered down, one by one, demolishing a group of saplings, finally shrieking to a stop several feet from Harry. The reindeer were nowhere to be seen.

Mike and Jonas had scrambled to the overhang and were staring at the wreckage.

I rushed at them, yelling, 'What the hell do you think you're doing? They could have been killed. Why didn't you warn them?'

'What do you mean, warn them?' Mike said, his attention still on the snowmobiles.

'For God's sake, you were right next to the machines.'

Jonas was frowning, the white cream round his eyes making him look like a ghoul. 'We were near the machines, yes, but when they slipped we couldn't stop them. It would have been danger-ous even to try.'

I looked from one to the other helplessly. 'But why didn't you warn Liz? And Harry?'

Mike peered over the edge, bewildered. 'We didn't know they were there.'

People were pouring out of the chalet, alerted by the noise. Shock registered on their faces as they reached us and saw what had happened.

Leo thrust his way through the crowd, his face as white as Jonas's. 'Sven,' he shouted, his voice breaking with shock.

Sven came running, zipping up his snow-suit. He stopped dead at the overhang. When he saw the wrecked snowmobiles, his expression hardened. His hands were trembling.

I pushed past and climbed down.

Liz had emerged from the trees, and she and Harry were gazing at the metallic heap. Beyond them, round a bend in the path, came the Bibbys. They stopped and gaped. Wilson's face was grim.

Marcellus hurried over. 'What in God's name happened here, Maggie?' He looked intently into my eyes. 'Are you okay?'

I nodded back towards the overhang. 'I was up there. It was Harry and Liz who . . . who . . .'

He squeezed my arm gently. I turned away.

Harry tried to inject a brave note into his voice. 'We're all right, Maggie. Shaken, but not stirred.'

I wasn't so sure. He and Liz looked as though they were in shock.

'I'm sorry, Liz,' I said feebly. 'I dropped your camera.'

'Oh, heavens, don't worry about that. No, really, that's what insurance is for.' She was shaking. 'Well, I don't know about you two, but I could do with a drink.'

Harry put an arm round her shoulders and we clambered up the overhang, slipping in the snow, helping each other. The Bibbys examined the wreckage, then followed us. Mike was arguing with Sven and Leo, and everyone else was talking at once. We ignored them and made our way slowly up to the chalet.

Halfway there, something made me look back. Jonas was standing apart from the crowd. He was watching us, motionless, his red eyes staring out of the white mask.

At the final count, the damage wasn't as bad as Sven had thought. There were enough working machines to get us back, provided we doubled up. Harry looked distraught and, understandably, refused my suggestion that he drive.

'My dear, if I'm at the helm, we won't be in a safe pair of hands.' He lifted his arms. 'Look, I'm still quaking.'

This was not the time to insist. I climbed into the front seat without another word.

We had to wait for Sven who was huddled with Leo by the trees. He was speaking quietly but firmly. Leo was shaking his head, disbelief on his face.

'Looks as if Sven might be sending Leo the bill,' I said, hoping to lighten the mood.

When there was no reply, I glanced over my shoulder. Harry was watching Sven and Leo, his face pale, a faraway look in his eyes.

On the coach, I made sure I sat next to him. He remained

subdued, eyes closed, head against the backrest. I made a mental note to think up something fun to do later. His arm was lying on his thigh, palm upwards. I slipped my hand into his and squeezed hard, but there was no response.

Liz was sitting with Olof, laughing at something he was saying, behaving as though nothing had happened. Jonas was staring at her, his face expressionless. He caught me watching and turned away, but not before I'd seen the look in his eyes. My mouth went dry. Was he feeling guilty at not having acted quickly? Or did he have something to hide?

Harry's eyes were still closed. 'What happened back there, Maggie?' he said quietly. 'I was in the hollow with Liz, and saw nothing until it was too late.'

'All I know is that you and Liz climbed down after the reindeer and, a second later, the snowmobiles toppled. Mike and Jonas were standing next to them.' I hesitated. 'They said they didn't see you, but I can't understand that. They must have watched you climb down.'

Harry opened his eyes. 'What I can't understand is why the machines fell over in the first place. Don't you think it odd?'

'It was an accident,' I said firmly. 'They were badly parked.'

'Were they? I thought the guide checked them before we went for lunch. You were with him when he did it.'

'I didn't see him check them all. I left after he'd looked at mine.'

'But he would have checked each one, wouldn't he? They were his machines. He wouldn't be sloppy about a thing like that.'

I felt the small hairs on the back of my neck rise. 'What are you saying, Harry?'

'Nothing, my dear, except I can quite believe that Mike and Jonas may not have seen us. No, what I find strange is that the snowmobiles, which had all been checked by an expert, slipped their brakes.'

CHAPTER 8

In the late afternoon, I ran into Liz in the foyer.

'How are you feeling?' I said anxiously.

She shrugged off the question, smiling. 'Absolutely nothing a stiff gin couldn't cure.'

'You and Harry could have been badly hurt. It makes my toes curl just to think about it.'

'Well, we weren't, so let's not dwell on it. Talking of Harry, where is he?'

'Working on his book. I tried to entice him out for a walk, but he insisted on doing his writing. He and that book are joined at the hip. You'd never think we were here for a holiday.' I paused. 'So how was the tour of the church?'

'Where were you? I made the guide wait but you didn't show. Marcellus was asking after you,' she added, a gleam in her eyes.

'Was he?'

'I have to confess, Mags, he does rather give me the creeps.'

'I like him,' I said defensively. 'Why does he give you the creeps?'

'I don't know. But that's why he gives me the creeps. If I knew why he gave me the creeps, he wouldn't be giving me the creeps, if you see what I mean.' She ran a hand over her ponytail. 'I have to say he's not someone I'd ever exchange body fluids with.'

I stared at her, wondering if this was her way of warning me off him.

'Well, why didn't you come to the church, Mags?'

'I had a nap and didn't wake in time. Did I miss anything?'

'It's interesting enough if architecture's your thing. You could pick the church up and transport it to Italy, and it really wouldn't look out of place. Inside, though, it's pure Scandinavian. All the original Italian stuff was taken away centuries ago.'

'And the platform in the tower?' I said eagerly.

'Marita was right. There's a notice telling you about viewing the aurora.' She studied me. 'It's a bit of a climb. Are you absolutely sure you want to do it?'

'Later in the week, perhaps. Tonight after dinner, I'm going out on the river.'

'Wow, you are keen. But how do you know there'll be anything to see?'

I nodded at the noticeboard. 'They're expecting a display tonight. There's something about a solar flare.'

She shook her head slowly. 'I really can't understand what it is with you and this aurora. It's just pretty lights in the sky, isn't it?'

'Did Mike go on the tour?' I said, suddenly curious.

'Yes, as a matter of fact he did.'

'And?'

'And nothing.'

'And afterwards?'

'We're only just back.' Her voice was measured. 'Mags, do I detect a subtext here?'

I was annoyed now that I'd missed the tour. Not because I'd wanted to see the church, which I could visit any time, but because I'd wanted to see how Mike and Liz behaved together.

She pulled a face. 'Wilson kept interrupting the guide, asking daft questions. At one point, I thought Mike was going to wallop him.'

'If he had, he'd have come off badly. You saw how Marcellus handled himself.'

'You don't think Mike would be a match?' There was a glint in her eyes. 'They're the same height and build.'

'I suppose you think Mike would have Marcellus's nuts in a jar.'

'You always did have an elegant turn of phrase, Mags. But, yes, I happen to think he would.'

She seemed determined to defend Mike. But she was my best friend, and I had to tell her. 'Liz, there's something you need to know about Mike. He told me he's into gambling in a big way. He goes to poker matches in Dundee.'

She was clearly undecided as to which stance to take. 'Well, what of it?' she said finally. 'It gives him a certain cachet, don't you think?'

'I don't. Put him back where you found him. People who gamble often ruin their lives. And the lives of others,' I added meaningfully. 'If this is how Mike likes to spend his time, give him a wide berth.'

'It's just a bit of harmless fun,' she said, in a tone that suggested she didn't believe it. 'I'm hoping to get to know him better.'

'Be careful what you wish for. You didn't see the lust on his face when he told me.'

'Lust?'

'Yes, lust. And it's not just the gambling. There's something about him I find disturbing. I can't put my finger on it. He's all charm and smarm on the surface, but underneath I think he's mad, bad and dangerous to know.'

She angled her head. I knew what she was thinking: *Are you really such a good judge of men, Mags?* But she had the good grace not to rub it in.

'It's ages till dinner,' she said, when the silence had gone on too long. 'There's time for a sauna. Are you coming?'

I was disappointed she'd dismissed my suspicions so readily. 'I'm going to the lounge.'

'You're not drinking already? Do go easy, Mags. Remember, it's Purple Kiss after dinner.'

'I'm not going for a drink. I feel like a game of chess.'

I watched her leave, suddenly remembering the fright in her eyes when she'd seen the pile of twisted snowmobiles. Had she known that Mike was above the overhang when they'd fallen? And hadn't shouted to warn her? Had Mike really not seen her?

Was I becoming paranoid?

The only guests in the lounge were the Ellises and Jane Galloway. They were huddled in an alcove, Robyn and Jim sitting one on either side of Jane. She was holding her mobile so they could all see the screen.

I took the seat opposite. 'Are those of the snowmobile trip?'

'The Ice Hotel tour.' Jim looked up. 'I wish I could have brought my boys to see that Scottish room.'

'Your children?' I said, smiling.

'My pupils. Robyn and I are teachers.' He glanced at his wife. When she didn't respond, he added, 'We both teach English literature.'

'That was some trip today, Maggie,' Jane said.

'The accident with the snowmobiles?'

'We were at that viewing place and didn't see anything. What in heaven's name happened?'

It wasn't a topic I wanted to dwell on, but I could see they expected me to tell them what I knew. 'One minute the machines were on the slope,' I said. 'The next, they were in a heap. It was a bizarre accident.'

'If bizarre accidents are going to happen—' Jim said.

93

'Oh, stop being neurotic,' Robyn replied. 'Nothing is going to happen, bizarre or otherwise.'

Jane put the phone away. 'According to Mr Bibby, those machines cost a packet. But I'm sure Sven has insurance.'

At the mention of Sven, Harry's words drifted into my mind: *What I find strange is that the snowmobiles, which had all been checked by an expert, slipped their brakes.* Sven *was* an expert, so how could those machines have fallen? I kept coming back to it: Mike and Jonas had been standing beside them.

The others were watching me as though I held the key to the puzzle. There was nothing more I could tell them.

'I'm forgetting my manners,' Jim said kindly. 'Can I get you something to drink?'

'Thanks, but no. I came for a game of chess. Any takers?'

'Sorry, I don't play,' Jane said.

'Nor do we,' Robyn added, with finality.

Jim was opening his mouth to speak when a deep voice said, 'I'll give you a game, ma'am.'

I turned slowly. 'Excellent,' I said, hoping the tone of my voice was consistent with its message.

Wilson fetched the wooden box from the bookcase. He set up the board and pieces at the table beside the window. 'How long have you been playing chess, Maggie?' He was studying me through narrowed eyes.

Of course, a shrewd businessman would evaluate the opposition first. I smiled disarmingly. 'Since I was a child.'

'Not too long, then.' He held out his arms, hands clenched into fists.

I pointed to his left. He uncurled the fist to reveal a black pawn.

A soft smile touched his lips. Something about his expression made me suspect he'd played chess all his life. But perhaps not with a board and wooden pieces.

He began with the traditional opening: pawn to king four.

'Are you enjoying your stay here, Wilson?' I said, making a show of concentration.

'This place is something else, isn't it? The snow conditions are just right.'

I lifted the pawn in front of the queen's knight and moved it forward two squares.

'Ah, the Sicilian defence. A good response. I see you'll be keeping me on my toes.' His hand hovered over the board. 'Yes, I was saying that the snow conditions are right for just about everything. I'm hoping to go on the snowshoeing trek tomorrow.' He made his play, moving another pawn.

'Today's accident hasn't put you off?'

'Nah. Why would it?'

We played silently for a while. He moved his pieces quickly and confidently, seeming impatient at my hesitation.

'Are you going back to the States at the end of the week?' I said.

'I have unfinished business in Stockholm.'

'To do with your schools' programme?' I glanced up. 'Marcellus told me about it.'

'I've a few things to conclude there. Then there's the obligatory reception at the palace.'

'It sounds like a great thing you're doing,' I said quietly.

'I'm proud of it.' A strange look came into his eyes. 'Possibly more so than any of my other initiatives.'

'Including the Bibby Foundation?'

'The Foundation is my son's pigeon now. I have little to do with it.'

'Including the decision on what to fund?' I said, hoping I wasn't being too blunt.

He didn't look up. 'I will always retain control over that.'

'And does Marcellus agree with your funding decisions?' I said, suspecting that now I *was* being too blunt.

'Not always.' Wilson's voice was hard. 'He has this romantic view of academics, because he has no idea what it is to be one. If I left it to him, he'd continue your friend's research grants, and bankrupt the Foundation.'

That was one I hadn't seen coming. I felt my cheeks flush. 'And after you've set up your schools' programme, have you any plans for similar initiatives?' I doubted he'd tell me, but I was smarting from his remark and had to say something. I moved my knight into the centre of the board, exposing my queen.

He didn't hesitate. He advanced his bishop and took my queen. 'Check.'

I moved my king out of danger.

'After my schools' programme is off the ground?' he said. 'I've no particular plans,' he added, in a noncommittal way. He repositioned his knight. 'Check.'

I took the knight. 'Checkmate,' I said softly.

He stared at the board, then slowly pushed the white king over. 'I shouldn't have underestimated you, Maggie.'

'I wasn't aware that you had. Your play didn't show it.'

'Don't patronise me, young lady.' He leant back, studying me. 'I'm not used to losing.'

I smiled hesitantly. 'Another game?'

Before he could reply, Marcellus entered. He caught his father's eye and brandished his mobile. Wilson rose, excusing himself, and they slipped into an alcove where Marcellus made a call.

'Hello now, Maggie,' a familiar voice said. 'We'll have to stop meeting like this.'

Mike took the seat vacated by Wilson. He surveyed the board. 'Ah, yes, the chess grandmaster.' He lifted the white king and rubbed it with his thumb. 'Who were you playing?'

'Wilson Bibby.'

'Did he win?'

'No.'

A slow smirk spread across Mike's face. 'And did he take it well?'

'No.'

'You know what they say: good losers don't make good winners.'

'That's crap, Mike.'

He glanced towards the alcove where the Bibbys were deep in conversation. 'Would you look at Bibby sitting there, like the grand lord? I can't imagine why he's prepared to mix with the plebs. He could buy the Ice Hotel several times over, he and his fat-cat friends.' He sneered. 'But, then, the rich have a reputation for salting their money away.'

'I've never seen the point of that. I intend to run out of money and breath at the same time.'

Mike's lips twisted. 'It must be lovely to have so much you don't know what to do with it.' He set the piece upright on the board but kept his fingers round it.

'You obviously know something I don't.' I lowered my voice. 'Tell me what you've got against Wilson Bibby. I don't believe it's just the money.'

'It's how you make it. I assume you don't know the story of how Wilson became a billionaire.'

'The way everyone does? Lots of hard graft?'

'By ruthlessly exploiting people.'

'Now that's good coming from someone who works for an IT company.'

'Says someone working for a pharmaceutical company.'

'Look, Mike,' I said, in a placatory tone, 'I'm sure Wilson made his fortune perfectly legitimately.'

He shook his head. 'His grandfather, Wilson Bibby the First, did that.'

'How?'

'Property deals.'

'How big was the fortune?'

'I don't think anyone knows, but big enough that the family could have lived like billionaires just on the interest.'

I moved the chess pieces to their starting positions. 'I presume Wilson is just continuing the family tradition.'

'Well, you presume wrong,' Mike said nastily. 'Listen and learn. Bibby's father, Wilson Bibby the Second, squandered most of the fortune.'

'How?' I said, intrigued.

'The casinos at Vegas.'

'How on earth did he get through that much money?'

'It took him a lifetime.'

'And did the current Wilson Bibby make the money back?'

'He did it in the worst possible way. On the backs of his workers.'

'In the States?'

'He couldn't touch those – they're heavily unionised.' Mike tapped the white king with a fingernail. 'The ones he exploited were in South America.'

'Tell me about it.'

He gazed at me without blinking. 'When I was in Dublin, I had a Venezuelan girlfriend, Consuela. She came from a large Maracaibo family. Her father worked for Bibby's company, a manual worker, not a professional. Well, the workers tried to form a union. It was groundbreaking, that sort of thing, but they didn't succeed. Bibby crushed it.' Mike dropped his voice. 'According to Consuela, he had the politicians in his pocket. Sure, and that didn't surprise me, given his wealth and the corruption in the government at the time. There was talk he was involved in narco-terrorism, although I find that hard to believe. He strikes me as a man who doesn't take unnecessary risks.'

Mike lowered his voice further and I had to strain to hear him. 'After destroying the union, he carried on doing what he'd done from the outset: increasing the workers' hours and reducing their pay. It was always in stages. He promised it was a short-term measure because of the global oil crisis. He was constantly reassuring them that things would soon return to normal.'

'But they didn't.'

'And that's not all. There was no health and safety legislation, and Bibby took advantage of it. The ventilation in the factories was expensive, and he cut corners. As his workers became sick, they were replaced – there were always queues of men at the gates. It was just a matter of time before Consuela's father contracted lung disease and was laid off. Everything went down-hill from then on.'

'Did he get sickness benefit?'

'There was no such thing. To make ends meet, Consuela's mother took a second job, cleaning offices. One of her sisters went on the game, although she didn't tell her family. Only Consuela knew.' Mike stared at the chessboard, his face grim. 'The real irony? Consuela was a bright kid and got a scholarship to study in Europe. You know who paid for it?'

'The Bibby Foundation?'

'Got it in one. She earns enough now that she can send money home. It keeps her family going.'

'What happened to her father?' I said quietly.

'He died a year after he lost his job. His wife never recovered, poor woman.' Mike was staring into his drink, his mouth working.

Pieces of the jigsaw were falling into place. 'You've not told me the whole story, have you?'

The silence lengthened.

'Let me guess,' I said. 'You got a scholarship too.'

He nodded dumbly.

'And it was the Bibby Foundation that paid for it,' I added.

After a pause, he said, 'My parents couldn't afford to give us a decent education. We were so poor we didn't have a pot to piss in. It was watching my mam boil potato peelings and my da working all the hours God sends that made me want a decent education so I could earn real money. And in the type of job where I'd be in demand, and could put two fingers up to my employer and leave if I wanted to.'

It said much about Mike's state of mind that he was prepared to disclose these details to a relative stranger. Seeing Bibby must have removed his inhibitions.

He rubbed the underside of his jaw. 'My school advised me to write to the Foundation. They offered scholarships to study at Trinity College, so I applied and won a place. My saving grace is that I didn't know about Bibby. But it doesn't make me feel any better.' He lifted the white king and rolled it between his palms. 'It makes me feel contaminated. Can you understand that?'

I looked away, unable to think of a reply. I knew what was going through his mind: the one thing worse than accepting tainted money was accepting it, not realising, then making the discovery too late. Now I understood why he'd been so hard on me and my acquaintanceship with the Bibbys: he was really being hard on himself.

'Don't beat yourself up, Mike,' I said, as kindly as I could. 'It's not your fault. You weren't to know.'

He stared balefully at the Bibbys.

'All these years, you haven't been able to let it go, have you?' I said. 'You've been keeping tabs on Wilson, following his career. That's how you know so much about him.'

I nearly said: *And perhaps why you've followed him to the Ice Hotel.*

Mike said nothing but, from across the table, I could feel his body tighten. He seemed to buzz with hatred, vibrating and thrumming like a wasps' nest.

CHAPTER 9

It was 8 p.m. We were in the Activities Room, dressing appropriately for the Ice Bar.

Mike was sprawled on a bench in his snow-suit, watching us struggling into ours. Of us all, he was the only one who'd mastered the art of slipping into a snow-suit quickly and gracefully.

His good humour had returned. 'Did you see the aurora, Maggie? I noticed you didn't stay for coffee.'

'Did I hell. I froze my backside off for half an hour and saw damn all. And the sky was clear, too. I was pretty fed up.'

'That's the trouble with natural phenomena, I'm afraid,' Harry said, zipping up his light-blue snow-suit. 'You can't see these things to order. You're always at the mercy of Mother Nature.' He pulled on a blue hat, and yanked it down over his ears.

'Maybe I was too early. They have a good idea of the date, but they can't predict the time with any accuracy. There might be something later tonight.'

'But, my dear, you'll be too blotto to go out. That's if this Purple Kiss lives up to its reputation.'

Liz was pulling on a pair of oversized fur-lined gloves. 'Does anyone know how on earth we're supposed to hold our glasses in these things?'

'We'll find a way, that's for sure.' Mike got to his feet. 'There's not much that can come between an Irishman and his drink, not when he has a throat on him. So, are we going?'

The bar was packed. We pushed our way to the counter or, rather, Mike pushed his way and we followed in his wake. Marita and a dark-haired girl, whom she addressed as Karin, looked harassed trying to serve the crush of customers. From the number of jugs on the counter, they were expecting a full house. We picked up our drinks and backed away carefully.

We found a free ice table. Mike ran a hand over the coarse hair covering the seats. 'Do you think these reindeer skins are going to keep our lovely arses from freezing?'

'They seem to work extraordinarily well for the reindeer,' Harry said, lowering himself gingerly. He took a sip of the purple liquid. 'Not bad, not bad at all. Try it, Maggie.'

But I found Purple Kiss too sweet, with a sickliness that set my teeth on edge, and so cold it gave me sinus pain. I set down the ice glass, wondering what else there was to drink. A mark on the rim caught my eye, an imprint where the warmth of my lips had melted the ice. 'I think I read somewhere that you have to drink quickly from these glasses before they disappear.'

'There's no time to waste then,' Mike said, downing his in one go. 'It's a bit on the sweet side. I'd take a pint of the black stuff over this any day.'

Liz had abandoned her gloves. Her fingers were turning blue clutching the glass. 'What's that strange taste?' she said, dabbing at her lips with a handkerchief.

'Violet cordial,' Harry said. 'Wonderfully refreshing, don't you think? Do you like it, Maggie?'

'I'm afraid it wouldn't be my first choice.' I took another sip, but I had to leave it. Nothing else seemed to be on offer. If this was indeed all they were serving tonight, I'd be the only one sober at the end of the evening. Brilliant.

A commotion at the entrance heralded the arrival of the Danes. They jostled their way to the bar and crowded out the people standing there. In a matter of minutes, they'd emptied the jugs. Marita refilled them, protesting at their conduct, but they ignored her. Jonas propped himself up against the counter and tried to engage Karin in conversation, but she picked up a tray and strode past him as if he didn't exist.

Jonas snatched up a jug and staggered round the room, refilling empty glasses. On reaching our table, he stopped and stared, glassy-eyed. 'Have a drink, Mike.'

He started to pour, holding the jug high, but was so wide of the mark he missed Mike's glass altogether. The liquid spilt on the table, sending out long purple fingers. Jonas swayed and lost his footing, sprawling across the table and knocking the glasses on to the ground. Mike clapped him on the back and hauled him to his feet. Laughing loudly, they dragged each other towards the bar. Liz groped in the snow for the glasses, moving her feet away from the purple stain. I watched in fascination as the top of the table began to dissolve.

Harry was eyeing Jonas. 'It seems that young man has recovered from yesterday's drinking binge. Or maybe it's the hair of the dog. Do you think, when it comes to alcohol, he's a match for Mike?'

'I doubt it,' I said. 'No one's ever won a drinking contest with an Irishman.'

But Jonas didn't make it to the bar. He collapsed and lay in the snow, despite the efforts of Mike and Olof to revive him.

I shook my head. 'Who was it who said, "When enough people tell you you're drunk, it's time to sit down"?'

The Bibbys had appeared. They didn't queue at the bar, but made for the table next to ours. Wilson produced a cigar and lit it slowly, sending clouds of smoke billowing up to the ceiling. I caught Marcellus's eye. He smiled, as if to say, 'Don't look at me, he's always like this.' But he murmured something to his father, who sighed and dropped the cigar on to the floor, where it lay in the snow.

Marcellus waved Karin over, and she arrived with a jug and glasses. He produced a wallet and offered a tip, but she shook her head and hurried away. Wilson drank greedily, licking his lips with relish, savouring the taste.

Mike had returned with a fresh jug.

'Not drinking with your buddies?' I said.

'That big feller, Jonas, may be good company in the gym, but he's beginning to get drunk.'

'*Beginning* to?'

A loud guffaw from Wilson made us turn. Marcellus was smiling, murmuring into his father's ear. Wilson's eyes were streaming with tears of laughter. He lifted a hand to wipe them and accidentally knocked his elbow into Karin, who was rushing past. She stumbled and the jug went flying, showering purple liquid over him and Marcellus.

Wilson got to his feet. 'I do apologise, ma'am.'

Karin looked close to tears. 'It's all over your clothes,' she wailed. She began to wipe the front of Wilson's suit.

He took the cloth from her hand, smiling sympathetically. 'I can do that, ma'am. Please don't worry yourself, it was my fault.'

She threw him a look of gratitude before retrieving the jug and slipping away.

Marcellus seemed unfazed, and poured another drink for Wilson. I noticed he'd left his own untouched. Someone else who was finding Purple Kiss too sweet. He glanced at the stain on his blue snow-suit, and ran a hand over it to remove the purple stickiness. Our eyes met, and he grinned. I couldn't tell what he found amusing: the fact the accident had happened, or his father's behaviour towards Karin. He held my gaze briefly, then turned his attention back to his suit.

Liz leant towards me, her eyes gleaming. 'I think he fancies you, Mags.'

'Who? Wilson?'

'Marcellus.'

'He does not.'

'I wouldn't let him near your drink, though.' She smiled, nodding eloquently. 'Remember Marcia Vandenberg?'

'Honestly, Liz, I wonder about you sometimes. Do you really believe that story?'

'Don't you?'

I thought through my interactions with Marcellus. 'I think Marcellus is a decent man.'

Her smile widened. 'I rather think that's what Marcia thought too.'

I turned away.

It was quieter now. The Danes were leaving, probably to continue their drinking in the Excelsior. Mike left us to sit with Jane and the Ellises. He refilled Jane's glass, leaning in close, his thigh hard against hers. I tried to envisage a seduction scene in the gelidity of the Ice Hotel, but my imagination failed me. I glanced at Liz, wanting to gauge her reaction to Mike's sudden change of amour, but her interest was taken elsewhere.

'Harry.' She gripped his arm. 'Look, sweetheart.'

Harry, who was gazing deep into his glass, jerked his head up so sharply the bobble on his hat shook.

Wilson was standing at our table. He inclined his head deferentially towards Harry. 'I believe we met in Stockholm, sir.' There was a slight burr to his words.

Harry lifted his chin. 'I would hardly call it meeting you, Mr

Bibby. You snubbed me, I seem to remember. And there was absolutely no call for it.'

Wilson held out his hand, swaying with the effort of keeping his arm extended. 'Please accept my apologies.'

Harry ignored the gesture, his face red with suppressed anger. 'Mr Bibby, I don't much care for your manners. I'm afraid I cannot accept your apology. Now, please leave us.'

I closed my eyes, unable to believe what I was hearing. Harry was being given a chance to impress Wilson with his magnanimity, yet he was behaving like a complete idiot. And all because of his stupid pride.

Wilson's expression changed. He lowered his arm. 'Ah, the hell with you,' he said under his breath.

Marcellus was returning from the bar with a full jug. Seeing his father reeling, he hurried over. He put the jug down in time to catch him before he fell and, supporting him gently, set him on his feet. I was surprised at the distress on his face, and wondered if he'd witnessed Harry's rejection of his father's apology.

Wilson made a show of brushing down his suit. He shrugged off Marcellus's arm and drew himself up. 'Come on, son. We're going to the Excelsior for a nightcap. I need a Scotch.' He let Marcellus put an arm round his shoulders. They left the bar.

Liz was gazing at Harry. 'Darling, you were quite magnificent.'

I played with my glass. Magnificent, yes, but he could kiss goodbye to any hope of further funding.

Harry was still shaking. He reached for the jug. 'I don't normally behave like that. I think I need another drink.'

'Me too. Here, let me do it.' Liz took the jug from his hand. 'What about you, Mags? Your glass is empty.'

'Thanks, but I've had enough.'

Mike had returned. 'So what did Bibby want?' he said quietly.

'To apologise to Harry for offending him at the airport,' I replied, watching his reaction.

His features tightened, but he said nothing.

Harry took a long drink of Purple Kiss. 'It's because he was plastered, dear boy. He wouldn't have made the gesture otherwise. And I'm sure he won't remember it in the morning.'

'You told him where to get off, though,' Liz said. 'I rather think you won that round.'

Mike smiled. 'Grand.'

Now that Mike was with us, the jug emptied rapidly. I checked my watch. It was nearly 10.30 p.m. 'I think I'm turning in,' I said.

'I'm ready for bed, too, children. It's been quite a day, what with one thing and another.' Harry stood up, swayed, then sat down again. He gazed up at Mike, a look of puzzlement on his face. 'Dear boy, do you think you could help me back to the Excelsior? My legs don't seem to be following my brain's instructions.'

I knew Harry enjoyed drinking, but I'd never seen him drunk. From the expression on Liz's face, neither had she. But once Harry was on his feet, he walked as steadily as always, and I could only conclude he'd put on an act for our amusement.

CHAPTER 10

We returned to the Excelsior and collected what we needed for the night. In the Locker Room, Liz and I said our goodbyes to Mike and Harry, who headed off to the men's changing room.

The women's area was packed. People were milling around in various stages of undress, drinking hot lingonberry juice and all talking at once. Clothes littered the benches.

I stared at myself in the long mirror. I was wearing a giant Babygro. 'I can't believe this sleep-suit is all we'll need, Liz. It'll be minus five.'

'I've never heard of anyone dying from hypothermia,' she said, smoothing cream over her face and neck. 'I really think the Ice Hotel would have closed down if they had.'

We secured our belongings in our personal lockers, removed the keys and slipped the rubber bands over our wrists. Then, clutching the sleeping bags, we made our way to the washroom, where we took hot showers.

I tensed myself for the now familiar sharp drop in temperature, and stepped outside. Despite the shower and thick snow-suit, the warmth leached out of my body and I started to shiver violently. The side door to the Ice Hotel was feet away. Liz pulled the antler handles and I followed her in. She took a couple of steps, then stopped short, drawing her breath in sharply.

Along the walls of the corridor, tiny yellow candles, like minia-ture runway lights, had been fixed into the snow. Their amber glow faded into the distance, narrowing to a single point, yet still bright enough to light our passage.

We started down the corridor, our feet swishing in the dry snow. The candles flared as we passed, throwing giant shadows on to the snow-covered walls. The shadows moved in silent congre-gation, growing and then dying in the flickering light, spirits of the Ice Hotel creeping after us.

We'd gone a little way when Liz pointed to a side corridor. 'My room's down here, Mags. Sleep well. I'll see you at brekkie.'

I waited until she'd disappeared before following the signs to number 16. By now, Harry would be asleep in number 15, Pan grinning lecherously down at him. Wilson was on my other side in number 17, and Marcellus in number 18. But the Bibbys would still be having their nightcap. I pictured Wilson sitting in the bar, drinking sullenly, ignoring everyone.

I drew back the velvet curtain, seeing my room for the first time. It was plain, identical to Harry's in size and layout. Candles were scattered across the floor, the light dancing in the draught from the corridor. Facing the double bed was the alcove. In it was an ice statue, lit from behind.

It was a Knight Templar. He was holding his helmet under his right arm. His gauntleted left hand was holding his shield, which partly obscured his great sword, still in its sheath. The crosses on his chest and shield had been roughened, like the clown's face, or they wouldn't have been visible in this light. He stood erect, legs planted in the snow, head thrown back, nobly scanning the dis-tance for some unseen enemy. I ran my hand over the pepperpot helmet, fingering the detail and wondering how the Templars could see through such narrow slits.

I brought my face close to his. His hair was swept back from his aristocratic forehead, and curled thickly at the nape of his neck. His eyes were clear and unflinching as they gazed towards a limitless horizon. And his mouth was set in grim determination, as a knight's should be. My honour would be safe with him tonight.

I touched his face. As my skin brushed the ice, I felt a light pricking as though static had discharged through my hand. Slowly, I ran my fingers across his cheek. The knight's features dissolved. Instead of the pale-blue ice face with its wide-set eyes and high cheekbones, I saw a face made of flesh and blood.

From the condition of the skin, he'd been dead for some time. His sunken eyes were closed and his lips were parted, the tips of his teeth just visible. His features were familiar, that thin mouth and prominent nose, but I couldn't place them. My fingers were still touching his face, making indentations in his cheek, the flesh cold and sticky. Suddenly, his eyelids fluttered and snapped open. His eyes rolled back until only the whites were showing. A foul stench filled the room.

I sprang back and fell against the bed, crashing to the ground and jarring my back so badly I cried out. I stared at the statue, half dreading, half wanting to see the face again. But it had vanished. The knight's ice features gazed out steadily. I tried to recall the image, but the memory was fading, and a moment later I could no longer remember what I'd seen. I struggled to my feet and touched the knight's cheek again. He continued to stare loftily into the distance.

I sat on the bed, waiting for the feeling of anxiety to subside. I was sweating heavily, uncomfortably aware of the chafing dampness in my armpits and between my legs. It was that bloody drink. I'd had only a few sips but something in Purple Kiss had disagreed with me. I scooped up a handful of snow and rubbed it over my face.

But I was fooling myself. It wasn't the oversweet Purple Kiss. I'd drunk nothing before my visit to the chapel except half a glass of champagne, and I'd still seen that thing in there. There was an explanation behind these ghastly images. An explanation hidden to me. I stared into the Templar's sightless eyes, remembering other sightless eyes, those of my neighbour's son, whose wrecked body I'd seen two days before he died. I walked round the room, running my hand over the snow-covered walls as though I would find the explanation there. But the Ice Hotel was telling me nothing.

There were voices in the corridor. Something brushed past the curtain, stirring it, causing the candles to gutter. I wondered whether I should blow them out. But the room had no ceiling window, and I'd need light if I wakened in the night.

I spread the sleeping bag on the reindeer skins and undressed quickly, dropping my outdoor clothes on the snow as there was nowhere to put them. After zipping myself up, I drew the hood over my head and tied the toggles. I lay quietly, cocooned in a long brown tunnel that ended in a tiny circle of light.

I turned over. The movement drew cold air into the sleeping bag, throwing me into a mild panic. But I grew warm again and drifted off into an uneasy sleep. Yet each time I turned, icy air on my face woke me. Eventually, I pulled the toggles loose and, shaking off the hood, peered round the room.

The candles were low but not out. They cast an eerie, shimmering light on the Templar, illuminating his sword and shield but keeping his face in shadow. I peered at my watch – it was after midnight.

I'd forgotten the aurora. It would be in full flow. And definitely worth getting up for. I threw back the sleeping bag, pulled on the snow-suit and followed the signs to the back exit. The Ice Hotel was silent: I met no one as I crept along the dark corridors.

I reached the exit and pushed against the handles. The doors swung open silently and I stepped into the night, my breath pluming white in the cold air. The moon had not yet risen, but the snow seemed to exude a ghostly light, outlining the frozen blocks of ice like pieces of giant Lego.

I made for the river, my feet crunching against the frozen snow. A thin layer of fog shrouded the ice, swirling slowly as I moved. I found a spot with an unobstructed view of the sky and stared up into the blackness, startled by the sudden harsh call of a bird deep within the forest.

The sky was cloudless except for a single faint band. It grew slowly, lengthening at both ends until it spanned the sky in a perfect arc. As it brightened, it changed colour from white to pale green, then to yellow. Folds of ghostly curtains appeared, rippling across the black vault. They dissolved into fingerlike threads, which pulsated rhythmically, as though spectral hands were playing chords on a celestial organ. As they faded, leaving a faint imprint, others emerged to take their place.

I threw back my head and watched, exhilarated, until my neck and shoulders ached. The warmth bled from my body, chilling my bones and making my teeth chatter. When I could no longer stand the cold, I pulled the hood tightly round my head, and trudged back reluctantly across the snow. The night bird called again. It had left the forest and was gliding across the river, dipping so low that I felt the brush of its great wings.

The Ice Theatre loomed like a dark battleship, menacing against the glowing sky. But, instead of retracing my steps, I decided to take the path at the side of the chapel and return to my room via the main entrance. It would be worth the detour to see the columns and fountain by the shimmering light from the chandelier.

I crept to the front of the Ice Hotel.

I was pulling at the antlers when a faint creaking to my right made me turn. The Locker Room door was opening, throwing a sudden stream of light into the darkness. Someone was at the entrance, on the point of stepping inside. He turned and looked at me. The hood of his suit was down and there was no mistaking his features.

I was about to call out when something stopped me. Something about the way he stood immobile, staring in my direction, making no attempt to acknowledge me. With a sudden movement, he pulled the hood over his head, hiding his face.

I hurried into the Ice Hotel and ran through the foyer, anxious to get to my room. The candles were mostly out, and those that weren't sputtered angrily. I'd reached my corridor when a thought stopped me. Perhaps Marcellus wasn't going late to bed. Perhaps he'd followed me to the river, and that was why he hadn't wanted to be recognised. The realisation that he might have been spying on my movements as I watched the aurora brought cold sweat to my brow.

I was about to enter my room when I saw Harry's curtain swaying. A second later, it was drawn back and Harry stepped out. In the gloom, I could just make out the woollen hat and the bulky frame in the blue snow-suit. He moved briskly away.

'Goodnight, Harry,' I called to his retreating back.

He stiffened, then continued as though he hadn't heard. Strange. That wasn't like Harry. But I put it down to his bladder problems. He might be desperate to get to the washroom.

In my room, I undressed and re-enacted the ritual of the sleeping bag. I writhed around for what seemed like hours before I finally fell asleep.

My dreams were vivid: we were on snowmobiles and Marcellus was chasing me and, however hard I pressed against the accelerator, I couldn't rev up enough speed to get away.

★ ★ ★

I woke early – my watch said 6.10 a.m. – and wriggled around trying to get comfortable, but I knew I wasn't going to get back to sleep. I dressed and tiptoed to the washroom. Standing under the hot jet, I worked shampoo into my hair. The others wouldn't be up for another hour but, rather than kill time in the lounge, I would take a walk on the river.

The sun was rising as I left the Ice Hotel, bathing the landscape in clear morning light. Ahead was the long stretch of river ice, pink in the sunrise, and fringed with snow-laden trees. A walk to the forest and back should take no more than an hour.

The snow was deep, and I had to lift my feet to clear the drifts. It was heavy-going but I was determined to cross the river. I was nearing the opposite bank when I saw a man on cross-country skis. Instead of a snow-suit, he wore a close-fitting red woollen jacket, patterned knee breeches and yellow socks. As he approached, he raised his ski pole in greeting, then, gliding grace-fully, he overtook me. At the edge of the river, he removed his skis and lifted them over his head. For a second, I thought he was going to scratch his back, but he pushed them neatly through a strap on his rucksack and disappeared into the forest.

I reached the bank, breathing hard, and collapsed on to a rock.

The sun had risen well above the horizon, and the shadows of the trees were creeping back to the river's edge, like a defeated army. There was more activity now: the harvesting of the day's ice had begun, a sledge pulled by eight yapping huskies sped across the river and dozens of people on skis moved soundlessly past each other. It was hard to believe this was the same river of a few hours before, deserted, washed pale in the cold light from the aurora.

My thoughts crept back to the scene outside the Locker Room. Why had Marcellus deliberately concealed his face? Was he afraid that Wilson would find out he was up late, and disapprove?

Unlikely. My assumption that he'd followed me on to the river seemed far-fetched now. Yes, he could have peered through his curtain, seen me leave and followed me out, but why had he re-entered the Ice Hotel via the Locker Room? Why not return to his room the same way, by the back? No, he hadn't been watching me. He'd been coming from the Excelsior. But why would he worry about being recognised? It made no sense.

The wind was strengthening. I rose, buttoning my hood, and started back. The going was slower as I needed my wits about me to avoid careering into traffic. The temperature had dropped, and huge pillowy clouds were forming. By the time I reached the back of the Ice Hotel, snow was falling soundlessly from a white sky.

I slipped inside, and paused to listen. No one was up. Yet as I padded along the corridors, following the signs to my room, I heard faint scratchings behind the curtains.

It was as I was nearing my corridor that I heard it – a scream that sent a jolt of fear through my body. It was a woman's voice, high-pitched and strong, tearing through the stiff fabric of silence. A second later, it was joined by another.

CHAPTER 11

The screaming stopped as suddenly as it had started. And then chaos erupted.

People rushed out of rooms, and ran down the corridor towards the sound. Others stood about, looking dazed. Instinctively, I joined the runners.

We rounded the corner, bursting on to the crowd. Karin and Marita were standing sobbing, their shoulders shaking uncontrollably. Tears streamed down their faces, smearing their make-up. A woman in a sleep-suit was trying to soothe them. She had an arm round Marita, who seemed in a worse state than Karin.

I elbowed my way through the crush. Someone was holding back the curtain to one of the bedrooms, and people were peering in, babbling to one another. I stood on my toes, craning my neck, and looked inside.

A tray and paper cups lay abandoned on the floor in a patch of reddish-purple mush. A sleeping bag, folded open, was spread neatly on the skins. And, on the floor at the side of the bed, a figure dressed only in a sleep-suit was lying on his back.

I felt a tightening in the pit of my stomach. It was a well-built man and, for one lurching moment, I thought it was Harry. Then I heard Harry's voice. He was standing next to me, gazing into the room.

'It's Wilson Bibby,' he said.

I looked through the bobbing heads at the figure. The blood had drained from his face, giving his skin the texture of parchment.

'He's frozen stiff, my dear.' There was an unnatural calmness in Harry's voice.

I stared at him, shocked that he seemed without emotion. He turned to look at me, and smiled faintly.

The people in front were pushing their way out, and we found ourselves at the entrance to the room. I saw the body clearly now.

It was like a waxwork in a horror show. Wilson's head was turned to the side. In this position, the hooked nose was unmistakable, and I wondered how I could have mistaken him for Harry. His mouth was open and a dribble of saliva had run down his chin and solidified. Mercifully, his eyes were shut.

Then my mouth went dry. This was the face I'd seen when I'd touched the statue of the Templar. The flesh-and-blood face. I shivered uncontrollably, grateful for Harry's arm round my shoulders.

The crowd was growing, pushing us into the room. We fought our way out, but not before I'd taken a final glance around. On the other side of the bed, a snow-suit and boots lay abandoned on the floor.

We stumbled into the corridor. Liz came running towards us, shock registering on her face.

She looked from Harry to me. 'What's happened?' Her voice was almost a whisper.

'It's Wilson Bibby,' I said.

The colour left her face. She made to go into the room.

'No, my dear,' Harry said firmly, grabbing at her arm.

But he was too late. She was at the entrance, staring at the corpse. 'Oh, my God, Mags,' she cried. 'He's dead. Wilson's dead.'

'He must have fallen out of bed and frozen to death,' I said, licking my lips nervously. 'Although—'

Harry interrupted me. 'Let's get out of here. I've never been good in crowds.'

He started to lead us away but I pulled back. Karin and Marita were huddled against the wall, shaking, their arms round each other. A feeling of dread swept over me. What I saw in their faces was not shock, but fear. Karin's sobbing was coming in small hiccups. Marita was gazing into space, wide-eyed, her mouth slack.

Harry took my arm. 'There's nothing we can do here, Maggie,' he said gently.

We joined the guests leaving the Ice Hotel. Some were in their nightwear, dragging their sleeping bags over the snow, others partially dressed in outdoor clothes. In a daze, I let the multilingual babble wash over me as we climbed the path to the Excelsior. I no longer felt tired.

The hotel manager was gibbering to the receptionist with the round glasses. They turned anxious faces towards us as we entered.

The manager rushed forward. 'Please do go up to the restaurant,' he shouted, ushering people towards the stairs. 'Breakfast is being served.'

Neither Liz, Harry nor I could face food, so we trudged to the lounge and ordered coffee.

Liz drained her espresso. 'I needed that,' she said, massaging her temples. 'I had too much of that damn drink last night.' She reached into her bag for paracetamol. 'Has anyone seen Mike?'

'He's probably upstairs having breakfast,' I said listlessly.

She swallowed two tablets. 'He may not know about Wilson. I'd better go up.'

She returned five minutes later, looking puzzled. 'He wasn't there. The manager checked his list. He's not been in the restaurant all morning.'

Harry smiled. 'I should think he's in the gym, building that glorious body of his. He'll be unaware of what's happened.'

And I wondered what his reaction would be when he found out.

'Pity we're not allowed to smoke in here,' Liz said. She threw me an embarrassed smile. 'Don't look so surprised, Mags. I haven't had a cigarette for a long time. But I could really do with one now.' She ran a hand over her eyes. 'I've never seen anything like that. It was simply dreadful. Poor Wilson.'

At the mention of Wilson, the memory of his corpse returned. That skin, like wallpaper paste. My stomach churned.

Leo Tullis hurried into the lounge. He called our group together. 'Can everyone hear me? Right. You'll know by now that there's been a tragic accident.' He swallowed hard. 'Mr Wilson Bibby was found dead this morning, most likely from hypothermia. Clearly, this changes everything. The Ice Hotel has been placed out of bounds, so you'll be sleeping in the Excelsior for the rest of the week.'

His expression changed to one of extreme discomfort. 'I have another message. The police are here, and they're going to question everyone.'

'Everyone?' Robyn Ellis said, outrage in her voice.

'It's routine when there's an unexpected death. There will be two teams of police conducting the interrogations simultaneously. They should get through them today, but we've been asked to keep tomorrow morning free, just in case.'

'Young man,' Harry said stiffly, 'I don't like the word, "interrogation".'

'I'm just quoting Inspector Hallengren, the officer leading the investigation.' Leo ran a hand through his mop of hair. 'Look, I'm sure there's nothing to worry about.' He failed to sound reassuring.

'So what are we allowed to do?' Jane said. 'May we leave the building?'

'That's the other message. Everyone is to stay in the Excelsior. And the police are taking your passports.'

This produced uproar. 'It's just routine,' he said miserably. 'They'll be returned.'

'When are we going to be questioned?' Jim said.

'The interviews are starting immediately. One of the hotel staff will call your name. The problem is I haven't been given a schedule, so you could be called at any time today. Or tomorrow.'

'That's utterly ridiculous,' Robyn said. 'Surely we can't be expected just to hang around.'

'That's precisely what you *are* expected to do. And it would be best to stay in the lounge. The management are going to make refreshments available all day.'

Her face was taking on the colour of a tomato. 'I will have to protest.'

Leo had had enough. 'Then protest to Inspector Hallengren,' he said harshly. 'These are his rules. The sooner the police can get through their questioning, the sooner things will return to normal. I'm sure you can understand that.'

Mike breezed in, brushing past Leo, who looked glad to leave.

Mike's hair was wet and he had the healthy glow that accompanies strenuous exercise. He flopped down and reached for the coffee pot. 'I don't know about the rest of you, but I've got the mother of all hangovers,' he said, pouring.

I kept my voice light. 'Where have you been, Mike?'

'Working out and trying to clear my head. I took a sauna, then went up to the restaurant, hoping to get a late breakfast. They sent me here without saying why.' He looked up. 'Has something happened?'

Liz was the one to break the silence. 'Wilson Bibby's body was found this morning. It seems he died from hypothermia. The police are here to question us.'

Mike's cup was halfway to his mouth. He set it down slowly, looking straight ahead.

There was a sudden cry behind me. Jane Galloway was gripping the edge of the table, rocking gently. The barman, a middle-aged man with a pronounced paunch, was standing over her, holding a tray. He was whispering conspiratorially.

Harry leant across. 'What's that you're saying?'

The barman turned the tray in his hands. 'It was last year, at the Maximilian, and in other hotels in Stockholm also. Many guests were murdered, one by one.' He spoke the words slowly, and with relish.

'Jesus, Mary and Joseph,' Mike said, under his breath. 'So what's this, now?'

'It's old news,' I said. 'Those murders took place last year. We heard something at the airport. What did they call them, Harry?'

'The Stockholm hotel murders.'

'You must have heard about them, Mike,' I said, looking directly at him.

He ran his tongue over his lips. 'I haven't.'

I stared at him in amazement. How could Mike not know about these murders? From what he'd told us, he practically lived in Stockholm. And he'd been in Stockholm when we saw the newsflash.

He glanced at me, then turned quickly away.

'What happened?' I asked the barman, anxious to hear him tell us the police had the killer behind bars.

'They never found him,' he said dramatically. 'We think he has come to the Ice Hotel.'

The conversations in the lounge stopped.

'Why do you think he's come here? We're miles from—'

Liz interrupted me. 'How were the guests murdered?'

I caught sight of Jane's complexion. 'Liz, I don't think we want to hear that right at this moment.'

Jane was shaking visibly. 'Why don't you come and sit with us?' I said, taking her hand.

But as she picked up her bag, one of the hotel staff came in and called her name. She left with him.

Harry raised his eyebrows. 'What do you make of that? The hotel killer, no less.' He tried to force a smile but I could see he was shaken.

'Wilson Bibby wasn't murdered,' I said firmly. 'You heard Leo tell us it was an accident.'

'Then what was he doing on the floor, my dear? Why was he out of his sleeping bag?'

'He had a weak heart. I saw him take medication for it. He must have got up in the middle of the night, and it gave out.'

Mike looked doubtful. 'From the shock of the cold, was it? I suppose it's possible.'

I thought back to the scene in Wilson's room. Something wasn't right. Something that was staring me in the face, but I couldn't see it.

'There's probably a perfectly rational explanation.' Harry frowned, nodding at the barman, who was speaking in hushed tones to the Ellises. 'But this talk about the hotel killer is unnerving me.'

Harry was anxious, Liz looked like a phantom, and I was feeling queasy. The only person unaffected by Wilson's death was Mike. He ordered coffee and sandwiches, and tucked into them greedily.

First the snowmobiles. And now Wilson. What the hell was happening? I stared out of the window. The wind had died, and the snow was falling steadily, dusting the ground like sieved icing sugar.

Mike was the next to be interviewed. He returned fifteen minutes later, in good spirits. We threw questions at him, but he shrugged them off. 'I told them the truth. I said I slept all night, and saw and heard nothing.'

Liz had been listless all morning, eating nothing. She popped out to light cigarette after cigarette on such a regular basis that it was impossible to believe she hadn't smoked for years. She was called at midday. On her return, she continued to be subdued.

'How did it go?' I said.

'It was terrible. The inspector's awfully intimidating. I nearly burst into tears.'

'He's a policeman, Liz.' I tried a smile. 'Those people intimidate for a living.'

'He looked at me as though he knew I was wearing Marks & Spencer underwear.' After a brief silence, she said, 'I do wish I'd paid more attention to that newsflash. You don't think there's anything in this hotel-killer story, do you?'

'I doubt it. I think Harry's right, and there's a simple explanation for Wilson's death. I expect Leo will tell us tomorrow.' I put a gentle hand on her arm. 'Chin up. It'll be all right.'

She didn't seem convinced. I did my best to steer the conversation away, but she kept returning to the hotel-killer story. I left her briefly to join the Ellises, who were marching round the foyer in mild protest at being confined to the lounge. They were as rattled as the rest of us and their jumpiness soon got on my nerves. I returned to find Liz talking earnestly to the barman. She broke away when she saw me, and brushed off my questions, saying she'd been ordering sandwiches.

'I'm going to call the twins,' she said. 'I'll be in my room if anyone needs me.' She picked up her cigarettes and left.

I flopped into the armchair and huddled into a ball. Liz was taking this harder than most. If only Harry had caught her before she'd seen Wilson's corpse.

After lunch, it was Harry's turn. He reappeared a short while later, and announced he was going to his room to work on his book.

By mid-afternoon, tempers had become frayed. The barman switched on the television, but the only channels were in Swedish. Jonas and his friends crowded round the screen, drinking beer.

I was at the bar ordering coffee when a familiar image appeared on the television. It was the hotel I'd seen at the airport. The stone façade and Swedish flag were unmistakable.

Jonas reached up to change the channel.

'No, wait,' I blurted.

The men turned in surprise.

I stared at the screen. A reporter was standing in front of the hotel, microphone in hand.

'What's he saying?' I said.

Olof was looking at me with interest. 'Someone was found dead there. Just a few days ago.'

'Did they say anything about the Stockholm hotel murders? Is it the same killer?'

'They haven't said he's been murdered. Just that he's been found dead.'

'So you know about the hotel killings?' Jonas said softly.

I couldn't tear my gaze from the screen. 'The barman was talking about them.'

'It all happened last year,' Jonas said, with a dismissive shrug. He put the bottle to his lips. 'There have been no murders since.'

'People are saying that the killer has come to the Ice Hotel.'

Jonas shook his head and turned away. But not before I'd caught the look that passed between him and Olof.

I returned to my seat and continued to gaze out of the window. I felt numb.

As people were called, the lounge slowly emptied.

It was nearly four o'clock when my name was called.

The manager's assistant accompanied me to the office at the end of the corridor, and asked me to wait outside.

I peered through the glass panel in the door.

Marcellus was seated, shoulders slumped, his posture suggesting either defeat or despair. Someone I couldn't see was speaking to him, but I couldn't make out the words. Marcellus shook his head vehemently once or twice. More murmuring from the invisible man. He must have hit a nerve because Marcellus leapt out of the chair and lunged forward. A fair-haired man who'd been standing out of sight darted forward and restrained him. This man was huge, broader even than Marcellus, and taller by a good six inches. Marcellus struggled, and the man said something into his ear. He nodded, relaxing visibly. The man released him.

Marcellus remained standing while the hidden man spoke again. Then Marcellus turned and stumbled towards the door. I sprang back and flattened myself against the wall, not wanting him to know I'd been watching. After throwing a final angry glance towards the men, he left the room, slamming the door so violently I thought the glass would break. He saw me then and paused, an expression of bewilderment on his face. I opened my mouth to speak, but he turned away and strode down the corridor.

I'd handled it badly. He must have known I'd been spying. But it was too late, I couldn't run after him. I wiped my hands down the sides of my jeans, and knocked timidly.

The blond officer turned. He had typical Swedish looks: tanned skin, blue eyes and white-blond eyebrows. But a boxer's face. One side was misshapen, and the nose had been broken more than once.

He opened the door. 'Please come in,' he said, with a slight accent. His tone was warm, and I felt my nervousness evaporate.

I was curious to see the other man. He was half sitting on the desk, one foot on the floor, the other dangling. He watched unsmilingly as his colleague ushered me forward. He seemed as unwelcoming as the other man was pleasant. I guessed I was in for the good-cop-bad-cop routine.

He stood up. 'My name is Thomas Hallengren.' He gestured to his colleague. 'This is Lars-Erik Engqvist. We are from the National Criminal Investigation Department.' He spoke slowly, with more of an accent than Engqvist, but his English was faultless.

His dark hair was cropped close, accentuating the outline of his skull. He, too, was tanned but, unlike his colleague, not entirely clean-shaven. They were both wearing the same blue uniform, but the markings must have indicated differences in rank because Engqvist deferred to him as superior. They towered over me. I doubted either could sleep with his feet in the bed. Perhaps it was government policy to recruit giants into the police force.

Hallengren continued to stare, his blue eyes holding mine. Then his gaze travelled slowly down my body, and back to my face. In other circumstances I wouldn't have let this go, but something about his manner told me to hold my tongue.

He motioned to the chair. 'Please sit down.'

Engqvist parked himself on the desk, evidently not expecting to have to restrain me. I drew my head back, wondering how long I could keep it in this position. Hallengren nodded to his colleague, who hurried to fetch chairs. He placed them in front of the desk. Hallengren sat opposite me.

He opened a notepad. 'Your name is Margaret Stewart. Is that correct?'

'Yes.'

'Miss Stewart, I need to ask you some questions about the death of the American. You were in . . .' he ruffled through his papers '. . . room sixteen. Am I right?' He looked up.

'Yes, room sixteen.'

Engqvist was watching, a smirk on his face.

Hallengren scribbled quickly. 'Can you tell me what time you went to bed last night?'

'Round about eleven. I can't be more specific.'

'Alone?' He continued to write.

Engqvist's smirk broadened into a smile.

'Of course,' I said, the blood rushing to my face.

Hallengren looked up in surprise. 'Why do you say that? Many couples sleep in the Ice Hotel. There are even honeymoon suites.'

I wondered when Engqvist would stop grinning. 'I went to bed alone,' I said.

'Did you stay in your room until morning?'

I rubbed the front of my jeans. 'I left the Ice Hotel later in the night.'

Hallengren studied me. 'Can you remember what time that was?'

'It was some time after midnight.'

'Why did you leave the Ice Hotel?' he said softly.

'To watch the aurora. The notice said there would be a display. I was disappointed there was nothing earlier, so I decided to try again. I didn't sleep well, so I—'

He interrupted me. 'You did not sleep well? Are you a light sleeper?'

'Not particularly.'

He and Engqvist exchanged glances. Engqvist muttered something I couldn't catch, and Hallengren replied in Swedish.

'Miss Stewart,' he said, 'you are the last person we are interviewing. Everyone said they slept exceptionally well. Some even said they could hardly stand on their feet after the snowmobile excursion. Were you on that excursion?'

The directness of the question threw me off guard. I hesitated. 'Yes, I was.' I looked at Engqvist. When I turned my head back, I caught Hallengren staring at my hair.

'What time did you return to the Ice Hotel?' He was writing again.

I tried to sound flippant. 'No idea.'

He waited in silence.

'I can't have been watching long. How long can you stay out before freezing to death?' I regretted my words instantly. 'I was probably out for about half an hour,' I said, running a hand over my face.

'Did you see anyone?' His expression was unchanged. There was no indication of what he was thinking. They must teach that at Detective School.

'No one. No, wait, I did see someone. It was when I was returning. I was coming in through the main door when I saw him. Marcellus Bibby. He was going into the Locker Room.'

I had their attention now. They sat up straight, gabbling to one another in Swedish.

Hallengren leant forward, searching my face. 'The son? Are you sure?'

'The light in the Locker Room was on. His hood was down and I saw his face. And his dark ponytail.'

Hallengren sat back, studying me. 'Did he see you?'

'He turned and looked at me – that's how I saw his face – but I was standing in the dark with my hood up. He may not have recognised me. But—' The breath caught in my throat as I remembered how he'd tried to conceal himself.

'Yes?'

'He was acting strangely. He turned in my direction and then pulled his hood up over his head.'

'So that you could not see his face?'

'I assumed that was the intention. It was too late by then, of course.'

'He may not have known that.'

'But why would he do it?'

'Some people are naturally suspicious, and do not want anyone knowing their movements, especially after dark.' He paused. 'Even if they are doing nothing wrong.'

'I suppose.'

'And then, Miss Stewart, did you go straight to bed?'

'Yes,' I said flatly. 'Alone.'

A faint smile touched his lips. 'You saw no one else?'

'Only Harry.'

He consulted his notepad, leafing back several pages. 'Professor Harry Auchinleck?' He pronounced it Ow-hin-lek.

'He was leaving his room as I reached my corridor.'

'Did you speak to him?'

'I called out goodnight. Not too loudly as I didn't want to wake the place. But loudly enough so he'd hear.'

'Did he reply?'

'No.'

'Are you sure he heard?'

That stiffening of the shoulders. Yes, Harry had heard. But something made me say, 'I might have been mistaken.'

Engqvist was running a hand through his hair from the back of the neck upwards. He had stopped smiling.

Hallengren studied his notes. 'Miss Stewart, Professor Auchinleck tells a different story. According to his statement . . .' he read from his notes '". . . I went out like a light and didn't surface till morning. The screaming woke me."'

'But that can't be true,' I said quickly. 'I saw him leave his room.'

'You are sure it was Professor Auchinleck?' Hallengren said, watching me.

'I've just said so. He was wearing the same blue snow-suit and the bobble hat, pulled down over the ears the way Harry does it. And he was walking exactly like Harry.'

'Where do you think he was going?' Hallengren said, after a pause.

'Given the amount he'd had to drink, probably the loo. The lavatory,' I added, seeing their faces. I could tell they didn't believe me. 'Look, it's just possible he's forgotten.'

But Harry had the memory of an elephant. And he wasn't hung-over this morning, so he couldn't have been so drunk that he'd forgotten he got up in the night. Why had he simply not told the police the truth?

Hallengren consulted his notes. 'Your room is next to Mr Wilson Bibby's.'

As this was a statement, not a question, I said nothing.

He waited silently.

I nodded.

'Did you hear anything from his room? People talking?'

'It was as silent as the proverbial grave.' I closed my eyes briefly. Why in heaven's name was I making these crass remarks?

Hallengren raised an eyebrow. 'How well did you know Wilson Bibby?'

'I met him for the first time on Monday.'

'And when did you see him last?' He was writing again.

'At the reception in the Ice Bar.'

'Ah, yes.' He glanced up. 'Purple Kiss. Did you enjoy it?'

'It was too sweet.'

He sat back, studying me. 'Miss Stewart, how do you think Mr Bibby came to be outside his sleeping bag? Do you not think it strange he was without a coat and boots?'

'I haven't a clue. His heart may have given out, and he collapsed before he had a chance to get dressed.' I shrugged. 'It's your job to find out, not mine.'

Hallengren smiled for the first time. The effect was stunning. 'We will find out, Miss Stewart,' he said slowly. 'The Swedish police are nothing if not efficient. The body is already at our laboratories.'

'A post-mortem?'

'When there is an unexpected death, there is always a post-mortem. It is the same in your country, I believe.' After a pause, he said, 'There is something I would like you to do.' The smile had vanished. 'I would like you to tell no one that you saw Professor Auchinleck leave his room last night.'

'Why?' I said coldly.

He leant forward. 'Because I am asking you.' His voice was equally cold.

'Very well.'

'One more thing, Miss Stewart.' He was speaking briskly now, his tone businesslike. 'You say you saw Marcellus Bibby outside the Locker Room. I would like you to keep that to yourself also. You must tell no one that you were even up and about last night, let alone that you left the Ice Hotel. Have I made myself clear?'

'Perfectly.' I was beginning to dislike him.

He said something in Swedish to Engqvist. They got to their feet.

Hallengren held the door open, watching me, unsmiling. 'You have been very helpful, Miss Stewart. If I need to see you again, I will let you know.'

I stepped into the corridor. As I glanced over my shoulder, I caught him looking at my backside.

CHAPTER 12

I was still smiling to myself when I reached the lounge.

I'd hoped to find the others but they'd vanished. Yet the room was fuller than it had been before. A group of men in suits were mobbing the bar. As I moved towards the window, one glanced at me, then turned and watched me.

The Ellises were on the three-seater. 'May I join you?' I said.

'Of course,' Jim replied, with a kindly smile. He shifted to make room.

'I take it you've just been interrogated.' Robyn's lips stabbed at the word.

There was sympathy in Jim's voice. 'The inspector's quite fierce, isn't he?'

'I suppose he's just doing his job.' I nodded towards the bar. 'Who are all those people?'

'Reporters,' Robyn said, wrinkling her nose. 'They've come to cover Wilson Bibby's death.' She fixed me with her stare. 'Did you know he was a billionaire?'

'Yes.'

'That explains the interest. Talking of which, one of those reporters seems unduly interested in you.'

The man who'd been watching me was heading to our table.

'Have you spoken to them?' I said.

'Once they realised we knew nothing, they moved on to pastures new,' Jim said.

'Miss Stewart?'

I looked up.

'I'm Denny Hinckley, from the *Express*. Would you mind if I asked you a couple of questions?' The accent was strong, from the East End of London.

He was short and slight with bandy legs, a thin face and silky brown hair that was receding early: if he hadn't told me he was a reporter, I'd have taken him for a jockey. His smile was friendly, but the expression in his eyes was pure insolence. I'd had dealings with reporters before, as Bayne Pharmaceuticals were often in the spotlight. I took an instant dislike to him.

'I'm with friends, Mr Hinckley,' I said, turning away. 'Another time, perhaps.'

He pulled out a chair and sat down. 'You were in the room next to Wilson Bibby.'

For a second, I wondered how he knew, but there was a number of ways a reporter could have found out.

'Mr Hinckley, I said I'm with friends.'

'You see, neither me nor the other lads can get into the Ice Hotel. It's cordoned off. So I wondered if you could describe Wilson Bibby's room for me. I hear there are statues and all sorts.' He whipped out a notebook.

I glared at him. Whether it was a reaction to my interview with Hallengren, or lack of sleep, something inside me snapped. 'Which part of "I don't want to talk to you just now" did you not understand?'

Something other than insolence appeared in his eyes. 'Come on, love,' he said testily. 'Surely you'd like to see your name in the papers.' An oily smile spread across his face. 'I'll make it worth your while, if you catch my drift.'

'Oh, hold me back,' I said, under my breath.

Before he could reply, a heavy hand was placed on his shoulder. 'Don't you understand what the lady's saying? No? Then here it is in your language. Piss off.' Mike took him by the shoulders, lifted him off the chair, and swung him round. I thought he was going to propel him towards the bar, but he released him.

Hinckley threw him a look of loathing before slinking off.

'What did he want?' Mike said, sitting down.

'He wanted me to describe Wilson's room in the Ice Hotel.'

'And did you?'

'I never saw it. Apart from a brief peek this morning over the heads of the crowd.'

'You should have made something up and pocketed a fat fee,' Jim said. 'He'd never have found out.'

Mike nodded at the reporters. 'I saw one of them filming in front of the Ice Hotel. I take it you've seen the TV vans outside? They've been trying to get a story from everyone. As soon as Harry heard there were reporters here, he vanished.' He grinned. 'But not before exchanging a few choice words.'

'How did they get here so quickly?' I said. 'It takes hours from the UK. And I can hear some American accents.'

'They've come from Stockholm. They've been covering Bibby's big splash there.'

'Of course. So where are they staying? Surely not here.'

'There's nowhere else. And the Excelsior's half empty.'

'Just peachy,' said Jim. 'Bang goes our holiday.'

'Don't talk so wet.' Robyn snapped her jaws at her husband. 'The excursions will be back on tomorrow. We'll be mushing with the huskies.'

Jim smiled unhappily.

I glanced towards the bar. Denny Hinckley was drinking

from a tall glass, studying me over the rim, the insolence back in his eyes.

Liz had been missing at dinner. A tray of half-eaten food lay in the corridor, a full ashtray among the plates. There was no reply to my gentle tap at the door. I tried turning the handle, but the door was locked. At this time of evening, there was only one other place she could be.

Mike and Harry were already in the computer room. On the large screen, I could see Annie in yellow pyjamas. Lucy, in pink, was rubbing her eyes.

'Hello, sweetie-pops,' said Liz. 'You look awfully sleepy.'

Lucy climbed on to a chair and leant forward, her face filling the screen. 'We've just been getting ready for bed, Mummy.' Her expression brightened. 'Maggie! Have you seen Father Christmas yet?'

'No, pet,' I said. 'But I will soon.'

'You haven't forgotten what you were going to ask him? About the doll's house?'

I registered the expectation in her voice, but was unable to remember when I'd made this particular promise. But I was an expert at thinking on my feet. 'Absolutely. He's going to be bringing it personally.'

Annie shoved her sister off the chair. 'I want to talk now.' She pointed at the screen. 'Who's that strange man, Mummy?'

'This is Mike. Say hello.'

'You look like the giant who lives at the top of the beanstalk,' Annie said, her voice a challenge. 'There's a picture of you in my story book.'

Mike put his face close to the webcam. 'I'm the handsome

137

prince, darling. The one who rescues the princess from the wicked stepmother.'

'You made that up. There's no such story.'

'What's a stepmother?' Lucy said.

Annie was glaring at Mike. 'You talk funny.'

He flashed her his smile. 'Well, now, that's how handsome princes talk.'

She didn't look convinced. 'Don't go away.' She left the room quickly.

Lucy, delighted at having us to herself, climbed back on to the chair. 'The Ice Hotel's been on the telly, Mummy, but we didn't see you.'

I exchanged a glance with Liz. It was inevitable that the news of Wilson's death would have been reported at home. 'When were you watching telly?' Liz said sternly.

'We weren't. It was Siobhan. I came into the room and saw the picture of the Ice Hotel. It looked just like in your magazines.'

Annie bounced in, clutching a large book. 'I want to show the giant his picture.' She pushed Lucy off the chair, and held the book up to the webcam. 'See? He looks exactly like you.'

The balding giant had yellow teeth, a bulbous nose and warts on his face. But the eyes were brown and flecked with amber, and their expression was pure Mike. He was evidently at a loss for words. I felt a twinge of pity. His ego would be taking a knock.

Annie dropped the book on to the floor. 'Harry, do the flower trick.'

'Alas, my lovely, I've no carnations. It's far too cold for flowers here.'

She stared, open-mouthed. I had to suppress a smile. This was probably the first time Harry had refused her request.

Lucy spoke hesitantly. 'Can you do magic tricks too, Mike?'

'Of course. Close your eyes and count to ten and, when you open them, I'll have disappeared in a puff of smoke.'

'Can you really do that?'

Annie looked sceptical. 'Bet you can't. Even Harry can't make himself disappear.'

'Talking of disappearing,' said Liz, 'it's time you two disappeared to bed.'

'Do we have to?' whined Annie.

'We'll be back tomorrow, sweetie-pops. Now scoot. And ask Siobhan to come in.'

Annie tilted her head back and shouted so loudly that Lucy cringed. 'Siobhan! Mummy wants you.'

Siobhan was a work colleague, a single woman who lived nearby and babysat for Liz. She was plump and cheerful, and had an easy way with children. The twins adored her, something I hadn't failed to notice, and I felt a prick of jealousy whenever I saw them all together.

Siobhan arrived and jerked her thumb in the direction of the door. 'Bed.' The girls scuttled away, giggling.

'How have they been, Siobhan?' Liz said.

'Wonderful. No trouble at all,' came Siobhan's lazy voice.

'What have you heard about the Ice Hotel? Lucy said it was on the news.'

'Not much. Just that some billionaire had a heart attack.'

Liz was playing nervously with her ponytail. 'The girls didn't see that, did they?'

'I always sit with the remote in my hand. They saw a bit of the building, but I switched off before they heard anything. It's been in the papers, too.'

'What specifically, Siobhan?' said Harry.

'The same stuff, Professor, only in more detail. I suppose these

139

things happen, even on holiday. I hope it's not spoiling things for you.'

'Not at all, my dear,' he said cheerfully.

'Can you try to keep the twins from finding out?' said Liz. 'You know what children are. They'll jump to all sorts of conclusions. I really don't want them fretting.'

'I'll be careful. Enjoy the rest of your holiday.' Siobhan pressed a key and the image disappeared.

'Your children are adorable,' Mike said, getting to his feet.

Liz seemed distracted. 'Thank you.'

'And you're good with kids,' I said to Mike.

'You sound surprised. I'm the eldest of eight. I helped my mam bring up the young ones.'

The statement said much about Mike. I had thought his interest in Liz's children was a ploy to wangle his way into her affections. Perhaps I was wrong, and it was genuine. Yet, despite his friendliness, there was still something about him I didn't trust.

'You've got that thirsty look on your face again,' I said, turning to Harry.

'Well spotted, dear girl. Are you children ready to hit the bar?' He glanced at Liz.

'I'll pass, sweetheart.'

'Come for a quick nightcap, Liz,' I said. 'I promise I'll keep Denny Hinckley at bay.'

'All right. But just one. And who's Denny Hinckley?'

'So you've not met him?' said Mike. 'He's from the *Express*.' He said it as though it tasted bad. 'He's been giving Maggie a hard time.'

'I can handle him,' I said defiantly.

He threw me an old-fashioned look, but said nothing.

In the lounge, we took the window seat near the piano. Liz sat half hidden behind the curtain, her head turned towards the window. Her anxiety had deepened. But, then, if I had children, I'd be worrying about what they'd be hearing at school. I squeezed her hand, but there was no response.

Harry was sitting at the baby grand, looking thoughtfully at the keys. I imagined him in a sparkling gown, like Liberace, raising his hands high before launching into Schubert's 'Serenade'.

'Will you play for us, Harry?' said Mike.

'Alas, dear boy, I can't. I've never learnt.'

'But you've one at home,' I said, remembering the piano with its lacquered shine.

'I bought it for one of my boyfriends. He was very good, actually, although he only ever played Scott Joplin. But it didn't last. He left Dundee with a rich man who ended up keeping him.' He added, as an afterthought, 'I ended up keeping the piano.' He closed the lid and took a seat beside Liz.

As Mike fetched the drinks, my thoughts wandered to my interview with Hallengren. I couldn't put out of my mind the one thing that bothered me: Harry, a scrupulously honest man, had lied to the police.

'How did you sleep in the Ice Hotel, Harry?' I said, trying to keep the interest out of my voice. 'Did you hear anything? People moving in the corridor?'

'That's precisely what the detective inspector asked me, dear girl, apart from my name, rank and serial number. But I didn't hear a thing. Never do in the watches of the night. I was oblivious to everyone and everything, probably because I'd drunk too much in that Ice Bar.' He winked. 'I must find out what they put in Purple Kiss. Do you think it would go down well at my parties?'

Liz's head jerked round. 'Oh, for heaven's sake, Harry, this is hardly the time to think about parties. In case it's escaped your notice, a man has died.'

His smiled faded. 'I'm aware of that, my dear. Yet life goes on.' He put a hand on her arm but she snatched it away.

'I'm sorry, sweetheart,' she said, her voice quivering. 'It's just a migraine.'

'I've got a packet of tablets upstairs,' I said.

'Please don't bother, Mags. It's an early night that I need. Will you all excuse me?'

At the door, she collided with Denny Hinckley who was coming into the lounge. He stopped and stared after her, his mouth open.

Harry sighed. 'Another who's smitten. Wherever Liz goes, heads turn like sunflowers.'

But I wasn't sure it was Liz's beauty that had stopped Denny in his tracks. It wasn't desire I'd seen in his eyes. It was more like calculation.

CHAPTER 13

I woke earlier than usual on Thursday. I dragged myself out of bed and drew open the curtains. Light lay in strips on the horizon under a slate-coloured sky. Yesterday's snow covered the ground in soft dunes, faintly grey, reflecting the colour of the clouds. I shivered as I watched the men arrive on the river for the ice cutting.

It wasn't yet 6 a.m. Although the restaurant was open, Liz and Harry would still be asleep. I considered snuggling back into bed, but taking breakfast now would mean avoiding the reporters.

In the dining room, I nodded to the Ellises, who were sitting at the window, eating quietly. The only other person in the room was Leo Tullis. He was at the buffet, helping himself to scrambled eggs as though he didn't want them. He was wearing chinos and a coffee-coloured shirt, his thatch of fair hair uncombed. There were large smudges under his eyes.

He glanced up as I approached. 'You couldn't sleep either, then, Maggie?' He sounded miserable.

I piled my plate high with reindeer sausages. 'I usually wake early. Something to do with long commuting times.' I tried to inject a cheerful note into my voice. 'Are the excursions back on?'

'For God's sake, don't talk to me about excursions.'

I laid a hand on his arm. 'Come and sit with me, Leo,' I said quietly.

We took seats out of earshot of the Ellises. I waited for Leo to speak, but he bent his head over his plate.

'So was the bill for the snowmobiles large?' I ventured.

'It's not the bill. Sven's insurance is huge. It has to be.' He glanced towards the Ellises, then lowered his voice. 'Something's happened.'

'What?'

He hesitated.

'Tell me, Leo.'

He laid his fork aside. 'Sven doesn't believe it was an accident. He examined the snowmobiles.' There was an edge of panic to Leo's voice. 'The brakes weren't on. None of them.'

Harry's words flew into my head: *What I find strange is that the snowmobiles, which had all been checked by an expert, slipped their brakes.* I felt a sudden shiver through my body.

'Someone loosened them, Maggie. After Sven had gone up to the chalet.'

'How can he be sure? Look, you've ridden those machines many times. It would take only a flick of the finger to loosen the brakes. If a machine started to slip, that would jolt the brake loose, wouldn't it? You saw the angle on that slope. It's the most likely explanation.'

'That's the whole point, though, with that model. If the brakes are on, then the slightest movement causes them to lock firm. Something to do with an extra ratchet. Sven explained it, although I can't say I took it in.' He passed a trembling hand over his face. 'He says there's no way the brakes could have come loose on their own. No way.'

My mind was reeling. 'Then the only explanation—'

144

'Someone loosened them deliberately.' He leant forward. 'I'll be honest with you. This thing is way over my head. And now someone's died. I don't know what to do. I'm tempted to contact Head Office, but they'll think I'm not competent to deal with the situation and reassign me.' An earnest expression came into his eyes. 'What would you do in my place?'

I thought for a minute. But there was only one thing he could do. 'Go to the police,' I said firmly.

'Sven's already done it. He reported it yesterday.'

'Did he speak to Inspector Hallengren?'

'He didn't say who.' The furrows in Leo's forehead deepened. 'Why would someone do that, Maggie? If it was a prank, then I might understand it.' His voice broke. 'But I don't think it was meant as a prank.'

I felt my heart pumping. 'Why do *you* think someone did it?'

He said nothing. He didn't need to. I knew with a terrible certainty what was going through his mind. 'There were people on the path,' I said. 'Below that overhang.'

He nodded dumbly, tears at the corners of his eyes. He glanced towards the Ellises. 'Jim and Robyn went down there to look at the view. And Jane.'

And not just Jane. Liz and Harry had been on the path.

'My God, Leo, whoever loosened those brakes intended to kill someone.'

'That's the conclusion Sven came to. It's the conclusion I've come to.'

I could almost smell his fear. 'Sven did the right thing in going to the police.' I squeezed his hand. 'They'll know how to handle this.'

'What about the excursions? Should I cancel them?' The appeal in his eyes was distressing.

'Go and speak to Inspector Hallengren. He'll advise you.'

Leo's face cleared. 'That's a good idea,' he said, half to himself. He pushed his plate aside, the eggs uneaten. 'Thanks, Maggie,' he added, with feeling.

After he'd gone, I sat for a long time, watching my coffee grow cold. Something was niggling. Something about the snowmobile trip. I tried to remember who else had been below that overhang.

In a flash, it came to me – Marcellus Bibby.

And Wilson.

Wilson, who was now dead.

My conversation with Leo had shaken me. I needed space to think. I grabbed a snow-suit from the Activities Room and tugged it on over my clothes.

The sun had risen into an ice-blue sky. I stepped on to the path and was instantly dazzled by the light bouncing off the snow. It wasn't until my eyes had adapted that I found I was standing next to a figure in a black snow-suit. He was leaning against the lion-tamer as though waiting for a bus. A pall of cigarette smoke hung in the air.

'Is it always as cold as this?' he said, gazing into the distance. His voice was deep, with a pronounced American accent.

'You think this is cold?' I said, remembering Leo's words. 'The temperature starts dropping about now.'

He stared at me, the cigarette partway to his lips.

He had an interesting face, with mild eyes, and bushy brows that almost met in the middle. The plaster of black hair was combed in a way that emphasised his slightly domed head. It was impossible to tell if he was tanned, because the black snow-suit leached the colour from his skin.

'The temperature's about to drop? That's just dandy. How's a Manhattan boy expected to survive in a goddamn freezer?'

I studied his snow-suit, which was unfastened at the wrists and ankles. 'You could put your hood up for starters,' I said lightly. 'And I'd get rid of that cigarette and find some gloves. Sneakers aren't such a good idea, either. You need fur-lined boots.'

He continued to smoke, his gaze sliding down my snow-suit. As he brought his hand to his lips, the light reflected off his signet ring. 'You sound like an expert. Been here all week?'

'By "here" I take it you mean the Ice Hotel.'

'You slept in there?' he said slowly, eyes focused on the tip of his cigarette.

'Yes.'

'What was it like?'

'Cold.'

He half closed his eyes. 'How cold?'

'Cold cold. Minus five cold.'

A look of alarm crossed his face. 'Fahrenheit?'

'Celsius.'

His cigarette was burning down. 'A man could freeze to death at minus five,' he said, looking at his feet.

'If he's not properly dressed.'

'Or if he's out of his sleeping bag.'

After a brief silence, I said, 'Which newspaper are you with?'

The thin smile didn't reach his eyes. 'I'm not a reporter.' He drew on his cigarette, letting the smoke drift from his mouth. 'I'm a lawyer.'

When I said nothing, he added, 'Aaron Vandenberg.' He turned and gazed at the Ice Hotel.

A lawyer. Of course. Bibby's lawyers would have arrived on the next plane.

'I thought you were one of the press, Mr Vandenberg. You didn't strike me as someone who's come here on holiday.'

He swivelled his head. 'A holiday? Here? Are you nuts? I'm out of this place the minute I've wound things up.'

'Things to do with Wilson Bibby?'

'You guessed right. I'm Wilson's lawyer.' He corrected himself. 'I *was* Wilson's lawyer.' A strange look came into his eyes. 'I was also his friend.'

There was little I could say. 'I'm sorry.'

He stubbed out the cigarette against the lion-tamer's chest. 'Did you ever meet him?'

'We spoke a few times. And we had a game of chess.'

'I bet he won. He always does.'

I was surprised. It hadn't taken me long to uncover Wilson's strategy. 'Always?'

'Every time. You could make book on it.'

I was inclined to throw back a caustic remark, but it would be bad form to criticise a dead man's chess-playing skills. And Wilson had been his friend.

'How is Marcellus coping?' I said. 'We've hardly seen him since Wilson's accident. I have to confess I'm a bit worried about him.'

'He's in that hick town, at the coroner's office.'

It wasn't an answer, but I let it go. A lawyer wasn't going to discuss his client's feelings with a stranger.

'I take it you were with Wilson in Stockholm,' I said.

The man seemed preoccupied. 'Stockholm? Yes, Stockholm,' he said slowly, turning his restless gaze on me. 'I flew up this morning.'

'Well, I'm off for a walk.' I motioned to the Excelsior. 'If you're staying here, perhaps I'll see you later.'

I made to go, but he put out an arm, barring my way. I was surprised at the gesture.

'You say you've been speaking to Marcellus?' There was a hint of menace in his voice.

I stepped back. 'That's right.'

'May I ask what about?'

I was tempted to tell him to mind his own business. 'It was small-talk, mainly. He told me about his work with the Bibby Foundation. And Wilson's schools' programme.'

The man relaxed visibly.

'Why are you so concerned about my conversation with Marcellus, Mr Vandenberg?'

His composure had returned. 'I'm not concerned.' He spoke lazily. 'If I sounded concerned, it was for Marcellus's wellbeing. He's had a nasty shock. He was close to his father.'

'Have you known Marcellus long?'

'Long enough.' He dismissed me with a look of indifference. 'Enjoy your walk.'

Interesting. Aaron Vandenberg might well be concerned for Marcellus's welfare, but he seemed more concerned about the nature of his conversations. What secrets did he think Marcellus was going to spill? Marcellus was an experienced businessman, someone who'd know when to keep his counsel. Yet something was rattling the family lawyer.

I trudged down the path between the ice statues, leaving him standing, a statue himself.

I took the route past the chapel, and made for the bank. The sun was rising. The ice-cutters had been hard at work here, and the river looked like a dark scar on a white face. Ice crusted the edges like a scab.

As I stepped off the path, Denny Hinckley materialised from behind the trees. He parked himself beside the brazier and warmed his hands as though he'd been there for hours.

'Well, hello there,' he said, in mock surprise.

149

I was in no mood for politeness. 'Not again, Mr Hinckley.' I took in the thick white snow-suit, the hood up, fur framing his face. 'Are you in camouflage so you can lie in wait for people?'

'Look, Maggie, I know we've got off on the wrong foot—'

'It's Maggie now? You seem to be taking a lot for granted.'

'Give me a break, love. I was trying to put you at your ease.' He produced a packet of cigarettes and shook one loose. 'All I'm after is some detail of the room. Wilson Bibby's. Then, Scout's honour, I'll leave you alone.'

'Is this the only tune in your repertoire?'

He gestured to the Ice Hotel, its blue colour bleached white in the sunlight. 'No one can get in. It's like Fort bloody Knox.'

'I bet you could if you wanted to,' I said carelessly. 'There are no locks to pick. The handles are taped, but it wouldn't take much to cut through them.'

He sneered, lighting his cigarette. 'You think I'd try a caper like that? Have you seen the A-list detective running this case? He's marked my card and no mistake.'

'Don't tell me you tried to interview him.'

Denny drew his head back and blew smoke into the air. 'We all did. We won't get much change out of him. He's issuing press statements but nothing else. And there's not much there. Nothing I can go back to my boss with.' He chewed his lip. 'Please, Maggie, you're my only hope. Give me something. I need a break. My boss has got me by the short and curlies.'

The man was a walking cliché. 'You're wasting your time,' I said. 'I don't know what Wilson's room looks like.'

'But you were in the one next to his.'

'That doesn't mean I went in.'

'What about the morning his body was discovered? Was it you who found him?'

'It was the girls who bring the drinks.' I felt a twinge of guilt. He'd be pestering Karin and Marita now.

He dropped his cigarette and began to scribble furiously. 'Go on.'

'There's nothing more to tell. Harry and I saw a little way into the room, that's all.'

'That's Harry Auchinleck?'

I was no longer surprised at the extent of Denny's knowledge. 'I suppose you've already pumped him for information.'

'Fat chance, love. We've locked horns in the past. He can clam up tighter than a virgin's thighs.'

'Locked horns?'

'I've seen him in court.'

'Ah, yes. Harry's been an expert witness many times.'

'That's as may be, darling, but me and the boys never get anything from him. Zippo. Zippo. Zippo.'

I grinned. 'Why am I not surprised?'

'These professors are all the same. They think they're anointed rather than appointed. I'm sure he's got a funny handshake, if you catch my drift. And I bet he eats muesli for breakfast. My paper offered him top whack for a story. Cash on the nail. And he turned us down. You'd think, from the way he dresses, he could use the dough.'

'You may find this hard to believe, but it's not money that floats Harry's boat.'

'He can't be a carbon-based life form, then.' Denny played with his pen. 'So what about it, love? I'll give you an exclusive.'

'Look, Mr Hinckley—'

'Denny.'

'Denny, there were loads of people around when Wilson's body was discovered. Why don't you go and harangue someone else?

And here's some friendly advice – it might be helpful not to rush in with both guns blazing.'

'I've tried everyone. No one can remember a thing,' he said, in disgust. 'As soon as I appear, it's a case of galloping amnesia. And my editor won't let me offer money.' He added quickly, 'You were going to be the exception, of course.'

I smiled. 'Well, without money, you're going to have to rely on that winning personality.'

He stared at the Ice Hotel. 'If this godforsaken place weren't on the edge of the known world, I might have got here before they'd taped it off.' He scratched his nose. 'I suppose I could ask Mr Hoity Toity Detective to send an officer in with me.'

'Forget it, Denny. You'll spend all your time filling out forms in triplicate.'

'Why? The place isn't a crime scene.' A gleam came into his eye. 'In my line of work, it's easier to be granted forgiveness than permission. Maybe I should break in after all.'

'Do that, and stuff's going to happen.' I looked squarely at him. 'You know, I don't see you as the type to go looking for trouble.'

He spoke with feeling. 'Oh, I don't need to. I know where it is.' His face sagged. 'Listen, Maggie, I have to find a big story. I can't afford to let the grass grow under my feet. There are young guys coming up behind me, if you catch my drift.'

I was starting to feel sorry for him. Something about his look of desolation made me ask, 'Do you have family, Denny?'

He seemed surprised at the sudden shift in the conversation. 'My ex remarried so we don't see each other any more. Maybe it's just as well. I don't have to continue with the payments. She likes the high life.'

'Any children?'

His eyes filmed over with sadness. 'I thought we were trying for kids till I discovered she'd been taking the pill. Secretly, like, behind my back. So no. No kids.'

I had a sudden desire to help him. 'Listen, Denny, if you're after a scoop, forget Wilson Bibby and the Ice Hotel. There's another story you could pursue.'

'Another?' He'd put his notebook away and was turning in a tight circle, holding his mobile above his head.

'Have you heard of the Stockholm hotel murders?'

He stopped. 'Hotel murders?' His eyes glittered. 'Tell me more, lovely girl.'

'I don't know the details, but the barman does. And so do the staff. There was nothing in the British papers, as far as I can remember, so maybe you can make a splash.'

'Stockholm, eh? But what's this got to do with Wilson Bibby?' A slow grin spread across his face. 'You think he was murdered, then?'

'Of course not. It's got nothing to do with him – he died of a heart attack. All I'm saying is you might get more mileage from the Stockholm hotel murders. There was a death in Stockholm last week. Maybe coincidence. Maybe not.' I was about to add that Harry could tell him things when I remembered that Denny was likely to get short shrift in that department.

He seemed undecided. He was gazing at the Ice Hotel. I could see he couldn't let it go. It had taken hold of him the way it took hold of everyone, reaching with its icy hands, caressing softly.

'Breathtaking, isn't it?' I said, watching him.

He didn't reply. His eyes were glazed, the expression vacant.

I left him standing by the brazier.

'Maggie! Wait for me!'

It was Jane, waving wildly. She was wearing a red snow-suit and

Russian-style fur hat with flaps over the ears. Corkscrews of hair were stuck to her forehead. She was stomping over the ice, breathing hard.

I gazed at her feet. 'Why are you wearing plastic tennis racquets?'

'These were all that were left. The wooden snowshoes have gone.' She stooped, supporting herself by gripping my shoulder, and eased them off. 'Here, take a look,' she added, handing me one.

I tapped the hard mesh. 'Looks painful.' I passed it back. 'I'll stick with boots.'

She tucked the snowshoes under her arm. 'At least I can say I've given them a go.' She glanced at the forest. 'You going for a walk?'

I hesitated, seeing my chance for solitude spinning out of sight. I could have put her off, but the last time I'd seen her, she was rocking in terror listening to the barman tell his tales of murder. I took her arm. 'Let's find the trail,' I said, guiding her towards the forest.

The path was narrow but well trodden, and lined with pine trees. They were heavy with snow, their branches bending inwards and meeting those of the trees opposite. The slanting light filtering through the pine needles threw splashes of brilliance on to the ground. Amid such whiteness, the tree trunks looked black, the ribbed bark with its dusting of snow like filigree lace.

'Have you seen who's here?' Jane said, after we'd walked a little way. When I didn't reply, she added, in a voice beating with excitement, 'Aaron Vandenberg.'

'Yes, I met him earlier. I suppose it's hardly surprising, the family lawyer descending.'

'He's not just the family lawyer. Doesn't the name Vandenberg ring a bell?'

I shook my head.

'Have you heard of Marcia Vandenberg?'

'Of course,' I said, remembering. 'The heiress who died from the overdose. Was she his wife?'

'Aaron and Marcia were brother and sister.'

'And she was Marcellus Bibby's girlfriend, wasn't she?'

'Not only that.' Jane lowered her voice, hardly necessary considering where we were. 'The police suspected him of complicity in her death.'

'So what do you think? Was Marcellus involved?'

'I know next to nothing about their relationship.' She tugged her ear flaps down. 'Only what was in the tabloids.'

Yes, the Bibbys seemed always to be in the papers. And there was going to be a damn sight more about them after this week was out.

I glanced at her. 'How are you coping with what's going on here, Jane? Wilson Bibby's accident, I mean.'

She didn't reply immediately. I watched the passage of emotions on her face. 'Well enough,' she said.

'You're not just being brave?' I said gently. 'You don't think Wilson was the victim of the Stockholm hotel killer?'

'Leo said it was a heart attack.'

'Tell me about yourself,' I said, wanting to change the subject. 'What do you do?'

'I'm a dentist's receptionist.' She flashed her thousand-watt smile. 'It's not very grand. You know what it's like. You start out with these dreams and you end up doing something totally different.'

I smiled. 'Real life gets in the way. So what were your dreams?'

'I've always wanted to be a journalist. I thought that coming here would give me inspiration for a travel article. I mean, how many people come to the Ice Hotel?'

A whole lot more would be coming now, I thought cynically. 'And have you started writing it yet?'

'I don't know where to begin.'

'Maybe you need an angle. What about Wilson? He's attracting as much attention now that he's dead as he ever did when he was alive, if those reporters are anything to go by.'

'That's the problem. They're the ones making the splash. They'll be describing this place, as well as everything that's happened here. By the time we go home, it'll be too late.'

'But you've an advantage they don't have. You've been holidaying with Wilson. You've had insight into the person, not the billionaire businessman. People will be more interested in that than in anything Denny Hinckley writes. His articles will be tomorrow's chip paper.'

There was bitterness in her voice. 'Denny has a good reputation.'

'He wasn't the one on that snowmobile trip. It was you and Wilson. Now, that would make a great article. You could write about—'

I stopped, remembering my conversation with Leo. The revelation about the loosened brakes wasn't something I intended to share with Jane. I'd been stupid even to mention it. I wondered whether Leo had seen Hallengren yet, and what Hallengren intended to do with the information.

She was watching me. 'Is something worrying you, Maggie?'

'It's just that I find this place a bit . . . Well, spooky is the wrong word. But you know what I mean.'

'The forest?'

I hesitated. 'The Ice Hotel.'

She swallowed rapidly. 'It's as if it's watching you. When I can see the Ice Hotel, I can't bring myself to talk about it.'

'As though it's listening.' I glanced around. 'This forest is the only place where you can't see it.'

'There's another. You know that road leading to the church? It bends into a small clearing enclosed by trees. The church is in that clearing. You can't see the Ice Hotel from there.' The muscles of her face tightened. 'You can see it from the top of the tower, though.'

'Wow, you've been up?' I said, making a show of being impressed. 'I've still to go.'

'If you do, then don't take the road. There's a path inside the forest. You can just see it from the road if you peer through the trees. It's easier walking, and won't take nearly as long.'

'So when did you climb the tower?'

'After the tour of the church.' Her expression brightened. 'The church is lovely. I felt a great sense of peace. Apart from the tours, no one seems to go there. The pews are all dusty. Strange that the candles were lit, though.'

'And the view from the top?'

'Magnificent.' The light faded from her eyes. 'But you can see the ice buildings in the distance. Including the Ice Hotel. And the chapel.'

'Have you been inside the chapel?' I said slowly, my mind immediately back at the image of the snow-covered corpse.

'I wanted to, but something prevented me.' Her voice sounded strange. 'I couldn't get through the door. I pulled at the handles, but it was as if something was pulling from the other side. I pushed hard, and it pushed back. I let go, and the door swung back and forth. When I pulled again, the same thing happened.'

'Someone must have been inside, larking around,' I said nervously.

'There was no one inside, Maggie.'

I wondered how she could know that. But I said nothing. The most likely explanation was Mike, or Jonas, having a laugh.

She gripped my sleeve. 'Don't go in there. The place is evil.'

157

'Nonsense,' I said, with a bravado I didn't feel. 'It's a consecrated chapel.'

'And what about those statues?' she said, in measured tones.

'The circus statues?'

'Have you noticed they're different every time you look?'

'That's impossible.'

'Look closely.'

'Okay, I will, but I doubt I can remember what they were like before.' I suddenly found myself shivering. 'Let's go back, Jane. I'm getting cold.'

We walked in silence through the forest and on to the ice. Aaron Vandenberg had gone, but Denny Hinckley was loitering at the river's edge, kicking the snow. He waved as we passed, but made no attempt to detain us.

Jane stopped at the roadside. 'I'm taking the bus into Kiruna. Jim and Robyn are meeting me for shopping and then lunch.' Her face brightened. 'Would you like to join us?'

'Thank you, but I won't.' I looked past her. 'Good timing. Here's your bus. Give me the snowshoes and I'll return them.'

'Thanks.' Her gaze drifted to the path that led to the Excelsior. 'Remember, Maggie. The statues.'

I watched the bus until it disappeared behind a bank of snow, then turned and walked slowly up to the hotel.

I examined the statues. The clown was still crying. His bowler was pushed back off his face, his arms lowered, the sticks touching the skin of the drum. The ballerina stood *en pointe*, one arm above her head, the other lowered. The juggler was staring balefully at the clown. Was this how I'd seen them that first day? I could no longer remember. I continued up the path. Jane was mistaken. Ice statues couldn't change. Not unless the staff slipped out in the morning, partially melted the ice and rearranged the figures for the amusement of the guests.

I stopped at the front door. My stomach cramped with fear. The lion was one figure I did remember. But he was no longer crouched beneath his master's whip, ready to leap. He was standing proud, on all fours, his head turned in my direction.

CHAPTER 14

'Miss Stewart.' The manager was hurrying towards me. 'Inspector Hallengren wishes to speak with you.'

I was in the foyer, pulling off my boots, watching the lion through the window. 'Inspector Hallengren? But he's already interviewed me. What's this about?'

'The inspector didn't tell me.'

'Is he here?' I said quietly, hoping this didn't mean a trip into Kiruna.

'He's in my office. I'll take you now.'

I glanced at my snow-suit.

'I'll return that, Miss Stewart. And the snowshoes.'

I struggled out of the suit quickly. The manager sped along the corridor. I padded after him in my socks.

The door to the office was ajar. The manager knocked hesitantly before pushing it open.

Hallengren was at the window. He turned as I entered. I wondered how long he'd been there. Had he watched me scrutinising the statues?

I heard the door being closed behind me.

'I believe you wish to speak to me, Inspector.'

He motioned through the window. 'I have always loved the view from this office.'

'I can understand why.' I went to stand beside him. 'You see all the way to the forest.'

He looked at me with interest. 'Have you been out to the forest, Miss Stewart?'

'There's something about snow-covered trees I simply can't resist.'

He smiled easily. 'Then you should try cross-country skiing. There are tracks through the forest, and they are well signposted.'

I thought of the loudly dressed man I'd seen the previous day. 'I'm sure it's harder than it looks.'

'That is true of most sports. But skiing cross-country does not take long to master.'

I looked into his eyes. 'I still think I'd need someone to show me.'

After a pause, he said, 'Miss Stewart, I asked to see you because I have some further questions concerning Wilson Bibby.'

'But I've told you everything I know.'

He nodded towards the desk. 'Please sit down.'

If Hallengren wanted to question me further, I intended to be comfortable. I ignored the straight-backed chairs and took one of the maroon armchairs. He hesitated for a second, then lowered himself on to the sofa.

'My questions are not about what happened in the Ice Hotel,' he said, turning the pages of his notebook. 'They are about your conversations with Wilson Bibby.' He looked up. 'You sat next to Mr Bibby on the plane to Kiruna.'

'That's right,' I said slowly, wondering how he would know. We hadn't been allocated seats so it couldn't have been from the plane's manifest.

He must have guessed what I was thinking. 'One of the passengers told me you and Mr Bibby sat together.'

'What do you want to know, Inspector? What we talked about?'

'Can you remember?'

'Why is it so important?' I said in exasperation.

'It may not be. Shall we just say it is part of a line of enquiry?'

'What sort of a line?'

'When there is an unexpected death, we establish the circum-stances leading up to it. So, can you remember what you talked about?' he added patiently.

'The usual stuff you talk about to strangers on a plane.'

He raised an eyebrow. 'Specifically?'

'Wilson gave me his family history. That more or less took up the entire flight.'

The corners of Hallengren's mouth twitched. So he did have a sense of humour.

'He opened up to you remarkably quickly, Miss Stewart. Do you not find that strange?'

'Americans are always quick to talk about their Scottish roots, Inspector.'

'What else did he tell you about himself?'

'It was just social chat . . . He told me that Marcellus acts as his bodyguard.'

Hallengren looked surprised. 'He told you that?'

'I can't remember what led to it. He mentioned being stalked.' I looked at my nails. 'I was rather rude to him. He'd snubbed Harry in Stockholm, and I told him so in words of one syllable. Once I get started, I find it difficult to stop.'

Hallengren nodded, a half-smile on his face.

'Inspector, what exactly is this about? If you gave me some hint of what you're after, I might be able to help you.'

'Did Wilson Bibby tell you anything about his business affairs?'

'To a complete stranger?' I said in amazement. 'Why on earth would he? Hold on, are you talking about this schools' exchange thing?'

'Possibly.'

'He didn't tell me anything. I learnt about it from Marcellus after we arrived here.'

'So Wilson said nothing about what he was doing in Stockholm last week?'

'Only that he'd be returning to continue whatever it was. Come to think of it, he told me that later.'

'I understand he showed you his diary.'

'Your spies are well informed, Inspector. Whoever this passenger is, he's observant.'

Hallengren waited in silence.

'He showed me his diary,' I said, my voice level. 'What of it?'

'What exactly did he show you, Miss Stewart? Think carefully.'

'The cover in the family tartan, which he was very proud of. And he showed me the pages.'

Hallengren leant forward. 'Did you see pages with writing? Or carbons?'

'I just saw the pages at the back, for December they must have been. They were blank.'

'You definitely did not see the date on the last page that had writing on it?'

'I've just said I didn't.' I studied his face, but he was giving nothing away. 'Look, Inspector, I don't understand this line of questioning. If you're so interested in Wilson's diary, why don't you look through it yourself? It'll still be in his locker.'

His eyes were without expression. He got to his feet. 'Thank you, Miss Stewart, that will be all for the time being. If you do remember anything about the diary, anything that you have not told me, please get in touch immediately.'

He walked over to the door, and held it open.

I stepped into the corridor. And then I had it.

'You're asking me these questions because you haven't got the diary, have you, Inspector?'

His gaze was steady. 'Thank you for your time, Miss Stewart.' He closed the door softly.

I leant against the wall, my mind buzzing. Wilson's diary was missing. What did that mean? He'd mislaid it? Hardly. Given what he'd said on the plane, he never let it out of his sight. He might even have kept it with him in the Ice Hotel. The only explanation was that it had been stolen. So what could have been in his diary that had made someone want to steal it?

But, more to the point, why would a detective be so interested in the diary of a man who'd died of a cardiac arrest?

I ran into Harry on the stairs.

'Lunchtime, dear girl. Man cannot live by champers alone.'

'You haven't been hitting the Bollinger already?' I said in mock disapproval.

'Far too early.' He winked. 'But I must confess to having had a small hock and seltzer by way of aperitif.'

I took his arm. 'Tell me what you've been up to this morning, Harry.'

'I went for a long walk with Liz and Mike.'

How quickly Mike had become a part of our group.

'I didn't see you on the river,' I said.

'We went in the opposite direction. There are several cross-country ski paths behind the Excelsior.'

'Don't tell me you went skiing.'

'Surprised?' he said, in a playful tone. 'It was great fun. And good exercise, especially for the waistline.' He patted his stomach. 'I must keep it up when we return to Dundee. Liz tells me there's that kind of skiing somewhere in Perthshire.'

'How is she today?'

'Much better. But I do wish she'd lay off the cigarettes. Smoking will ruin her complexion. She and Mike are waiting for us in the restaurant.' Harry dropped his voice. 'We're going for the early sitting in an attempt to avoid the jackals.'

'By jackals, I take it you're referring to the gentlemen of the press.'

'If they're gentlemen, I'm a Dutchman,' he said, pulling open the dining-room door.

Liz and Mike were at the long central table, leaning into one another, talking quietly. Marcellus had abandoned his window and was sitting a few seats away from them. Aaron Vandenberg was absent. Perhaps it was his turn at the coroner's office. That's what lawyers were for, I thought with satisfaction, and Marcellus would be needing a break.

It was the first time I'd seen him since the police interviews. He looked tired and ill at ease, shoulders sagging, head bent over his plate. His mouth was fixed in an expression of hopelessness. I went over to speak to him, but he rose as if from a deep sleep and left the room.

'I take it you've met the lawyer, Mags,' Liz said, watching him go.

I reached for the chicken salad. 'When he told me his name, he seemed to expect me to recognise it.'

'Well, I'd never heard the name Vandenberg until I read it in the papers last week,' said Mike.

'And what did they say about him?'

'He's the architect of this schools' thing. He's Wilson's right-hand man, been with him these last few weeks, doing the deal.' Mike piled pasta on to his plate. 'So what's this about his sister overdosing?'

'That was in the papers too?' I said, not surprised.

'And can someone tell me the rest?'

Liz filled him in briefly.

'I don't understand,' he said in a puzzled voice. 'If he's related to Marcia, who Marcellus may have killed, doesn't it strike you as odd he's the Bibby lawyer?'

I put my fork down firmly. 'That's the least of it. Everything about what's happening here is odd.'

I described my recent conversation with Leo Tullis, specifically Sven's theory that the snowmobile brakes had been deliberately loosened. I left out that Leo had concluded it was with the intention of killing someone.

Harry was staring blankly.

Liz's face was ashen. She would have come to the same conclusion I had. She had been one of the people beneath the overhang.

'Jesus, Mary and Joseph,' Mike said under his breath. 'I don't believe it.'

'That there's a nutter going around loosening brakes?' I said. 'And that's not all. Hallengren told me that Wilson's diary has been stolen. So what's that all about?'

Mike sneered. 'It's obvious what's happened. Now that he's dead, some journalist wants to publish the grand man's ramblings.'

'It's not just a diary. His business decisions are recorded in it. And signed and witnessed, which I suppose makes them legally binding.'

'So someone wants to know what he's been doing in Stockholm? But the whole world knows. Why steal his diary? I don't get it.'

But I got it. I got it in a flash. It was nothing to do with what Wilson *had* been doing. It was what he was *intending* to do. Someone had stolen his diary with the express purpose of uncovering his next business move. But who? A reporter wanting to expose his plans? The diary might well be of interest to someone like Denny Hinckley, who'd probably not be above a little judicious thievery. Yet the reporters hadn't arrived until the afternoon, and the Locker Room was out of bounds by then. Whoever had stolen it had taken it on the night Wilson had died, or early in the morning before the police were called. I kept coming back to it: why would the theft of Wilson's diary be of such interest to Hallengren that he'd trek out to the Excelsior to question me about it?

Harry leant forward, his cowlick flopping over his eyes. 'Maggie, getting back to the snowmobiles, if there's a nutter on the loose, as you so eloquently put it, then don't you think Leo should tell the police?'

'I think he's already been to see Hallengren.'

'You don't suppose the brakes were loosened with the intention of killing someone?' Mike said.

'Of course not. It was a prank.'

But I was only half listening. My mind was still on the diary. If Hallengren hadn't found it by now, he was unlikely ever to. It was too recognisable for a thief to keep it long. My bet was that it was at the bottom of the river. But if the inspector was so interested in the diary, why hadn't he taken the Excelsior apart searching for it?

'There's the trip to the Sami village this afternoon,' Liz was saying, brushing at the tablecloth. 'Are you coming, Mags?'

'I think I'll go to the church. I'd like to check out that tower.' And I wanted somewhere quiet to sit and think.

She didn't even try to dissuade me. She turned to the others. 'I'll see you in the Activities Room.' Without waiting for a reply, she left the room, avoiding my gaze.

'I'd better catch her up,' Harry said quickly, getting to his feet. 'She seems quite shaken.'

Mike was playing with his coffee cup. 'Liz has been smoking non-stop. It's got so she's spending more time outside than in. Is she always this jittery?'

'It's my fault,' I said wearily. 'I should have kept quiet about the brakes. And those stories about the hotel killer coming here can't have helped. I wish that barman had kept his mouth shut.'

Mike lifted his head. 'You don't think there's anything in that story, do you?'

'It seems too far-fetched. I thought the Stockholm hotel killer did his work in Stockholm. What's he doing here? Kiruna's a long way from anywhere.'

'Jonas Madsen told me he used to stay regularly at the Maximilian,' Mike said, sifting the sugar in the bowl.

'He told me that too. But lots of people stayed there. And they're not all killers.'

He gave me a strange look.

After a brief silence, I said, 'Mike, didn't you say you'd spent much of last year in Stockholm?'

'What of it?'

'Don't take this the wrong way, but I had the impression that the first time you'd heard about these murders was when the barman talked about them yesterday.'

'Your impression's correct, Maggie. Where's this going?'

'I'm just amazed that you missed the story. It's all anyone talked about, from what Harry said.'

'It must have been a seven-day wonder.' He was looking at me steadily. 'And I don't remember hearing anything.'

I almost believed him. But everyone in Sweden knew, so his denial made no sense. Yet why would he lie?

He gulped his coffee, rose, and left the room.

★ ★ ★

The church was a good twenty minutes from the Excelsior. I walked briskly, grateful for the exercise. Wands of smoke curled from the chimneys of the tightly crowded buildings, and disintegrated in the still air. The houses soon thinned, giving way to clusters of pine trees. Every so often, snow fell soundlessly from their branches as the burdened trees released their load.

I met no one on the road. A flock of birds flapped low, but this served only to enhance the sense of solitude. The forecast was for good weather, although the colour of the sky suggested otherwise. A sudden gust of wind blew yesterday's snow into puffs, which eddied like tiny sandstorms around my ankles.

I took the bend in the road. The church stood a couple of hundred feet away in a cul-de-sac, protected on three sides by forest. The rectangular tower, the tallest structure for miles, dwarfed the building.

The going was easier here, as someone had swept the snow off the gravel path. I walked round to the side of the church. An iron ladder, riveted to the tower, led to a wooden door near the top. I brushed the snow off the lower rungs. They were free of rust, solid and deep, although a climber would still need to take great care. I gripped the rungs with both hands and hauled at the ladder, letting it take my weight, but it didn't budge. I wondered why it was there. Surely there was a way of climbing the tower from the inside.

I returned to the main entrance and twisted the iron ring in the wooden door. It opened with a pained creak. A thick cloak of musty air enveloped me, bringing with it strong memories of childhood attendance at Mass. I shut the door behind me.

The pencil windows set into the pastel-coloured walls cast narrow bands of light on to the floor. Other than the altar, there was nothing in the building except the painted wooden pews. Their gaudy colours had faded unevenly and the paint was peeling off, exposing bleached pine ravaged by woodworm. But the pews were solid enough. This would be a good place to sit and think.

The altar stood on a platform behind waist-high black railings, which were fastened with a padlock. On the cloth was a carved altarpiece. It was a tree in full leaf, painted in primary colours. But instead of tropical birds, saintly figures were perched in the branches. At the top was the crucified Christ, his flattened hands and feet nailed to the trunk, blood gushing into cups held by cheerful angels. In front of the tree, a row of candles striped in red, blue and yellow stood like papal guards. The smell of hot wax filled my nostrils, making me want to curl up and sleep.

There was a stone column half hidden in the shadows at the far left of the nave. On it was attached a yellowing notice, the typescript faded but readable. I found the section in English: a brief history of the church, specific mention of the Italian architect and an account of the removal of the ancient bells to the museum in Kiruna. The outside ladder and side door in the tower were for the convenience of the bell-ringer, who could come and go without disturbing the congregation. I scanned the text. It was possible to climb the tower from the inside and, once through the trapdoor at the top, a walled platform 'afforded an unparalleled view of the aurora borealis'.

The door to the tower was tucked away in the corner behind the column. I pushed it gently.

There was nothing inside, only darkness and a chill like that of a mortuary. I opened the door wide, letting the warm air waft in from the church, like breath on my skin. A rusty candelabrum was set into the wall, its ivory candles unlit. I stared into the windowless room until my eyes had adapted. But there was no other door, no ladder, no means of climbing the tower.

Then I spied it at the back – a flight of wooden steps, wide and deep. Easy to miss in the gloom.

I gripped the railings and stared up into the tower. The steps spiralled into blackness. The trapdoor was closed.

I was about to leave when I heard the creak. The front door was opening. Men's voices. I tiptoed to the door and peered out cautiously.

Marcellus and Aaron Vandenberg had entered. They were at the far end of the nave, Marcellus's bulk partly hidden by the column.

'You sure we can speak freely here?' I heard Aaron say.

I moved back, but not so far that I couldn't hear. It was as Marcellus was replying that I remembered the only way out was through the nave. But it was too late now. I'd committed myself to eavesdropping.

'For Chrissakes, Aaron, chill out. This place is deserted.'

'And you know this how?'

'There's one tour a week, and I've been on it.'

'Well, someone's lit those candles.' A pause. 'C'mon, son. Let's sit down.' A creaking.

Aaron again, gentleness in his voice. 'So how are you bearing up? They keeping you in town a lot?'

'There's a million forms to be filled out. Has to be done and, anyway, it keeps me from thinking too much.'

'I'm truly sorry, Marcellus.' A deep sigh. 'You know, the minute your dad said he wanted a vacation, I knew it would monkey-wrench our plans. But when he said he'd be coming here, I thought it might work for us. It's so remote.' More creaking, suggesting he was shifting his weight. 'This place really is something else.'

'The church?'

'Nah. The location. All this snow, masses of it, even in town.' A snort. 'I was glad to get my ass out of there. The Excelsior might not be the Hilton, but it's better than that shitty little hotel in Kiruna. One night would have been enough, but I've been there since Monday.' A long pause. 'So do you think the cops suspect anything?'

'If they do, they're giving nothing away.'

'What did they ask you?'

'The questions you'd expect them to ask. Where were you? Were you up and about, et cetera, et cetera?' Irritation in the voice. 'Do I have to write a book about it? I'm sure you can guess what they wanted to know.'

'And they said nothing about Stockholm?'

'What do you mean?'

'They gave no hint they thought anything was going on?'

'They already knew about my father's schools' initiative, if that's what you mean.'

'Are you being deliberately obtuse? No, that's not what I meant.'

'They only asked me about the schools' programme. And what our movements had been last week.'

'Given there was a daily account of where your father was every second of the day, I'm surprised they bothered. I suspect they just wanted you to corroborate it.' A note of anxiety crept into Aaron's voice. 'You told them only about the programme?'

'Of course. As you say, they'd be checking all that anyways.'

'Well, provided you keep your nerve, we'll come out of this smelling of roses.'

'Now who's being obtuse?'

'Lighten up, son. You'll soon be in the big league, no question. So when can we get out of here and back across the Pond?'

'You and I need to wind things up in Stockholm first.'

'We can do that tonight.'

'And I guess once I get the coroner's go-ahead for release of my father's body, we can go back to the States.'

'You got a timescale for that, son?'

'They're doing an autopsy.' A brief silence. 'Our passports are still being held by the police. We're allowed to go to Kiruna, and on the excursions, but nowhere else.'

'Says who?'

'The cop, Hallengren.'

'Forget him.'

'He's not some peach-fuzzed rookie, Aaron. He's sharp. Watch yourself when you speak to him.'

A thick laugh. 'There ain't a cop alive who can outsmart me. I've not been the Bibby lawyer all these years for nothing. This guy had better not jerk me around if he knows what's good for him.' A pause. 'So, is there anything else, or are we done here?'

'There's a problem with the diary.'

'Well, that came right out of left field. What sort of a problem?'

'The cops found pages torn out.'

'Did they, by God? Which particular pages?'

'All the ones from last week. They may ask you about them, Aaron. Your signature is on most of the memos.'

'The Swedish education minister has copies of those pages too. The cops'll find them soon enough if they're as smart as you say. And there's nothing there that will remotely interest them.'

'But it's the entry on the final day that *would* interest them.'

'I'm assuming that page was torn out along with the others. My guess is it's been destroyed.'

'Only a fool would keep it.' A pause, heavy with meaning. 'And the copy?'

'It's in a safe place, son.'

A harsh laugh. 'Why am I not surprised?'

'Which leaves us with only one thing we haven't talked about, Marcellus.'

'Like?'

'Like – how shall I put it? – my remuneration.'

'You'll get your remuneration. Once I know how much there is.'

'I've never been one for playing the long game. But for you, son, I can wait.' A creaking. 'Now, that's a weird thing, and no mistake.'

'What?'

'On the altar.'

'I hadn't noticed.'

'I thought you said you'd been on the tour. And what's in there, through that door?'

'A tower. There used to be bells or something.'

A rustling, followed by more creaking. 'So can you get up the tower?'

'Sure.'

'Fancy a climb? Now, don't look at me like that. I've no designs on you. Right now, we need each other. You could say we're a mutual assurance company.' The rustling grew louder, followed by footsteps.

I sprang back, my heart lurching. They were heading for the tower. I hadn't a clue what they'd been talking about, but I suspected they wouldn't be best pleased to discover they'd been overheard. I glanced at the steps. If I climbed to the top, they might think I'd been there all the while. But they'd be through the door before I made it halfway across. There was only one thing to do.

I slipped behind the door and pressed myself against the wall, hoping they'd leave the door open to let the warmth in. A second later, I heard their voices.

'There's nothing here, son. Let's go.'

'Wait. There, at the back.'

'Ah, yes, steps. Shall we?'

The footsteps moved further into the tower. To my horror, I felt the door moving. In a second, they'd see me.

'Leave it open, son.'

'Why?'

'We won't see a goddamn thing otherwise.'

There was a sudden groaning of wood, followed by heavy thuds. They were climbing. After a minute that felt like an hour, I crept out and padded softly down the nave. Halfway to the door, I remembered the loud creak. If they heard it, they'd be down like a shot. Even if I succeeded in making it to the road, they'd still see me.

I tiptoed back and climbed over the rail. I crouched behind the altar. A few seconds later, I heard footsteps.

'Not without a torch, son. It ain't safe. Anyway, I'm not sure those steps will take your weight. The wood looks a bit flaky. C'mon, I need a drink.'

The sound of footsteps faded. The front door creaked open. I counted to a hundred, then edged out from behind the altar.

I left the church, intending to walk slowly, out of sight of the men, but then remembered my conversation with Jane. I swerved right, towards the forest. Under the trees, the path's red markers were visible despite the recent snowfall. If what Jane had told me was correct, I should arrive at the Excelsior before Marcellus and Aaron.

The going was surprisingly easy. I ducked under low-hanging branches, hearing tiny rustlings in the undergrowth and the dull thump of snow hitting ground. The forest grew lighter and I soon found myself at the back of the Excelsior. The fire door in the Activities Room was just feet away.

I slipped round to the front where the courtesy bus was waiting. I boarded and settled myself in the back. As we moved off, I turned to look through the rear window. Marcellus and Aaron had reached the circus statues.

CHAPTER 15

As the bus bumped along the road to Kiruna, I went over Marcellus's conversation with Aaron in my mind several times so as not to forget it. There was no time to analyse it. I would leave that task to someone else.

The police station was a modest single-storey building on the outskirts of town, its walls a regulation steel grey. The impression it gave was that the only thing that engaged the occupants was a small number of petty crimes.

The interior was painted in muted shades of blue and yellow, and smelt of floor polish. One wall was covered with posters. The more recent ones obscured those underneath, rendering them unreadable as if the sole intention was to leave no inch of paintwork showing. A row of moulded plastic chairs stood underneath, blue alternating with yellow in a way that I found almost frivolous.

A young fair-haired man dressed in the familiar blue uniform was typing rapidly at a keyboard. He stopped and watched me approach.

'Do you speak English?' I said.

'Of course. How may I help you?'

'Is Inspector Hallengren in?'

The officer sat back. 'He is certainly in.'

I forced a smile, hoping this wasn't going to be hard work. 'And is he busy just now?'

He tapped a couple of keys. 'He is free.'

'May I speak with him?'

'I will check. What is your name, please?'

'Margaret Stewart.'

He spoke into the phone in rapid Swedish, then listened intently, his shoulders straightening. For a second, I thought he was going to jump to his feet and click his heels.

He replaced the receiver. 'Inspector Hallengren will see you now. Please follow me.'

The room was at the end of the corridor. The door was open, but he still knocked loudly.

Hallengren's voice came from within. The young man stepped back, motioning to me to enter, then left quickly.

If I'd expected clues to Hallengren's private life, I was disappointed. There were no family photographs or children's drawings. Only office furniture: filing cabinets, a cluttered desk, a table and chairs. A single bed, too short for Hallengren, was made up in the corner.

He got to his feet. 'Miss Stewart, this is an unexpected pleasure.' He motioned to a chair. 'Would you like some coffee?'

'No, thank you.' I sat down.

He lowered himself into his chair. 'I am hoping this is a social visit,' he said, a smile playing on his lips.

'It isn't, Inspector.' I hesitated. 'I've come about the diary.'

'I see.'

I'd expected more of a reaction. 'You told me it was missing,' I added.

'I do not believe that I did. I asked whether you had seen the contents. I did not say it was missing.' He clasped his hands behind his neck. 'What precisely have you come to see me about, Miss Stewart?'

'I overheard a conversation between Marcellus and Wilson Bibby's lawyer.'

He raised an eyebrow. 'His lawyer?'

'Aaron Vandenberg. I think you might not have met him.'

'I had no idea Wilson had brought his lawyer with him.' He reached for a file. 'He has not been staying at the Excelsior. I would have remembered the name.'

'He's been in Kiruna since Monday. He's at the Excelsior now.'

Hallengren studied me, frowning. 'You heard him speaking to Marcellus Bibby about the diary?'

I nodded.

'When was this, Miss Stewart?'

'An hour ago. I was in the church tower when they came in. They sat on a bench and talked.' I chewed my lip. 'I hid behind the door.'

If Hallengren had a view as to my behaviour, he kept it to himself.

'Inspector, I can only just remember what I overheard,' I said impatiently.

He opened a drawer and produced a portable recorder. 'Do you mind speaking into a machine?'

'No.'

'Then tell me what you remember. I will not interrupt.'

He listened intently, making notes while I recounted the conversation between Marcellus and Aaron as well as I could remember it. After I'd finished, he rose and paced the room, deep in thought.

'Miss Stewart,' he said, sitting down, 'you must promise to keep this information to yourself.'

'Again?' I said, with mild irony. 'Will you tell me why this time?'

He drew his brows together, saying nothing.

'Look, Inspector, we're crammed into the Excelsior like sardines, Aaron and Marcellus included. If what I've told you is of interest, and I think it is or you wouldn't be asking me to keep quiet about it, I may be able to help you further. I may overhear things, but I won't know if they're useful unless you tell me what's so important about this diary.'

He must have seen the force of my argument. 'The diary is not missing,' he said reluctantly. 'It never was. But there are pages that have been removed.'

'I know that. But what's so unusual about pages removed? They doubled as memo slips. Memo slips are meant to be removed.'

'But not the carbons. All the pages from last week, the week Wilson Bibby stayed in Stockholm, have been removed, carbons included. They were torn out by someone in a hurry.'

'From what Aaron Vandenberg said, you can get them from the Swedish minister.'

'Maybe not the final page.'

'Aaron has a copy,' I said, wondering if Hallengren had missed that point.

He nodded, saying nothing.

'Inspector, do you think Aaron and Marcellus are involved in something illegal? And it's on that last page?'

'If it is, Miss Stewart, then Wilson Bibby would have been involved too. It is his diary.'

'I suppose.' I sat back. 'There's something else I should tell you. I spoke with Aaron Vandenberg earlier, before I went to the church. He told me he'd flown down that morning from Stockholm.'

'What time did you speak to him?'

'A little before eight o'clock.'

'Then he cannot have. The first plane from Stockholm to Kiruna is not until ten thirty. He could have chartered a plane – I can easily check – but, even so, it contradicts what he said to Marcellus about staying in Kiruna since Monday.'

'What do you think's going on with the two of them?'

'I have no idea, Miss Stewart.'

'But you know that this diary is important. Otherwise you wouldn't have asked me to keep quiet about it.'

'I asked you to keep quiet because it *might* be important.' After a silence, he said, 'Miss Stewart, did you look into Wilson Bibby's room on the morning his body was discovered?' He was watching me, his gaze steady. 'You seem surprised by the question. I cannot think why – I understand half the guests in the Ice Hotel took a good look at the corpse.'

I shifted in the chair.

'Did you notice anything unusual?' he said.

'About the room?'

'About the corpse. Apart from the fact that Wilson Bibby was not wearing his snow-suit.'

I cast my mind back to the scene. At the time, something had seemed wrong. I couldn't put my finger on it then, and I couldn't now.

'There was something else he was not wearing, Miss Stewart. There was no locker key round his wrist.' Hallengren waited for the information to sink in. 'We checked every inch of his room – we even sifted the snow – but we could not find it. And we know that he used the locker because there are witnesses who not only saw him leave his clothes there, but saw him use his key.'

'I take it he hadn't left it in the lock.'

'He hadn't. In the end, we opened the locker. All his effects were there, according to Marcellus. The money, the credit cards. It was Marcellus who drew our attention to the diary. He was looking through it, and discovered that some pages had been torn out.'

'He volunteered this information?'

'He was very helpful.'

I felt like saying, 'Then why were you giving him such a hard time when you interviewed him?' But I said nothing. From what I'd overheard in the church, Marcellus wasn't exactly squeaky clean.

'How would you account for the missing locker key, Miss Stewart?'

'Wilson dropped it on the way to his room?'

'We combed the entire Ice Hotel.'

A thought struck me. 'Did Marcellus tell you he needs the pages found?'

'You must understand that I cannot divulge the nature of my conversations with other people.' Hallengren smiled. 'However, thanks to your information, we can now trace those pages.'

Then Marcellus couldn't have told Hallengren he could get them from the Swedish education minister. So he hadn't been entirely helpful. But it was the last page that seemed important to him and Aaron. Yet something told me Hallengren would never find it. I pictured the scene: Aaron coolly blowing cigarette smoke into Hallengren's face, denying all knowledge of the last page, laughing to himself because it was in an offshore bank vault.

'Tell me what you're thinking, Inspector.'

'You know I cannot do that.'

'Then I'll tell you.'

'Go on,' he said softly.

'Wilson Bibby never let that diary out of his sight, so he would have taken care with the locker key. You've turned the Ice Hotel upside down, but you haven't found it. Ergo, someone must have stolen it. Someone who wanted those pages removed.'

Hallengren leant back and folded his arms across his chest.

'Someone removed the key from Wilson's wrist,' I went on, 'opened the locker, and tore out the pages. They replaced the diary and secured the locker. But they didn't re-attach the key to Wilson's wrist.'

'And why would that be, Miss Stewart?'

It was difficult to think under Hallengren's gaze. 'He'd be taking a huge risk removing it in the first place – Wilson could have woken, after all – so he might not think it worth the risk to return it.'

Hallengren said nothing, but a smile had formed on his lips.

'He wouldn't dare keep it. He'd walk on to the ice and throw it into the water, or bury it in a drift.'

'Why did he not just leave it in the lock?'

'Because, in the morning, Wilson would see it in the lock and remember he hadn't left it there. He'd raise merry hell and call the police.' I shrugged. 'Actually, whether the thief left the key in the lock, or disposed of it, either way Wilson would notice it was no longer on his wrist. He'd check the locker and find the diary pages missing. Unless—'

The smile had vanished.

'Unless whoever removed the pages knew he was already dead,' I said slowly.

Hallengren raised an eyebrow. 'Then why did he not replace the key round Wilson's wrist? He was dead, after all. By not doing so, the thief forced us to scrutinise the locker's contents. If he had replaced the key, Marcellus may not have discovered the missing pages for some time, possibly not until he'd returned to the States. That delay may have given the thief an advantage.'

I thought rapidly. 'It can only be because he couldn't return it. He was somehow prevented from getting back to Wilson's room. Or—' My breath came out in a rush. 'His timing was out. He might have opened the locker shortly before Karin and Marita arrived. By the time he'd returned to Wilson's room, a crowd had gathered outside. He was too late.'

From Hallengren's demeanour, I suspected he agreed with me. 'If someone had wanted to remove pages from Wilson's diary, Miss Stewart, the Ice Hotel would have given them the ideal opportunity. The rooms have no doors. Anyone can creep in under cover of darkness and steal.'

'But why not take the whole diary? Why just tear out pages?'

'I can think of a number of reasons. Disposing of a complete diary, especially one as thick as Wilson's, would be time-consuming. A few pages, on the other hand, can be flushed down a lavatory. My guess is that those pages were destroyed well before Wilson's body was discovered.' Hallengren rubbed his chin. 'We have one thing in our favour. Whoever stole the key must have been familiar with the contents of the diary.'

Yet who would know what was in it? Some of Wilson's business associates, definitely. But who else?

'Inspector, who do you think did it? And why?'

He lifted his arms and let them drop. 'Who knew that Wilson would be coming to the Ice Hotel?'

'Oh, everyone. Half the guests, anyway.'

'Everyone? Everyone was remarkably quick to tell me they had never heard of him.'

Brilliant. More interviews. That was going to make me Miss Popularity.

His expression hardened. 'Can you tell me who these people are?'

I hesitated.

He picked up a pen. 'I am waiting, Miss Stewart.'

'Mike Molloy knew.' After a pause, I said quietly, 'And Harry.'

'And your friend, Miss Hallam?'

183

'She didn't even know who Wilson was, let alone that he'd be coming here.' I cleared my throat. 'And, of course, the reporters will have known.'

'Will they?' Hallengren said softly. 'I doubt that.' He put the pen down. 'Miss Stewart, apart from the missing locker key, did anything else in the room strike you as odd?'

'Something did, but I can't think what.'

A look crossed his face, a look that said he'd seen it too and knew what it signified. But he wasn't going to tell me.

'Well, Miss Stewart,' he said finally, 'I do not need to remind you that what has passed between us must stay within these four walls.' He frowned. 'You have not told your friends about overhearing the conversation?'

'I've come straight from the church. I've told no one.'

'Please keep it that way.' He smiled. 'If you stumble across anything that might be useful, by all means come to see me. But do not go seeking it out. However tempting, please do not play detective. We are well paid to do that.'

I glared at him, my resentment rising at his patronising manner. And after all the information I'd given him.

He took me to the reception area, and exchanged words in Swedish with the young man. 'I have arranged for a car to take you to the Excelsior, Miss Stewart,' he said.

We looked at one another briefly. Then he walked away.

The first stars were appearing in the sky as we drove out of Kiruna. I sat back in the car and thought through my conversation with Hallengren.

He'd not said it in so many words, but he was thinking the same as I – Wilson's key had been removed after his death. But why, and by whom? What was so important about those pages, especially the last one, that would make someone remove a key from the wrist of a dead man in order to steal them?

Who knew that Wilson would be coming to the Ice Hotel?

Obviously Aaron and Marcellus. Both had had the opportunity to take the key. Aaron had been in Kiruna the night Wilson died, but he could have hired a car. Yet whatever the two of them were involved in in Stockholm, it didn't seem to have anything to do with the diary: Marcellus had raised the subject almost as an afterthought.

Then there was Mike. He'd known Wilson would be at the Ice Hotel: *One of the Yanks I was drinking with is working with Bibby. He told me.* Could that Yank have told Mike something about Bibby's dealings that would make him want to steal pages from his diary? Unlikely. What could possibly interest Mike?

I leant back, weary from the day's events. Who cared about Wilson's diary anyway? How important was it in the grand scheme of things? If Hallengren had nothing better to do than chase missing diary pages, he was welcome to it. What intrigued me more was what Marcellus and Aaron had been up to in Stockholm. Perhaps it involved the Bibby Foundation and would be to Harry's benefit. His research funding might come through after all. I pictured his happiness at discovering he could continue with his work.

Harry. I sat up slowly. He'd known from the Foundation's newsletter that Wilson would be in Stockholm, if not the Ice Hotel.

Yes, Harry had known. Harry, whom I'd spied in the corridor the night Wilson had died, who'd denied being up, saying he'd slept through without waking. Had he been on his way to the lockers, having crept into Wilson's room and taken his key? If so, he must have known what was in the diary. Something to do with the Foundation? Marcellus had said that the decision to stop funding pure research wasn't definite. Perhaps Harry had wanted to remove all trace of that decision, carbons and all, hoping that Marcellus, who was better disposed towards academics, would continue the funding.

I sank back into the upholstery. If Harry was the thief, he must have been desperate to take such a chance. What would Wilson have done if he'd woken to find Harry looming over him? Yelled for Marcellus. The scenario didn't bear thinking about. No, I couldn't see Harry taking the risk, research funding or not.

Unless, of course, Harry had known that Wilson was already dead.

CHAPTER 16

Leo Tullis was waiting for me as I entered the Ice Hotel.

'You got a moment, Maggie?' He sounded anxious.

'Of course. Shall we go into the lounge?'

'We need somewhere private. The manager lets me use his office.'

I followed him down the corridor, wondering what could have happened now.

'Have you been to see the inspector?' I said, after we'd sat down.

'I went straight after breakfast.'

'And you told him about the brakes?'

'He already knew. Sven had reported it. But he had a few questions for me.' Leo pushed his hands through his hair. 'He asked if I remembered who'd been near the machines.'

'What did you tell him?' I said slowly.

'That I was inside the chalet when the snowmobiles toppled, and I didn't go down to the path until I heard the noise and saw everyone running out.' He stared hard at the floor. 'Then I remembered I'd seen Mike and Jonas standing near that ledge. I assumed they'd been there the whole time, so I gave the inspector their names.' He lifted his head. 'Did I do the right thing?'

The directness of the question surprised me. 'What was the inspector's reaction?'

'He seemed cool. I asked him what he thought was going on. He said he didn't know, and that it could have been a prank. Or an accident.'

'But you told him what Sven said about the brakes?'

'The way the inspector talked, he sounded as much of an expert on snowmobile brakes as Sven. I don't know who to believe now.'

I'd believe Sven, I was tempted to say. But I kept quiet. Leo seemed a man at the end of his resources, grateful for a mandate to carry on with his job. I wondered what Hallengren would do with this new knowledge about Mike and Jonas. If he believed it was an accident, he'd do nothing.

Leo looked at me searchingly. 'The inspector said that the excursions could continue, which is why we went to the Sami village today. That's something, I suppose. Perhaps now everything will be okay.' He said it as though he didn't believe it.

'Yes,' I said, squeezing his hand. 'Perhaps now everything will be okay.' But I didn't believe it either.

With the arrival of the reporters, the restaurant was crowded.

Jane was sitting with the Danes, who seemed to have taken her under their wing. The Ellises were wedged between Denny Hinckley and another reporter, who were talking across them. I wondered how long it would be before Robyn lost it and smacked one of them. Marcellus and Aaron were missing.

Liz and Mike were so absorbed in one another that they hardly noticed my conversation with Harry.

'So how was the trip to the Sami village?' I said.

'My dear, it's such a shame you didn't come. It was simply marvellous. We met the village leader. He was dressed in a wonderfully colourful costume. Anyway, he described how the

Sami live, tending the reindeer the way they have for generations. I must say they looked splendid.'

'The reindeer?'

He peered at me over his soup spoon. 'The Sami.'

'And where did the chief live?'

'Well, I'm not sure they live there now, but he took us into a huge tent. You know the sort of thing, rugs and skins all over the place. There was a log fire, which was smoking so badly I thought we'd all suffocate. He had to open a flap in the top to let the smoke out. Then he started to tell us about his ancestors, and how this way of living and these old traditions are so important. Which they are, of course.' Harry's eyes were gleaming. 'But do you know what happened then?'

Harry could hardly contain himself. 'Tell me,' I said, smiling in anticipation.

'His mobile phone went off. He started to laugh, and then we all did. I do wish you'd been there.' Suddenly he sat up straight, staring over my shoulder. 'My goodness. An inspector calls.'

I turned round. Hallengren had entered with the hotel manager, who hovered nervously at his side.

The manager raised his voice. 'Could I have everyone's attention, please?'

The conversations tailed off into silence.

'Inspector Hallengren has something to say.' He looked expectantly at the detective.

'I am sorry to disturb you at dinner, but I have come on police business.' Hallengren spoke with his customary slowness. 'My men are here to search the Excelsior. That includes your rooms. Please be assured that we will do this rapidly and efficiently, with the minimum of inconvenience.'

Harry broke the stunned silence. 'And what are you looking for, Inspector? Perhaps if you told us, we might be able to help.'

'I am not at liberty to say, Professor Auchinleck.'

Jonas shouted something in what might have been Danish or Swedish and which, from the tone, sounded like a question. Hallengren was unfazed. He replied quickly and firmly. Jonas turned his attention back to his food.

Robyn stood up, ignoring her husband, who was trying to pull her back down. 'This is preposterous.' She raised her voice so the room could hear. 'I know the law. You can't do this without a warrant. I intend to file a complaint with the embassy.'

Hallengren smiled. 'Be assured, madam, that I have all the documents I need.' He scanned the room. 'Please continue with your dinner, ladies and gentlemen. By the time you have finished, we will be gone. My men are under strict instructions not to disturb your rooms more than is necessary.' Ignoring the sudden commotion, he left, the manager following gratefully.

The reporters had pulled out their notebooks and were conferring with each other. Denny Hinckley was staring at Liz, as though this must somehow be her doing.

'What's that all about then, Maggie?' Mike said. 'You think it's something to do with Wilson's diary?'

My mind was in a whirl. Why had Hallengren chosen this moment to turn the Excelsior upside down? He'd known about the missing pages since yesterday. 'I've no idea,' I said slowly.

Harry pushed his chair back, his expression grim. 'I can't have them disturbing my papers. No, I can't have that.' He rose and made for the door.

'Oh, Harry, do come and finish your dinner,' Liz called after him. 'You heard what he said, sweetheart, they're not going to mess up your papers.'

But Harry had disappeared.

'They won't let him into his room,' I said.

'You don't think they'll arrest him, do you?' she said, alarm in her voice.

'Only if he misbehaves.'

'That's lovely now,' Mike said. 'And is he likely to?'

I exchanged a glance with Liz. When it came to his papers, Harry was like a bear with her cubs. I sighed. 'He is.'

'Then hadn't someone better go after him?' Mike said angrily.

'I'll go,' I said, getting to my feet. 'But I'm not promising I can bring him back.'

I'd reached the foyer, and was passing the lounge when I felt a strong grip on my arm.

'And where do you think you are going, Miss Stewart?' The voice was cold.

I swung round. Hallengren raised an eyebrow, waiting for my response. 'I was running after Harry. He's gone back to his room.'

'I see.' He released my arm. 'May I suggest you return to the restaurant?'

'But Harry—'

'My men will deal with Professor Auchinleck.'

'That's what I'm afraid of.' I looked at Hallengren pleadingly. 'Harry's writing a book, Inspector. He spreads hundreds of papers all over the room in what is a cleverly calculated system. He's afraid your officers will muddle them up.'

'My men will be careful.'

'Then promise me you won't arrest him.'

He inclined his head. 'I will do my best, Miss Stewart, but I cannot promise.'

'What if Harry brings a book down on an officer's head?' I said, seeing the scene unfold.

The corners of Hallengren's lips lifted. 'The officer will have to restrain him.'

191

He didn't believe Harry would do it. I imagined the mayhem that would be taking place in his room.

'None of my officers will use unnecessary force,' he added.

I found myself smiling. 'You're not taking me seriously.'

He moved his face closer to mine, returning the smile. 'On the contrary, I am taking you very seriously. And now, Miss Stewart, shall I escort you to the restaurant?'

'There's no need, Inspector. I know the way.'

He bowed. 'I will bid you goodnight, then.'

I walked away, resisting the urge to look back at him.

The restaurant was still buzzing.

'Where's Harry?' Liz said, as I took my seat.

'I didn't get past the lounge. The police were there. Harry must have slipped past.'

She beckoned to a waiter, who brought a tray of venison.

'What do you think he's doing?' she said, watching me eat.

'Probably decking one of Hallengren's men. Can you pass me the vegetables?'

Minutes later, Harry returned, his face flushed. He resumed his seat without a word.

Mike poured him a glass of wine. 'You've not been clapped in irons, then.'

'They wouldn't let me into my room,' he said, his voice a child's.

'Could you see what they were doing?' I said.

'It's strange. I had books and papers everywhere but they didn't touch them. One policeman was searching the pockets of my waistcoat, while another was examining the soap dish.'

'The soap dish?' Mike said. 'What the hell's going on?'

I knew even before Liz told him.

'Whatever they're looking for,' she said gloomily, 'it isn't Wilson's diary.'

★ ★ ★

We left the restaurant and made our way towards the lounge. Hallengren's men were still milling around the foyer. Their voices carried through the building.

'Who'd have thought tiny Kiruna had so many police?' Liz said.

'I suspect they've been drafted in,' I replied.

Hallengren arrived and spoke in low tones to the manager, then turned to the men and jerked his thumb at the door. They filed out in silence. As he glanced back, his gaze met mine. He nodded briefly, and left.

'The bar?' Mike said.

Liz glanced at her watch. 'I can't. I've arranged to talk to the twins.'

'And I need to look through my papers,' Harry said sombrely. 'I'll see you children later.'

In the lounge, Mike left me to fetch our drinks.

Denny Hinckley peeled away from his friends and ambled over. He lowered himself into a chair. 'What's this about, Maggie?' He licked his lips. 'What was Sherlock looking for?'

'I don't know,' I said quietly.

'I saw you talking to him,' he said in a provocative tone.

I wondered where he'd been when I was with Hallengren, and what he'd overheard. Nothing, I decided, or he wouldn't be needling me now.

'I take it he wasn't asking you out on a date, lovely girl.'

'What do *you* think he was looking for, Denny?'

'Must be something to do with Wilson Bibby. Question is, what?'

'I'm sure the inspector will be giving the press a statement in the morning.' I glanced across at the bar. Mike had our drinks in his hands. Remembering his earlier treatment of Denny, I thought I should warn him. I kept my tone friendly. 'I'd scarper, if I were you, before my weight-lifting friend returns and finds you here.'

'Point taken. By the way, I need to thank you for that hot tip. The hotel murders.' He smiled, his eyes lazy. 'I've made some enquiries of my pals in Stockholm.'

'And what did you discover?'

'That death you spoke about? The American? It wasn't natural causes.' He paused for effect. 'Very unnatural, if you catch my drift.'

I felt a cold hand touch my heart. 'What do you mean?'

He leant forward, and his breath came to me stinking of beer. 'His neck was broken. Whoever did it didn't need to use much force. From the marks on the victim's neck, the killer used only one hand to snap the spinal column.'

I stared at him, unable to speak.

He was on his feet. 'Must have been strong, eh? With big hands.' He threw his parting words into the air. 'Maybe even a weight-lifter.'

CHAPTER 17

After breakfast on Friday, I decided to join the walking tour. I needed exercise to clear my head. I hadn't slept after Denny's bombshell, specifically his final comment about the weight-lifter. What had he been implying? Every male in the Excelsior seemed to be into weight-lifting. Perhaps he'd simply wanted to rattle me.

Aaron Vandenberg was pacing the foyer, smoking furiously.

'I don't think you're allowed to do that in here,' I said.

'Can you tell me what the hell's going on?' He was boiling with anger. 'Is it true the cops have turned this place over?'

'They searched our rooms at dinner time.'

'They should have checked with us first, let us oversee what they were doing.'

I was tempted to say that Hallengren had picked that time precisely to avoid any overseeing of what they were doing. 'They were very considerate, Mr Vandenberg. They did me a favour, in fact. After they'd searched my room, it was tidier than it had ever been before. And, in fairness to the inspector, he did tell us what he was going to do.'

'I don't give a rat's ass about that. Marcellus and I weren't at dinner.' He spoke with more control. 'He should have waited until we were there.'

'The police work to their own timetable.' I couldn't resist adding, 'As a lawyer, you'll know that.'

His expression was glacial. 'I'm not an attorney. My dealings with the police are non-existent.'

I bet they're not, I thought. He'd have had to deal with the police over his sister's death. And Aaron Vandenberg looked like a man who'd had more than one brush with the law. For the first time, I wondered how many of Wilson's dealings had been above board. Whatever scam Aaron and Marcellus were involved in may have included him too.

I glanced round the foyer. 'Is Marcellus here?'

'Why do you want to know?' Aaron said, suspicion in his voice.

I was getting used to his sudden changes of mood. 'I'm concerned, that's all. I haven't spoken to him since his father's death.'

'I'm sorry, ma'am,' he said, waving a placatory hand. 'That was impolite of me. He's keeping to his room. He doesn't want to be disturbed.'

'Perhaps you could pass on my best wishes?'

He threw me a veiled glance, nodding, but saying nothing.

The front door opened and Engqvist entered with another policeman. He spoke hurriedly with the receptionist. Alarm registered on the man's face, and he stared in our direction.

Engqvist swung round. 'Are you Mr Aaron Vandenberg?' he said politely.

Aaron dropped his cigarette butt and ground it into the carpet. 'I am. What of it?'

'I must ask you to come with me.'

'May I know why?'

'Inspector Hallengren wishes to speak with you. That's all I can tell you.' He smiled. 'We have a car outside.'

Aaron's voice was hard. 'Very well.' He let the officers escort him out of the building.

'What do you think's going on?' I said to the receptionist.

He polished his glasses. 'I have no idea. The other American went to Kiruna this morning.'

'Marcellus?'

'He is still there.'

'At the coroner's office?'

The man lowered his voice. 'He was taken also to the police station, personally by Inspector Hallengren. The inspector arrived at seven o'clock. It's a bad business. First a death, then the hotel is searched.'

Then why did Aaron tell me that Marcellus was in his room? Did he know he'd been taken to Kiruna and didn't want this information to leak out? Or was it simply that at seven o'clock he'd been asleep and knew nothing of Marcellus's arrest?

The receptionist seemed willing to talk, so I seized the opportunity. 'Do you know what the police were looking for when they searched the hotel?' I played with the desk bell, avoiding his gaze. 'Did the inspector tell you?'

'He said nothing. But they searched everywhere. Even the kitchens. I should say, especially the kitchens. They spent more time there than anywhere else. And they took things away.'

'What sort of things?'

'Food, drink.' He straightened, seeing the hotel manager.

They spoke in Swedish, not bothering to keep their voices down, and I had the impression the receptionist was being repri-manded. The manager glanced briefly in my direction. I hurried away before he turned his attention to me.

I sat in the Activities Room, my chin cupped in my hands. So Hallengren had finally hauled in Marcellus and Aaron. It could only be about the diary. I wondered how much he was prepared to reveal to them. If he told them about the missing last page he'd

197

be showing his hand, which would signal to them he had no other cards to play.

But what was more intriguing was what the receptionist had just told me. Hallengren hadn't been looking for the diary last night. That much was obvious. Yet what could possibly interest him in the Excelsior's kitchens?

After lunch, I found Harry outside, examining the circus statues.

'Where is everyone?' I said.

'Mike's on the trip. He thought you'd like to come but he couldn't find you. Liz cried off.' Harry scrutinised the ballerina's flowers. 'You know, Maggie, these are extraordinary.'

'The tears have gone,' I said softly, staring at the clown.

'What tears?'

'When we first came here, the clown was crying.'

Harry straightened. 'Are you sure, my dear? I don't recall the tears.'

'Don't you think these statues are different now?'

'That's not possible. Statues can't change. That's why they're statues.'

After a pause, I said, 'So which trip did Mike go on?'

'Reindeer racing. Oh, and the huskies.'

I pulled a face. 'He can keep them.'

'Not keen?'

'I can't stand yapping dogs. You weren't tempted yourself?'

'The reindeer racing is down as a fairly strenuous activity, so not something I'd do straight after eating. Exercise is bad for the digestion, my dear. Anyway, I couldn't look a reindeer in the eye, having just eaten one for lunch.'

'What about the huskies?' I had a sudden vision of Harry, arms full of wriggling puppies trying to lick his face.

'Dogs? I don't get on with them. They're always trying to mate with my leg.' He brushed snow from the clown's drum. 'You know the trouble with this climate? It's impossible to play any proper sports.' He made a motion with his arms, as though wielding a cricket bat. 'The thwack of leather against willow is a sound they've never heard here.'

'And you said Liz cried off the trip?'

His voice grew serious. 'She isn't sleeping. The cross-country jolly this morning finished her off, so she's lying down. She seems in better humour today, though.'

I hesitated. 'Is it me, or are Liz and Mike joined at the hip?'

'I wonder if he's bedded her yet?' Harry squinted into the distance. 'If he has, it'll be the best thing for her.'

'I wouldn't say that.'

'Do I see the green-eyed monster rearing his head? I can understand that. I feel envious, too, when I see a new-minted relationship.'

'I'm not jealous,' I said firmly. 'Mike isn't my type.'

'My dear, Mike is everyone's type. Including mine. But I rather think you've set your cap at the detective inspector.' Harry gazed at me until I looked away. He'd always been able to see through me.

'You couldn't be more wrong,' I said too quickly.

I could tell he was trying not to laugh. 'Well, if you do get your leg over, that would also be the best thing for you, my dear. A bit of uncomplicated sex would be just the ticket.' He cocked his head. 'Maybe not, though. You try to kid us on that you chew men up and spit them out, but I've known since the day I met you that you're an incurable romantic. It's one of your most admirable qualities.'

'Yours too, Harry.'

He smiled wistfully. 'It's taken me many years to discover that you only ever love, I mean *really* love, once in your lifetime.' He stopped suddenly as though he'd said too much. 'Have you ever thought of having children, Maggie?' There was softness in his voice.

'You know how it is,' I said, running my fingers over the clown's face. 'My career's going so well. There's plenty of time.'

'I used to think like that,' Harry said sadly. 'Now I have no choice in the matter.' He drew back his shoulders. 'But I've no cause to feel envious. Annie and Lucy are all the children I need. And Liz is very good about letting me spend time with them.'

My heart went out to him, the gay bachelor, with a generosity matched only by his intellect. What a fine father he would have made.

'Tell me,' he said, 'what was your first boyfriend like? Do you remember?'

'Who doesn't remember their first? He was impulsive, always writing poetry. He'd waylay me in the street, then, on one knee, he'd start spouting it in front of everyone.' I smiled at the memory. 'We slept outdoors once or twice, watching shooting stars.'

'It would have to be a damned sight warmer than it is in Scotland before I'd do that. But, at a May Ball once, I did have sex in a meadow.'

'I've done that too. It's exhilarating.' I slipped an arm through his. 'I don't know whether it's the fresh air, or the feeling that you might be discovered. The only downside is picking grass seed out of your knickers afterwards.'

'Ha! Indeed. Well, whatever your preference in bed, the detective inspector looks like your ideal man.'

'You don't know what my ideal man is, Harry.'

He smiled impishly. 'Do tell.'

'A man who knows how to take his time,' I said, without hesitation.

He laughed. 'That's my definition too. But you never met my

soulmate. He was from my Cambridge days, before your time. Mad as a box of frogs, but he was my greatest love, probably my only true love.' Harry brought his head close to mine. 'It was sex at first sight. He was absolutely brilliant in bed. We still keep in touch.' He pulled his bobble hat down over his forehead, and looked intently into my eyes. 'Maggie, my dear, don't take this as a criticism, but I have the impression you know more than you're letting on.'

'Everyone knows more than they're letting on,' I said, astonished by the sudden statement. 'Are you talking about anything in particular?'

'This business with Wilson's diary. Why did the detective inspector tell you it had been stolen? Police aren't usually so free with their intelligence.' His voice was cold. 'Unless it was you who supplied the intelligence in the first place.'

'Hallengren mentioned it because someone told him I'd seen it,' I said helplessly. 'Wilson showed me the diary on the plane.'

'Showed you?' Harry gazed into the distance. 'And did you see anything of interest?'

'Nothing about the Bibby Foundation. Anyway, I presume Wilson's decision to stop funding research can't go ahead now.'

'Not unless he had already signed off on it.' He ran his fingers over the rim of the clown's bowler. 'And with the diary gone now, we'll never know, will we? Well, work calls, my dear. Time's wingèd chariot, and all that.'

'More writing?'

'Dragon Control has been sending text messages, requesting sample chapters. She's absolutely no idea what's involved in writing a book. So, what are your plans for the afternoon?'

'A sauna and a massage. Then I'm off to buy presents for Annie and Lucy.'

'Kiruna?' he said vaguely.

'There's a gift shop near here that sells wooden toys. On the road to the church.'

'Yes, well, don't spend it all at once, my dear. See you for cocktails.' He strolled up the path, patting the penguins as he went inside.

I lay on the table, half asleep. The Swedish masseur, a thickset, dark-haired man with hands like hams, worked my back, smoothing away the knots in my muscles.

So Harry thought the entire diary was missing. He couldn't have been the one to have torn out the pages, then. Unless, of course, he was bluffing. If he thought I was having little chats with Hallengren, he might want me to pass on this snippet of information. Was Harry that devious? How well did I really know him? With all that was happening here, how well did I know anyone?

I closed my eyes and abandoned myself to the masseur.

The gift shop was the last of a small cluster of buildings before the bend in the road. It sold clocks, wooden toys and glassware.

The assistant was wearing a knitted wimple hat and the same style of clothes as Marita. 'Are you staying in Kiruna?' she asked pleasantly, wrapping my gifts in coloured paper.

'At the Ice Hotel.'

Her smile faded and fear shrouded her eyes, the same fear I'd seen on Karin and Marita's faces. The news of Wilson's death had spread. And the rumours about the hotel killer, no doubt fuelled by the recent murder in Stockholm. Was she afraid the Ice Hotel would close down and she'd be out of a job? Or was it something else?

I gathered up the parcels and left.

The sun was close to setting but it was still light, and the air was sharp with the smell of woodsmoke. I heard a faint sound and, thinking it was geese, peered into the sky. The sound grew louder before I recognised it as the barking of dogs. The husky sledges were out on the river. Mike would be with them.

The dying sun was gilding the rooftops, making the landscape shimmer in a soft apricot-rose light. I reached the Excelsior and took the path at the side of the chapel. The ice-harvesting machines had finished for the day, but the skiers were still out, calling to each other as they zigzagged towards the bank. The sky, streaked blood-orange and crimson, threw its burning reflection on to the ice. I watched the colours deepen as the sun sank towards the horizon, then retraced my steps.

A slim, red-suited figure was teetering in the snow. It was Liz, holding her arms out like a tightrope walker. Unable to keep her balance, she sank into a drift and fell heavily.

'Mags,' she said, in surprise, her face white against the red hood. 'I didn't expect you back so early.' She scrambled to her feet. 'This snow's absolutely marvellous, isn't it? Just like powder. Do you remember those snowball fights we used to have?'

I grinned. 'I always came off badly. No hand-to-eye coordination.'

'So how were the huskies?'

'I went shopping instead. I've bought some fabulous things for the twins. But I'll tell you inside. If I don't get out of this cold, I'll collapse.'

She started to shiver uncontrollably, and wrapped her arms round herself.

'Your hands are blue, Liz,' I said, frowning.

'It's not my hands I'm worried about. My backside's frozen solid.'

'Now, there's an image.' I studied her. 'Harry told me you were taking a nap. How are you feeling now?'

'Wonderful. You really can't overestimate the restorative powers of sleep.' She looked past me at the sunset. 'You know, this sky is absolutely glorious, isn't it? I've never seen such colours. It's the sort of thing Turner would paint.'

'Never mind the sunset. Think hot chocolate and rum.' I took her arm and steered her towards the Excelsior.

She stopped at the chapel door. 'Oh, let's just take a quick peek inside, Mags. The light will be streaming in through that big window. It'll be amazing.'

I had to smile. For all her sneering about auroras, Liz had her romantic streak. 'Five minutes,' I said, 'and then we're out of here.'

She pulled at the antlers. The door swung open smoothly.

As I stepped in behind her, a movement to the right caught my eye and, for an instant, I thought I saw someone disappear behind a column. I was about to call out when a strangled noise made me turn. Liz had stopped dead. She was trembling, staring towards the far end of the chapel.

I looked along the nave.

Two figures were lying near the altar. One was curled up in a grotesque foetal position, the other lay sprawled, arms outstretched as though crucified. They and the ground beneath them were soaked in blood.

I backed towards the door, colliding with Liz. She was shaking convulsively, her face devoid of colour, her breathing laboured. I gripped her arm, unable to tear my gaze from the figures.

I was groping behind me for the handle when I heard a sudden gurgling from the direction of the altar. I pushed past Liz and bolted down the nave.

But I'd been mistaken. There was only one body. The curled-up figure was just a crumpled red snow-suit. I touched it gingerly with my boot, then pushed it over, exposing the bloody ski mask and gloves underneath.

I took a deep breath and turned to the figure spread-eagled by the pulpit. From the build, it looked like a man. Bile surged into my mouth and I gagged uncontrollably. Someone had hacked at his head so brutally his features were unrecognisable.

Deep gashes scored his face. His nose had been sliced off and his jaw so badly crushed that most of the lower teeth were missing. One eye was a pulpy mess, the other stared straight ahead, unblinking. His chest had been slashed, exposing part of the ribcage, the bone pink-white and smooth. Between his legs was a yellow-brown stain.

The altar and pulpit were smeared with great patches of red. Blood was trickling into the snow, mingling with the spattered flesh and splinters of bone. There was a sweet, heavy stench, like the inside of a butcher's shop.

A loud retching sound came from behind me. Liz was facing the wall, one hand against it for support. She was vomiting violently.

Suddenly, the man began to twitch as though an electric current were passing through his muscles. The spasms grew so severe that at one point his body jerked clear of the ground. I moved in close and forced myself to look, seeing what I'd missed earlier – the ice axe, its tip clotted with flesh and hair. I fell to my knees, gasping for breath, my mind unravelling.

The man's strength was failing and his groans had dwindled to a soft keening. A stream of bloody bubbles oozed from the gash that had been his mouth. He was trying to say something. Steeling myself, I put my ear close to his face and strained to listen.

The blue woollen hat was lying at an angle across his forehead. Strangely anguished by this indignity, I reached across to straighten it.

Then I saw his hair. The shock was so great that I felt as if someone had punched me in the stomach. The cowlick and salt-and-pepper colour were unmistakable. It was Harry! Harry was dying in front of my eyes.

He drummed his heels, furiously at first, then more slowly until finally he lay still. I marshalled what was left of my strength and slipped my arms under his shoulders. Kneeling in the melting snow, I cradled him, my keening joining his, and watched his lifeblood seep away.

I rocked back and forth, gazing at Annie and Lucy's scattered parcels, my body growing cold along with Harry's. A sudden breath of wind blew through the rose window and stirred the neatly tied ribbons.

I felt strong arms prise my own from Harry's body, and I was lifted to my feet. I heard voices, first Swedish, then English. I was led away, supported on either side. There were faces, Mike's, Hallengren's, a crowd in the Excelsior gaping at me, a hot bath, Liz and another woman sponging me down, Liz spooning some-thing into my mouth, then me gagging, unable to swallow.

I was dressed in a nightshirt and helped into bed. The woman rolled back my sleeve and inserted a needle into my arm. The last thing I saw before sinking into oblivion was her head close to mine, concern etched into the lines of her face.

CHAPTER 18

I drifted in and out of sleep. My dreams were sharp and brightly coloured. I was with Harry and Liz. We were on the ice, skating. But something was wrong. We were skating too quickly. Whenever the blades cut into the ice they made a sharp clicking sound, rhythmical and hypnotic. It grew louder.

I woke with a strange sense of guilt. Daylight was pouring into the room. A woman was sitting in a chair next to the bed. She was knitting something colourful, moving her fingers rapidly. Whenever she worked a stitch, her needles made a sharp clicking sound. It was rhythmical and hypnotic.

I watched listlessly. My eyes started to close, but I made myself stay awake because there was something I had to remember. I moved my head.

The clicking stopped. 'How are you feeling?' the woman said, in a thick accent.

There was something familiar about her face. I'd seen it before, that look of concern.

She smiled then, and memory returned with such force that I couldn't breathe. I pawed at the bedclothes in a frenzy. A second later, there was a loud hissing and something hard was pushed over my face. I took huge, rasping gulps as though I'd never draw in enough air, until gradually the constriction in my throat eased.

The woman removed the mask and laid a hand against my forehead. She spoke soothingly, but I couldn't understand the words. Tears rolled down the sides of my face and into my ears. She spoke again, and her expression changed from sympathy to regret. I turned away and, lying on my side, cried as I hadn't cried since I was a child. My breathing came in huge sobs, racking my body and giving me hiccups. From somewhere far away, I heard the door open and close.

I turned to the woman. But it was Hallengren sitting in the chair. He was leaning forward, elbows on knees, hands loosely clasped.

'Shall I come back later?' he said softly.

I shook my head. I didn't want him to leave. I wanted him to tell me it was a horrible mistake, and Harry was alive.

He went to the bathroom, and I heard a tap being run. He reappeared with a glass of water and handed it to me without a word. I struggled to a sitting position and, cupping the glass in both hands, drank greedily, spilling water down my nightshirt. I held out the glass.

'More?' he said.

I nodded.

Along with the water, he brought a wet towel. I rubbed it over my face, feeling the welcome coldness against my hot, sore eyes.

'Miss Stewart,' he said, resuming his seat, 'I would like to ask you some questions about yesterday. Do you feel up to it?'

'Yesterday?' I said vaguely.

'Today is Saturday. You were given a sedative and slept through the night.' He spoke with his usual slowness. 'I need you to tell me what happened in the chapel.'

The chapel. I remembered his face as I was being led away. Surely he'd know everything. What else could I tell him? 'But hasn't Liz—'

'Miss Hallam has given us a statement, but I need you to fill in the gaps,' he said gently. 'She told us she met you outside the chapel. Where were you before that?'

'In the morning—'

'I know where everyone was in the morning. Where were you after lunch?'

'I went to the spa.'

'And afterwards?' He was writing.

'I went to that shop.' I ran a hand across my eyes. 'The one on the way to the church.' I saw again the parcels and ribbons, reddening in the dying light, and drew in my breath sharply.

He glanced up. 'Please go on,' he said, after a moment.

'Then I went back to the Excelsior. Liz was there on the path.'

'What time would this have been?'

'I don't know. The sun was setting. Liz might know what time it was.' I felt a great heaviness press against my eyes. 'She can tell you the rest.' I let my eyelids droop.

'Miss Stewart, I know it's difficult but please try to answer my questions. Your friend was killed with an ice axe. You were the last person to see him alive.'

I gazed at him helplessly.

'Miss Hallam told us that she remained at the back of the chapel and it was you who went up to the altar. Is that correct?'

I nodded.

He spoke softly. 'Was Professor Auchinleck alive when you reached him? Miss Hallam could not confirm it. If we could establish that, it would help us greatly.'

'He was alive when we came in.'

'And did he say anything to you? I know it is painful to think about it, but can you remember?'

I could remember. That keening would stay with me until I

died. 'Harry said nothing. I don't think—' I closed my eyes. 'I don't think he was capable of speaking.'

After a silence, Hallengren said, 'You and Professor Auchinleck were close, I think. Were you lovers?'

'What damn business is it of yours?'

He raised an eyebrow, but said nothing.

'Harry was gay,' I said quietly.

'Did he have any enemies? Anyone who might have wanted to kill him? Anyone homophobic, perhaps?'

'No one I can think of.'

'What about the Irishman, Mr Molloy?'

'We met him for the first time only a few days ago. But he and Harry got on fantastically well.'

'And Miss Hallam?' His expression was unchanged.

I felt myself losing control. 'My God, what are you suggesting? Do you think Liz did this?'

He was watching me closely.

'Look, Harry was a wonderful man. Everyone liked him.' I felt the tears welling, but I was determined not to cry again.

Hallengren put away the notebook, and walked to the window. The light from the snow-covered landscape whitened his skin, making him look ill.

'Inspector.'

He turned his head.

'Do you have any idea who did this?'

He gazed out of the window again. 'No, Miss Stewart.'

'There's been talk about a hotel killer. We saw a newsflash at the airport.'

He returned to the chair. 'It does not surprise me. It has been widely reported.' He smiled thinly. 'Every time there is a death in a Swedish hotel, even from natural causes, someone resurrects the Stockholm hotel killer. It does not help that a tourist was found dead last Saturday. That is what the newsflash would have been about.'

'Yes, the American.'

'So you have read about it. Initially, we did not suspect – how do you say it? – foul play.'

'But Denny Hinckley told me his neck was broken.'

Hallengren looked at me with interest. 'The Stockholm police have only just released that information. To have found that out so quickly, your reporter friend must have contacts in high places.'

'His contacts are all in low places, Inspector,' I said, trying a smile.

He raised an eyebrow. 'Do not all reporters have such contacts?' He studied me, frowning, as though trying to make up his mind about something. 'A press statement is due to go out today, Miss Stewart, so I can tell you now. We believe Wilson Bibby was murdered.'

'Murdered?' I whispered, my heart thudding against my ribs.

'The post-mortem was on Thursday. The report reached my desk the same evening.' He ran a hand over his head. 'We were suspicious when we saw Bibby's body on one side of the bed, and his clothes on the other. If he had wanted to use the bathroom, why would he not have got out of bed on the same side as his clothes? But, yes, people do get out of bed on the wrong side. However, we discounted that when the pathologist's results arrived.'

I saw again Wilson's corpse, stiff as a board, the parchment-like skin, the frozen trickle of saliva. But there was no sign of violence. And no murder weapon.

Hallengren leant forward. 'The temperature and state of the body put the time of death at somewhere between three and four a.m. For a man of his bodyweight to freeze to death, he must have been out of his sleeping bag between one and two a.m.

But even more interesting was what we discovered in his blood and urine.'

'Was he poisoned?'

'He was drugged. Our forensics team found a powerful sleep-inducing drug, marketed under the name Phenonal, in his body. Phenonal is a barbiturate.' He stumbled slightly over the word. 'Is that how you say it?'

I nodded.

'The quantities of both Phenonal and the chemicals that the body . . .' Hallengren was clearly trying to remember the word '. . . metabolises from it indicate that he was very heavily drugged.' He was watching me closely. 'Wilson had taken a dose of Phenonal so large that he would have been unconscious at one a.m.'

I stared at him, not understanding.

There was a note of exasperation in his voice. 'He was too deeply drugged to get up by himself. Someone pushed him out of his sleeping bag.'

'So he didn't have a heart attack?' I said, stunned.

'The autopsy showed that his heart was not as weak as every-one had thought. No, Miss Stewart, Wilson Bibby did not die of a heart attack. He was drugged, pushed out of his sleeping bag and left to die.' After a brief silence, he added, 'That is what Thursday evening was about. As soon as I knew Bibby had been drugged, I had my men search the Excelsior for Phenonal. We turned the kitchens upside down. I am still waiting for the results of the tests but I do not expect to find anything. Like most hotels, the Excelsior disposes of unused food quickly.'

'I thought you were looking for the pages from Wilson's diary. That is, until Harry saw your men examining his soap dish.'

'We looked for the missing pages too, and for the locker key. The search was originally organised for that purpose. The autopsy results came in as we were leaving.' He gave a dismissive shrug. 'It would have been a miracle if we had found anything. But we had to try.'

'So Wilson was pushed out of bed around one a.m.,' I said half to myself.

Hallengren got to his feet and zipped up his suit. 'I suggest you eat something, Miss Stewart, even though you may not feel like it. You need to regain your strength.' He was looking at me strangely.

It was only after the door had closed that it struck me: my statement put me awake and in the corridor outside Wilson Bibby's room around 1 a.m. – the time he'd been pushed out of his sleeping bag and left to die.

CHAPTER 19

An hour later the woman returned with a tray. She encouraged me in broken English to eat, then gave up and left.

I had no appetite. My mind was a tumult of unformed thoughts and hypotheses, analysed, and rejected.

Wilson had been murdered.

The events since his death had been coloured by my conviction that he'd died of natural causes. Now I was seeing those events in a new light. The removal of the diary pages took on greater significance. Those, surely, must hold the key to his murder, and possibly to Harry's. Whoever had taken the pages had known that either Wilson was dead, or he was unconscious and wouldn't recover. The thief was therefore Wilson's murderer.

But someone else could have pushed Wilson out of bed, and the thief had arrived to find a frozen corpse. Yet what if he'd found Wilson still breathing? And hadn't raised the alarm, because it would have been in his interests to keep quiet? By leaving him to die, he'd become an accomplice to murder.

So could Marcellus have killed his own father? The thought was chilling. *The minute your dad said he wanted a vacation, I knew it would monkey-wrench our plans. But when he said he'd be coming here, I thought it might work for us. It's so remote.*

What were these plans? Had Marcellus and Aaron been plotting to kill Wilson in Stockholm, but his last-minute decision to take a holiday had necessitated a rethink? The Ice Hotel would have been the perfect choice. There were no doors to the rooms. Yes, a murder here would give the police a headache of monumental proportions. And why had Aaron been staying in Kiruna all week? To plan with Marcellus the fine details of Wilson's murder in the Ice Hotel?

I picked at the food. Things were starting to make sense. Marcellus, dismayed that Wilson was spending his inheritance on the schools' programme, had decided to kill him while there was still silver left in the kist. Silver, which would then go to Marcellus as next of kin. And Aaron would take a share as payment for his participation. *Which leaves us with only one thing we haven't talked about, Marcellus . . . my remuneration.*

Marcellus could easily have drugged Wilson, then pushed him out of bed. *I find myself nodding off over dinner and then I'm wide awake at one in the morning.* But was it jet-lag that had kept him up in the small hours? Or the execution of his plan?

And what was on the last page of the diary that was the subject of so much interest?

There was a soft knock.

Liz put her head round the door, her face paler than usual. 'Are you up for a visit? Mike's here, too,' she added, almost as an apology. She glanced at the tray. 'The receptionist told us the nurse was bringing you some food. Did you manage to eat anything?'

My last memory of Liz was of her holding a spoon to my mouth. Tears pricked my eyes. 'Liz—'

In a second, she was at my bedside. I flung my arms round her, and she buried her face in my neck. When her sobbing had stopped, she disentangled herself and fumbled for a handkerchief, releasing the scent of Paris, familiar and strangely comforting.

Mike was in Hallengren's chair, watching us. He reached into his jacket and produced a small bottle of schnapps. He handed it to Liz, who drank greedily before passing it to me. The liquid burnt my throat, but settled in my stomach, its warmth spreading through my body.

'Did you know Hallengren was here?' I said.

'For heaven's sake, why is he bothering you at a time like this?' Liz snapped. 'I told him what we saw in the chapel.' She ran a hand over her ponytail. 'We were all questioned last night.'

'They have to take statements from everyone,' Mike said. 'I had to give mine twice.'

She frowned. 'But you were miles away when it happened, weren't you?'

'I returned early with the Danish fellers and the husky manager.'

'Oh? What time would this have been?'

'Mid-afternoon.' He smiled ruefully. 'I went straight to the gym.'

I steered the subject back. 'There's something I need to tell you both.' I waited until I had their attention. 'Hallengren told me that Wilson Bibby was murdered.'

From the shock on their faces, I realised they hadn't yet seen the press release. 'They did a post-mortem,' I added. 'He was drugged.'

'You mean someone gave him an overdose?' Mike said.

'The drug wasn't intended to kill him, but to render him unconscious. He was incapable of getting up. Whoever did it pushed him out of bed. He froze to death, and the police are treating it as murder.'

'Oh, my God,' Liz said slowly. Her eyes were wide. 'Do they have any idea who it was?'

'They don't know anything.' I picked at the bedsheet. 'But now Harry's been murdered.'

'What's going on here? It's this hotel killer, isn't it? He's come to the Ice Hotel.' She took a huge swallow from the bottle, her hands trembling.

'Listen to me, Liz. It's not the hotel killer, okay?'

'How can you be so sure?'

'I just know, that's all.'

'What else did Hallengren tell you?' Mike said.

'Just that Wilson had been given a massive dose of barbiturate.' I sat up. 'Look, do you remember he left the Ice Bar before everyone else? He said something about wanting a Scotch.'

Liz nodded. 'He said he needed his nightcap.'

'Well, Marcellus went with him.'

She handed Mike the schnapps. 'Marcellus went everywhere with him,' she said.

'He could have slipped something into Wilson's whisky. You know about these things, Liz. How much would you put into a drink to drug someone so they're out? Is it easy to get hold of stuff like that?'

She looked unsure. 'You can buy barbiturates over the counter now. And mixed with alcohol—'

'So Marcellus could have done it. And he had the motive.'

'Money?' Mike said. 'But he stood to inherit when his daddy died. Which was going to be soon. Didn't Bibby have this heart condition?'

'Hallengren said Wilson could have kept going for years. I don't understand that. I saw him take Coumarinose.'

Liz was staring at the wall. 'He took it on the plane, Mags. It could have been to prevent deep-vein thrombosis.' She went over to the wardrobe mirror, and stood frowning at her reflection. She smoothed the dark circles under her eyes. 'Yes, Marcellus had the motive. But he wouldn't do it, would he? It's simply far too obvious. He'd be the prime suspect.'

'Perhaps he thought the police would assume his father's heart had given out.'

She looked at me in the mirror. 'There's always a post-mortem, though, isn't there?' She returned and sat on the bed. 'Did Hallengren say which barbiturate it was?'

'I think it was called Phenonal.'

'Some barbiturates metabolise quickly. Maybe Marcellus thought it would be out of the body by the time death occurred.'

'Maybe he just didn't think,' Mike said. 'Murderers don't always have a plan. They seize an opportunity.'

I was tempted to tell them about Marcellus's conversation with Aaron in the church, but I was mindful of Hallengren's warning. The fewer people who knew, the better. If those men were killers and came to learn I'd overheard their conversation . . . Thank goodness they hadn't seen me in the tower.

'Marcellus would have had to know what he was doing,' Mike was saying. 'If he got the dose wrong and Wilson woke up while he was rolling him on to the floor, he could kiss goodbye to his inheritance.'

'There's that history with him and Marcia Vandenberg. Wasn't there talk that he drugged her? If he did, then he got *that* right.'

'Lots of ifs and buts,' Liz said doubtfully.

'What about Harry?' Mike was weighing the bottle of schnapps in his hand. 'Marcellus might have killed his father for money, but why would he kill Harry?'

'I've been thinking about that,' I said. 'For a while, I wondered whether—'

'Whether what, Mags?'

I chewed my lip. 'There's something I haven't told you. It's about the night we spent in the Ice Hotel. I got up to watch the aurora. When I came back, I saw Harry.'

Her eyes widened. 'Harry?'

'He was coming out of his room. The thing is, when I told Hallengren, he said Harry's story was different. He told the police he'd slept through and didn't get up. Don't you think that's strange?'

'Why on earth didn't you tell us all this before?' She took the bottle from Mike.

I looked away, afraid she'd read my thoughts.

'There may be any number of reasons why Harry's story doesn't tally with yours,' she said. 'He might simply have forgotten – he'd been drinking, after all – and he was probably half asleep at the time.' She looked peeved. 'What's your point?'

'It's possible Harry didn't remember, but it's not likely. He wasn't as drunk as all that. And he wasn't walking like a drunk. What I'm saying is that maybe Marcellus didn't murder his father.' I chose my words carefully, only now remembering Hallengren's warning about keeping quiet that I'd seen Marcellus. 'Maybe he was up and about, saw Harry prowling the Ice Hotel, came to the conclusion Harry did it, and killed him.'

'I'm not joining the dots,' Mike said. 'Are you suggesting Marcellus killed Harry? Out of revenge?'

'It's possible.'

'Well, all right now, but there's still the question of who killed Wilson. If it wasn't Marcellus, then who?'

After a brief silence, I said, 'Harry might have done it.'

'My God, Mags, you can't be serious.' Liz was glaring at me, her mouth ugly. 'Harry wasn't capable of murder. He simply wasn't.'

'That's a despicable thing to say about your friend,' Mike said slowly.

I didn't like the expression on his face. 'I know,' I said, looking away. 'I'm sorry. I can't square the circle, that's all.'

'Just because Harry was awake doesn't make him a murderer. I only met him this week, but there's no doubt in my mind. I'm with Liz on this. He wasn't a killer.'

And yet Harry had been stricken when he'd learnt Wilson was about to withdraw his funding. And he'd shown no emotion when his body was discovered. Harry could have killed Wilson, taken the locker key, found the diary pages relating to the funding decision, and disposed of them, carbons and all.

Mike broke into my thoughts. 'If the motive was hatred, it could just as easily have been me. I had no love for Bibby.'

Liz shook her head. 'This really isn't getting us anywhere. Look, let's go back to the original premise that Marcellus killed his father for his inheritance. Why would he then kill Harry?'

'Because Harry ran into him on his way out,' I said irritably.

She looked thoughtful. 'But if Harry had seen Marcellus, don't you think he'd have told us?'

Yes, Harry would have made a great story of it, adding his usual embroideries. 'We're back to square one,' I said wearily.

I didn't tell them what I was thinking, that if Harry was innocent his silence was a mystery, but if he'd killed Wilson his silence explained everything.

'And the raid on the Excelsior?' Mike said. 'What was all that paddywhack about?'

'The police were looking for traces of the barbiturate.'

'And this missing diary must have something to do with it,' he said. 'Too much of a coincidence. Wilson gets killed. The diary goes missing. It must have been the same person.'

'I'm not sure it isn't more complicated.'

'Things are never complicated, Maggie. When people are

murdered, look for the simplest motive. That's what Hallengren's doing, I'll bet.'

'But murder investigations take an awfully long time, don't they?' Liz said, rubbing her eyes. 'I suppose any chance of getting our passports back has flown out of the window.'

'Grand,' said Mike. 'And I have to be back on Monday.'

'There's nothing at Bayne's that my staff can't deal with,' I said, in my best accountant's voice.

'Well, I'm going to ask Hallengren if he'll release me,' Liz said, her eyes filling. 'I'm not a suspect. I need to see the twins.' Her voice broke on the word.

Mike put an arm round her. 'That's not how murder investigations work,' he said, squeezing. 'We're stuck here till it's over.'

'You know, there's something not quite right about all this,' I said, half to myself.

'Two murders, and something's not quite right?' He smiled grimly. 'If that isn't the understatement of the year.'

'That's not what I mean.'

His voice was cold. 'What, then?'

'I'm missing something. You know, something you can't quite remember. It's there on the edge of consciousness, but when you think hard, it slips away. Like trying to remember a dream in the morning.'

'That's poetic,' Liz said. She put the bottle to her lips. 'Any idea what it might be?'

'It's something vital. When it comes to me, I'll be able to work everything out.'

Mike's lips curved into a smile. 'I'm betting Hallengren works it out first. He fancies you, so he does. He was waiting ages downstairs.'

I smiled to myself. The thought of sex with Hallengren hadn't exactly been at the forefront of my mind. But, then, it hadn't exactly been absent, either.

CHAPTER 20

The receptionist glanced at my snow-suit. His look of enquiry turned to one of alarm.

He put down his book, a Swedish Mills & Boon. 'How are you feeling, Miss Stewart?' he said, in the tone of an undertaker.

'I'm not too bad. I'm going out,' I added unnecessarily. 'For some air.'

He nodded. With a nervous movement, he peeled a leaflet from a pile on the counter. It was an advert for *Macbeth*, playing in the Ice Theatre the following evening. Liz had booked tickets, but I doubted we'd be going now.

'The rehearsal is under way,' he said cheerfully. 'You are allowed to watch. The actors don't mind. They encourage it.'

He seemed so eager to please that I kept the leaflet. I hadn't planned on visiting the Ice Theatre, but I had nothing better to do. I pulled on my gloves, drew up my hood and left.

The Ice Hotel and the chapel were cordoned off so the quickest route to the theatre was behind the Locker Room. The river snaked into view as I rounded the corner, the ice-harvesting machines moving over the frozen surface like giant worker ants. I trudged through the snow, following the trail of footprints, thinking about Harry.

The theatre towered in front of me, sparkling in the sunshine. It looked like a huge frosted cake.

Ice statues guarded the entrance. On the left was Bottom, his freakish ass's head tilted mockingly and his arms outspread in a gesture of welcome. On the right, a frightful creature I recognised as Caliban was hunched over, closed in on himself. If the statues and building didn't give enough of a clue as to the theatre's purpose, set over the doors, profiled in snow, was an unmistakable likeness of Shakespeare. Sconces bearing Olympic-style torches flanked the entrance. According to the leaflet, they would be lit for the performance.

I pulled back the doors and crept inside. Either the rehearsal hadn't started or I'd arrived during a scene change because nothing was happening. The actors, wearing padded, fur-trimmed gowns in silk and leather, were listening to someone in a red snow-suit. I couldn't help noticing their thick gloves, fur hats and heavy-soled boots.

The stage was a low semicircular platform made of pale-blue ice. Workmen were spreading snow on to the surface and patting it down with large plastic shovels. Behind the stage a snow-covered wall was carved with strange shapes: snowflakes, concentric circles and huge spider's webs. A rope of miniature lights climbed, like an exotic twining plant, up the sides and along the wall. The few props were minimalistic: crude, throne-like ice chairs covered with reindeer skins, and columns at either end of the stage.

I trudged up to the top of the auditorium and took a seat below one of the glassless windows. As the building had no roof, the torches fixed to the wall would illuminate the night sky. Not so good for the aurora watchers.

The theatre was full. Strange for a rehearsal but, as the temperature dropped to minus twenty at night, people were probably giving the evening performance a miss. Even now, in the early afternoon, it was cold enough that everyone wore thick suits and ski masks.

'You haven't missed anything,' the woman next to me said. She was not from our group, but one of the Ice Hotel's many day-trippers.

The man in the red snow-suit climbed on to the stage and announced in fluent English that the play was about to begin.

'Who's that?' I murmured to the woman.

'The director. Someone famous who comes every year.' She pointed to the leaflet. 'It's all in there.'

The actors moved to the wings and waited in full view of the audience. The director signalled to a technician, the music started and he hurried back to his seat.

The strident music grew louder, filling the auditorium, then stopped suddenly.

Three witches slipped on to the stage. They danced in a circle, swaying rhythmically, howling and gesticulating. After spinning round, they huddled over an imaginary cauldron, and the play began. As they spoke, they tried to convey the meaning of their words through the movement of their bodies.

'It works, doesn't it?' the woman said. 'You don't need to know Sami.'

'Just as well. It sounds like a cross between singing and gargling.'

I watched, fascinated, as the drama unfolded. As far as I could tell, the players were word-perfect. The director intervened only twice to reposition the actors.

The lighting changed and Lady Macbeth floated on to the platform, her head hidden under a fur-trimmed cowl. Her velvet gown was red, light at the neck but deepening in colour from the waist to the end of the long train, as if the blood she'd waded in had soaked through the hem and was seeping upwards.

I stared at the gown. Oh, God, the blood in the chapel . . .

I looked away quickly, my mind in turmoil. And then I saw him. Harry was sitting two rows further down.

I leapt to my feet and was about to call out when I saw my mistake. It wasn't Harry, but a large woman in a blue snow-suit, her hair the same colour as his. I sank into my seat and leant against the wall, breathing rapidly. My sanity was leaving me. The day-tripper put her face close to mine and asked if I felt unwell. I shook my head, not wanting to talk. With a monumental effort of will, I kept my gaze fixed on the platform.

Lady Macbeth stopped abruptly and, with a dramatic gesture, threw back her hood. The audience gasped. Her eyes, heavily defined with kohl, stared out from her white face. Her blue-black hair was twisted into fat braids, coiling round her head like snakes. She parted her blood-red lips and spoke her opening lines. The audience fell silent. Her voice was deep and resonant, a male actor playing a woman.

I sat in a daze, still thinking about Harry. With an effort, I dragged my attention back to the performance. As it ended, with Macduff brandishing Macbeth's severed head, the music reached a jarring climax, which rang off the walls, deafening the people near the loudspeakers. It faded slowly, and then the actors spilt on to the stage. They bowed, smiling, acknowledging the applause.

The woman next to me had slipped out. People were drifting away. The Harry-lookalike heaved her bulk out of the auditorium. The technician packed his equipment into plastic boxes, and hauled them outside. The director in the front row was conversing with a couple of spectators in the row behind. I felt no desire to move. I wrapped the reindeer skins round my shoulders and leant back. Drained of energy, I closed my eyes and fell asleep.

A sudden noise woke me: an ice-harvesting machine was shutting down. I glanced around, conscious of a growing feeling of apprehension. The theatre was empty, except for the director and the spectators, all in the front row now, talking earnestly. I dragged myself to my feet and made to leave.

A movement caught my eye. Someone else was in the auditorium.

A hooded, black-suited figure at the end of the front row was staring up at me from behind his ski mask. From the build and the way he held himself, I recognised Jonas Madsen. What on earth was he doing just sitting there? I looked around for another exit, but there was only the one door and I'd have to pass him to get out. I pretended to be asleep, watching from under half-closed eyes, hoping he'd lose interest. He continued to gaze at me, glancing now and again at the director and spectators, but they were engrossed in their conversation and showed no signs of leaving.

After several minutes, he rose heavily and lumbered out. I waited until I thought he'd be back at the Excelsior, then threw off the skins, ran down to the front and almost fell outside.

It was snowing. The wind had lessened, and the fat flakes drifted lazily, carpeting the ground in soft white. I drew up my hood and fastened the straps. A feeling of unease crept over me. Why had Jonas been watching me?

I reached the Excelsior as Liz was leaving.

I clutched her arm. 'Liz, stop a minute.' I peered past her into the foyer. 'Have you seen Jonas?'

'Well, yes, I have, about a minute ago. He's in the lounge.'

'Did you see him come in? Could you tell which direction he was coming from?'

She was looking at me strangely. 'I've absolutely no idea.'

'What is he wearing? Is he in a black snow-suit?' Even to my own ears, my voice sounded desperate.

'Why are you asking me these questions?'

'I saw him in the Ice Theatre.' I swallowed hard. 'He was watching me, at the end, after everyone had gone.'

'You're sure it was Jonas?'

'Of course I'm sure.'

'Did you see his face?' she said slowly.

'Yes. No. Look, I didn't need to. He was sitting hunched over the way he does, you know, like he's about to pounce. It was him, Liz, I swear.'

'And what if it was?' she said, with a small shrug. 'Maybe he likes Shakespeare.'

I stared at her. She was behaving as if it didn't matter. 'You don't think it's odd?' I said. 'Everyone goes. He stays behind and watches me.'

Her mouth formed into a smile. 'I can think of any number of reasons why a man would stay behind and watch you. Half the men here are on heat.'

'This is no time for jokes. Don't you realise what this means? He could be the killer.'

'Please, Mags, this is stretching credibility. He can't be the killer. He's bladdered most of the time.'

'Okay, so he drinks,' I said, bristling, 'but not every minute of every day.'

'I suppose that's true. In fact, when he's sober he can be quite jolly. I've had a few chats with him.'

The conversation wasn't going the way I wanted. 'Liz, it's possible he killed Harry.'

'I do believe you're serious,' she said softly.

'And not only Harry. Maybe Wilson, too.'

'And now you think he's after you? How did you jump to that conclusion?'

'Oh, I don't know,' I said, rubbing my face. 'But there's a killer on the loose, and Jonas's behaviour at the theatre was strange. I thought it was, anyway.'

'So this is you working it out? Just like you told us you would?' She tilted her head. 'But have you got the motive for Wilson and Harry's murders? And the proof it was Jonas?' She paused, seeming unsure. 'Because if not . . .'

'Would it kill you to listen to me for one moment?' I said angrily. 'Of course I don't have the proof. Or the motive . . . I'm not even sure it was Jonas, now.'

'Then under the circs I'd keep quiet, if I were you. Hallengren isn't going to take kindly to wild, unsubstantiated accusations. And neither is Jonas,' she added meaningfully.

I stared at her, struck by the force of her argument.

'You're not yourself, Mags. It's understandable after what you've been through. You're tired. We're all tired.'

'You think I'm imagining it, don't you?' I blurted.

She sighed. 'All right, then. If it'll make you feel better, go and tell Hallengren. I'll come with you, if you like. But I would just give him the facts. Don't jump to conclusions. Men, especially detectives, hate it when you try to outsmart them.'

'So what's the quickest way?'

'Right now?' She glanced at her watch. 'I think it'll be the courtesy bus. It's a pity you didn't tell me this earlier. We could have shared with Mike. He's just gone in by cab.'

'Mike's gone to Kiruna?' I said, in dismay. Despite my misgivings about him, I thought Mike at least would have had more faith in me.

'He said he's maxed out on these winter sports, and wants a change of scene. He heard there's a small casino in Kiruna.' She gazed at me anxiously. 'When we get there, do you think you could persuade Hallengren to return my passport? He'd listen to you if you told him that, well, you know . . .'

Liz was desperate to get back to the twins. I suddenly felt exhausted. Why raise her hopes? It would be futile to speak to Hallengren. He wouldn't let her or anyone else leave until everything was solved. And he'd be furious if I wasted his time with some nonsense about Jonas.

'I've changed my mind,' I said, without preamble.

She smiled faintly. 'Well, that was quick.'

'I think you might be right about Jonas.'

'Fine. It's really up to you.' She sounded deeply disappointed.

'I need to warm up. Tell you what, let's ditch our snow-suits and go to the lounge. We can play Scrabble or something.'

'Maybe later. I think I'll try the computer room. Perhaps I can catch the twins.'

I watched her return to the Excelsior, hoping for her sake that, whatever Hallengren was doing to solve the case, he'd do it quickly.

The lounge was empty except for the Danes. Jonas was at the bar, waving a full beer glass and spattering his companions with flecks of foam.

All conversation stopped as I entered.

Avoiding their gaze, I ordered a hot chocolate and took it to the seat nearest the door.

A minute later, a shadow fell across the table. 'May we join you?' a deep voice said.

I glanced up. Olof was pulling out a chair. He sat down without waiting for an answer. Jonas took the chair on my other side.

He was looking at me with a serious expression. The door suddenly seemed far away.

'We are sorry about your friend,' Olof said. 'Finding him like that must have been terrible.'

They unbuttoned their black snow-suits and opened them out, revealing jeans and fishermen's sweaters underneath.

'If there is anything we can do, then please just say,' said Jonas. 'Perhaps you would like a trip into Kiruna. We don't have to wait for the bus. We could go by taxi.'

Olof said something in Danish. Jonas nodded and pulled a mobile out of his jeans.

'I don't want to go to Kiruna,' I said, unable to tear my gaze from Jonas's snow-suit.

He put the phone down. His face brightened. 'Have you been on a husky ride yet? I have a friend who runs a kennel. He can take us.' He paused. 'Would you like that?'

The Danes at the bar were watching silently.

I was shaking so badly, I was spilling the chocolate. I glanced at the door, wondering what would happen if I made a run for it.

'Are you cold?' Jonas said, concern in his voice. 'You're trembling.'

He placed a gentle paw over my hand, hunching his shoulders the way he'd done in the Ice Theatre.

My pulse was racing. I jerked my arm away and jumped to my feet. 'Don't touch me,' I cried.

His face wore a startled expression. 'But I was just—' He made to rise but Olof put a restraining hand on his arm.

'Keep away from me,' I said, stumbling over the words.

I turned and ran out of the room.

I grabbed a snow-suit and boots and rushed out the Excelsior, skating past the ice penguins, which stared up in surprise. When I reached the clown, I stopped for breath and leant against him, shivering. After shaking out the snow-suit, I clambered into it awkwardly.

I sat at the clown's feet and watched the shadows deepen. Dusk had softened the edges of the buildings, and the falling snow made the distance to the Ice Hotel seem greater than it was.

'Who's the killer, Charlie?' I glanced up. 'You know who it is, don't you?'

The clown gazed at the ballerina, his arms high above the drum, ice tears glistening on his cheeks again. I dragged myself to my feet and wrapped my arms round him. 'Tell me,' I whispered. 'Tell me who it is.'

For an instant, I thought I saw his head move, but it was a trick of the light.

I placed my hand against his cheek and felt a sudden rush of warmth. The tears had dissolved under my fingers. I lifted them to my lips, startled by the unexpected taste of salt.

The snow was falling heavily now. I thrust my hands deep into my pockets and peered into the clown's eyes.

And I asked myself again: why had Jonas been watching me?

CHAPTER 21

After dinner, I sat in the lounge with Liz, although neither of us felt like socialising. She was tearful, talking first about Harry, then about the twins. After a while, Mike joined us, but his banter appealed less to me than it did to her. I only half listened to his attempts at flirting, grateful his attention was directed elsewhere.

My thoughts turned once again to Harry. They would have finished the post-mortem. God knows, it wasn't necessary. The cause of death was obvious. What more was Hallengren expecting to find? I tried to imagine Harry dissected, his brains packing the scales, but all I saw was his ruined body spread-eagled on the chapel floor.

Leo came and sat with us. His face was gaunt and he looked as though he hadn't slept for days. 'How are you doing, Maggie?' he said.

I forced a smile. 'Right at this moment, better than you, I think.'

'I doubt that. I wasn't the one who found Harry.' He stiffened. 'I'm sorry. I didn't mean—'

'It's all right.' I squeezed his arm. 'Hang on in there. Come on, have a drink with me.'

He sipped his beer, unable to keep up his end of the conversation. I was glad when he excused himself and left.

The atmosphere remained restrained. The Danes were nowhere

to be seen. The reporters huddled at the bar, Denny Hinckley among them. I was relieved he made no attempt to come over. Some guests smiled sympathetically, but turned away when I met their gaze. Others spoke in hushed tones, throwing veiled glances in my direction. After an hour of this, I'd had enough. I finished my coffee, said my goodnights and left.

In the corridor, I ran into Jonas and Olof. They were still in their black snow-suits, and were heading for the Activities Room. Jonas's lips tightened when he saw me, but he said nothing, just nodded courteously and stepped back to let me pass. I put my head down and hurried to my room.

I lay on the bed, fully clothed, picking through the events of the afternoon, specifically Jonas's behaviour. Strange how attentive he'd been to my welfare, suggesting a trip into Kiruna, or husky riding. Could I have been wrong, and the figure at the Ice Theatre was someone else? But who?

The phone rang, grating my nerves.

'Maggie, it's Jane.' Her voice sounded tinny and far away. 'We're going on the river to see the aurora. Everyone's here, Jim and Robyn too. We thought you might fancy coming with us. I've had a quick peek and it's stopped snowing. The sky's clear but it might not stay that way for long.'

The aurora was the last thing on my mind. But their kindness touched me. 'I'm not sure, Jane . . .'

'Well, have a think about it. If you do decide to join us, we'll be taking the path at the side of the chapel. You can't miss us.'

'Are you going now?'

'Everyone's in the foyer.' A pause. 'I hope you can make it, but I'll understand if you don't want to.' She rang off.

I continued to lie on the bed, cradling the phone. The television clock told me it was only 11 p.m. I was wide awake and unlikely to get to sleep. Fresh air would help. I replaced the receiver and left the room.

A faint murmuring, punctuated by laughter, came from the lounge. So, not everyone was out. I wondered whether Jonas and Olof would be on the aurora watch or, as I suspected, they'd bedded themselves in for another night in the bar. I crept away, hearing the laughter swell and fade as I passed the room.

I pushed against the door to the Activities Room, and stepped into darkness. That was odd. The light was always on. I ran a hand over the wall, groping for the switch, but couldn't find it. No matter. A faint glow was visible through the windows.

The racks of clothes disappeared into the shadows. I fumbled around in the gloom for the extra-thick snow-suits and chose one at random. A minute later, I'd found boots and gloves.

I was sitting pulling on a ski mask when I heard the door open. I stiffened. Another aurora watcher? Without knowing why, I crept to the nearest rack and hid among the suits.

Whoever had entered was in a hurry. He didn't bother with the light switch. He paused for a second, then walked purposefully towards the racks. I dropped to my knees, feeling the blood pulsing through my temples. I parted the snow-suits carefully and peered out. A pair of boots marched past.

I sank back, my heart thumping wildly. I was being ridiculous. This was someone getting dressed for the aurora.

But the ice axe that had butchered Harry – this was where the killer had come to fetch it.

Suddenly, the rack began to shake. There was a rustling, followed a moment later by the heavy creak of a bench. He'd taken a snow-suit and had sat down to remove his boots.

I slipped out of the rack on the other side and edged towards the exit. As quietly as I could, I pulled open the door and stepped into the corridor.

I padded quickly towards the foyer. Halfway there, something made me look back. The door to the Activities Room was swinging. Had I done that? Or had he followed me out? But the corridor was deserted.

I hurried past Reception, instinctively turning away from the man on the desk.

'Are you going to watch the northern lights, Miss Stewart?' he said, smiling happily. 'The party has just left. You should see them from the door.'

I nodded, fastening the hood securely. I wondered whether I should ask for a torch. But I wouldn't need one: there should be enough ambient light. I drew on my gloves, and opened the front door.

The freezing air filled my lungs, settling like fog. I was getting good at estimating the temperature. It would be minus fifteen tonight. I scanned the sky. It had snowed earlier, but the clouds had dispersed and, despite the light from the Excelsior, the aurora was faintly visible.

In my hurry to catch up with the group, I collided with the penguins. I lost my footing and slithered down the path, bringing myself to a stop by grabbing the ballerina's outstretched arm. I peered at the statues. The snow lay at bizarre angles on their heads and arms, sparkling in the reflected light and ready to fall at the merest touch. I had the strangest sensation that the figures were coming to life, and the ghostly company would follow me to the river.

I took the path through the trees, my steps creaking in the new snow. The ground was strewn with tiny crystals, winking in the feeble light, and the temptation to kick them into a glittering arc was almost irresistible.

Ahead of me was the crowd of watchers. In the still night air, their voices carried clearly.

They had just reached the path beside the chapel when a dark figure detached itself. He hung back, waiting until the others had disappeared, then turned and moved stealthily towards the Ice Hotel. He was in a crouch but it was impossible not to recognise the bandy legs and jockey's build. I watched from behind a tree. He dropped under the police cordon and, on reaching the main doors, bent to examine the taped-up handles. So that was it: Denny Hinckley was going to get his photographs if it killed him.

He straightened suddenly, then wheeled round and stared in my direction. I felt a pricking on the backs of my hands. He must have heard me or perhaps sensed my presence. A shutter closed with a bang in one of the upstairs windows. He turned away, apparently satisfied.

He moved silently past the Ice Hotel, then, all pretence at stealth gone, walked confidently to the Locker Room. Something about his swagger made me suspect he wouldn't be letting a little thing like taped handles stand in his way. The sensible thing would have been to leave quietly. Instead I decided to follow him.

I skirted the trees and, with a final furtive glance around, crept into the Locker Room. A faint square of light from the window lay, like an open mouth, on the giant molehill of sleeping bags. I hurried through the washroom and crossed the passageway to the Ice Hotel. Strangely, the handles on the side door hadn't been taped – surely an oversight on Hallengren's part. So much for Swedish efficiency, I thought, smiling to myself. I gripped the antlers and stepped inside.

The candles were unlit and the lights were off. I should have known: why burn electricity in an out-of-bounds building? I debated whether I should go back for a torch, but if I asked the receptionist, his suspicions might be raised. He looked like the type who'd report it to Hallengren. And the last thing I wanted was to be reported to Hallengren.

As I stood, undecided, my eyes slowly adapted. Then I saw him at the far end of the corridor, his shape inked against the wall. He was on tiptoe, peering at the signs. With a rapid movement, he unzipped his suit and produced a torch. After playing the beam over the wall, he disappeared abruptly through a curtain. It was the way to my corridor, I realised then. And to Wilson's room.

I followed at a safe distance, catching the last bobbing light from his torch as I rounded the corners. But I'd miscalculated. I turned into my corridor to find that he'd vanished.

I squinted at the room numbers, counting off the curtains to Wilson's room. Perhaps now was the time to blaze in and challenge Denny. Perhaps not. I was tailing someone at night in a deserted building, which had been placed out of bounds after someone had been murdered. Perhaps it was time to go. Perhaps even time to call Hallengren.

I was sneaking away when I saw a flash from under the curtain. A second later, there was another. So Denny was prepared to trample over the crime scene to get his photographs. He'd scoop his law-abiding colleagues and make a big journalistic splash. I decided there and then that, even if it meant a night in the Swedish cells, I was going to report him.

More flashes, coming fast now. Denny must be nearing the end. I decided to hide in my room, wait until he'd left, then creep away. My hand was on the curtain when something made me stiffen. I looked back down the tunnel-like corridor, but there was nothing. Nothing but shadows. I was becoming jittery. I pulled aside the curtain and stepped into my room. Too late, I remembered there was no ceiling window. The curtain fell back and I was plunged into darkness.

I heard a soft singing. I moved the curtain an inch and peered out. Denny was standing smiling, his teeth glinting in the light from the torch. He stuffed something inside his snow-suit, then zipped it up carefully. But instead of turning left the way he'd come, he went right. A strange decision as that way would take him longer. Of course. He'd thought of everything. His intention was to exit by the back. He'd slip out and rejoin the aurora watchers. And deny he was ever in the Ice Hotel.

I watched him go. At the end of the corridor, he switched off his torch. I could still make out his form, a thickening of the darkness. Then he disappeared.

I let the curtain drop and shuffled into the room, like a blind woman. My foot struck something hard. I patted the reindeer hides and sat on the bed. What would Denny have found in Wilson's room? Only skins. The sleeping bag would have been removed for forensic tests, along with Wilson's clothes. Maybe he'd wanted a picture of where the billionaire had died. He must have gone into Harry's room, too. The double bill would earn him a nice, tidy sum. Mr Paparazzo. I had to hand it to him, he had balls. If Hallengren ever found the images on his camera, it would be Denny seeing the inside of a Swedish jail.

I'd give him another minute before leaving, to be sure he was out of the building. I lay back on the skins and spread my arms out, counting silently.

That was when I heard the sound.

There was no mistaking it. Someone else was in the Ice Hotel.

I held my breath, straining to listen. Moments later, I heard it again, muffled but louder. A spasm of fear ran through my body. The sound came from within the room. Had Denny returned? But why? And why to my room? No, this wasn't Denny: Denny was long gone. I leapt off the bed and thrust my arms out, wheeling in a circle, ready to scream if I touched anything.

To my horror, something brushed against my face. I jumped back and dropped to my knees, my heart racing. I had one thought – find the curtain or I would die there in the blackness of the Ice Hotel.

I felt around frantically until I found the bed. I paused to listen, but could hear nothing except my ragged breathing. I crawled round the block of ice, my shoulder rubbing against the skins, and stopped when I thought I'd be in front of the curtain. Silently, I shifted into a crouching position and held out my arms, like a sleepwalker. Praying I wasn't in front of a wall, I sprang forward and ran. My hands hit the curtain. I beat it out of the way and rushed out of the room.

The corridor stretched endlessly in either direction. I'd never make it. I'd have to hide. I ran into Harry's room, holding the curtain down behind me to stop it swinging. The ceiling window cast a strange light, silvering the objects in the room. I looked around swiftly. The only hiding place was behind the bed, but I had no intention of lying on the floor. As I backed away, my stomach cramping with fear, I collided with something hard. It was the statue of Pan, his manic leer faintly visible in the dim light. I squeezed into the niche behind him and flattened myself against the wall.

From the back of the alcove, the curtain wasn't visible, but its weak reflection smeared the wall opposite, like a bloodstain. I waited, my body tense, and was starting to think it was safe to leave when I heard the slow swishing of footsteps in the snow. He was in the corridor outside. Numb with fear, I pressed my body deeper into the alcove.

I listened, holding my breath. The footsteps were dying away. Relief flooded through me. He'd gone. He'd have left the Ice Hotel by now, even reached the Excelsior. But to be on the safe side, I would leave by the back and join the aurora watchers. I slid out from the alcove and was squeezing past the statue when, in the half-light from the ceiling window, I saw the bloodstain ripple and gently dissolve. The curtain was drawn back, and a black-suited figure lumbered into the room.

He was huge, much bigger than Denny. His hood was drawn over his head and his face was hidden under a ski mask. He moved his head purposefully left and right. I slipped back behind the statue, my heart hammering against my ribs.

The figure lurched towards the bed. As he swung his arms, I caught the glint of metal. I felt myself grow cold as though the blood had drained from my body. He was holding an ice axe, not by the handle but near the top where the shaft meets the blade. He pawed at the jumbled heap of skins, sifting through them and hurling them on to the ground. I had to think quickly or I wouldn't leave the Ice Hotel alive. I had one chance. Dressed in a white suit and hood, I was camouflaged against the snow. He just might not see me. And his movements were sluggish. With luck, I'd outrun him.

As he leant forward to look behind the bed, I crept out of the alcove. Then, with my back against the wall, I sidled towards the curtain. But as I reached it, I overbalanced and fell, jarring my knee so badly that I cried out. The figure straightened.

God knows how – I was exhausted by fear – I struggled to my feet and, ignoring the pain in my knee, ran thrashing through the curtain. I bolted down the corridor. If I could find one of the doors, I didn't care which, I would be safe. I would scream my lungs out the moment I was outside.

But he'd been quick. I heard him pounding behind me. I tore through the maze of corridors, searching desperately until I found the double doors. Without pausing to fumble for the handles, I rammed my body into them. They swung open, banging off the walls and slamming back against my shoulders. Panting heavily, the blood thundering in my ears, I ran out into the night.

To the left was the great curve of the Ice Theatre. I rushed on to the frozen river, my knee pulsing with pain, and my breathing coming in huge gulps. As I sped past the wall of ice blocks, I heard a deep bellow behind me. A metallic taste filled my mouth. The dark figure was close. In a second, he'd reach me. I was sobbing now, my throat and lungs on fire, my breath streaming in a white vapour. I summoned all my strength and ran on, no longer caring where I was going.

Without warning, the ground gave way and I stumbled, still running, into water. My face scraped against something hard and I felt a sharp stab of pain. I flailed my arms, thrashing blindly at the ice, kicking my legs in a vain attempt to find a foothold. And then the sky disappeared and silence closed round me. My descent slowed, leaving me suspended in a murky, alien world. A second later, icy water seeped through my suit, and I gasped, drawing water into my lungs, feeling the cold ripping through my chest. I tried to swim to the surface, beating my arms, willing myself to move upwards, but my legs seemed held in a vice. Exhausted, I let my body go limp.

I peered up through the spiral of water and saw a pale light far above. Giant figures swam into my vision – the circus statues and chess pieces, the Knight Templar. And Denny, his eyes wide with fright, bubbles streaming from his open mouth. They tumbled heavily towards me, completing huge somersaults before taking up position in a circle. From somewhere far away, I watched myself drifting in the water, with Denny and the ice statues jigging and reeling furiously round me. An eternity later, the silence was broken by a roaring that I felt rather than heard. I made a last desperate attempt to save myself, wriggling feebly, trying to free my legs. The water turned red, my vision tunnelled, and then it faded altogether.

CHAPTER 22

'Miss Stewart. Miss Stewart!'

I opened my eyes into an unfamiliar world. Everything was a blur, like seeing through someone else's glasses. A faraway voice was calling, insistent. It was familiar but I couldn't identify it. My face hurt and there was a dull ache in my knee. I tried to move but the pain in my head worsened, shooting bright lights, which left firework trails before my eyes. My eyelids drooped and I drifted back into a fitful sleep.

It seemed only minutes before I woke again. The world was back in focus. My knee ached but the pain in my head was gone.

An open suitcase lay on the table, its contents scattered. Clothes were strewn untidily over the armchair. Others were crumpled on the carpet. The mess was all too familiar – I was in my room in the Excelsior.

Something near the door caught my eye, a chair with damp clothes hanging over the back, the carpet underneath stained dark. I lifted my head. Among the clothes was a white snow-suit. In an instant, I remembered everything – Denny and the Ice Hotel, running on to the river, falling through the ice. And the figure with the ice axe. Fear closed round my throat, threatening to choke me, and I sank gasping against the pillow.

'Miss Stewart.' The voice again. 'How are you feeling?'

Hallengren was sitting near the door, his long legs stretched out.

'The back of my throat's on fire,' I said hoarsely.

'I am sorry. We had to pump the water out quickly. The paramedic may have been a little rough.'

I swallowed experimentally, wincing at the wave of pain.

He poured from a flask. 'Drink this.' He handed me a mug.

I realised only then that I was naked under the bedclothes. I clamped the sheet across my chest and struggled to a sitting position. The towel round my head unwound, and damp hair fell in a tangled mass over my shoulders.

The drink was hot lingonberry juice with honey. I sipped carefully, ignoring the burning sensation in my throat. 'Is it still night, Inspector?'

He poured a drink for himself. 'It is nearly one a.m.'

I'd been unconscious for about an hour. It felt longer.

I studied him over the rim of the mug. He was unshaven, his eyes red. And he was without his uniform. He wore faded jeans and a purple crew-neck sweater. He would have been asleep when they called him. Alone?

'How long have you been here?' I said.

'Since shortly after you were pulled out of the river, which was just after midnight.' He paused. 'The hospital is on the other side of Kiruna. We thought it best to bring you here rather than risk a journey in a poorly heated ambulance. The paramedics assured me that what you needed most was warmth and rest.'

'And I've been asleep all this time?' It was a ridiculous question, but I wanted to hear him tell me he'd been in the room with me.

'You woke only once.' He smiled, arching an eyebrow. 'This is the second time in twenty-four hours that I find myself in your bedroom, Miss Stewart.' When I said nothing, he added, 'So do you think you could answer a few questions? Or would you prefer it if I returned in the morning?'

'No, please don't go,' I said, too quickly. 'Now will be fine.'

He held my gaze briefly, then pulled a notebook from the black snow-suit at his feet. 'Let us start with the reason you were in the Ice Hotel.'

'How did you know I was in the Ice Hotel?' I said faintly.

'You told me just now.'

I ran a hand over my face. God, I was such an idiot.

His voice was hard. 'You knew it was off limits, so what were you doing there?'

I hesitated. Denny's photographs would be in this morning's edition of the *Express*. Hallengren would find out soon enough, so what was the point of giving Denny up? And I had a vague sense of guilt that I was the one who'd planted the idea in his head. But I had to tell Hallengren something. 'I saw someone going into the Ice Hotel and decided to follow him.' I tried to look innocent.

'Do you know who it was?'

'I couldn't see his face,' I said truthfully.

'Height? Build?'

'Short. And slightly built.' If that didn't identify Denny, Hallengren should be back in Detective School.

'Why did you follow him, Miss Stewart?'

It was a good question and one to which I had no good answer.

He sat back, shaking his head slightly. 'There is always one.'

'Excuse me?'

'In every investigation. An amateur sleuth.' He injected just enough irony into his voice. 'Someone who wants to be Hercule Poirot.'

'It wasn't like that,' I said, writhing inwardly.

'No? Then how was it? Tell me, Miss Stewart.'

I looked away, unable to bear the disdain on his face.

'I warned you against playing detective,' he said, his voice harsh. 'And this is what happens when you ignore my warnings.' He frowned. 'Were you not afraid to go into the Ice Hotel?'

'Why should I be afraid?' I said, surprised.

'A man died there, in a room close to yours. It would deter many people.'

'I think ghosts appear only to those who believe in them, Inspector.'

The instant the words left my mouth, I understood with a rush of clarity what I'd been seeing these past few days. In the chapel, when my fingers had brushed against the pulpit, I'd seen Harry's corpse, his lifeblood draining away. And Wilson's face, the flesh decaying, had appeared when I'd touched the Templar's cheek. Wilson and Harry. Both murdered. It was as though the ice had knowledge of the future, guarding that knowledge patiently, yet releasing it at the merest touch of a human hand.

Hallengren was watching me. 'So how did you and this mystery man get inside the Ice Hotel? The front door was sealed, and the seal has not been broken.'

This was not the time to be smug. 'The side door from the washroom wasn't taped up,' I said quietly.

He muttered in Swedish. Someone's head was going to roll. I wondered whether the culprit was Engqvist.

'So you entered from the Locker Room.'

I nodded.

'And then?' He was writing.

'I followed him. He went into Wilson Bibby's room.'

Hallengren frowned, but said nothing.

'I saw flashes of light coming from under the curtain.'

'He was taking photographs?'

'It seems the only explanation.'

'Continue, Miss Stewart.'

'He left by the back. At least, that was what I assumed. He went into the corridor that leads there.'

Hallengren glanced up. 'So why did you also leave by the back? And why were you running?'

'Because someone was chasing me,' I said, keeping my voice steady.

'With so much traffic in the Ice Hotel, I do not suppose you managed to see his face either.'

'I didn't see his face, but he had an ice axe.'

Hallengren stopped writing in mid-sentence. He looked up sharply.

'I stayed in my room until I thought the mystery man had left the Ice Hotel. But someone else came in. It was pitch black, but he was there. I heard him.' I stopped as the memory returned. A knot formed in the pit of my stomach.

'Go on,' Hallengren said softly.

'I ran out and hid in the next room, the one with the statue of Pan. I don't know why, I just panicked. But he followed me in.'

'That room has a ceiling window. Did you see his face?'

'He wore a ski mask. He was huge.' I shuddered, remembering how he'd swung the ice axe casually, his fingers under the blade.

'Was there anything unusual about him? Anything that might identify him? Think hard, Miss Stewart.'

'His snow-suit was black.' I glanced at the suit on the floor. 'Like yours. But that's not going to help.'

'Had you seen anyone follow you to the Ice Hotel?'

I shook my head.

'So what happened? He saw you hiding?'

'I slipped out from behind the statue. He saw me then. I ran out and somehow found the back door. I heard him running after me. He called out before I fell into the water.' I closed my eyes briefly. 'He was right behind me—'

'It may not have been him calling out. One of the people watching the aurora shouted to you to stop. He saw you running past the blocks of ice and tried to warn you.'

'Then he must have seen this man.'

'Everyone we questioned said they saw you running past the Ice Theatre. They saw no one else.'

'Then maybe he ran away when he saw the crowd,' I said helplessly. 'Or even joined them.'

'It is possible.' Hallengren didn't sound convinced.

I sat up, ignoring the bedsheet. 'Look, why else would I be running out of the Ice Hotel like a person demented?'

He said nothing.

'I'm not making this up, Inspector.'

'No, I do not think you are.' He sounded tired, and spoke more slowly than usual. 'You have had a lucky escape, Miss Stewart. You were wearing a thick snow-suit. It saved your life. At these temperatures, without adequate insulation immersion can be fatal. And your legs became entangled in weeds. If there had not been people nearby, you would have drowned.'

I searched his face. 'Someone was in the Ice Hotel with me. Do you believe me?' If he told me he believed me, then somehow everything would be all right.

'I believe you.' He opened the notebook again. 'Now, shall we go through it once more, and in some detail?'

He listened, not interrupting. After I'd finished, he leant back and looked at me.

'Is this your first visit to Sweden, Miss Stewart?' he said, after a while.

I was surprised by the change of subject. 'Yes, my first.'

'Where do you normally take your vacation?'

'I usually head south to the sun. Coming here broke a long tradition. Why do you ask?'

'Just curious.' His gaze drifted to my hair. 'What sorts of things do you like to do on vacation?'

'I'm a city girl. I love poking around old Europe. You know, cathedrals, tram rides, coffee and cake. Nothing too energetic, though. I'm unbelievably lazy.'

The corners of his mouth lifted.

'I'm guessing you're the opposite, Inspector. You mentioned cross-country skiing.' I glanced at his body. 'I'd say you're into hard sports. I see you as an ice climber.'

His smile widened. 'Perceptive, Miss Stewart.' His expression softened. 'So, I take it that this location was not your idea?'

'It was Harry's. He suggested skiing, then Liz found this place in the winter catalogue.'

Hallengren nodded. He seemed in no hurry to leave.

'Tell me something,' I said. 'You're surrounded by snow. Don't you ever get tired of it?'

'Never. It is in my blood.' He raised an eyebrow. 'But I have been known to lie on a beach.'

'That's the kind of holiday Harry usually goes for. To think, if we'd done that, he'd be alive now.'

A look of sadness passed across Hallengren's face. 'You know the worst thing about losing someone?'

'The grief,' I said, without having to think.

'Not grief.' He refused to meet my gaze. 'Guilt. You do not feel that?'

'You've lost someone, haven't you?' I said softly.

'My parents died when I was a boy. I feel guilty that I no longer remember them.' After a pause, he said, 'I am afraid, Miss Stewart, that your grief will eventually turn into guilt.' He got to his feet. 'But enough talk. You need to rest.'

He came over to the bed, and pushed a strand of damp hair away from my face, brushing my cheek with his finger. 'Your hair is still wet, Miss Stewart.' He turned away slowly.

'Are you going?' I said, watching him clamber into his snow-suit. It was a stupid question, but I asked it anyway.

'Would you feel safer if I posted an officer outside?'

I nodded, disappointed he wasn't going to stay himself.

'Very well.' He drew on his gloves. 'Now try to get some sleep.'

He stared at me. Then he left.

I woke with a start. Someone had drawn back the curtains and light was flooding into the room, daubing a wash of brightness on the floor. Dust particles floated in the thin shafts, disappearing whenever a cloud hid the sun, only to reappear and drift aimlessly.

I peered at the television: it was 11.05 a.m.

I showered quickly, running the water hot. I was towelling my hair when my glance fell on the white snow-suit lying over the back of the chair.

I left my room, nearly falling over the young man sitting dozing behind the door. He jumped up in surprise. Another giant. I took in his blue uniform, and the array of coffee cups on the floor.

'I'm going to the lounge,' I said.

He nodded, rubbing his eyes.

I smiled. 'Does this mean you can go?'

'My orders were to stay until you left.'

'You drew the short straw, then.'

'Excuse me?'

'Just an expression. Thanks for looking after me.'

He smiled shyly. 'It is my job.'

★ ★ ★

249

The lounge was empty except for the barman. He was standing behind the counter, whistling and polishing glasses. After two attempts to get his attention, I ordered coffee and a croissant and took them to the sofa by the window.

I thought through the events of the previous week, trying to make sense of them. Someone had killed Wilson Bibby. Someone had killed Harry. And someone had tried to kill me. Were Wilson and Harry's deaths related? And was the person who'd killed Harry the same person who'd tried to kill me? There was the ice-axe connection, but anyone could take an ice axe from the Activities Room. Two different people could have done it.

No one had followed me to the Ice Hotel, so the black-suited figure must already have been there. Perhaps I'd surprised him and he'd felt he had to kill me in case I could identify him. Yet what was he doing there? Was he Wilson's murderer come back to the scene of the crime? But why? To wipe out clues? Then why would he be carrying an ice axe? And he hadn't run after Denny. He'd run after me, as though he'd known who I was under my hood.

I swirled the croissant in the coffee, watching the flakes crumble off. If I hadn't been so lost in my thoughts, I'd have seen him come in. I jumped when I heard the voice.

'Miss Stewart.' Hallengren had shaved and was in his uniform. 'How are you feeling this morning?'

'Medium rare,' I said, smiling.

He smiled back. 'May I join you?'

I motioned to the chair opposite.

He turned his head towards the barman. A second later, the man hurried over with a double espresso.

Hallengren studied my face. 'Did you get any sleep after I left?'

'A little.'

He nodded sympathetically.

'Inspector, what's happening here? Two people have been murdered, and last night someone tried to kill me. Do you think it's the same person?'

He lifted the cup to his lips. 'It is possible that there is more than one killer.'

'Okay, but how do you make that out?'

He looked at me speculatively. 'Have you considered the different ways in which Wilson Bibby and Professor Auchinleck were killed? Wilson's murder was meticulously planned. Someone drugged him and waited until night to push him out of his sleeping bag. Harry was killed with an ice axe, during the day, in the chapel where anyone could have walked in. It could not have been less planned.' He set down the cup. 'In your testimony you stated that Harry was alive when you found him. Given the nature of his wounds, it means that the killer would have been close by, so . . .' He looked hard at me, and his expression changed.

The killer would have been close by.

A shiver ran through my body. The killer had still been in the chapel. He could have butchered me too. And Liz. I watched helplessly as my mug shook and coffee spilt on to the table.

Hallengren reached across and took the mug from my hands. Then everything went black round the edges. I heard the table being pushed away and a chair overturn with a clatter. A second later, he was on the sofa, forcing my head between my knees. I swallowed repeatedly, willing myself not to faint, staring at a spot on the carpet until my head cleared.

He pulled me up gently, leaving his arm round my shoulders. His face was so close I could smell the coffee on his breath.

'Are you all right?' There was concern in his eyes.

'I think so,' I stammered.

The barman was fussing, pulling the chair upright, mopping the spilt liquid. Hallengren looked at him and he slunk off.

'Breathe deeply,' he said, squeezing my shoulders encouragingly. The desire to lean against him was overwhelming.

'You need more rest, Miss Stewart.' He released me. 'What are you doing today?'

'We've no plans, except for tonight. It's *Macbeth* in the Ice Theatre. I saw the rehearsal but my mind wasn't really on it, so I'd like to see it again.'

The barman had brought more coffee.

'I had forgotten,' Hallengren said, spooning sugar into my mug. 'Shakespeare is always on a Sunday. Are you a fan of Shakespeare?'

I took the mug and sipped, wincing at the sweetness. 'Isn't everyone?'

'So which is your favourite?' he said lightly.

'Probably *Hamlet*. Or *Julius Caesar*.'

'Ah, political intrigue. Mine is *Romeo and Juliet*.' He glanced at me. 'You may find it hard to believe, but I am a great romantic. So remind me, please, what time does the performance start?'

'Nine. We're leaving early to get seats.'

'And this afternoon? What do you intend to do?'

'I'm going to stay here.'

But I didn't want to talk about Shakespeare, or this afternoon. 'Inspector, you just said Harry's killer was nearby. I think I saw him.'

He drew his brows together. 'Where?'

'In the chapel. Didn't I tell you? As I came in, I thought I saw someone behind a pillar.'

'Could you describe this person?' he said softly.

'It was a movement out of the corner of my eye. Nothing more. When I heard Harry groaning, I forgot everything else.'

'If the murderer was behind a pillar and realised that Harry was still alive when you ran up to him, he might have concluded Harry told you who he was. Or gave you some hint.'

Fear caught at my throat. Here, then, was a possible motive for the attempt on my life.

Hallengren must have seen the shock on my face, but he continued, 'He might have assumed you would uncover his identity eventually, so he would be seeking the next opportunity to kill you.'

My stomach clenched. 'Why are you telling me this?'

'Because, Miss Stewart,' he said, emphasising the words, 'he may still be looking for an opportunity to kill you. You need to be aware of that.'

'Maybe it happened differently,' I said faintly. 'Maybe the killer followed me to the Ice Hotel thinking I was someone else. You can't tell who people are in these snow-suits.'

Hallengren said nothing.

'Wasn't there any evidence in the chapel? He left his snow-suit behind. Was anyone nearby not wearing one?'

'There were dozens of guests in the Excelsior without snow-suits. And many people, Swedes in particular, go outside for short periods without one. I am not wearing a snow-suit today, as you can see.'

My mind was racing. 'Perhaps the killer didn't follow me to the Ice Hotel last night. Perhaps he was already there.'

Hallengren smiled apologetically. 'And what would the killer be doing in the Ice Hotel?'

'Covering his tracks?' But I was clutching at straws.

'There were no tracks to cover, Miss Stewart. Fingerprints cannot be lifted from compressed snow, footprints from snow-boots are all the same and, anyway, the ground in the Ice Hotel and chapel is always well trampled. Our forensic team found nothing we could use for DNA-testing at either crime scene.'

'Maybe Denny saw him too,' I said eagerly.

'Mr Hinckley?' Hallengren raised an eyebrow. 'The reporter?'

'I'm sure he was the man I followed to the Ice Hotel.'

'I had worked that out for myself, Miss Stewart,' he said wryly. 'Unfortunately, Mr Hinckley seems to have left.'

'Already?'

'Early this morning, we think. The maid found his room empty, and all his personal effects gone. The manager is concerned. It appears that Mr Hinckley left without paying his bill.'

'Typical,' I said, smiling. 'Now that he's got his precious photographs, he's hightailed it back to Stockholm.'

'He will not get far. There is only a limited number of ways he can travel.'

'You're not going to arrest him?'

'Because he deliberately disturbed a crime scene?' Hallengren's lips twitched. 'That is indeed an arrestable offence.' He paused, letting the message sink in. 'But, no, we will not arrest him. However, I would like to speak with him about his escapade in the Ice Hotel. As you say, he may have seen your assailant.'

'And Wilson's diary? Any leads there?'

'The police in Stockholm were most helpful in supplying the carbons from the missing pages. There was nothing unusual or unexpected. A list of business appointments with Swedish officials.'

'I don't understand.' I set down my mug. 'Why would anyone want a list of business appointments destroyed?'

'I have no idea, Miss Stewart.'

'And the final page?'

'We were not able to obtain a copy. I am now convinced that is the only page the thief wanted to destroy.'

Yes, a thief in a hurry would have grabbed the last few pages without bothering to read them.

'And the incident with the snowmobiles?' I said. 'Is that connected to the murders?'

'Mr Tullis was not able to tell us anything other than the identity of the people on the path. Given that two of them are dead, it is possible that was the killer's first attempt.'

If it was, then he botched it. But he surely wouldn't have expected to kill two birds with one stone. So which was the intended victim? Harry? Or Wilson?

'Miss Stewart, if it was indeed a murder attempt, then whoever loosened those brakes must have known he might kill the wrong person. It tells us something about him that he went ahead anyway.' A note of impatience crept into his voice. 'But I have my doubts that it was intentional. The brakes can easily come loose on that model of snowmobile if it is not serviced regularly. I have one like it myself.'

I gazed at him. 'Inspector, do you have any clue at all as to what's going on?'

'There is one possibility we are seriously considering.' He looked at me curiously. 'How much do you know about the Stockholm hotel killings?'

'Next to nothing.'

'It was in spring last year. I was brought in on the case, as were half the police in Sweden.' He played with the sugar, sifting it slowly. 'The guests were murdered in one of Stockholm's top hotels in what appeared to be random killings. Later that year, the same happened in another hotel. Both were forced to close down because business became so bad. The profile of the killer was that of a psychopath. He was never caught.'

'How does one recognise a psychopath?' I said uneasily.

'If only it were that simple. Psychopaths are surprisingly difficult to recognise. They can be charming, manipulative, experienced liars with a greatly inflated opinion of themselves. You may not be able to distinguish them from people you meet every day. I certainly cannot.'

'Half the people I know are like that.'

'And, of course, they are highly dangerous. They have no conscience.'

I took the spoon from his hand. 'So what happened in these
hotels?'

'At first, we thought there might be two killers. The killings
in the second hotel were a – how do you say it? – a cat copy of
the first.'

'Copycat.'

'Copycat. But we eventually concluded it was the same person.'

'And you think he's come here?' I said slowly.

'In the Maximilian, the first murder was a drowning in a bath.
Then two people were poisoned. The fourth was a woman who
was hacked to death with a meat cleaver. But the last murder was
something I have never—'

His expression changed and, for the barest instant, I saw
reflected in his eyes the same fear he must have seen in mine.

I sank back into the sofa, my heart clenching.

'As I said, Miss Stewart, the killer was never caught. The trail
went cold. The case remains open.'

The Maximilian.

'Inspector,' I said, sitting up, 'one of the Danish guests here, Jonas
Madsen, told me he used to stay regularly at the Maximilian on
business. So . . .' I tailed off, not knowing how to finish the
sentence.

'We are of course conducting investigations.' Hallengren smiled
patiently. 'You will understand why I cannot discuss the details
with you.'

I examined my hands, feeling foolish. I was glad now that I
hadn't told him about seeing Jonas at the Ice Theatre. Liz was
right: it wasn't proof of anything. And I was coming to the

conclusion that I might have been wrong, and the figure watching me, whoever he was, had had no malicious intentions.

'Who were these people who were murdered in Stockholm?' I said.

'We looked for a link, but there was little to go on. The only thing they had in common is that they were in business or financiers. The hotels catered for the business community, so it may not be significant. We established that two of them knew each other but, again, that is unsurprising given the nature of their business.' The furrows on his forehead deepened. 'When Wilson Bibby was murdered, we thought the killer had struck again. Bibby's programme with schools has been widely publicised. There cannot be many people who do not know he was in Sweden last week.'

'Why would anyone want to kill a bunch of businessmen? And in such terrible ways?'

'We asked ourselves the same question.'

'And what about Harry? He wasn't a businessman.'

'Which is why I am less inclined to believe that the hotel killer has come to the Ice Hotel.'

'But he is still killing,' I said softly. 'In Stockholm.'

'The American whose neck was broken?' Hallengren nodded. 'We think so.'

He turned his body round and looked directly at me. 'Miss Stewart, there is something you need to understand.' His voice was hard. 'Whether the Stockholm hotel killer has come to the Ice Hotel is not the point. There is a murderer on the loose here. I will be issuing guidelines to Mr Tullis today. You should all be careful about what you say, and to whom you say it. And you, Miss Stewart, should not be alone at any time. Will you promise me that?'

'You think the killer is coming after me,' I said, my voice wavering.

'Or he may have another victim in mind and see your – how shall I put it? – amateur investigations as an impediment.'

'But this has nothing to do with me. I never met Wilson before this week. How could the killer be after me?' I caught my breath. 'I refuse to believe it.'

Hallengren gripped my shoulders. 'Believe it, or do not believe it, but promise me you will be careful.' His face was so close I could see the purple flecks in his irises.

'Very well,' I said faintly. 'I promise.'

He released me, and got to his feet. He dropped a few coins on to the counter, nodding to the barman who'd been watching with curiosity. Then, without a backward glance, he left the room.

I curled into the sofa and clutched at the cushions, burying my face in their softness.

CHAPTER 23

I threw the cushions aside and set up the chessboard, reconstructing one of my favourite games, the 1918 match between José Capablanca and Frank Marshall. I moved the pieces automatically as I sipped the sweet coffee.

Hallengren's words played in my mind: *The killer would have been close by.*

A sudden sound made me look up.

He was in the doorway, watching me. I took in every detail: the huge bulk, the black hooded snow-suit and ski mask. And the ice axe in his hand. An ice axe, which he was holding firmly by the shaft.

He took a step towards me. I scanned the room, searching helplessly for the barman. Snatches of laughter drifted in from the kitchen. The figure came closer. I tried to lever myself up, thinking I might make a run for it, but my limbs refused to move. He reached the table. Another second, and the axe would smash through my skull. In that moment, the spectre of Harry's mutilated body rose before me and I nearly passed out with fear.

'Maggie? Are you all right?' The Irish accent was unmistakable. In a single flowing movement, he raised his hand and pulled off the ski mask. 'You should see yourself, you've gone a whiter shade of pale.'

The barman breezed in and busied himself washing glasses.

Liz arrived. 'So this is where you are, Mags,' she said, taking the seat next to me. 'You've no idea how relieved I am. Leo told us at breakfast what had happened. It must have been absolutely dreadful.' She reached across and squeezed my fingers. 'Your hands are like ice.'

I let her blow on my fingers. I was unable to take my gaze off Mike.

'We wanted to come straight away,' she was saying, 'but Hallengren gave strict instructions you were not to be disturbed. I saw the policeman outside your room.' She glanced at the table, and an expression of exasperation crossed her face. 'And here you are playing chess as though nothing's happened.'

Mike stepped smartly out of his suit. 'For the love o' God, what were you doing out there on the ice? We thought you'd gone to bed.'

I was on the point of telling them about Denny, the figure with the ice axe, the whole bloody lot. But something stopped me.

They were waiting for an answer.

'I went out to watch the aurora.' I tried to sound convincing. 'I got too close to the edge and stepped into the water. Stupid of me. Fortunately, there were people around.'

They exchanged glances but didn't press me. I wondered what else they'd heard.

'Have you seen Hallengren?' Liz said.

'Just now.'

'And what did he say about going for little night-time walks on the ice?' she said sternly.

I chewed my thumb. 'He let me have it. Both barrels.'

'You and your auroras. You were damned lucky, you know. If you'd been alone . . .'

I glanced at Mike. He was twirling the ski mask on the end of his finger.

We were in the restaurant, finishing lunch.

'Would you girls like to do something this afternoon?' Mike said. 'The excursions have been cancelled again.'

Before I could reply, Leo Tullis arrived with Jane.

'How are you doing, Maggie?' he said anxiously.

I smiled, wanting to reassure him. 'Nothing a good night's sleep couldn't cure.'

There was a slight flush on Jane's cheeks. 'I've been feeling bad all morning. If I hadn't rung you and told you about the aurora, you'd never have fallen into the water.'

'For heaven's sake,' I said playfully, 'it's not your fault. I'm a big girl now. I make my own decisions.' I felt like adding: *And my own mistakes.*

She seemed grateful for my answer. 'So are you going to the play?'

'*Macbeth*?'

Her expression changed to one of shock. 'The Scottish play, Maggie. You should never call it by its name.'

'I rather think I've had all the bad luck I'm going to get,' I said, forcing a laugh.

She looked unconvinced. I could see she wanted to leave. She glanced questioningly at Leo, who nodded.

They were moving away when Leo said, 'I meant to ask. Have any of you seen Denny Hinckley?'

'The reporter?' Mike said.

'I lent him my brochure on the Ice Hotel and I'd like to have it back.'

'You're out of luck,' I said. 'I understand he's left.'

261

'What do you mean?'

'He's gone AWOL. And he didn't settle his bill.'

Liz glared at Leo. 'How is it that he's got his passport back, and we're still here? That's not very fair.'

'I don't know anything about his passport,' Leo said, tugging at his hair. 'Maybe the press didn't have to surrender theirs.'

But the police hadn't let the press leave. They'd been around when Harry was murdered, so they were marooned like the rest of us.

Liz's glare intensified. 'Look, Denny can't possibly have left the hotel without his passport, so he must have had it returned. Either that or he's still here somewhere.'

'He had more than one,' Jane said timidly.

We stared at her.

'From the way he said it, I think at least one of them was a forgery.' She smiled nervously as though this was somehow her fault. 'He bragged about being able to get out of trouble faster than he got into it.'

Mike grinned. 'The sly dog. But in this case I don't think it's trouble that's made him do a runner. He's legged it to avoid paying his bar bill. I saw how much he put away.' He shook his head. 'That man's got Irish blood in him somewhere.'

'About our passports, Leo,' Liz said wearily, 'is there really nothing you can do to persuade the inspector to let us go home? He can't keep us here much longer. Murder investigations can go on for months, can't they? What about all that awful paperwork he'll have to keep filling out if we stay?'

'Everyone keeps asking me that. When I next see the inspector, I'll put the question to him.'

'Do you know how far they've got with catching Harry's killer?' Mike said.

'We may learn something at the next press release.'

'Which will be when?'

'Can't tell you, I'm afraid.' Leo glanced at his watch. 'Sorry, but I've got to run.' He and Jane left.

'Well then, ladies?' Mike said. 'This afternoon?'

'I need to go into Kiruna to the coroner's office,' Liz said. 'There are some final things that need doing.' It was Liz who'd been dealing with the paperwork over Harry's body.

'But they must be closed on a Sunday,' Mike said.

'They told me they'd open the office. I think they want to get it over with as quickly as I do. They gave me a time, four thirty. I thought of going now and doing a spot of shopping. What about you, Mags? How are you feeling?'

They were watching me.

'Look, you don't need to keep tiptoeing round me,' I said. 'We should make an effort. It's what Harry would have wanted. So tonight we're going to see the play. The Scottish play.'

There was an awkward pause. 'And Kiruna?' Liz said. 'Is that something you'd like to do?'

I was tired and about to decline when I remembered Hallengren's warning about not being alone. What safer place than in the centre of town, surrounded by people?

'Let's go,' I said firmly. 'Now.'

She looked surprised at this show of assertiveness. 'Fine. We can take the courtesy bus. Are you coming, Mike?'

He was peeling an orange. 'I'll give it a miss, I think.' A slow smile spread across his face. 'I know what it's like when girls go shopping.'

'What are you going to do instead?' I asked lightly.

He was arranging the orange segments into a star pattern. 'I haven't decided. I went ice climbing this morning. I may try snowshoeing. Then I can cross it off my list of winter sports.'

263

'Let's go, then, Mags.' Liz drained her espresso. 'We'll need snow-suits.'

At the mention of snow-suits, I glanced at the black suit draped across Mike's chair. He saw me looking and stared back silently, eating the orange segments, one by one.

We were leaving the Excelsior when I saw the notice.

'Liz, there's another aurora tonight.' I scanned the text. 'It's supposed to be magnificent. The best yet.'

'You can't be serious. After your escapade last night, do you think anyone will let you back on to that river?'

'Pity there's nowhere else.'

'Can't you watch it from your window?'

'The trees get in the way.' I gazed at the photograph of the ice-cream colours swirling into the velvet sky.

'There's the church tower,' she said hesitantly. 'It's awfully high. But think of the view.' She shook her head firmly. 'It's out of the question, though.'

'Too right. Only a lunatic would climb up there when there's an axe murderer running loose.' I took her arm. 'Come on. Kiruna.'

A queue had formed at the bus stop. The cancelled excursions and the realisation that this might be the last opportunity for shopping must have accounted for Kiruna's sudden popularity. Jonas and his friends were there, dressed in black, larking about and shoving each other. They wore ski masks but there was no mistaking their voices. I pulled my hood up and turned away, not wanting them to see me.

The bus dropped us at the park on the outskirts of town. Kiruna had been built on several hills, a strange decision for a town snowbound for most of the year. The trees had been brushed clear and strings of fat lanterns, like miniature Cinderella carriages, hung from the branches. I studied the map I'd picked up at the reception desk. The quickest way to the centre was through the park. We found the exit, clinging to each other, losing our footing despite the tread in our snow-boots.

After a while, we arrived at a residential area.

'We've gone wrong somewhere,' I said, scrutinising the map. 'We should be in town by now.'

I swung round to get my bearings, and saw a figure in a black snow-suit step smartly out of sight.

Liz took the map from me. 'We turned too soon. It should have been the third left, not the second.'

I decided to say nothing. As we retraced our steps, I glanced down the side road. It was empty.

We reached the town centre and strolled along the high street, taking in the shops. But the black figure had given me a shock, and I couldn't rid myself of the feeling we were being stalked. Every so often, I glanced over my shoulder. After a while, I saw him again, sauntering a respectable distance behind us, peering into shop windows.

I told myself I was being ridiculous. Many people were wearing black snow-suits. It might be Mike coming to join us, having changed his mind. Except Mike wouldn't be dawdling. He'd have caught us up by now.

We were nearing a café. 'I could do with something hot, Liz,' I said. 'My knee's throbbing.'

'Of course,' she replied quickly.

I opened the door. The thick, warm air, scented with vanilla and cinnamon, wrapped itself round me like a blanket. We ordered two hot chocolates.

I steered Liz to a window seat. 'That was some news about

Denny doing a runner to avoid paying his bill,' I said, gazing out. 'I thought journalists are on expenses.'

'Only if they're with a paper, I think.'

'He worked for the *Express*, didn't he?'

'Really? I didn't know.'

I dragged my gaze from the window. 'Yes, you did. Mike told us.'

'Anyway, Denny Hinckley didn't talk to me,' she said, running a fingernail over the yellow tablecloth.

'You're lucky. He talked to everyone else.' I sipped my chocolate. 'I just don't get it, though. Why would he do a bunk if the *Express* are paying his expenses? There must have been another reason.'

'You're not saying he killed Harry, are you?' There was a trace of irritation in her voice.

'Of course not. I find it strange he left so suddenly, that's all.' Denny's words came back to me: *I have to find a big story. I can't afford to let the grass grow under my feet.* 'A journalist leaves before the case of a murdered billionaire is solved? It doesn't wash.'

'Just leave it, Mags.'

I studied her, seeing how much she'd changed this last week. There were dark smudges under her eyes, which no amount of expensive foundation could conceal, and her hair, released from its hood, reeked of cigarette smoke. I guessed what she was thinking: Denny had left, and she was stuck here indefinitely, away from her children. I took her hand and squeezed it.

She let it lie in mine, not looking at me. When she spoke, it was with weariness in her voice. 'What's wrong?'

'To do with Denny?'

'You've not been yourself since we stepped off the bus.'

For a second, I considered not telling her. But she had a right to know: her life might also be in danger. 'We're being followed,' I said. 'He's wearing a black snow-suit and a ski mask.'

On cue, a black-suited figure strolled past the window. A moment later, we saw another, moving more quickly. Then two figures in black snow-suits wandered along, deep in conversation.

Liz relaxed visibly. 'Everyone seems to be wearing black, Mags.'

I felt foolish. 'Maybe I imagined it.' I finished my chocolate. 'Come on, let's go.' We pulled up our ski masks and left.

But as we picked our way along the crowded street, I continued to search for the figure, hoping his actions would give him away.

'You're driving me nuts,' Liz said suddenly. 'I can see what you're doing.' She stopped and scanned the street. 'There are people in black suits, there are people in red suits, blue suits and white suits. I've even seen a pink suit.'

'Okay,' I said sheepishly. 'You're right. I'll stop.'

We wandered into the main square. Despite the cold, the whole of Kiruna seemed to have turned out, and a market was in full swing.

We trailed around, ignoring the sharp eyes and brittle smiles of the stall-keepers. They were calling raucously to each other, and stamping their feet to warm them. The shoppers searched in packs, eyes roaming hungrily for gifts, jostling each other with an easy indifference.

I stopped at a candle stall, attracted by the warm, waxy smell. The girl was lighting the candles with a taper, and wiping her dripping nose on her sleeve. The expression in her moist eyes, mournful and hopeful as a spaniel's, decided me. I bent over the scented candles and inhaled deeply. More for her benefit than mine, I took my time making up my mind, and settled on a miniature Christmas tree, which smelt of pine needles.

The stall-keeper opposite was winking at me, inviting me to buy the decorations hanging from the frame. The wind had strengthened and a sudden gust swung them alarmingly. One fell to the ground, tinkling as it smashed. The man frowned, muttering in Swedish, and kicked the glass away. Unable to clear the shards, he ground the remains under his boot. He saw me watching then, and called out, but I couldn't understand him.

I felt a sudden grip on my arm. Liz was staring at something behind me.

I turned to look.

He was tall and well built, wearing a black ski mask and suit. He was leaning over a stall that sold tablecloths, fingering the merchandise and deliberately not looking in our direction.

Liz's voice was almost a whisper. 'You were right, he's been following us. He's been stopping whenever we have so that he's always a couple of stalls behind. And he's been looking us over.'

I pulled her away. 'For heaven's sake, don't let him see that we know.'

'I owe you an apology, Mags. I should have believed you.'

'He won't try anything in a crowd. It shouldn't be difficult to lose him.'

'Oh, no, we're not losing him. We're going to challenge him,' she said, in a tone that brooked no argument.

'You can't be serious. If he knows we're on to him, it's a whole new situation.' I glanced at the figure. 'He could be someone unconnected with the Ice Hotel, who's doing this for a lark.'

'A pervert, you mean?'

'They exist, Liz, even this far north. Let's just leave it.'

But Liz wouldn't leave it. 'Hey, you,' she called, striding towards the black-suited figure.

He looked up, dropped what he was holding, and walked briskly away.

'What the hell do you think you're doing? Hey, I'm talking to you.' She broke into a run.

The figure glanced over his shoulder, then took off like a

rocket. I dashed after them, trying to keep up despite the pain in my knee.

For a brief moment, I thought he'd lose us but he slipped, knocked into a stall, and fell crashing to the ground. Liz reached him in seconds. He tried to haul himself up but she delivered a vicious kick to his groin.

'Right, who the hell are you?' she yelled.

He howled, curling into a ball, and lay on his side, rocking. She struck out savagely at his ribs.

I dragged her off him. 'Liz, for God's sake, that's enough.'

She broke free of my grip. 'Why were you following us?' she shouted at the man.

When he didn't reply, she reached down and tore off his mask. I stared at his face.

'Do you speak English?' Liz said roughly.

A crowd had gathered and was watching silently.

Sweat was running into the man's eyes. He was having difficulty breathing. 'A little.' His accent was French.

'You've been following us since we left the park,' I said quietly. I glanced at Liz, afraid she'd have another go at him.

'I was not following you.' He managed to get the words out. 'But when you ran at me, I thought—' He motioned to Liz's face. 'I thought you were a man.'

She removed her ski mask and pulled down her hood, shaking out her hair. He made an attempt at a smile but it was more of a grimace. 'A misunderstanding on both sides,' he gasped.

He started to drag himself up but fell back, wincing. I reached down and took his arm, signalling to Liz to do the same. She stepped away. I threw her an angry look. What on earth was she playing at? The man was obviously a tourist. One of the crowd came forward and, supporting him under the shoulders, lifted him to his feet.

I hooked a hand under Liz's elbow. 'Let's get out of here before we're arrested for GBH.'

She was frowning at the Frenchman. 'Have you been anywhere near the Ice Hotel?' she said rudely.

'Madame, I am in Kiruna only for today.' He was breathless from the effort of standing upright. He inclined his head. 'Please accept my apology for anything I have done to offend you.'

He limped towards the road. The crowd parted to let him pass.

I stared at Liz as though seeing her for the first time.

'Why are you looking at me like that?' she said sullenly.

'Unbelievable, Liz. You could have broken his ribs, to say nothing of what you've done to his ability to procreate. That was totally uncalled for.'

Her eyes blazed. 'Oh, that's rich, coming from you. You've been bleating on about being followed by an axe murderer, and when I take action this is your response. Yes, of course, now I see he's a tourist, but for all I know he could have been the man who killed Harry.'

'Hold on, press the pause button.' I tried to keep my voice level. 'Okay, but when you saw he wasn't the murderer you could at least have apologised. I had no idea you can be so vicious. If you'd wanted to immobilise him, why didn't you use a judo hold instead of whacking at his ribs?'

Her anger dissolved. 'I'm sorry, Mags,' she said quietly. 'I'm so sorry. I know what I did was awful. I really don't know why I'm behaving like this.' Her voice shook. 'I just want to get home to Annie and Lucy.'

I put my arms round her and held her shaking body against mine, unable to bear her tears. 'It's not your fault,' I murmured.

I took her to a stall that sold drinks, and bought her a glass of hot, spiced wine. I made sure she drank it all.

She wiped her eyes. 'Thanks, Mags.' She drew up her ski mask, smiling bravely. 'So shall we go shopping?'

In a large department store, I watched her spend money on things she didn't need. My mind was still at the scene with the Frenchman. Her uncharacteristic behaviour was a nervous reaction to the strain she was under, the strain we were all under. But when would Hallengren let us leave?

I was playing with the testers at the perfume counter when Liz said, with a glance at her watch, 'Whoops, I'm going to be late. I need to get to the coroner's.'

'Already? I'll come with you.'

'It's away at the other end of town. You should get back, Mags. Go and warm yourself up with a sauna.'

I frowned. 'You sure you don't want me along?'

'There's no need to worry. I'm fine now, really I am.' She nodded at the bottle in my hand. 'I'd buy that, if I were you. According to the label, it's supposed to drive men wild with desire. I'll see you at dinner.' She hurried away.

I sat in the bus and soon forgot the black-clad Frenchman. My thoughts turned to the reason for our trip into Kiruna. Would Harry's body be released? I closed my eyes, seeing his flaccid corpse, the Y-shaped scar livid on his chest.

In the far distance, the Excelsior was a tiny red pillar box in an expanse of white.

CHAPTER 24

I was removing my ski mask in the foyer when Leo Tullis came running out of the lounge.

'Maggie? Thank goodness we've found you.' He ran a trembling hand through his hair. 'They've got them. Marcellus and Aaron. Marcellus is already at the station. Aaron is being arrested now.' He looked past me. 'There he is,' he murmured.

Aaron, his wrists handcuffed, was being frogmarched down the corridor by two policemen. Hallengren was with them.

Hallengren ignored the crowd gathering in the foyer and pushed his way to the door. As Aaron passed us, he stared at me. He opened his mouth to speak, but the officers pulled him away. The front door closed behind them. A minute later, I heard the whine of a car engine.

'They're being charged with murder,' Leo said, his voice strange. 'They hatched a plan in Stockholm to kill Wilson. I don't have the details yet.' He nodded at the receptionist. 'Mr Karlsson had a few words with one of the officers. They're being charged with the murder of Harry, too.'

'Harry,' I whispered, closing my eyes.

'We'll get the press release in the morning. But it's official.' Leo clasped my fingers and squeezed hard. 'It's over.'

'I don't know what I'm supposed to feel,' I said weakly.

'Well, I feel like a drink, a stiff one. Join me?'

'But why did they murder Harry?' I said, my mind a whirl.

'We'll get the details soon enough.' Leo sounded greatly relieved. 'Mr Karlsson said they're not looking for anyone else. We can rest easy. The killers are under lock and key.' Seeing my tears, he put an arm round my shoulders. 'Come on, Maggie, chin up.'

I let him lead me away. Relief flooded through me. Harry's killers had been caught.

There was time for a drink before the play. We pushed our way into the lounge, and took the last free table. Everyone was in high spirits, especially the reporters.

'I can't believe it,' Mike was saying.

'That Marcellus and Aaron are guilty?' I said.

'That it took your ace detective this long to bring them in.'

'What do you mean, "this long"?'

Mike said nothing, but a smile flickered on his lips.

'Can we talk about something else?' I said.

He turned to Liz. 'So how are the twins? You were ages at the computer.'

Liz was pale. 'Lucy's not feeling terribly well. She's been throwing up all day. Siobhan thinks it's something she ate. I'm sure it's not serious but I've given her the Excelsior's number just in case. My phone's reception comes and goes here, I'm afraid.'

'We should make our flight tomorrow,' Mike said reassuringly. 'Leo sounded hopeful we'll be getting our passports back.'

'Oh, thank goodness,' she said, with feeling.

Mike raised his glass. 'Well, then, here's to the Bard.'

'Listen, how about a last look at the aurora?' I said, glancing from one to the other.

'Are you for real?' His voice grew hard. 'You're not going on that river, Maggie.'

'No, not the river. The light from the Ice Theatre will wash everything out.'

He lowered his glass. 'Where, then?'

'The only place far enough away from illumination is the church. The bell tower. The view will be to die for.' I looked pointedly at Liz. 'So who's coming?'

She laughed. 'I give in, Mags. You've been droning on about this aurora all week. I absolutely have to see what the fuss is all about. You can count me in.'

Mike was looking at me strangely. 'You can count me out.'

Liz leant into him. 'Oh, come on, Mike. Please.'

'I'm going to see *Macbeth*.'

'You mean the Scottish play?' I said. 'Now you've brought us bad luck.'

'There'll be time for both, you know,' Liz said pleadingly. 'We'll only stay out half an hour. Then we'll go straight to the theatre. If we leave now, we won't miss much.'

'It's not that.' He hesitated. 'I'm no good up towers. I get vertigo.'

It was a strange remark from someone who'd been ice climbing. But I let it go.

He looked into his beer. 'You girls have fun. But mind yourselves up there.'

I glanced at my watch. It was 8.50 p.m.

'We'll need hot showers first,' Liz said, getting to her feet. 'It'll be perishing up there. I'll meet you in the foyer, shall I?' She sounded excited.

I pushed back my chair, gulping my drink.

Mike laid a hand on my arm. 'It's not the height, Maggie.' He seemed anxious I hear him out. 'It's the tower, the enclosed space.'

I was surprised at this admission of weakness. 'We all have our phobias, Mike,' I said, smiling. 'I'm no good underwater, but you already know that.'

He seemed grateful for my flippant remark.

'*Macbeth*'s about to start,' I added. 'I mean, the Scottish play.'

In the Excelsior, I took a shower, running the water as hot as I could bear until my skin glowed red. It was now nearly 9.30 p.m. If we hurried, we'd be at the church by ten.

The receptionist with the glasses was deep in another Mills & Boon. He looked up at the sound of my footsteps. 'Are you wanting to see the play? It began half an hour ago, I'm afraid.'

'We're going to the church.'

'The church?' He looked puzzled.

'To watch the aurora from the tower.'

His eyes grew wide behind the lenses. 'I can't remember the last time anyone climbed up there,' he said slowly. 'It's a long walk. Are you sure you want to go?'

'It'll be our last chance. We're flying home tomorrow. Could you lend me a torch?' I added, remembering the darkness in the tower.

He opened a cupboard and removed a heavy rubber one. After checking it was working, he handed it to me without a word. I nodded my thanks.

'Ah, here is your friend.'

Liz was marching down the corridor, drawing on her gloves. 'Ready?' she said, smiling.

We were at the door when the manager appeared. 'Miss Hallam, there is a phone call for you in my office,' he said.

'It must be Lucy.'

'I'll wait here,' I said. 'Or should I come with you?'

'No, no, it's fine.' She hesitated. 'Look, Mags, do go on and I'll catch you up. I really don't think it's serious. Children are always

275

being sick. Awful, but there you are.' She saw the doubt on my face. 'Go on, go on, or you'll miss it.'

'Are you sure?'

'I'll be along as soon as I can. Or I'll meet you up there.' She disappeared with the manager.

I hesitated for only a second, then left the building, conscious of the receptionist's accusing stare.

The damp air was filled with the scent of woodsmoke. I studied the sky. It was cloudless, and there was no moon. The night gods were smiling on me.

I slithered down the path between the statues, and found the road to the church. Ice was forming and I had to watch where I trod. Despite taking care, I lost my footing a couple of times and slipped, crashing painfully on to my side.

Eventually, the streetlights thinned out and, at the edge of the cluster of houses, I switched on the torch. The yellow cone of light pushed back the darkness, illuminating the road ahead. I swung round, moving the torch in a wide arc and catching the snow-covered trees in the beam. I thought I saw an answering flash from the forest but it must have been a reflection. I trudged on. The only sound was my feet crackling on the ice.

I took the bend in the road. In the distance the church and the tower looked eerie in the torchlight. The ground was almost free of ice as the surrounding forest gave a measure of shelter.

I was nearing the church door when something made me stop. It wasn't a sound, more a feeling that someone or something was close by. It couldn't be Liz. I'd have heard her. And she'd have seen the torch and called to me. I ran the beam over the entrance, even moving it up the walls, but there was nothing.

I pulled the wrought-iron ring, bracing myself for the loud creak, but the door swung open silently.

The familiar cloying smell of wax filled the church. I played the beam over the floor, listening to the muffled sound of my footsteps as I walked up the nave. Would Liz think to bring a torch? Probably not.

The door to the tower stood half open. Yet I thought it had been closed when I'd entered the church. I pushed against it, tensing as the rush of cold air chilled my face. There was no point in leaving it open to try to warm the room. I'd soon be out on the platform.

The candles in the wall were lit. Their tiny flames flared in the draught, throwing faint shadows on to the floor. At the bottom of the steps, I shone the torch into the tower. The trapdoor was just visible, the size of a postage stamp.

I started to climb, one hand on the rail, the other gripping the torch. As I shifted my weight, the wood creaked alarmingly. *I can't remember the last time anyone climbed up there.* After misjudging the first few steps, I found my rhythm. The ascent seemed never-ending. I trudged up spiral after spiral, but each time I peered up, the trapdoor looked no larger.

I was transferring the torch from one hand to the other when I lost my footing. I dropped the torch and seized both rails, slithering about on the step and trying frantically to regain my balance. From far below came a dull thump, followed by the sound of breaking glass. The tower was plunged into darkness.

I clutched at the rails, listening to the echoes banging off the walls. Cursing my clumsiness, I ran a hand over the step. The wood was split. I'd had a lucky escape. But, God, it was dark. I couldn't climb in this. If I hadn't gone far, the smart thing would be to turn back. But how far had I climbed?

A faint current of air brushed my face. I tilted my head back and felt it again, colder and stronger, an indication that I was near the top. I continued to climb, counting the steps until my head hit something hard. I lifted a hand slowly. My fingers scraped against rough wood. I pushed gently, raising the trapdoor several inches, and was instantly chilled by a blast of cold air. I pushed harder. The trapdoor swung back with a clatter.

The thick mantle of snow cloaking the landscape reflected what little light there was, silhouetting the platform and its surrounding wall. Above my head was a curved metal contraption, which must have held the bells. Above that, there was a dilapidated stone roof, high enough not to obscure the view of the sky. I clambered out, leaving the trapdoor open, and stationed myself in a corner to wait for Liz. The white forest stretched to the horizon, crowned by the dome of ink-black sky.

There was no sign of the aurora. I moved briskly round the platform, beating my arms. Any minute now and it would start. An hour had passed since I'd left the Excelsior, so what had happened to Liz? Perhaps there was a real crisis with Lucy. I felt a sudden twinge of guilt at not having stayed.

I was searching the sky for signs of life when I heard the faint sound. I leant over the trapdoor, holding my breath. Silence. I must have imagined it.

Then I heard it again, louder. The door into the tower was opening. A second later, I heard the unmistakable thud of someone climbing the steps. Liz had finally arrived. I let my breath out in a rush. Whatever was wrong with Lucy, it wasn't serious, thank goodness.

I'd need to warn Liz about the broken step. I shouted into the tower, 'Liz, can you hear me?'

There was no response.

I yelled at the top of my voice. 'Liz!'

But Liz didn't reply. She continued to climb the tower, heavily, and with purpose.

I sprang back, my heart thudding. This wasn't Liz. She would have shouted back. And she was much lighter on her feet. Someone else was coming to watch the aurora. Yet everyone was at *Macbeth* – the light from the theatre was visible as a distant glow. So who was it? And why hadn't he shouted back?

With a sudden rush of fear, I knew why.

I ran to the edge of the platform and, clinging to the parapet, peered down. The tower fell away in a sheer drop.

I sank to my knees. My mind was racing. I ran my hands over the floor, searching for something I could use as a weapon. Nothing. Perhaps the trapdoor could be locked from the outside. I felt around the latch, but there was no bolt or key. And even if there had been, a few blows from an ice axe would splinter the wood in seconds.

The footsteps were close. Another minute and his head would appear through the opening. I struggled to my feet but my legs gave way. Leaning against the parapet, I sank to the floor. I was sick with fear. I was going to die like Harry.

But not without a fight. I had one chance: if I kicked his head hard enough, I could knock him off the steps. I crawled to the trapdoor, hauled myself to my feet, and positioned myself where a well-placed boot in the face would send him backwards. As I steadied myself, I heard something that made my heart lurch – a splintering, followed by a high-pitched shriek that scorched the air. The screaming went on for ever, merging with its echoes, filling the tower until there was nothing else. There was a sickening boom. Then silence, quivering in the air like the skin of a drum.

I stumbled back and collapsed on to the platform. As I lay weak with shock, staring into blackness, the aurora burst into the sky, flooding the night with incandescence.

The cold seeped through my suit, chilling my body and bringing me to my senses. I dragged myself to my knees. After several attempts, I lowered myself over the edge of the trapdoor and started the climb down. My legs were trembling, and I clutched the rails so tightly that my hands hurt. Speed was impossible as a section of railing was missing. After passing the broken step – I gave silent thanks that I'd counted – I went as quickly as I dared.

As I neared the ground, I paused to look over my shoulder. In the feeble candlelight, I glimpsed a black heap lying crumpled in the corner. Pieces of broken railing were scattered across the floor. A sudden draught from the door caused the candles to flare, throwing moving shadows over the shape and making it writhe as if in agony. But he was dead. He had to be. No one could survive that fall. Yet, something was wrong. The figure was stirring. He began to rise. Dear God, he was still alive . . .

I jumped the last few steps and bolted for the door, feeling glass crunch beneath my feet. The risen figure leapt forward. He slammed the door shut, and I crashed into it, unable to stop in time. Dazed, I grappled with the handle, but he threw his arms round my body and held me in an iron grip so powerful that he lifted me off my feet. I struggled and kicked viciously at his shins, finding a strength I didn't know I possessed. He loosened his grip, but I couldn't shake him off. Panic overwhelmed me and, filling my lungs, I screamed in pure animal terror.

He relaxed his grip and wheeled me round to face him. But he towered over me, and my chances of fighting him off were slim. In desperation, I raised my fists and pummelled him about the head, sobbing, lacking the breath to scream.

He grabbed my wrists and pulled them away. 'Miss Stewart,' he cried. 'It is me, Thomas Hallengren.'

I stopped struggling and peered up at him, but it was impossible to see his face in the dark. He released his hold on my wrists and drew back his hood.

My voice caught in my throat. 'So it was you climbing the tower?'

He turned and looked behind him. And I saw then what I'd missed earlier – he'd been crouching over someone.

'The receptionist told me you were here. I came as quickly as I could. I arrived in time to see him fall.' He brought his face close to mine. 'It is over, Miss Stewart.'

I stared at the body. 'Who is it?' I said, in a whisper.

Hallengren picked up his torch and cast the beam on to the slumped figure.

The fall had twisted his body into an unnatural position. His legs were crossed as though, even in death, he had a need to relieve himself. One arm was trapped behind his back, the other stretched out, palm upwards, in an attitude of supplication. His shoulders were propped against the wall, his head lolling sideways at an obscene angle. Around him were pieces of wood and the glass shards from my torch, glinting like jewels in the uncertain light.

Hallengren moved the torch and caught the face in the beam. I stooped and looked into the staring eyes. Death had smoothed his features, but I recognised him instantly.

Blood was spreading across the uneven floor. I watched it gather in the grooves of the flagstones, realising too late that it was staining the soles of my boots.

CHAPTER 25

I was shaking violently.

In a second, Hallengren had his arms round me. I clutched at him, burying my face in his chest, feeling his warmth seep through my suit and into my body.

'You are in shock, Miss Stewart,' he murmured, rubbing my back. He lifted my chin gently. 'Can I leave you for a moment? I need to call my men.'

He helped me into the church, where I sat while he used his radio. He spoke softly, staring up at the altarpiece. The call finished, he sat down beside me and slipped an arm round my shoulders.

'Marcellus,' I said. 'But why?'

'There will be time for explanations later. But right now I need to take you away from here. My men will arrive in a few minutes.'

I leant against him, trying to dispel the image of Marcellus's staring eyes. A loud creaking made me jump: the front door was opening.

Engqvist entered with several uniformed men. They hurried up the nave, flashing their torches, their boots thudding on the wooden floor. Hallengren left me, and he and the men huddled round the altar like conspirators. The singsong of their Swedish voices echoed through the church.

He returned to the pew. 'Engqvist is taking over. It is a bit of a walk to my car. We need to go back to the road.' He took my hands in his. 'We will go to Kiruna first, then I will take you to the Excelsior.'

Kiruna. Of course, Hallengren would need a statement.

He helped me to my feet, but my legs buckled. He caught me, and half carried me outside where we hobbled down the path to his car. He settled me into the passenger seat and fastened the seatbelt as though I were a child.

As he started the engine, I turned to him, thinking of the questions I badly wanted to ask.

He caught the movement. 'It is a good half-hour to the police station, Miss Stewart. Try to get some sleep.'

I lay back and closed my eyes. But sleep was impossible.

'How are you feeling, Miss Stewart?'

We were entering Kiruna.

I sat up, and moved my head carefully, massaging away the stiffness in my neck. 'Bloody awful, to be honest.'

Hallengren stopped the vehicle outside the police station. I swung my legs out and stepped on to the frozen ground, grabbing at the car door so as not to slip. The weather had changed: leaden clouds were forming, and the wind from the north was ballooning them, like wet sheets. As we entered the building, snow was already falling.

At the front desk, Hallengren spoke in Swedish to the uniformed policeman, who leapt to attention. The clock on the wall behind him told me it was midnight.

We took the corridor to Hallengren's office. He swiped a keycard through the door's security system, and stepped back to let me enter.

The room was as I remembered it, except for the maps pinned to the noticeboard. I recognised the one on the left as the floor plan of the Ice Hotel. On the whiteboard on the adjacent wall, scribbled Swedish words were interconnected with lines. And there were names: Wilson Bibby, Harry Auchinleck, Marcellus Bibby. My own.

Hallengren motioned to the chairs. 'Please sit down, Miss Stewart. The duty policeman is bringing coffee.'

He strode over to the whiteboard, and added more words and lines with a black felt-tip. I watched, studying his profile. He wrote quickly and confidently, pausing once or twice to rub his chin.

There was a knock at the door. He called out in Swedish, but continued to write. The policeman from Reception entered with mugs and a pot of coffee. He arranged them on the table, then straightened and waited. Seeing no response from Hallengren, he left, throwing me a look of curiosity as he closed the door. I sat patiently, but the smell of coffee defeated me. I reached for the pot.

The movement made Hallengren turn.

He hurried over and took the pot from my hands. 'I do apologise, Miss Stewart.' He studied me for a moment, then produced a bottle of brandy and two glasses from the filing cabinet. Setting the glasses aside, he poured a shot into the mugs, and added coffee. 'I think you need some fortification after what you have been through tonight,' he said, with a tilt of the head.

I could wait no longer. 'Inspector, why did Marcellus try to kill me?'

Hallengren cradled his mug, an amused look on his face. 'This is your only question, Miss Stewart?'

'I've others, but it'll do for a start.'

'You are owed a full explanation, I think. And what I tell you will be in tomorrow's press release.' He perched on the edge of the table, leg dangling, as he'd done that first day. 'The final piece of the puzzle came to us this afternoon, shortly before we arrested Mr Vandenberg.'

'And Marcellus. You arrested him too.'

'We put out a warrant, but we could not find him.'

I ran a hand over my face. Dear God, if I'd known that, there was no way I'd have gone up that tower, with or without Liz. Anger simmered inside me. 'The receptionist at the Excelsior told Leo that Marcellus was already in custody.'

'He was mistaken.'

'Inspector, please will you tell me what this is all about.'

'We need to go back to the beginning. To well before Wilson's murder. It all hinges on Wilson's diary, as we'd thought.' He sipped from his mug. 'As you might expect, Wilson Bibby made a will. There was provision for his wife, but the bulk of his fortune was left to his only son, Marcellus.'

'Marcellus told you this?'

'We asked him about his father's plans for his inheritance, but he referred us to his lawyer. Mr Vandenberg arranged for a copy of the will to be faxed through. He also gave us an indication of the sum that Marcellus would inherit.'

'I can imagine,' I said, with feeling.

'I doubt it, Miss Stewart. Even we were surprised. It gave Marcellus the strongest possible motive for murder. And made him our prime suspect, *non plus ultra*. Now, this is where it becomes interesting,' he said, as though murders of billionaires by their sons were an everyday occurrence in Kiruna. 'We interrogated Aaron and Marcellus separately about the final diary page. We asked them what was on it. Their answers were identical, and predictable. Neither could remember, nor did they have a copy. We knew they were lying, thanks to your information.'

285

'Did you tell them how you came by this information?' I said in alarm.

'Of course not.' Hallengren smiled thinly. 'They were greatly surprised at the extent of my knowledge. However, with no firm evidence, we had no option but to release them.'

'And the breakthrough you said you made this afternoon?'

'It was quite by chance. The Stockholm police had recently been tipped off that Marcellus and Vandenberg were plotting something there. They made their own enquiries, then called me. I thought they might have uncovered evidence of the plot to murder Wilson. But it was something completely different.' He was silent for a moment. 'Marcellus and the lawyer were indeed hatching a plan. But it was to kidnap Wilson, not murder him.'

'*Kidnap* him?' I said, stunned. 'At the Ice Hotel?'

'In Stockholm. Their plan was well advanced. They knew what Wilson's movements would be and they contracted with someone to kidnap him. The tip-off I mentioned led to the arrest of the would-be kidnapper today.'

'What was the point of the kidnap? Ransom?'

Hallengren finished the coffee. 'I wondered about the motive but in the end it was the money. My Stockholm colleagues told the kidnapper that Wilson had been murdered and, not wanting to be accused of a murder he did not commit and for which he had no alibi, the man gave them everything: dates, times, and the proof that Marcellus and Vandenberg were in on it. Marcellus and Vandenberg's phone records link them to the kidnapper and the plot.'

'But Wilson wasn't kidnapped.'

'Unfortunately for him, he decided to take a last-minute holiday. Had he stayed in Stockholm, the plan would have gone ahead, and he would probably have been kidnapped and ransomed.'

'And still be alive.'

'The kidnapper told us that Marcellus, having seen the Excelsior, felt that snatching Wilson here was out of the question. In the end, I think he and Vandenberg abandoned the idea.'

'And they decided to murder him instead?'

Hallengren inclined his head. 'Much easier, do you not think?'

'I've no idea.' I rubbed my eyes. 'I've never planned a murder. Or a kidnap.'

'I should hope not, Miss Stewart,' he said, refilling the mugs. 'Once I knew about the failed kidnap attempt, I put out word to arrest them. We found Vandenberg at the Excelsior. When we presented him with the evidence, he admitted everything.'

'That he'd killed Wilson?' I said, astonished.

'Everything but that. He denied it strenuously. He said he was in Kiruna when Wilson was killed. He had gone there to coordinate a new kidnap plan with Marcellus. It was to take place when Wilson returned to Stockholm. But then Wilson died.'

'Do you believe him?'

Hallengren made a gesture of impatience. 'He was booked into a hotel in Kiruna. No one saw him come and go. It is a small hotel. However, I am convinced that Vandenberg is lying, and he and Marcellus killed Wilson. There is no hard evidence, so we will have to try for a confession. Vandenberg did admit the kidnap plot, so with a little pressure he may admit to murder.' A look of contempt crossed his face. 'He thought he could save his skin by giving us evidence that would implicate Marcellus.'

I took a wild guess. 'The contents of the final diary page.'

'Indeed, Miss Stewart. The final page was a memorandum by Wilson, countersigned by Vandenberg, to change his will.'

'Cutting Marcellus out?'

'In effect. Marcellus would still be provided for, but he would have to greatly curtail his lavish lifestyle.'

'Do you think Marcellus saw that page?'

'Vandenberg said he told him what was on it. It provides the motive for the kidnap.'

'So where was Wilson leaving his money? His schools' initiative?'

'He wanted that to continue after he died. But there was another beneficiary, an obscure working-men's charity in South America.'

I thought back to Mike's account of his girlfriend's family history. So Wilson had found a conscience at last. 'Was it in Venezuela?'

Hallengren raised his eyebrows in surprise. 'Maracaibo.' He looked amused. 'The things you know, Miss Stewart.'

I tried to get my head round it. 'So Wilson was to be kidnapped and ransomed before he could give away his money.'

'Once he had been ransomed, Vandenberg was going to launder the money by creating companies jointly owned by himself and Marcellus. When Marcellus learnt about the new will, he was not particularly worried as he would soon be getting millions from the ransom.'

'But when the kidnap plans fell through, he saw his inheritance going down the drain, so he and Aaron murdered Wilson. And with the final diary page removed, no one would know about the new will. The old will, leaving everything to Marcellus, would still be the one in effect.'

Hallengren nodded appreciatively. 'You should have been a detective, Miss Stewart.'

It all made sense. What had Aaron said about the copy of that last page? *It's in a safe place.* With Wilson dead, and Marcellus standing to gain a fortune under the old will, Aaron could still get his share by blackmailing him.

'Which of them do you think went into Wilson's room?' I said.

'My money is on Marcellus. His room was next to his father's. He could have slipped a drug into his father's food or drink, and pushed him on to the floor later that night. He would have expected everyone to be asleep between one and two a.m.'

Yes, Marcellus had had the opportunity. But would he really have killed his father just for money? 'What did Aaron say when you pressed him?'

'Vandenberg tells a different story. He says Marcellus claimed that he had not gone into his father's room until shortly before the police arrived. He saw his father was dead and immediately understood the consequences regarding his inheritance. He removed the key from Wilson's wrist and hurried to the Locker Room. In a panic, he tore out the last few pages with writing on them. The only one he needed to remove, of course, was that final page.'

'Marcellus did this after he'd seen his father was dead?'

'So Vandenberg claims, but I do not believe it. I think that Marcellus took the key and went to the Locker Room as soon as he had pushed his father on to the floor.'

'He took a hell of a risk.'

'There is always a risk,' Hallengren said, with a thoughtful nod, 'but Marcellus must have thought it was acceptable. He was in a nearby room. He could slip in and out of his father's quickly.'

'But wasn't Marcellus the one to alert you to the missing pages?'

'That was a whole day later after he had had time to do a bit of thinking. It was a good tactic. I suspect he hoped it would throw us off the scent.'

'Wouldn't it draw attention to the fact that Wilson might have been murdered?'

'Marcellus must have thought there would be no post-mortem. He stressed that Wilson had a heart condition. He even showed us the medication.'

'Yes, I saw Wilson use it on the plane.'

'Wilson's doctors advised us that his heart had a slight arrhythmia for which they had prescribed Coumarinose.'

'So if it hadn't been for the post-mortem, they would have pulled off the perfect murder,' I said, half to myself.

Hallengren laughed then, a rich deep sound. It was the first time I'd heard it.

'Believe me, Miss Stewart, there is no such thing. Marcellus was a bit too quick to tell us about his father's heart condition, and our suspicions were raised. The post-mortem put an end to the weak-heart theory.' He paused. 'There was something else, however, something one of my men remembered. Marcellus's name had been linked to an incident in the United States. A woman he had been seeing had been found dead of an overdose.'

'Marcia Vandenberg? The heiress?'

'We requested the file from the New York police, hoping we would learn something useful. A particular detail caught our attention – traces of a barbiturate in her body. Phenonal. The same barbiturate as in Wilson Bibby's bloodstream. The New York police concluded that the killer had first sedated Miss Vandenberg by drugging her drink, then injected her with a lethal dose of heroin. It had to be someone she knew well enough to let into her apartment and have a drink with. Their prime suspect was Marcellus Bibby.'

'But he wasn't convicted.'

'He had an alibi for that night. But I put little stock in alibis.'

'The same barbiturate?' I said doubtfully.

'And I put even less stock in coincidences, Miss Stewart.'

I played with the mug. 'I don't get it. She was Aaron Vandenberg's sister. Would Aaron be such a buddy to someone suspected of murdering his sister?'

'If it was also in his interests that his sister die. She was a stepsister, in point of fact, and he was her only surviving relative.

And she was very wealthy.' Hallengren looked at me thoughtfully. 'Perhaps the kidnap of Wilson Bibby was not the first – how shall I put it? – criminal enterprise the two were involved in.'

I rubbed my face hard, saying nothing.

'We became suspicious when Marcellus's story about not being outside the Locker Room did not agree with yours. He told us he spent the entire night in the Excelsior.'

'Why did you believe my story and not his?' I said, curious.

Hallengren looked surprised. 'Because you had no reason to lie and Marcellus did. I can usually tell when people are lying, and Marcellus struck me as a habitual liar from the moment I met him. He must have known he would be our prime suspect. Of course he would lie about going into the Locker Room. Admitting he was there would put him near the scene of the crime at the time of the crime. With no witnesses, there would be no one to challenge his version of events.'

'But there *was* a witness,' I said softly.

'He must have concluded that he had not been identified.' Hallengren's mouth tightened. 'It is just as well that he was not able to identify you. Otherwise, Miss Stewart, he would have killed you the same night.'

I gulped my coffee, my hands shaking.

'Marcellus told us that he had stayed drinking in the Excelsior after his father had retired for the night. His story was that he had drunk too much and could not face the cold, so decided to sleep in the Excelsior. We checked, of course. His bed in the Excelsior had been slept in, but that proved nothing. He could have disturbed the bedclothes. Or pushed his father out of bed, taken the diary pages, then gone to sleep in the Excelsior. We learnt that some time between one and two a.m. the Excelsior's Reception had been left unattended for about half an hour. Marcellus would

291

have seen the empty desk, and slipped out. The only people left in the lounge were guests who were blind drunk.'

'So there'd be no one who could credibly challenge his story.' I hesitated. 'But if he hadn't identified me, why did he try to kill me tonight?'

Hallengren poured from the bottle. 'Because he'd learnt that Harry was still alive when you found him,' he said, handing me a glass.

'But how would he know? And what does Harry's death have to do with it?'

'Marcellus would have overheard people in the Excelsior talking about Harry, and that you'd found him alive. I did, as soon as I arrived. It may have been speculation, but Marcellus must have assumed it was true. We believe that he killed Harry, and he tried to kill you because Harry had given you the name of his killer.'

'But if Harry had named him, I'd have told you, and Marcellus would have been arrested. Surely he'd know that.' I rolled the glass between my hands. 'It makes no sense.'

'Maybe not a name, then, but a clue. Although Marcellus should have known that we would need evidence beyond a whispered suggestion from a dying man before arresting someone for murder. But I believe that by then he was not thinking straight. When we interviewed him after Harry was killed, he was greatly altered. Who knows what his state of mind was? Not all killers are cold-blooded, Miss Stewart. He may have planned to kidnap his father, but I think he was a reluctant murderer.'

'You think he was pushed into it by Aaron?'

'It is possible.' Hallengren gulped the brandy. 'My theory is that Marcellus thought you would work things through and identify him as Harry's killer. He could not wait. He tried to kill you that same night in the Ice Hotel.'

I felt a sudden stab of fear. The black figure with the ice axe. So it had been Marcellus.

Hallengren spoke clinically, as though counting off items on a shopping list. 'Following you to the Ice Hotel gave him a great opportunity. After he saw you fall through the ice, he slipped away, assuming you would drown or die of hypothermia. But when he learnt you were still alive, he searched for another way. Falling to your death from the church tower would be seen as an accident.'

My head was spinning. 'Hold on, Inspector, can we back up a bit? Let's go back to Harry. Why did Marcellus kill him?'

'That is the part of the puzzle we cannot solve. We cannot find a motive.' He poured more brandy. 'But I am convinced it is linked to your and Harry's contradictory accounts of the night you spent in the Ice Hotel.'

I searched his face. 'You know, although Harry told you he was asleep the night Wilson was murdered, I did see him leave his room. You must believe me.'

'So why would he lie, Miss Stewart? What reason would he have?'

'I can't help you there,' I said sadly. 'But on the subject of motive, could Harry have passed Marcellus on his way from the Locker Room? Maybe Marcellus thought he would put two and two together later and name him as the killer.'

Hallengren brushed the suggestion aside. 'If Marcellus thought Harry had seen him, he would not have waited. He would have murdered him the same night.' He went over to the noticeboard and studied the plan of the Ice Hotel. 'But perhaps we have been coming at this from the wrong direction. Perhaps what you saw was something different. You say you re-entered the Ice Hotel by the front door?'

'Yes.'

'In the time it took you to reach your room, Marcellus could have run through the Locker Room into the Ice Hotel, taken Wilson's key and rolled him on to the floor. So maybe it was *Marcellus* you saw in your corridor, not Harry. Take a look at the floor plan.'

I walked round the table, swaying from the effects of the brandy. Hallengren traced the path Marcellus would have taken from the Locker Room. I saw immediately that, even if he'd been walking, he'd have reached his father's room well before I turned into the corridor.

That stiffening of the shoulders as I called goodnight. If it was Marcellus, it would explain why he hadn't turned round. But something wasn't right.

As if reading my thoughts, Hallengren said, 'Are you absolutely sure that you did not mistake the room?'

'Yes. The man I saw came out of Harry's room.' I stared at the map. 'Why would Marcellus be coming out of room fifteen?'

'Because he had just murdered his father.'

'His father was in room *seventeen*,' I said, in exasperation. 'Marcellus, or whoever, came out of room *fifteen*.'

'The person you saw came out of room fifteen?' Hallengren frowned. 'Are you certain?'

'That's why I told you I thought it was Harry. Number fifteen was Harry's room.'

He was staring blankly.

I ran my finger over the last three rooms in the corridor. 'Look, Wilson Bibby in room seventeen, me in room sixteen, and Harry in room fifteen.'

'What did Harry's room look like?' he said softly, gazing at the map.

'It had a statue of Pan. Harry was afraid he wouldn't be able to sleep with it grinning at him. He said—' I stopped, remembering his remark about the erection.

Hallengren muttered something in Swedish. He snatched up a folder from the desk and leafed through it rapidly. His expression changed.

He thrust out a sheet of paper. 'The receptionist gave me this on the morning Wilson's body was discovered. It was printed from the hotel computer as I waited.'

It was a list of names and room numbers. I scanned it, searching for my name and Harry's.

There was an edge to his voice. 'It shows without a shadow of doubt that Wilson Bibby was in room fifteen, and Harry Auchinleck in room seventeen.'

I stared as though seeing him for the first time. 'But that's wrong,' I said slowly.

'How were you told which room you would be in?'

'It was on Monday. Leo explained everything on the bus. And he posted a list of names and room numbers on the noticeboard in the foyer.'

Hallengren grabbed the phone. A minute later, the duty policeman entered. Hallengren spoke briefly, showing him the sheet, and the man left running.

'I have sent for the receptionist who was on duty on Monday. Perhaps now we will get to the bottom of this mystery.' He poured more brandy, watching me. His expression was composed, almost sympathetic. 'I would drink this, Miss Stewart. You may be glad of it by the time we have finished.'

CHAPTER 26

Hallengren strode across to the whiteboard, and stood thoughtfully for a moment. Then his pen moved quickly over the surface. My mind was in a whirl but, after the quantity of brandy I'd drunk, I was in no condition to work anything out. I sat down and settled back to wait.

A while later, there was a knock at the door and the duty policeman entered with the receptionist. I recognised the man with the round glasses who'd been on the Excelsior desk all week. He was agitated, and licked his lips repeatedly. I felt sorry for him. Hallengren had a talent for making even innocent people nervous.

'Please sit down, Mr Karlsson,' Hallengren said, motioning to a chair.

The man placed a folder on the table, and straightened it with little taps of the hand.

'Mr Karlsson,' Hallengren said, keeping his tone friendly, 'I need you to explain something that is puzzling me. How are rooms allocated in the Excelsior and the Ice Hotel?'

The man looked bewildered, glancing from Hallengren to me and back again. 'There is no secret to it. Guests are allocated the same number in both hotels. It makes it easy for them to remember.'

Hallengren smiled encouragingly. 'And how are guests notified of their number?'

'When they check in, we give them their key.' Karlsson lifted a finger, as though to command our attention. 'For tours, we vary the procedure. Rather than have them queue at Reception, we leave the key in their door and post a list on the noticeboard.'

'In the foyer?'

'Yes.'

'What happens to that list?'

'It's taken down the following day and kept until the end of the week. Then I give it to the tour guide as a record of who stayed in which room. Some tours issue commemorative certificates.'

'You still have the list?'

'I was asked to bring it,' the man said defensively. He drew a sheet from his folder and handed it to Hallengren.

Hallengren scanned it, his face expressionless. 'Mr Karlsson, when we were called to the Excelsior after the discovery of Wilson Bibby's body, the manager gave me a list of names and room numbers of the Ice Hotel's occupants.' He held out the computer printout from his own file. 'As you can see, it does not quite match the list you posted in the foyer.'

Karlsson took the sheet and stared at it, his hands trembling. There was a faint sheen on his forehead. 'I can't see—'

'Rooms fifteen and seventeen,' Hallengren said patiently.

There was a stir of recognition in the man's eyes. 'I remember now,' he said, relief in his voice. 'Originally, we assigned room seventeen to Mr Bibby – Mr Wilson Bibby – and room fifteen to Professor Auchinleck. But later that day—'

'Which day?' Hallengren interrupted.

'Monday, Inspector, the day the tour party arrived.'

Hallengren nodded to him to proceed.

'On Monday afternoon, Mr Wilson Bibby asked to have his room changed. He explained he was a light sleeper. His room at the Excelsior was above the lounge and he was afraid the noise would keep him awake. So I put him in the room round the corridor, room fifteen, which is the quietest.' He paused, blinking rapidly. 'Room fifteen was Professor Auchinleck's. I saw the professor later that afternoon and asked if he objected to a room change. He seemed willing to oblige – he didn't even ask who the guest was. He said he was a sound sleeper, and didn't mind which room he had. I explained then, as I'd explained to Mr Bibby, that this meant the rooms in the Ice Hotel would also be swapped. So Professor Auchinleck would be in room seventeen in both hotels, and Mr Bibby in room fifteen.'

The pieces were falling into place. I glanced at Hallengren, but his attention was on Karlsson.

The man took our silence as a signal to continue. 'I instructed my staff to move the luggage. Fortunately, neither guest had unpacked. And then I logged the change on the computer.'

'Which is why it showed on the printout,' Hallengren said.

'Exactly.' Karlsson removed his glasses and polished them with a handkerchief.

'So how do you explain the discrepancy between the printout and the list in the foyer, Mr Karlsson?'

The smile vanished. He stared at Hallengren. 'The list?' he stammered.

'It seems that you did not make the same change on the noticeboard.'

Karlsson looked from Hallengren to me, then back to Hallengren, a stricken expression on his face. 'I must confess that I did not. But there was no need, because both Professor Auchinleck and Mr Bibby knew where they would be sleeping.'

He smiled apologetically. 'They will get the wrong certificates from Mr Tullis, of course . . .'

I looked away. The only certificates they would be getting now were from the coroner.

Hallengren took the sheets. 'I will have to retain these for my records.'

'Of course. I understand.' Sweat was trickling into the man's eyes. 'May I go now?'

'Thank you, Mr Karlsson. You have been most helpful.'

He picked up the folder and almost ran from the room.

Hallengren looked amused. 'So we have been at cross-purposes, Miss Stewart. Is that the correct phrase — cross-purposes?'

'It's the correct phrase,' I replied automatically. My mind was in turmoil. The rooms had been swapped. So what did it mean?

He picked up the bottle. 'Let us examine the facts. Shortly after you saw Marcellus Bibby outside the Locker Room, you saw a man come out of room fifteen. Correct?'

'Yes.'

'You are certain it was room fifteen? Yes?'

'Yes.'

'And you assumed the man was Harry, thinking it was his room.'

'Yes.'

'You called out to him but he did not reply.'

'But I know he heard,' I said emphatically. 'He paused, then carried on walking. And he didn't turn round.'

'Why did you think it was Harry, apart from believing that he came out of Harry's room?'

'He was a big man, Harry's build, and he wore a blue snow-suit. Harry always wore blue.'

Hallengren studied me. 'If it had been Harry, would he have spoken to you?'

'Of course,' I said sadly. 'Harry wasn't someone who ignored people. He'd probably have suggested we go for a drink. It puzzled me at the time, but I said nothing to him, especially after your request I keep quiet.'

'It would explain why your story and his were inconsistent. Harry was in room seventeen, fast asleep, just as he claimed later. And if the man you saw was Marcellus, who had just pushed his drugged father on to the floor, of course he would not turn round when he heard you call Harry's name.'

I thought back to the day Wilson's corpse had been discovered. 'There was such a crowd outside the room that I couldn't see the number plaque. When I saw Wilson's body, I just assumed it was room seventeen.'

'Could you have seen the statue of Pan from where you were?'

I shook my head.

'Marcellus would have known about the room swap. His father would have told him. But Harry did not tell you or your friends. Why do you think that was?'

'It wouldn't have been important.' I played with my glass. 'Harry was always travelling and living in hotels.'

'After Bibby's death, his rooms in both the Excelsior and the Ice Hotel were sealed.' Hallengren scrutinised the Excelsior's floor plans pinned up next to the Ice Hotel's. 'Room fifteen in the Excelsior is round the corner from your room, so you could not have seen the tapes. And you would not have heard much from room seventeen because it is across the corridor. There would be nothing in the Excelsior to make you suspect there had been a swap.'

The brandy was doing its work. 'So Marcellus kills Wilson, and knows I see someone leave his father's room,' I said, my words slightly slurred. 'He hears me call Harry's name and therefore he knows he hasn't been identified. So . . . why kill Harry?'

'Why would he *want* to kill Harry?' Hallengren studied the whiteboard, frowning. His expression changed. 'The answer has nothing to do with the discrepancy between your story and Harry's. That has now been explained. No, it has to do with the discrepancy between your story and Marcellus's.' He looked directly at me. 'Miss Stewart, after we discovered that Wilson Bibby's death was not accidental, I sent Engqvist to re-interview you, Harry and Marcellus. We had to understand why there were differences in your accounts.'

'When was this?'

'Friday afternoon – the afternoon that Harry was murdered.'

'But I wasn't interviewed,' I said slowly.

'No one could find you. For that matter, no one could find Harry. But Marcellus *was* interviewed.' Hallengren searched through his papers, and opened a buff-coloured folder. 'We interviewed Marcellus at three p.m. in the hotel manager's office, an hour and a half before Harry was murdered. He did not change his story. He persisted in his claim that he did not leave the Excelsior the night his father was killed.' He glanced up. 'Unfortunately, the hotel manager came into the office as Marcellus was leaving. Before Engqvist could stop him, he announced that he had been unable to find Professor Auchinleck. Marcellus would have heard him.'

'So he assumed Harry was also going to be questioned?' I said, my mind racing.

'Yes, but listen carefully. When we questioned Marcellus, we interrogated him hard about timing and his precise movements. And, for the first time, we told him that a witness was prepared to make a statement putting him outside the Locker Room at the time of his father's death.' He lifted a hand to ward off my protest. 'Do not be alarmed – Engqvist was careful not to say who. It was a tactic that might have forced a confession. It did not. If it had, we would have arrested him there and then. But my point is this: if Marcellus thought that Harry was also about to be questioned, he might have jumped to the conclusion that Harry was the witness.'

'He thought Harry had been called in to make the statement?'

'To make it, and to sign it. Even if he had any doubts, he could not take the risk. He had to find Harry and kill him before he was questioned.'

I stared at Hallengren, finally understanding. 'It should have been me who was killed. I was the one who saw Marcellus.'

'You must not think like that, Miss Stewart,' he said firmly. 'The fault was ours.' He rubbed his face. 'There was a crowd in the foyer that afternoon. Harry could have slipped past the receptionist. Marcellus must have seen him. He fetched an ice axe, saw Harry enter the chapel, followed him and killed him. It explains the great risk he took in doing this in broad daylight. He had no choice. He had to move quickly.'

So the large, bloody snow-suit abandoned in the chapel was Marcellus's. He would have slipped back into the Excelsior in his own clothes and mingled with the crowd.

'And this connection that Marcellus made? That Harry was the witness?' I said angrily. 'That didn't make him an immediate suspect in Harry's murder? You've realised it only now? Why didn't you arrest him straight after Harry was killed?'

Hallengren spoke calmly. 'We interviewed everyone in connection with Harry's murder, Marcellus included. We questioned him for hours. He told us that after he had left the manager's office he went to Kiruna. We tried to break him but he stuck to his statement.'

I glared. 'And you believed it?'

'There was no evidence either to corroborate or refute his story.'

Of course Hallengren couldn't make an arrest without hard evidence. My anger evaporated. 'I'm sorry I shouted at you, Inspector.' I pressed my fingertips into my eyes. 'Let me get this straight, then. Even knowing about the room swap, you've still no real evidence that it was Marcellus who came out of that room, and not Harry.'

'That is correct. But I believe it was Marcellus. And he had just killed his father.' Hallengren reached for the brandy. 'Anyway, neither you nor Harry fits the profile of a murderer.'

I gasped. 'You suspected us?'

He looked surprised. 'At the outset, everyone is under suspicion. Your evidence put you and Harry close to the scene of the crime at the time of Bibby's death. I would be a fool not to consider you suspects.'

And Hallengren was no fool. 'So when did you decide we weren't?' I said.

'With Harry, it was when he was murdered. But we discounted him early on. Harry was not a killer.'

'And me?' I said, after a pause.

'You ceased to be a suspect when you fell into the river. You nearly died, Miss Stewart. No one would endanger their life like that just to throw the police off the scent.'

'That was yesterday. What about earlier in the week?'

He smiled. 'We could not find a motive for you to kill Wilson Bibby.'

'Did you think I could have killed Harry?' I said warily.

'You might have had time before you met Miss Hallam. However . . .' his gaze travelled slowly down my body '. . . I doubt you have the strength. Whoever killed Harry was strong. We could tell that from the wounds on his body.'

I pictured the scene in the chapel: Harry raising his arms, trying desperately to ward off his attacker, and Marcellus, bringing the ice axe down again and again.

Hallengren's voice broke into my thoughts. 'After you told me about the axeman who chased you out of the Ice Hotel, I had Engqvist tail you. He followed you and Miss Hallam to Kiruna.'

'That was Engqvist?' I said, astonished.

'You saw him?'

'I saw someone who I thought was following us,' I said quickly, not wanting to get the man into trouble, 'but it turned out to be another tourist.'

'Engqvist should have been well disguised,' Hallengren said, his voice hard. 'He lost you in the evening in the crowd going to the Ice Theatre. He called me straight away. We had to find you quickly. We did not have Marcellus in custody. You might have been his next victim. We questioned Karlsson, who remembered that you had gone to the church.'

'So how did Marcellus discover where I was?'

'That we will never know, Miss Stewart. All we have managed to learn of his movements that day is that he had an appointment at the coroner's office. He must have returned to the Excelsior unseen. Perhaps he saw you leave the hotel and followed you.'

I felt a chill in the room. 'The church tower would have been ideal. An accident. Like falling through the ice.'

'Marcellus must have left just before we reached the Excelsior. I sent Engqvist to search the hotel in case he was there, while I hurried to the church. The rest you know.' Hallengren leant forward, his eyes blazing. 'And now there is something *I* would like to know.'

The anger in his voice took me by surprise.

'What in the name of God were you doing up that tower?' he said. 'I specifically warned you against being alone at any time. Were you out of your mind?'

'I wanted to see the aurora,' I said miserably.

'The aurora? When there was a killer on the loose?'

I chewed my thumb. 'I thought the killer was behind bars. Leo told us about the arrests. Both of them, Aaron and Marcellus.'

Hallengren ran a hand over his head, staring at the ceiling.

'So what happens next?' I said in a small voice.

'Aaron Vandenberg will stand trial for conspiracy to kidnap. The evidence is clear cut.'

'And the murders?'

'Unless we can persuade Vandenberg to admit to murder, or to being an accomplice to murder, the case will remain open. There is not the evidence to bring anyone to trial. Vandenberg's likely course of action will be to pin the blame on his dead friend, Marcellus.'

'And that's it?' I let out a breath. 'That's the end?'

Hallengren smiled. 'Most people imagine that murder cases are solved beyond a shadow of doubt, but that rarely happens. Real murder cases are not like those in films or murder-mystery novels. There is always doubt unless you get a confession. And even then people confess to murders they did not commit. So perhaps it was the hotel killer from the Maximilian. Or Harry who killed Wilson. Or someone else.' He finished the brandy. 'Apart from greed, revenge is the strongest motive for murder. But there was no one with revenge as a possible motive. What will appear in my report is that, on the balance of probabilities, the killer of Wilson Bibby and Harry Auchinleck was Marcellus Bibby, with Aaron Vandenberg as accomplice.' He was studying me with an expression of mild irony. 'But even if we had the evidence, we cannot prosecute the dead.'

'I suppose not.'

He turned the glass in his hand. 'You have had some terrible experiences, Miss Stewart, the sort of experiences no one should have in a lifetime, let alone in the space of a week.'

I looked away.

He cupped my chin, turning my head to face him. 'I see the mark of the survivor in your eyes. You will go through bad times in the next few months, but they will not last for ever. You will come out on the other side stronger than you are now.'

I gazed into the deep blue of his irises, feeling the warmth of his hand against my skin.

He released me slowly. 'Now that my investigations are over, I will have your passports with Mr Tullis first thing tomorrow.'

'Well, Liz, for one, will be eternally grateful.'

'Miss Hallam?'

'She's had a particularly bad time of it.' I smiled ruefully. 'The idea behind this holiday was that she'd have some kind of respite from her children. Go back refreshed, that sort of thing.'

He raised an eyebrow. 'I hope it will not deter her from visiting Sweden again.'

I thought of Liz lighting up greedily, her hands shaking. She might visit Sweden again, but she wouldn't be coming back to Lapland.

He was smiling. 'And what about you?'

'I never did try cross-country skiing,' I said, avoiding the question. 'And now I've run out of time.'

'You are definitely leaving tomorrow?'

'Our flight's at midday.'

I thought I saw disappointment in his eyes, but it was probably wishful thinking on my part.

'Well, Miss Stewart, I must arrange to have you taken back to your hotel.'

He stood up briskly. I staggered to my feet.

'Tomorrow I fly to Malmö,' he said. 'A case in Lund requires my attention. We will not meet again.' He held out his hand, smiling. 'Goodbye, Miss Stewart.'

'Maggie,' I said, slipping my hand into his. 'My name is Maggie.'

There was an expression in his eyes that I hadn't seen before. 'Maggie,' he said softly. He slid an arm round my waist and drew me towards him.

CHAPTER 27

Liz's eyes were wide. 'No! Really? You slept with him?'

It was lunchtime and we were flying home. The tiny plane, still climbing, banked suddenly towards Kiruna. I craned my head and peered out of the window, catching a last glimpse of the Ice Hotel.

We'd said our goodbyes at the airport. Robyn and Jim were flying with us. Jane was travelling on a later plane, intending to stay in Stockholm to do some research for her article. We exchanged contact details and I made her promise to send me a copy of her travel feature. Jonas and Olof were with her, Olof holding her bag. I lifted my gaze to Jonas's and smiled nervously. He smiled back, an expression of understanding in his eyes.

Leo was the last to say goodbye. 'Keep in touch, Maggie.' He ruffled his hair. 'Let me know how you're doing.'

'You too. Another group coming today?'

'The last of the season. Life goes on.' He grinned. 'And so do tours to the Ice Hotel.'

And now we were flying south on a great circle to Stockholm. Mike was in the window seat, snoring like a warthog, sleeping off the after-effects of a post-theatre drinking bout with the Danes.

'Come on, then,' Liz was saying across the aisle. 'This isn't the time to daydream. Tell me about Hallengren.'

I kept my voice low, trying to sound matter-of-fact. 'We spent the night at his apartment. He drove me back to the hotel this morning.'

'Well? Oh, don't keep me in suspense, Mags. What was he like? I've been fantasising about him all week.'

'What can I say? It was the best sex I've ever had.'

It was true. Thomas Hallengren had been spectacular in bed.

He drove me to an apartment block on the other side of Kiruna. Neither of us spoke as we took the lift to the top floor.

The front door to his apartment opened directly on to a spacious, open-plan room painted in muted shades of green. The light was still on. Cream leather armchairs were arranged in front of a low glass-topped table, which was covered with newspapers and skiing magazines. At the far end, half a dozen chairs stood untidily round a dining table, the remains of a meal abandoned on the striped cloth.

I was on edge, conscious I'd drunk too much brandy. Hallengren was watching me in silence. He took my hand and led me into the bedroom. At first, I could distinguish only the double bed against the wall, then dark shapes resolved themselves into a wardrobe, a chest of drawers and a blanket box. He switched on the light, and immediately pressed a button that dimmed it.

I felt a gentle touch on my arm. Hallengren unzipped my snow-suit and sat me on the bed. He slipped off my boots, while I struggled awkwardly to shake my arms out of the suit. He sat back on his heels and smiled up at me, raising an eyebrow questioningly. In that instant, my nervousness evaporated. I leant forward and, clutching at his snow-suit, pulled him towards me. We kissed insistently, hungry for the taste and smell of each other.

He disentangled himself and stripped off quickly. We removed the rest of my clothes, doing it in the wrong order and getting in each other's way. He ran his hands lightly down my arms, and lifted my fingers to his mouth. Then somehow we were in bed, entangled in the sheets, grabbing at one another. He brought me to near-climax and away again so many times that I thought I was going to faint. Finally, he positioned his body over mine and entered me, waiting until he'd brought me to a shuddering orgasm before reaching his own. As the throbbing lessened, I lay back, panting and sweating like a marathon runner.

We made love more times that night than I would have thought possible. Towards the end, he was rougher, pinning my wrists, thrusting quickly, watching my reactions and timing his movements so that when we climaxed it was nearly simultaneously. He cried out and collapsed on to me, rolling away with a groan. Smiling sleepily, he reached over to trace the outline of my mouth. Then he dragged the damp sheets over our bodies and we slept, exhausted, his face buried in my hair.

In the early morning, he drove me to the hotel. The wind had dropped. A feeble sun was rising, its rays filtering through the trees, stippling yesterday's snow.

He stopped the car in front of the Excelsior. 'Will we see you here again, Miss Stewart?' he murmured. He drew back my hood and pushed his fingers through my hair.

I turned away, unable to look into his eyes. We both knew the answer.

Liz's words dragged me back to the present.

'You can call me old-fashioned, Mags, but I thought it wasn't the done thing for police to sleep with their suspects,' she said, resentment in her voice.

'I didn't sleep with him until afterwards. And I wasn't a suspect.'

'Oh, don't give me that. He could lose his job, you know, plying you with drink like that.'

'He didn't ply me.' I shifted in the seat. 'You can be so holier-than-though sometimes, Liz.'

'And after he got you drunk, he seduced you. But, then, I suppose you did say you only wanted one-night stands from now on.'

'It wasn't like that,' I said, remembering the touch of his hand on my cheek.

'You know, I still can't get over what you just told me about Marcellus and Aaron. It really is amazing.' She grew thoughtful. 'You were right about Marcellus being the killer, though.'

'You think that gives me any satisfaction?'

'I suspected something had happened when Leo returned our passports. There wasn't a lot he could tell us. I expect it'll be in today's papers.'

The stewardess was handing out the coffee.

'And that hell you went through in the tower,' Liz continued. 'If I hadn't been called away, it would never have happened. You've no idea how that makes me feel.'

'Hasn't it occurred to you we might both be dead?'

'You really can't make me feel any worse than I do now.'

'I'm sorry, it wasn't meant to come out like that. By the way, I've been meaning to ask. How is Lucy?'

Liz sipped the coffee slowly. She grimaced, then set down the cup. 'It was a false alarm. Too much ice cream. That's Lucy.'

Mike shifted in his sleep, and the snoring stopped.

But Liz couldn't leave it. 'What I still can't get over is that you returned to the Ice Hotel that night. We thought you'd gone to see the aurora.' She played with her hands. 'You've been keeping a lot from us, you know.'

I said nothing. She was right. I hadn't taken her into my confidence. Or Mike.

'You do realise you could have died,' she went on.

I leant back. None of it mattered now. 'It's over, Liz.'

'Yes, you can give that brain of yours a rest,' she said gently. 'It's time to move on.'

I remembered Hallengren's words about grief turning to guilt. 'Harry's dead, Liz. That's not something I can forget.'

'Nor I.' She looked straight ahead. 'But he would want us to get on with our lives, wouldn't he?'

We hit turbulence. My cup flew off the table and on to Mike's lap.

He sat up. 'Jesus, Mary and Joseph.'

'Good sleep, Mike?' I said into his ear.

His fingers flew to his temples. 'For the love o' God, will you turn down the volume?' He stared in dismay at the wetness spreading across his crotch. 'What in the name of—?'

'You missed the show,' Liz said. She raised her voice so the whole plane could hear. 'While you were snoring, Mags was telling us about her night of passion with that sexy Swedish detective.'

The Ellises, sitting in front of Liz, turned in my direction. Robyn glared. Jim, sitting so Robyn couldn't see his face, smirked and gave a slow wink.

The captain's voice crackled through, announcing our descent into Stockholm. I fastened my seatbelt, thinking of the last time we'd been there. Had it really only been a week?

Liz was right: it was time to move on. Harry would want us to get on with our lives. So why, then, did I have a feeling in my waters that there was unfinished business?

CHAPTER 28

'And that's the whole story,' I said, chewing my thumbnail. 'We flew back to Scotland.'

It was a while before Dr Langley spoke. 'What happened on your return?'

'We buried Harry.'

'How did that feel?'

'We laid him to rest in Balgay Cemetery. The place was packed.'

'That's not what I asked.'

What could I tell her? It had felt more like a comedy than a funeral.

We'd stood at the graveside listening to the minister, the rain gusting and lashing at us as it's supposed to do at funerals. The wind snatched up Liz's hat and nearly took it away. As she grabbed it, her umbrella turned inside out. Mike caught my eye, trying not to laugh. Then I saw the young man, one of Harry's old boyfriends, standing so close to the grave I thought he'd fall in. He was crying openly, not caring who saw him, lips parted and nose running into his mouth. The minister spoke quietly to him, but the young man just gazed at him uncomprehending. People were moving away when something happened that only I wit-nessed: the minister, believing no one was watching, turned away surreptitiously and pulled a half-bottle from his cassock. He took a good long swallow, then belched softly before wiping his mouth on his sleeve. Despite my grief, I had to smile. Harry would have approved.

'Was it a comfort having Liz and Mike there?' Dr Langley said.

'I suppose so.'

'You know, Maggie, I no longer attend funerals. I can't cope with the finality.' She made an arch with her fingers. 'Harry's was nine months ago. What is your last memory of it?'

I was back at the Boatman's Inn, its dark spaces too cramped for the crowd of people paying their respects. The dean of Harry's faculty, a waspish woman with permed grey hair, was speaking warmly of Harry's contribution to teaching and to his chosen field of research.

'My last memory?' I said. 'Seeing his students, thinking how gratified Harry would have been to know they were there.'

But that was a lie. My last memory was the drive along Glamis Road past the cemetery. I'd glanced out of the window and caught a last glimpse of the gravediggers. They were finishing their cigarettes, throwing their shovels into the back of a van. Behind them was a neat mound of wet, black earth, gleaming, like coal, on the grass.

'I had no idea how terrible it was,' Dr Langley was saying.

'The funeral?'

'The Ice Hotel.' Her voice softened. 'And after you buried Harry? What then?'

'We went back to work, Liz and I to Bayne's and Mike to his IT company. I see less of him now because he's always in Stockholm. Mane Drew's computers there keep falling over. It's really Liz who's kept up with him.' I played with my hands. 'She's been my rock. It was awful going back to work. I couldn't have done it without her.'

'How did your colleagues react?'

I shrugged. 'There'd been all this media coverage about Wilson, and then Harry. Our names weren't in the papers, but everyone knew where we'd been and they put two and two together. We told them nothing, but it was weeks before they stopped pestering us.' I paused. 'That was the problem. The Ice Hotel was constantly being pushed into my face. I couldn't go to a meeting without hearing the whispers as I came into the room. Or as I left it.'

'And your line manager?'

'To begin with, Andrew was very understanding. A month after the funeral, he called me in. He was holding a report I'd prepared. He said the figures weren't correct and I'd have to redo them. It was the second time since we'd come back that he'd pulled me up over my work. I'd never made mistakes before.'

'But he knew what had happened to you?' Dr Langley said, frowning.

'I told him in the end. He was pretty stunned. He asked me whether I was seeing anyone, and I said, no, I'm between boy-friends. He said, "I meant a doctor or a counsellor." I became angry. I told him I could deal with it myself, it was grief, nothing more, I just needed time.' I glanced up. 'I think he was embarrassed by the whole thing.'

'And how have Liz and Mike coped?'

'Liz gets tearful whenever we talk about Harry. She's lucky, though, she has a life with her children. She told me recently it keeps her from brooding.' I managed a tired smile. 'I suspect it's bravado. She's changed, although she won't admit it. She smokes openly now, more than I do, even though she's always singing me an aria about the evils of tobacco.'

'And Mike?' Dr Langley said softly.

'He's managed best of all,' I said, with resentment. 'Do you think it's a man thing?'

315

'Do you?'

'I think it's a Mike thing.'

'Why do you say that? He seemed to care about Harry.'

I ran my hands through my hair. 'I don't know what it is about Mike. I can't understand the way he behaves towards me.'

'Give me an example.'

'A few weeks ago, I went to his flat for lunch. Liz and the twins were at her parents, so it was just me. Mike was cooking Thai chicken and coconut rice, one of Harry's favourites and the kitchen smelt of lemon grass. I'd had the dream the night before. I'd never told anyone about it except Liz, but I described it to him. He just gazed at me as though I was reading the telephone directory . . . He took my hands and leant in close, and I thought, Hello, where's this leading? Then he suddenly sat back and demanded to know how much I'd had to drink.'

'Had you been drinking?'

'I'd had a couple of glasses before lunch. Anyway, he dragged me to the bathroom. He stood me in front of the mirror and asked me what I saw.' My mouth twisted into a sneer. 'His Irish accent's always more pronounced when he's angry.'

'And what did you see, Maggie?'

'I saw what you're seeing now,' I said brutally.

'What's his bathroom like? I'm assuming this wasn't your first time there.'

'I'd been to his flat before.' I picked at my cuticles. 'Large mirror, white tiles. Incredibly clean.'

'And the bath?'

I lifted my head. 'Sunken, like a swimming pool.'

'And are Liz and Mike an item now?'

'It's an on–off thing. I thought Mike just wanted to get into her knickers, but I was wrong. He seemed to want a meaningful relationship – God, how I hate that phrase – but now he's blowing hot and cold, and it's Liz who's hoping it'll become serious.'

Dr Langley placed her hands together. 'This session is about getting to the truth,' she said, choosing her words carefully. 'We both know you've been bottling something up, something you either can't admit to yourself, or won't admit to me.'

I shifted in my seat. I'd gone this far so there was no point in not going the rest of the way. 'Marcellus didn't kill Harry,' I said emphatically.

I'd expected a look of surprise, but what I saw was understanding. For the first time, I dared hope that salvation might be possible.

'And you want to find out who did,' she said.

I took a deep breath. 'I owe it to Harry.'

'Let me get this straight. It's because you want to see justice done for him?'

'And for the others, too. I feel I have a responsibility towards the dead.'

'All right. Tell me why you're sure Marcellus wasn't the killer. It seems a cut-and-dried case.'

I looked at her helplessly. 'I just don't see him as a killer. Yes, I know he was planning to kidnap his father, but I saw how the two of them behaved together.'

'Very well then, but what about Marcellus killing Harry?'

'If Marcellus didn't kill Wilson, it follows he didn't kill Harry.' I frowned. 'I keep thinking of the way Harry was murdered. Marcellus was built like a Sherman tank. He wouldn't have used an ice axe. He'd have slipped up behind him and snapped his neck like a twig.'

Dr Langley fingered her letter-opener. 'Can you remember when you came to this conclusion?'

'I saw a film on television about a group of commandos. One of them had Marcellus's height and build – he looked just like him from the back. He crept up behind an enemy soldier and broke his neck. He was fast and he was silent. He slipped back into the shadows before the soldier had even hit the ground. The others had their backs turned and didn't know anything had happened until they heard the man fall.' I stared at the ceiling. 'It was the strangest thing. The minute I saw it, I realised I'd known all along that Marcellus couldn't have been Harry's killer. It was as if I'd woken from a deep sleep.'

'And you began to have the dream at about that time.' It was a statement.

I looked at her in surprise.

'Remember what I said earlier, Maggie? The thing that's lurking under the water, yet never revealing itself, is something you want to discover.' She spoke slowly, emphasising the words. 'I now know what your dream signifies. What you want to discover is the identity of the killer.'

'Then why don't I see a body in the bath?'

She smiled gently. 'You don't yet know who the killer is.'

'And the smell of river water?' I said, looking at my hands.

'You fell into the river and nearly drowned. Your sleeping mind is associating a personally traumatic experience with the deaths at the Ice Hotel.'

I lifted my head. 'So where do we go from here?'

She rose and opened the window, letting in the faint early-evening sounds: the traffic, people shouting. She settled herself behind the desk. 'I'd like you to tell me what you really think happened. It doesn't matter how far-fetched or illogical it sounds.'

'I don't know if I can,' I said in a small voice.

'You've been thinking about it these past few months. All I'm asking you to do is to think out loud. Remember that I'm less interested in catching a killer, and more interested in helping you. What you say will stay within these four walls.' She leant forward. 'Tell me who you think killed Wilson and Harry.'

After a long silence, I whispered, 'I don't need to tell you. You know who it is.'

'The white tiles and the sunken bath. You saw those in his bathroom. They're always in the dream. It's Mike you're expecting to see in the bath, Maggie,' she added quietly.

I put my hands under my knees, not wanting her to see them shaking.

'Your subconscious is telling you it's Mike. But does the conscious you really think he's the killer?' When I said nothing, she continued, 'From what you say, Mike hadn't disguised his hatred of Wilson Bibby. But could he have done it? Did he have the opportunity?'

I gazed at her without blinking. 'He could have spiked Wilson's food or drink that evening, then pushed him out of bed later.'

'Would he have known about the room swap?'

'Harry could have told him, or he could have overheard Harry's conversation with the receptionist.'

'And the snowmobiles? You said you didn't think that was an accident.'

'Mike had been standing next to them when they fell. He had the opportunity to loosen the brakes.' I ticked off the possibilities on my fingers. 'He'd been back from the husky trip well in time to murder Harry. The suit in the chapel was extra-large, Mike's size. It was Mike who suspected that Harry had whispered his killer's name to me. And it was Mike, not Jonas, who sat watching me at the rehearsal.' I glared at her triumphantly.

'Could he have followed you to the Ice Hotel that night?'

'From the lounge, you can see people going into the Activities Room. He could have grabbed a suit and followed me out.'

'And when you and Liz went into that town? . . . Kiruna?'

'Mike hadn't come with us but he could have taken the next bus in. He might have been the figure I'd seen tailing us, waiting for an opportunity to kill me, or Liz, or both of us.'

'Wasn't that the policeman?'

'A trained detective would know how to follow someone without being seen.'

'Wouldn't he have seen Mike following you, and apprehended him?'

I felt as though I'd been slapped in the face. 'You don't believe me,' I said, my voice quivering.

'Maggie, please understand that I'm just working this through. It's not what *I* believe, but what *you* believe. I'm trying to understand your thought processes.'

I nodded. 'All right, Engqvist might have seen Mike, but perhaps he was under orders not to detain him, just see what he was up to.'

She seemed satisfied. 'Go on.'

'Mike had been absent for much of the week. He said he'd been in the gym, and perhaps he was telling the truth – perhaps he'd been plotting his moves there.' My head was spinning. 'To establish his alibi, he could have sent Marcellus to the church by persuading him I was his father's killer.'

'Marcellus's climb up the tower seemed to be the most difficult thing for the inspector to explain.'

'And I'm convinced Mike had a hand in it somehow.'

Her voice was guarded. 'You know, Maggie, Wilson's death was painless, as painless as death can be, I suspect. If Mike had killed Harry so brutally, Harry whom he seemed genuinely to like, then why hadn't he killed Wilson in a similar way? He had reason to hate the man, after all.'

'I don't know,' I said helplessly. 'Wilson was rarely alone. Marcellus was his bodyguard. Maybe Mike couldn't find any other way.'

'And the motive for killing Harry?'

'There isn't one. Psychopaths don't need a motive,' I added defiantly. 'Do you know what's clinched it? Mike's revelation that he'd travelled to Stockholm several times last year, the year the killings at the Maximilian took place. When we arrived at the Ice Hotel, he told us he'd just come from Stockholm. He said that at the weekend he'd hooked up with a group of Yanks.' I stared at her. 'At the weekend. A group of Yanks.'

Something passed across Dr Langley's face, a look of apprehension. 'What are you saying?'

'Don't you see?' I felt like screaming. 'An American tourist had died the Saturday before we arrived. Hallengren said the death wasn't accidental.'

'The Saturday that Mike had been there?'

'And he's still going back and forth to Stockholm.'

'Are the hotel murders continuing?' she said slowly.

'I've made a point of following the Swedish news.' I held her gaze. 'Each time Mike is away, there's a death.'

She said nothing, but there was no mistaking the shock on her face.

I ran a hand over my eyes. 'The first time my suspicions were raised was when Mike took Liz and me out to lunch. He mentioned he'd been in Stockholm for the May Day celebrations.' The restaurant was a seafood place in Broughty Ferry. There'd been nothing remarkable about the occasion, but when Mike had mentioned Stockholm, it had struck a chord. After I'd returned home, it was still vibrating. 'I went online and scoured the newspapers. There was an article dated May the second about a man bludgeoned to death in a Stockholm hotel.'

Anxiety edged Dr Langley's voice. 'You don't think this could be a coincidence?'

I put even less stock in coincidences, Miss Stewart.

I shook my head vehemently. 'Whoever killed those people in Stockholm could have killed Harry. You didn't see his body.' I swallowed rapidly. 'Or the inside of that chapel.'

When there was no response, I added, in a tired voice, 'You think I'm imagining this, don't you?'

'Your fears are real, and they are grounded in a form of logic. Everything you say is plausible. You're sane, if that's what you want to know. The question is, where do you think you should go from here?'

'Where do *I* think?' I said, with a gesture of helplessness. 'I was hoping you'd tell me.'

'The basis of your fear is that the police got the wrong man, and Harry's murderer walked free.'

'Is that a question?'

She smiled encouragingly. 'It's a beginning. We go forward from here.' She looked at her watch. 'I'm sorry, Maggie, we need to draw this to a close. But this session is not over.' She buzzed her secretary. 'Caroline, am I free tomorrow afternoon?'

'You have a meeting with the councillor,' came Caroline's voice.

'So I do. The day after, then?'

'I can make it free.'

Dr Langley glanced at me.

I nodded.

'Please rearrange whatever I have, Caroline, and make an appointment for Miss Stewart for two p.m.' She sat back, studying me. 'You've done well today, Maggie. You've taken a great leap forward.'

'Who was it who used that expression? Mao? Or Stalin?' I tried a laugh, but it came out as a cough.

She walked me to the door, smiling. 'My husband says I'm a bit like Stalin.'

I gazed at her. 'I haven't always been like this, Dr Langley. I used to be a nice person.'

She looked surprised. 'You still are.'

'There's something I need to know,' I said hesitantly. 'Why is there blood in the bath? Is it because of how Harry was killed?'

A veil came over her eyes. 'It could be that.'

'Or?'

'Blood in dreams can act as a portent. It may be that you think the killer will strike again.'

I felt the air leave my lungs. Yes, the killer could strike again. And not necessarily in Stockholm.

CHAPTER 29

I left Dr Langley's office and made for the Nethergate. An early moon was rising, skimming the rooftops and pouring its creamy light over the tiles. The first stars were out, like sharp points in the blue-black sky.

As I approached the Queen's Hotel, I collided with someone. I lost my balance and fell heavily. Raising my head, I gazed into the face of a well-dressed man. He looked me over casually, indifference in his eyes, then turned away, pulling his cashmere coat more tightly round him. I struggled to my feet and peeled the sodden jeans away from my legs. My scarf was half buried in the snow. Lacking the energy to wrap it round my neck, I dragged it behind me in the slush like a limp tail.

I needed a drink. More than one. If ever there was a time to get legless, this was it. I'd told Dr Langley everything, exhuming my deepest fears, and she'd confirmed that I was sane. That had to be grounds for celebration.

It was snowing. Large flakes, like communion hosts, fell gently. I tilted my head back and stared into the brooding sky, savouring the sharp tingles on my face.

I trudged along Perth Road. A few more steps and I was there.

The Highlander had become my local. It was dark and deep, and no one I knew drank there. It was cocktail hour and the pub was filling. I pushed my way in, fighting past the guests to reach the counter.

The barman watched me approach. He was built like a rhinoceros, with a head that hung slightly forward. He had eyes the colour of water, and his face was crisscrossed with scars. In a suit, he could have been the sort of heavy a debt-collection agency would employ. But he wore a kilt.

'You here again, lass?' He eyed me warily. 'That's twice in one day.'

I stared at the hairs in his nostrils. 'I can't keep away from you, Mac. It must be love.'

The barman and I always began by sparring, but we quickly came to an understanding. He hesitated for only a second before reaching for the bottle. I watched eagerly as he poured. Wine had become my friend, even the metallic white variety they served here.

'Are you going to behave, eh?' he said.

'It's nearly Christmas. Do you want me to be naughty or nice?'

He started to replace the cork, but I laid a hand on his arm. 'Leave the bottle.'

'That's not a good idea.'

'I'll drink slowly. You can give me a packet of pork scratchings to soak it up.'

'One drink at a time, lass.'

I snatched up the glass. 'You know, that sort of attitude is going to widen the cracks in our relationship.'

At a table in the corner, I sat rolling the glass between my palms, thinking back to my session with Dr Langley.

Mike. It was out in the open. Or, rather, out in my open. There was now no question of sitting back and doing nothing. Could I enlist Dr Langley's help? *Remember that I'm less interested in catching a killer, and more interested in helping you.* No, I'd have to return to Kiruna and see Hallengren. I felt a sudden tug of lust as I remembered the night in his apartment. I lifted the glass and drank deeply in the bleak and certain knowledge that he wouldn't recognise me: my hair was a mess, and I was so scrawny that I looked like an adolescent in her mother's clothes. I pictured the polite but puzzled way he'd greet me, the interest dying in his eyes as his gaze ran down my body.

A half-empty glass lay abandoned on the table. I fished out the sliver of lemon and shredded it, bursting the tiny juice sacs with my fingers. There was something pressing I had to do first, and that was to warn Liz. Was she likely to believe me? Without proof? For that matter, was Hallengren? The Stockholm police might, though, especially if they correlated Mike's movements with the hotel deaths. I was seeing Liz for lunch the following day. If I could persuade her that Mike was the killer, she might come to Stockholm with me. But what if she refused to accept it? Even told Mike? Where would that leave me? I couldn't help but wonder why Mike had insinuated himself into our lives so carefully. Was it with a specific end in sight? The thought made my flesh crawl. I dropped the lemon into the glass and wiped my fingers on my jeans.

A crash from the bar made me jump. Someone had dropped a beer glass and the customers were backing away from the spreading foam. I turned away in irritation.

No, I would have to tell Liz everything because I had no one else. And she was sensible, she'd know what to do. I'd hand the matter over to her and go with her decision. My spirits rose, as they always did when I'd formulated a plan.

A couple of drinks later, I decided I'd marinated my brain long enough. It was time for the one more I always had for the road. 'Hey, Mac,' I called to the barman, with my customary politeness, 'another wine, if you don't mind.'

He was pulling a pint. 'You'll have to fetch it yourself, lass. I haven't the time to wait on you.'

I dragged myself to my feet, and waited for the room to stop swaying before making my way to the bar. Service was slow, and it was several minutes before the barman reached me.

He eyed me with distaste. 'This has to be your last.'

'Better make it a large one, in that case.'

He watched me with his little piggy eyes, pouring the wine as though it was poison. I clutched the glass to my chest and picked my way back to the table.

The pub was teeming now. People were pushing towards the bar, jostling my chair as they squeezed past, their loud conversations drilling into my head. Suddenly, I had to get out of there.

I got to my feet. The room heaved like a sea in swell. My stomach tightened, and I crashed face down on to the table.

The noise stopped, and people turned to stare.

'Right, that's it,' I heard the barman say. 'Enough is enough.'

The customers watched in thinly veiled satisfaction as he marched over and hauled me to my feet. He thrust my arms into my duffel coat and pulled it roughly round me, not bothering with the toggles. I gazed in drunken detachment as he held me upright with one hand and lifted the scarf off the floor with the other. He glowered at me and, for a second, I thought he was going to strangle me with it, but he just slung it round my neck. I reached for the bag hanging from the chair but missed it by several inches. He snatched it up and, ignoring the items that fell out, looped it over my head. The pantomime over, he gripped my arm and dragged me to the door. As he pulled it open, an icy blast sent me reeling backwards.

I tried to make it outside, but collided with the doorframe.

'You need help, lass,' he said, doing up the toggles of my coat. 'Do you have far to go?'

327

I blinked at him.

His expression softened. 'Shall I call you a cab, eh?'

I shook my head.

Without ceremony, he took me outside and turned me round so I was facing the road. 'Merry Christmas,' he said sadly, closing the door.

I walked a few paces, then fell sprawling on the caked snow, somehow getting it down the neck of my sweater. After several attempts, I staggered to my feet and plunged headlong down Perth Road.

I was approaching the intersection with Airlie Place when I felt a spasm in my stomach. My throat contracted and my vision clouded. Afraid I would be cautioned again for being drunk and disorderly, I lurched into the University of Dundee's car park. I placed both hands on the wall and breathed deeply, willing the world to stop spinning, but my legs gave way and I sank to the ground.

It was as the wind was whipping icicles into my face that I realised, somewhere between there and the Highlander, I'd lost my scarf.

The taxi dropped me off at Liz's house on Abercromby Street. Normally, I'd have taken my car, but I'd given up driving since I'd lurched awake at the wheel with Liz screaming into my ear.

It was 1 p.m. and I was on time. There was no sign of Mike's banana-yellow Porsche on the street or in Liz's drive. That meant nothing. Like me, he could have arrived by cab. The opportunity would be wasted if he were present, to say nothing of how I'd feel about seeing him now.

The pink-white gravel, wet from the recent snow, sank under

my feet as I crunched up Liz's drive. Weeds grew everywhere, poking through the gravel and spoiling the lawn and flowerbeds.

I loved Liz's house, a sprawling mix of stone and white harling. The front door was framed with climbing roses, blooming despite the season, their peach-coloured buds blackened with frost. The bushes grew untethered and several branches had made a bid for freedom, entangling themselves in the profusion of dead honey-suckle that wreathed the windows.

A large Peugeot stood backed up so close to the door that I had to squeeze past to reach the bell. I knew what this meant: Liz had been on one of her mammoth shopping trips.

The bell jangled deep inside the house. Liz opened the door before it had finished ringing. She was wearing jeans and an Aran sweater, too large for her, the cuffs hanging over her fingers. I glanced at the thick-soled boots and the green parka in her hand. She was on her way out.

'You're here, Mags.' She smiled warmly. 'Excellent, we've just set the table.'

'We?' I said in alarm, trying to see over her shoulder. 'Is Mike here?'

'He's away. It was the twins who helped me. They've already eaten.' Her eyes narrowed. 'Are you all right? You haven't been drinking?'

My breath smelt from the evening before. 'I've not had a drop today, honest. I've even had a huge cooked breakfast.' I glanced at the parka. 'Did I get the time wrong?'

'I'm out of cigarettes, that's all. I was about to pop down to the petrol station and get you some.'

'Well, don't bother on my account. You know I've given up.'

Liz and I had taken to playing this game, each of us pretending she didn't smoke and the other did.

'So where's Mike?' I said warily.

329

'In Stockholm.' She was looking at me curiously. 'You know, he told me he's been to see you but you're never in, and you don't return his calls. He's even come into Bayne's and asked after you. He said the girls at Accounts Payable won't leave him alone.' She took my coat and threw it on to the hall stand. 'You're not avoiding him, are you?'

'Of course not,' I said too quickly. 'I've been meaning to get in touch, but I never get round to it.'

'That's easily solved. I'll have you both round for dinner one evening.'

I hesitated. 'Look, Liz, about Mike,' I said, my voice faltering.

'Yes?' She waited, studying my face.

I found my courage. 'There's something I need to talk to you about.'

'Fine, but shall we do it over lunch? Come through, the twins are dying to see you.'

I followed her into the living room, my courage evaporating.

The room was large with a high ceiling buried under ornate plastering. Both sides of the dado rail were papered with red and green floral damask, the wallpaper stained and torn in places. Fading curtains, too heavy for the sagging brass rods, bordered the sash windows, which were kept closed even in summer. Liz had inherited the dark furniture from the previous owners. Even the sofa was ancient, with its Queen Anne legs and striped silk upholstery. There was no sign that a fire was ever lit. Dried flowers, dust powdering the leaves, were crammed into a Chinese vase that stood in the grate. But the room was warm. Liz had had central heating installed.

It was weeks since I'd seen the twins. They were dressed identically in kilted skirts and bright red sweaters, with different-coloured grips in their hair. They were playing one of their let's-make-as-much-mess-as-we-can games. A blanket had been draped over a clotheshorse and they were pretending it was a house, stuffing it full of objects from the room.

'So school's over for Christmas?' I said, trying to inject a cheerful note into my voice.

Annie glanced up, then stared open-mouthed. 'You've cut your hair.'

I wondered what was coming next. Annie was not a child who minced her words.

'It makes you look like a boy,' she said.

'That's rude, Annie,' Liz said.

'Is it because you've got nits? Alastair in my class has got nits and his hair has been cut just like yours, only shorter.'

Another time, I'd have joined in the joke, but I was preoccupied with thinking of how to broach the subject of Mike.

'That's enough,' Liz said firmly.

Annie was known for her non sequiturs. She eyed me solemnly. 'Your clothes look funny. I bet your bra doesn't match your knickers,' she added knowingly. 'Mummy's always does.'

Liz shook her head in mock exasperation. 'Could you watch them for a minute, Mags? I won't be too long.' She took a ten-pound note from her purse. 'Mags is in charge while I go to the shops. Can I trust the two of you to behave?'

Lucy gazed at me blissfully, nodding. Annie said, 'Yeah, yeah,' in a bored tone and didn't look up.

I smiled at Liz. 'We'll be fine.'

She threw the twins a warning look and left the room. A second later, I heard the front door close.

I bent to stroke Lucy's hair. 'How did it go at the doctor's?' I said, pleased I'd remembered this small but important detail.

She raised her hand proudly. 'The nurse put a bandage on my finger.'

'That's nice, sweetie,' I said mechanically.

331

I sank on to the sofa, wishing now that I'd rehearsed what I would say to Liz. There were two ways she could react. She would agree I had a point, and that it would be worth going to see Hallengren. Or she'd be in denial, call me a lunatic and demand to see proof. Or she'd think I was fabricating some nonsense to keep her and Mike apart. Three ways.

'We've been practising ballet for the nativity play,' Annie was saying. 'We're angels and we wear white dresses with wings and we do a dance.'

'And we have sparkly stuff in our hair,' Lucy chipped in.

'Do you want to see me do the dance?' Annie said, nudging her sister aside. She scrambled to her feet and performed a little pirouette. But she overbalanced and knocked into a table. She lost her footing and fell, her heavy curls tumbling over her cheeks.

I turned away to hide a smile. 'That's wonderful, Annie.'

She struggled to her feet and brushed down her skirt, a cross expression on her pink face.

'Does Mike come here often?' I said, watching them play.

'He used to come a lot,' Annie said. 'He was always bringing Mummy flowers, big yellow ones.'

'Yes, lilies are Mummy's favourites.' I studied the girl's face. 'But he doesn't come so much now?'

'Mummy said he's too busy working.'

I hesitated. 'Do you like him, Annie?'

She turned away, shaking her head slowly.

That surprised me. I thought Mike would be well established in their affections by now. I was about to quiz her further when I felt a tug at my arm. Lucy had clambered on to the sofa.

'There's something I have to tell you, Maggie,' she said earnestly. 'We've got a computer at school and we're using the Wide World Web.'

'Wow, it sounds marvellous,' I said, running a finger down her cheek.

She slipped her little hand into mine and gazed at me with a hopeful expression. 'Will you play shop with us?'

'Of course I will, pet. What do I have to do?'

Annie took control, as always. 'We need money.'

Liz's handbag was on the chair. Annie opened it, and started to throw the contents out.

'Annie, I don't think that's a good idea,' I said quickly.

She brandished Liz's purse. 'Mummy lets us use her money provided we put it back,' she said with authority.

Before I could stop her, she'd tipped the purse upside down and was shaking it, showering the floor with the contents. After a final, violent jerk, she threw it over her shoulder. She and Lucy picked up the coins and busied themselves making neat piles of pennies. I bent to gather the scattered items.

I was zipping the bag shut when something under the chair caught my eye. It was a silver cigarette case.

I'd never seen Liz use a case. Like me, she took her cigarettes straight from the pack. I ran my finger over the monogram: EK. The curling letters spiralled outwards, looping over the edges on to the other side. I pulled at the clasp, wondering idly who EK was. The case sprang open. I'd half hoped to find cigarettes, but it was empty except for a few strands of tobacco. The workmanship was exquisite: tortoiseshell lining and two yellow silk bands, one on either side. I wondered why Liz kept the case in her bag but didn't use it.

I was about to snap it shut when I noticed that the lining on one side was loose. I prodded it back, pushing it under the rim, but couldn't get it to stay. Something was wedged behind it. I picked the tortoiseshell off carefully. A piece of newspaper was jammed in so firmly that it might have been glued to the silver.

I peeled it away and smoothed it open. The paper, yellow with age, had been folded so many times it was difficult to read.

It was a cutting from a London newspaper. There was a single article. The title jumped out at me from the page.

Leading civil servant commits suicide in prison

Richard Kellett's body was found hanging by his belt in his cell yesterday morning. The prison governor, Mr John Hickock, will deliver a full statement later today, but told our reporter last night that Kellett had been assessed as not being at risk to himself. His belt and shoelaces had therefore not been removed. Police have ruled out foul play.

Kellett had just begun a life sentence after having been convicted of treason in one of London's most sensational court cases for decades. Kellett, a leading civil servant at the Ministry of Defence, had been found guilty of selling information to several international terrorist groups. In his summing up after a trial lasting nearly six months, the judge, Mr Justice Cleveley, told the jury that the crime of which Kellett stood accused was treason and, until recently, would have carried the death penalty. The jury had taken less than thirty minutes to find Kellett guilty. Sentencing him to life imprisonment, Mr Justice Cleveley said that the sentence reflected the gravity of the crime and recommended that Kellett serve no less than thirty years.

The star prosecution witness was Professor Henry Auchinleck, a historian at Cambridge University. Professor Auchinleck, a researcher of international repute, had been commissioned by the government to help them trace the leak in the MoD. After months of painstaking work, he had finally uncovered the identity of the civil servant who had been leaking secrets to terrorist organisations. When initially questioned by police,

Kellett had vehemently denied any involvement in the affair. But after hearing the evidence given by Professor Auchinleck, and under intense cross-examination in the witness stand, Kellett had broken down and changed his plea to one of guilty. He had acted alone, he said, and purely out of greed.

Notable by her complete absence from the trial and the public eye in general was Kellett's wife, Elizabeth. A spokesman for the family confirmed that she had been eight months pregnant when Kellett was convicted, and had been too unwell to attend the trial. No one was available for comment at the family home yesterday.

I glanced at the date. The article was nearly six years old. Details of the case started to come back to me. I remembered the name Kellett as being unusual. Yet what had so interested Liz that she'd kept this cutting?

Below the text were two colour photographs, badly faded. One was of Harry, looking more youthful than when I'd known him. The other, grainier, was captioned: *Richard and Elizabeth Kellett on their wedding day*. A couple was standing smiling for the camera, their arms round each other, the man's head inclined towards the woman's. I recognised Richard Kellett's face from television.

His wife was wearing an ivory-coloured gown, the tight fit accentuating her slimness. Her blonde hair was piled loosely on top of her head, making her neck look longer than it was. She wore a simple headband of the same pink rosebuds that were arranged in her bouquet, and round her neck was a double strand of pearls, which matched her earrings.

I looked at her face. The paper was worn and the picture faded, but there was no mistaking it. I stared, feeling the shock of recognition blast through my body. That mole on her cheek. Elizabeth Kellett was Liz Hallam.

I sank on to the sofa, my mind reeling. So Richard Kellett had been Liz's husband. No wonder she never talked about him. I glanced again at the date and did the calculation. The twins had been born after Kellett's death, so would know nothing of their father. I scanned the living room, only then seeing what had escaped me before: the complete absence of photos of Liz's husband. There were several of Liz and of the twins at different ages, but none of Kellett.

But there was something else. Harry had been involved. He'd done the research that had brought Kellett down, even presented it in court. In all their years of friendship, had Harry known that Liz was Kellett's wife? It seemed unlikely – Liz had kept out of the spotlight. But she would have known who Harry was. She'd have followed the trial at home. Why, then, had she been such a good friend to him?

Engrossed in my thoughts, I didn't hear the door open.

'So, Mags, you've discovered my little secret.'

The voice gave me such a shock that I jumped to my feet.

I gazed at the newspaper cutting. And, suddenly, it was blindingly obvious.

CHAPTER 30

Liz was at the door, a packet of cigarettes in her hand. We stared at one another in silence.

Her expression changed, and she turned to the children. 'You two, up to your room and play,' she said sharply.

'Do we have to?' Annie said. She was sorting the silver coins and didn't look up.

'Stop whining. You can watch television.'

'Okay, but we have to finish our game first.'

'Now!'

The harshness in her voice had the desired effect. Annie kicked the piles of coins over, and she and Lucy marched sulkily out of the room. I heard their footsteps on the stairs. A door banged somewhere above my head.

Without taking her eyes off me, Liz reached behind her and pushed the door shut. She gestured to the sofa. 'Sit down,' she said quietly.

I remained standing, my mind in a turmoil.

'Well, now that you know, what are you going to do about it?' She was watching me, her gaze steady.

I tried to keep my hands from trembling. 'I don't know anything, Liz.'

'Oh, for heaven's sake, you've got a brain the size of a planet.'

I looked deep into her eyes. Then I dropped the cutting and sprinted for the door.

She grabbed me and held my neck in an arm grip, forcing me to bend over. I beat at her legs, my hands balled into fists, but she didn't budge. She released me suddenly, and placed the heels of her hands below my ears. As she pressed hard, my blows grew weaker, lights popped in my head, and then blackness rushed over me.

When I opened my eyes, I was lying on the sofa, the sleeve of my jumper rolled up. Liz was in the armchair, looking thoughtfully at me. A syringe lay on the table beside her.

'Please don't be alarmed, Mags. I've injected you with a muscle relaxant. It's not at all life-threatening, but I wouldn't try moving if I were you.'

I tried to sit up but my body felt pressed by a great weight. What in God's name had she pumped into me? I sank into the cushions.

'I use tiny amounts for sprains and muscle injury.' She motioned to the cocktail cabinet. 'All my goodies are kept in a locked drawer.'

I said nothing. I was concentrating on the mechanics of breathing.

She ripped the cellophane off the cigarette packet, then leant forward and took a lighter from the back pocket of her jeans. She lit up, inhaling slowly.

I watched these familiar actions with growing dread. 'What is this stuff, Liz?' I gasped. 'I feel like shit.'

'I'm so sorry.' Her voice softened. 'It'll wear off with no ill-effects, I promise you.'

I tried closing my eyes, but that made the queasiness worse.

'You're owed an explanation, Mags. And I know you'll want to hear it from beginning to end.' Her mouth twisted, as though what she was about to say would be painful. 'You see, after Dick's suicide, I simply couldn't live in London. There were far too many memories, and too many people knew me. I changed back to my maiden name, Hallam, and got the job here at Bayne's.'

I shifted on the sofa, only half listening. If I could keep her talking, the relaxant would wear off and I might find a way to escape. If only Mike were here, I thought, aware of the irony behind my wish.

She blew smoke through her nostrils. 'I've waited years, you know. Long, long years. You've no idea what it's been like, the strain of pretending to love him, watching him befriend my children, for God's sake. But I want to tell it from the start.' She looked directly at me. 'How I became a murderer.'

In desperation, I tried to move my legs. Liz watched my feeble attempts, then got up and locked the door. Terror surged through me. I sank back, gasping.

'Why did you kill Harry?' I said. My tongue felt thick, my voice sounding as though it came from far away.

'Harry was the only one I intended to kill. Wilson was . . .' she picked a tobacco strand from her teeth and examined it '. . . rather unfortunate.'

Wilson. She'd killed Wilson, too. My God . . .

'I saw Harry on television when it was all happening. After the trial, I thought I'd never have to see his face again. Then, surprise surprise, he just appeared out of the blue. He'd moved from Cambridge to Dundee, and it was all in the news again. That was what decided me, you see, the two of us here in the same city. It was Fate.' Her face was expressionless. 'But I really didn't need much persuading. He'd taken my husband from me.'

'Your husband killed himself,' I said, forcing out the words. 'All Harry did was uncover the truth.'

Liz's eyes blazed. 'What would you know about it? You've never had a husband, you with your casual affairs and one-night stands. You've never known what it is to be in love, not the kind of love Dick and I had.' Her face was distorted. 'That awful ache after he'd gone. Harry took everything away from me. Worst of all, he robbed my children of their father.'

Her anger hung in the air, like smoke from a pistol. I didn't dare reply.

She continued more quietly: 'Once I'd made up my mind, it wasn't terribly difficult. You know the sort of person Harry was, always giving lectures, attending book signings. The first time I spoke to him, I could see immediately that he didn't have a scooby who I was. I'd kept out of the limelight, you see.' She indicated the cutting. 'You know, I think that article carried the only photograph of me. Harry can't have seen it. I'd forgotten I still had that. Where did you find it?'

I nodded at the cigarette case on the floor.

She gazed at it for a while. 'How careless of me,' she murmured.

I had to keep her talking. 'Your parents,' I said slowly. 'Didn't they recognise Harry?'

'I kept them apart. My parents are too poorly now to travel all the way to Scotland.'

'But didn't the twins give the game away? They must have mentioned him.'

'Oh, children don't use surnames. My parents knew of a Professor Henry Auchinleck from Cambridge. They didn't suspect he was the Harry the twins were always talking about.' She stabbed out the cigarette and lit another. 'Things became more complicated when you got the job at Bayne's. I was sure you'd see through my relationship with Harry. But as time went on, I realised I'd fooled you.'

'You fooled us all,' I said, with difficulty. 'Especially Harry.'

Her mouth forced itself into a smile. 'I thought first about killing him here in Dundee, you know. I dreamt up one plan after another. There are drugs that can bring on a cardiac arrest, for example. I even thought about killing him with my bare hands. My karate would have come in handy there. But all these methods would lead back to me. Questions would be asked and the truth about Dick would come out.' She pulled on the cigarette. 'Then the perfect opportunity came up. Harry suggested a holiday.'

I closed my eyes, remembering that autumn afternoon in Liz's garden.

'It really couldn't have been better, Mags. You see, I could kill Harry abroad. If I took care to make it look like an accident, no one would dig up the past.'

That conversation Harry and I had had about the holiday. We'd been so worried Liz would back out. Now I understood why she'd accepted so readily.

She grew animated. 'Harry had brought those skiing catalogues. When I saw the Ice Hotel, I knew it would be the perfect location. It was the bit about sleeping in rooms without doors. Remember? It dawned on me then how awfully easy it would be to kill someone. Someone who'd been drugged.'

Yes, Wilson had been drugged. But what did that have to do with Harry?

'The Ice Hotel's website had all the details. That jolly reception in the Ice Bar, the Activities Room. There was even a picture of the snow-suits.'

I slurred out the words. 'How did you get the drug into Wilson's food?'

She laughed lightly. 'I didn't just drug Wilson, you little idiot, I drugged everybody.' She was enjoying the expression on my face. 'Remember Purple Kiss? Well, the website lists the Ice Hotel's cocktails and all their ingredients. On that first night, only Purple

Kiss is served at the reception. As it happens, *crème de violette* is the main ingredient.' Her eyes were gleaming. 'But this is the point, Mags. *Crème de violette* is only in Purple Kiss. None of the other cocktails has it. My plan was to drug Harry, then roll him out of his sleeping bag. But I had to do it with the minimum of risk. So I introduced Phenonal into all the bottles of *crème de violette*. That way, it would get into every jug of Purple Kiss, and all the guests, including Harry, would take it.'

It was devastatingly simple. I had to admire her. Who was the chess player now?

'There was always a teensy risk that Harry wouldn't drink Purple Kiss, but he had a sweet tooth so I thought it worth a try. And Phenonal has a sweetish aftertaste, you see, so Purple Kiss was ideal.'

'When did you get it into the bottles?' I said slowly.

'It was that first afternoon, after the tour of the Ice Hotel. We went our separate ways. You wandered off to look at the Ice Theatre, I think. I went exploring. You know, for a hotel, the Excelsior is remarkably insecure. Absolutely no one saw me slip into the storeroom. The purple liqueur bottles were all lined up ready to be taken to the Ice Hotel. It took only a minute to unscrew them and add the powder. Easy-peasy.'

'How did you get the stuff into the country?' I hadn't seen sniffer dogs at the airports but they must have been there.

'It was in a hermetically sealed packet, actually, which I stuffed inside a tin of strong-smelling talcum powder. I flushed what was left down the loo in the Locker Room.'

It was a plan worthy of a superspy. No wonder Liz looked smug.

'I planned it down to the last little detail,' she said, with a wide smile. 'Everyone would have a good night's sleep. Phenonal is a commonly used sedative that metabolises rapidly, so after a few hours it's completely out of the bloodstream. When a man's freezing to death, the metabolic rate slows, but even then I thought the drug would be out before hypothermia took its toll.' Her smile faded into a frown. 'I was wrong about that, as it happens.'

'What if Harry hadn't drunk Purple Kiss?'

'I'd have found another way.'

'But you drank it, too.'

She smiled again. 'Only a tiny amount. That drunken idiot Jonas was spilling it everywhere, so it was easy to spill mine. What I didn't know was that you weren't drinking it either.' The smile vanished. 'That was rather a pity.'

Blood was pounding in my ears. I placed my hands against the sofa and tried to push myself up. My arms buckled and I sank back, sweating heavily.

'I wouldn't, Mags. Adrenalin reacts badly with that drug. You'll be dreadfully sick.' She ran a hand over her hair. 'Where everything began to unravel was when Harry and Wilson's rooms were swapped. I didn't know, I really didn't. And as if that weren't bad enough, you saw me coming out of Wilson's room.'

'But I saw a man,' I said, stunned. 'A big man.'

She lit a cigarette, inhaling slowly. 'It was the website that gave me the idea. There was a detailed description of the snow-suits. It occurred to me as I read about the different sizes that I could put one on over the other. I'd look much bigger. And being tall helps. When I tried it, I saw immediately that I could be mistaken for a man.'

The room was spinning. All these years, and how little I knew her.

'After I'd spiked the bottles, I hid a large suit in my locker. Then at night when everyone was semi-comatose, I slipped out of my room. It was near that side entrance so it only took a minute to get to the Locker Room. I pulled on the outer suit, then crept into what I thought was Harry's room. It was too dark to see his face, and I was in a hurry, so I didn't look terribly closely. All I saw was tousled hair that looked like Harry's.' There was bitterness in her voice. 'When I discovered it was Wilson I'd killed, I really couldn't understand it. There was that frightful statue of Pan in there. To cap it all, I heard your voice as I was walking away. But as long as I didn't turn round, I knew you couldn't identify me.'

'The blue suit and the woollen hat,' I murmured. 'I thought it was Harry.'

'The blue suits were the largest. As for the hat, I considered putting my hood up, but it might have come down. The bobble hat really was perfect. I took the first that came to hand and tucked my hair under it. I didn't intend to look like Harry – it was sheer coincidence it was blue. And I wore a ski mask. But you wouldn't have known that.'

I saw it all now, how easily I'd got it wrong. How easily every-one had got it wrong.

'I didn't return the clothes to the Locker Room. I mean, why take the risk? I stuffed the outer suit behind the linen basket in the washroom. No one would think it strange finding a snow-suit there.' She sat back, staring straight ahead. 'I was stunned when I discovered I'd killed the wrong man. I'd done my homework so thoroughly, you know, I could have found Harry's room blindfold. All that careful planning gone to waste. I had to think quickly after that.'

I knew what Liz was going to say. She was going to tell me how she'd killed Harry. Muffled laughter from the girls' bedroom filtered through the ceiling.

'It wasn't planned. Not the way I had to do it. It was two days after the police interviews. You were off somewhere, and Mike had gone on that husky trip.' She paused, the cigarette halfway to her lips. 'Harry said he'd stay in the hotel and work on his book. He was behind with some chapter or other. I saw a chance, so I stayed too.'

A thud came from upstairs, followed by squabbling, which eventually died down.

'I really wasn't prepared to risk anything in the Excelsior. So I sat in the lounge, hoping coffee would give me inspiration. After a while, Harry came down. He told me he needed fresh air and was going to take a look inside the chapel, and did I want to come. I was so excited, Mags, you wouldn't believe. The problem was how to do it, exactly.'

She leant forward, her arms over her stomach as though nursing an acute pain. 'I said no, I couldn't go out, I was expecting a call from the twins. He went into the Activities Room. I waited ages, my attention on the door. Then I saw him at Reception. His hat was still in his hand. I would have missed him otherwise. People were coming into the foyer from one of those ice-climbing trips. When I saw what they were holding, I knew what to do. I ran to the Activities Room. There were only a couple of people there. No one saw me put on a ski mask and two suits. I made sure they were both red.'

'No, Liz,' I whispered. 'Please, no.'

'I took an ice axe, one of those big ones. I had to push through the crowd to get to the front door. It was deserted outside. I slipped into the chapel.' She was rocking back and forth. 'He was there, looking up at the big window. I crept over. He turned and saw me. We stared at one another. My hood was up and he didn't recognise me under the mask.'

'Liz, I'm begging you—'

She was staring into space, oblivious. 'I thought I should speak to him. Let him know who I was, you see, and why I was going to kill him. But I couldn't. Then he saw the axe in my hand, and

I knew I'd have to do it. I swung as hard as I could – God knows where I found the strength – but I missed his head and the axe ripped through his shoulder. He screamed and threw his arms in front of his face. I swung again and the axe went into his chest. He fell back, dragging me with him. And then I just kept going until he went down. After a while, he stopped thrashing.'

My breath was coming in short gasps. With a sudden wrench, my stomach convulsed.

She turned her head slowly and looked at me. Her face was flushed, her lips wet. 'You know, Mags, when I saw Harry lying there, his body twitching and his blood spraying on to the walls, God forgive me, it felt better than sex.'

I threw up then, over Liz's living-room carpet.

CHAPTER 31

I continued to retch, leaning over the floor and spewing up the contents of my stomach until there was nothing left. The phone rang. After six rings, the answer machine whirred into life with a loud click and Liz's recorded message came on. The caller rang off before it had finished.

I lifted my head in a daze. My stomach felt as though it had been tied in knots. My ears were buzzing and objects in my field of view were ringed with dark bands. I drew my legs up slowly, gasping with the effort, and curled into a ball.

The smell of vomit pricked my nostrils. With a rapid movement, Liz tore the blanket off the clotheshorse and flung it over the pizza-like splash.

'There's more to tell,' she said softly.

I knew what had happened next: I was there. 'I don't want to hear it,' I groaned. 'Please, Liz, please.'

'I had to get out of the chapel quickly. The screams could have carried. And anyone could have walked in. I stripped off the mask and the suit, trying not to get blood over myself. I was less concerned about the inner suit because it was red.'

A part of me had to hear it. I struggled to a sitting position.

'I ran into you outside when I least expected it.' She smiled crookedly. 'Sorry and all that, but I had to have an alibi, and you provided the perfect one. It wasn't difficult to get you into the chapel and have you be the one to discover Harry's body. I told Hallengren I was napping, then got up and saw you outside the Excelsior.' She paused. 'And in case you're wondering, it's really easy to induce vomiting when adrenalin is pumping through your body. It just needed a couple of fingers down my throat.' She wrinkled her nose. 'And that smell—'

The memory returned and I started to gag. Liz watched me, sympathy on her face.

'I saw someone in the chapel, behind a column,' I gasped, wiping my mouth. 'I assumed it was the person who'd killed Harry.'

'You know, that was absolutely the worst possible luck. I'd tried to avoid the reporters by keeping to my room, but it wasn't always possible. I was afraid one of them might have covered Dick's trial, you see. None of them would have heard of Liz Hallam, but Harry was with us and he's such a flamboyant character that anyone who'd followed the trial would have remembered him.' She looked away. 'It was a one in a million chance, but Denny Hinckley had seen my photograph in the papers. I didn't know it at the time but he was spying on me and Harry. He watched Harry go into the chapel and followed him in. He saw everything. Including my face as I removed the mask.'

Denny had witnessed a murder and said nothing? 'Why didn't he go to Hallengren?' I said.

'He made a fatal mistake in not doing so,' she said quietly. 'But I'll come to Denny later.' She was watching me thoughtfully. 'Your big mistake, Mags, was that you tried to work everything out. Starting with the snowmobiles. You were way off track there, though. You thought it was Mike or Jonas who'd loosened those brakes. Well, it wasn't.'

'You?' I said, my voice faltering.

'I went to join Mike, do you remember? He and Jonas were so busy arguing about whether the Danes or the Belgians made better beer that they didn't see me sidle past the machines. It needed a mere flick of the finger under each handle.' She smiled. 'That funny snowmobile guide had even shown me how to do it.'

'What were you thinking, Liz?' I said, confused. 'Harry was nowhere near those machines.'

'Ah, but I'd intended to entice him on to that path. The promise of the stupendous vista would have done it – you know what he was like when it came to views – but the reindeer provided a brilliant excuse.'

'You thought Harry would stand still while the machines fell towards him?'

'His reactions are slower than you might imagine. And he'd drunk more than his share of beer. But I agree it was always going to be a long shot. I wasn't even sure the machines would slip. Or at the right time.'

'I don't know why you bothered. Your Plan A was perfect.'

'Things can go wrong, you know, even with a perfect plan. It did – I killed the wrong man. I'd be a fool not to take any opportunity that presented itself. But I hadn't expected the guide to examine his machines so closely. It's really just as well that Hallengren didn't take his story seriously.' She massaged her temples. 'The morning after Harry's death, Mike and I came to see you, do you remember? You told us there was something wrong and you'd eventually work it out. I saw that you couldn't let it go, you kept trying. I suppose chess players do that. So in the end, I really couldn't take the risk.'

'What do you mean?' I said faintly, my fear returning in a rush.

'I was supposed to be in Kiruna dealing with the paperwork over Harry's death – you wouldn't believe how complicated it is when someone dies abroad – but I persuaded Mike to go instead.

He'd been telling me how concerned he was about you. I was glad to get him out of my hair.' She ran her hands over her knees. 'I overheard the receptionist talking to you about the rehearsal. I put on two suits – I don't know why, I had no plan.' She refused to look at me. 'I arrived at the Ice Theatre in time to see you climb up to the back. I waited until the play was over and everyone had gone. Except there was a group who really didn't seem to want to. And neither did you. In the end, I gave up and left.'

And I thought it had been Jonas. And then Mike, Mike who'd been so worried about me. Dear God, I was such an idiot.

'You didn't have a clue what was going on, even though that brain of yours was working overtime. But it didn't weaken my resolve. You see, I was so close, Mags, so close. I couldn't take any chances.' Her eyes were steady. 'You really were the only loose end left to tie up.'

A loose end that was still dangling. I flexed my muscles experimentally. Life was returning. But I'd never make it to the door.

'I had another chance after dinner,' Liz went on. 'You'd gone to bed early. A decent interval later, I excused myself and crept upstairs. I saw you leave your room.'

Saturday night: the night Denny had slipped into the Ice Hotel.

'I followed you to the Activities Room. I thought of killing you there. Although it was dark, I knew where you were among the snow-suits. But it was really too dangerous. You'd have screamed like Harry.'

I swung my legs painfully over the side. Dizziness overcame me and I sank back into the sofa.

Liz's voice reached me over the ringing in my ears. 'I heard the door swing as you left the Activities Room, but I was still in with a chance if I moved quickly.'

'So you followed me out,' I said dully.

'The Activities Room has a back door, a fire door. I'd taken a good look at it when I conducted my little exploration of the Excelsior. I went out that way. But there's no outside handle so I left it propped open. And I took an ice axe.'

I felt a deathly chill in the room. Upstairs, all was silent except for the faint sound of the television.

'I ran round to the front of the Excelsior and saw you disappear into the Locker Room. You know, a minute later and I'd have lost you. It simply never occurred to me that you were going to the Ice Hotel. I thought you were off to watch the aurora. You'd take the path beside the chapel. And that was where I was going to do it. But when I saw you were going back to the Ice Hotel, which was deserted . . .' She left the consequences unspoken.

'You were the figure in the black suit,' I said, half to myself.

'And the police also thought it was a man. No one believes that a woman can kill with an ice axe.'

Would Liz have split my skull? I looked into her eyes, unable to read the answer. But surely our friendship went too deep. No, she'd have come to her senses.

'At first, I couldn't see you. I concluded you must have gone to your room for something. I mean, why else would you be there? I'd memorised the layout so I could find Harry's room easily. That's how I was able to get to your room so quickly in the dark.'

I lay back, staring at the ceiling. Why had I followed Denny? I could no longer remember.

'You know the rest, Mags, you were there. I wouldn't have thought you could outrun me, though. But, then, it is rather difficult to run with two suits on.' There was a new respect in her voice. 'And you were running as though your life depended on it. When I realised I couldn't catch you up, I hung back. I heard a shout, then an almighty crash. I thought you'd either drown or freeze to death in the water, so I dropped the axe and crept back into the Excelsior through the fire door.'

Anger bubbled up inside me and boiled over. 'You murdering bitch. You would have killed me in cold blood.'

'I've never understood that expression. Blood isn't cold.' She looked away. 'Harry's was surprisingly warm.'

I pictured the scene in the chapel: Harry, butchered, lying at the altar like a sacrificial animal, his blood melting the snow. In an instant, my anger drained away, leaving an overwhelming sadness.

'I've thought about it non-stop ever since. I wish to God now that he'd frozen to death painlessly, unknowing.' The words came out in a gasp. 'The way he screamed—'

I closed my eyes. Tears spilt down my cheeks.

Liz played with the lighter, flicking it on and off. 'I went back up to my room. As I was turning the corner, I heard someone call my name. My married name, Mrs Kellett. Denny was leaning against the wall with a smirk on his face. He said he wanted to speak to me. I was terrified. I simply couldn't think – I had to stall for time. I told him it wasn't safe to talk there. We'd have to find a spot where we wouldn't be overheard. He suggested behind the chapel early the next morning. I agreed. I spent much of the night planning what to do.'

She went over to the drinks cabinet and poured herself a neat gin. I calculated the distance between the sofa and the door, shifting my weight as silently as I could.

'I wouldn't bother, Mags,' she said softly. 'Your legs won't carry you.' She flopped back into the armchair. 'The following morning, I slipped out of the Excelsior through the fire door. I got to the riverbank well before Denny. I wanted to do a quick recce, you see. He was so late in arriving, I thought he'd given up and gone to the police. But then I saw him sauntering down the path, whistling. Silly of me, of course he was going to come. He didn't bother with pleasantries, just came straight out and told me he knew who I was and who Harry was and that he'd seen everything in the chapel. I nearly fainted when he told me he'd taken pictures.' She mimicked Denny's Cockney accent. '"Got a nice one of you removing your ski mask at the scene of the crime, I'm going to write a big fat article and make my fortune. I've even got snaps of Harry's room in the Ice Hotel."' She sipped at the gin. 'He waved his camera at me and said he wanted money. Lots of it. I asked if the pictures were his only evidence. "Yes," he said, "but they're enough to put a noose round that lovely neck, if you catch my drift. They're still in the camera, safe and sound. I've told my editor nothing because I'm sure you'll make me a better offer."'

Oh, Denny, I thought bitterly. You idiot. You sad, sad idiot.

She turned the glass in her hand. 'He didn't see the stone. I hit him on the side of the head, not enough to kill him, just to stun him. I pushed him face down into the water and lifted his legs up. There was nothing he could do. He drowned very quickly. You see, I wanted them to find water in his lungs if they recovered his body. A small bump on the head would suggest he'd slipped on the ice, hit his head, then fallen into the river and drowned.'

My blood ran cold. How little time Liz had had to think up this scheme, but it was perfect.

'I removed the memory card from his camera. Then I took his room key and ran back through the fire door and up to his room. I packed all his stuff, including the camera, into his rucksack. That was the hardest bit, you know. I was afraid someone would hear me. I took the rucksack to the river and put it on his back. It must have weighed as much as he did, he had so much stuff with him. A quick push into the water and he slipped under. I didn't want there to be footprints so I swept the area with branches. I even thought of taking my boots off, you know, before sneaking back.' She drained the gin. 'A bit of an overkill, I decided in the end. The bank behind the chapel is popular with hikers. By the time anyone noticed Denny was missing, it would be covered with footprints.'

'They'll find his body. Denny will get washed up somewhere. They'll see him in the shallows.'

'You weren't listening to Marita, were you? The strong current when the snows melt? Remember all that? A few weeks later, Denny's body would be halfway to the Gulf of Bothnia. And goodness knows where it is now.' She smiled sadly. 'Everyone thought Denny had done a runner to avoid paying his bill. And that girl, Jane, supplied the icing on the cake when she told us he had more than one passport. I rather think no one went looking for him.'

Poor Denny, unloved and unlamented. He hadn't deserved this.

'Later that morning, the workmen had a fire going. I warmed my hands at the brazier, and slipped the memory card in. After that, things moved quickly. There was a chance we'd be getting our passports back, so I had less than a day left.'

My head was spinning. Once Liz told me the rest, it would all be over. My gaze drifted to the door. Only now did I see she'd left the key in the lock. I moved my legs cautiously. To have any chance, I'd need to get her away from her chair.

'Could I have a fag?' I said weakly.

She threw the packet and lighter. The lighter struck my arm and landed on the carpet, along with the cigarettes. As I reached for them, I caught a sharp whiff of vomit through the blanket. I lit up, sucking greedily, my actions studied as though I was doing this for the first time. Out of habit, I took several cigarettes from the pack and stuffed them into my jeans. I was about to pocket the lighter when Liz motioned to me to leave it on the sofa.

She was watching me, waiting to continue her narrative. How much more was there to tell? Yet the longer I could keep her talking, the more the odds increased in my favour. Perhaps the twins would tire of television and come down, demanding attention.

'And Marcellus?' I said. 'He has a part in this story too, doesn't he?'

'That's perceptive of you, Mags,' she said, with irony. She examined her nails. 'It was after that shopping trip to Kiruna. You returned to the Excelsior and I went to pick up Harry's death certificate. While I was in the waiting room, Marcellus came in. He seemed awfully depressed, said the police weren't telling him a thing. Then he started to talk about you. He'd heard you nearly drowned. My mind wasn't really on what he was saying, and I let slip that you'd returned to the Ice Hotel after it was placed out of bounds, and it was *afterwards* that you'd fallen into the river. He said he'd heard different. You'd told everyone you fell through the ice watching the aurora. That was when I had my lightbulb moment. I told him you were lying, you'd confided in me that you'd gone back to the Ice Hotel and it was because of something to do with Wilson's murder. He swore under his breath. I knew then that I could turn things round.' She raised a tense face. 'I could make it look as though Marcellus was the killer all along.'

'Why? Marcellus was already the prime suspect.'

'But, you see, I wanted him to be a suspect beyond a shadow of doubt. If I sent him to the church, it would look as though he'd gone to murder you, wouldn't it? The police would conclude he was the killer – why else would he climb after you at dead of night? – but, more importantly, *you* would conclude that he was the killer, too.' She sneered. 'I knew you simply wouldn't be able to resist one last look at the aurora. Especially if I came as well. I was going to suggest we view it from the top of the tower, but you did it for me.'

'How on earth did you persuade Marcellus to go to the church?'

'First, I really need you to understand that I had to do it. I tried so hard to find another way, I absolutely did. I wanted you to stay my friend.'

I looked at Liz in disgust. 'You'd have had an innocent man convicted just to keep our friendship?'

She lowered her head. 'I told Marcellus you were telling me nothing, so if he wanted to uncover the truth, he'd need to talk to you himself. He was convinced Hallengren was going to arrest him that evening and charge him formally with murder. Once I knew time was running out, it was easy to bait the trap.' She looked directly at me. 'I told him it wasn't just that you'd gone back to an out-of-bounds crime scene. You'd been acting really strangely ever since Wilson had died. As though you were feeling terribly guilty about something, and maybe you'd seen who killed him.'

'But if you told Marcellus all this, why didn't he go and see Hallengren?'

'I think he wanted to present him with evidence that would clear him. And he had to be sure of that evidence before he walked into a police station.' She paused. 'You didn't see him, Mags. He was like a wild man. He hadn't shaved, his eyes were bloodshot and there was a dreadful look in them that I can't describe. Don't get me wrong, though. I don't think he meant to harm you.'

I thought back to my encounters with him. No, whatever he may have thought about my actions, Marcellus wouldn't have hurt me.

'He said he was sure he could persuade you to go with him to see Hallengren. You know, the way he talked about Wilson, I think he genuinely loved him. He told me he'd even agreed to sleep in the Ice Hotel at Wilson's request, although he only got as far as the Locker Room. He wimped out at the last minute and went back to the Excelsior. He was really gutted by his father's death. Would you believe he nearly broke down? It was quite awful to watch, actually. I mean, who'd have thought Marcellus was such a marshmallow?'

So Marcellus had only got as far as the Locker Room. After leaving Wilson's room, Liz had dumped her outer suit in the washroom. If Marcellus hadn't returned to the Excelsior, he might have run into her. And how differently things would have turned out.

'He told me he had to wait at the coroner's for his father's death certificate, and there was some mix-up over paperwork so he wouldn't be free for ages. The timing simply couldn't have been better. I said our passports had been returned and we were flying out in the early hours. If he wanted to see you and he didn't find you at the hotel, his best bet was the church. You'd be there watching the spectacular aurora predicted for that night. And leaving for the airport straight after.'

Poor Marcellus. He must have been frantic to prove his innocence if he'd been prepared to follow me to the church and confront me there. And instead of uncovering the truth, he'd slipped and fallen to his death.

'I pointed out that he'd probably be under arrest shortly. That did the trick. I could see the determination in his eyes.'

My cigarette had burnt down, and ash was spilling on to the front of my sweater. There'd been little time for Liz to formulate this plan, yet it was staggeringly simple. And it had worked. Hallengren had come to the conclusion that the murderer was Marcellus. I was seeing Liz in a new light: the grandmaster, moving her pieces over the board, checkmate in one decisive move.

She mixed another drink, and swallowed it greedily. 'You and I were leaving for the church when I got that phone call from

Siobhan. It turned out to be nothing, really, but it gave me the opportunity I was looking for.' She looked hard at me. 'I'd intended to cry off once we got to the church. You see, I needed you up that tower alone.'

My heart hammered against my ribs. 'Why alone? Because Marcellus was coming?'

'I put on a second suit and left by the fire door. My plan was to slip into the Ice Theatre afterwards and return to the Excelsior with the crowd. That would give me the perfect alibi.'

'What do you mean by "afterwards", Liz?' I said slowly. 'An alibi for what?'

'I reached the church just minutes before you. When I think about it now, it was a miracle you didn't see me.'

I cast my mind back to that night. I'd seen no one. How could I have missed her on the road?

She was enjoying my confusion. 'I took that other route to the church. The path inside the forest? It's faster, and I had a torch. The guide took us that way on the tour, and he told us about the side door at the top of the tower, the one you reach by climbing up the outside.'

There was a strange taste in my mouth. 'What did you do?'

'Well, for a moment I did think about just pushing you off the top and being done with it. If you didn't break your neck, you'd freeze to death before anyone came looking. It would seem like a dreadful accident. But there'd still be those unanswered questions about Wilson and Harry.'

'Where were you?' I whispered.

'When you come in through that side door, you step on to a wide ledge with a safety rail. It's tucked out of the way. Anyone climbing up the inside simply wouldn't see it.' Her voice was steady. 'Especially in the dark, after they've dropped their torch.'

So she'd been there. As I was climbing.

'You came past me, so close I could have touched you. After you'd been up top for a while, I heard the creak of the front door. A few moments later, the door into the tower opened. Someone started to climb. It could only have been Marcellus.' She paused. 'He came level with me. And I pushed him hard. He lost his balance and fell.'

'My God, Liz . . .'

We sat in the thick silence, watching each other. Liz had killed an innocent man to throw the police off the scent, purely to keep our friendship. Liz, my best friend, someone I thought I'd known all these years.

I had to ask. 'What would you have done if Marcellus hadn't arrived?'

She was fidgeting with the hem of her sweater. 'I'd have gone to the top and pushed you off. Or done it as you came back down.' She lifted her head. 'You were jolly lucky.'

I saw again the scene in the tower: the candlelight flickering over Marcellus's twisted body, the staring eyes, the dark blood staining my boots.

'When I heard him hit the ground, I slipped outside and climbed down the ladder. I took the path through the forest and hurried to the theatre.' She pulled at a loose thread. 'I came home with the crowd, making sure I removed my mask so people could see my face. And having watched the rehearsal, I could discuss the play over breakfast.'

'When did you change, Liz?' The words caught in my throat. 'When did you stop being the person I knew?'

She stared at me in bewilderment, as though only now appreciating the full horror of her actions. Her face sagged, and she pressed trembling fingers into her eyes.

'What do you want?' I said sadly. 'Forgiveness?'

'Don't think this hasn't affected me, Mags. You're not the only one who's had nightmares, you know. I feel as though I've exchanged one kind of hell for another.'

'And I'm supposed to cry bitter salt tears over you?'

She wiped her face, sniffing loudly. 'At breakfast, we heard something about an incident in the church. You weren't there, of course, you were fucking your detective.'

I looked away, unable to meet her gaze.

'Leo Tullis told us a body had been found in the tower,' she said, pulling viciously at the thread. 'And the police were treating it as an accident. He announced we were getting our passports back. He looked awfully relieved. Poor Leo, I bet he's never had a week like that before.' She was unravelling the hem of her sweater. 'On the plane back, you told me that whole story about Marcellus and Aaron and the diary, and what Hallengren thought had happened. And how you wanted to forget and move on. I really thought it was all over, and if I kept my nerve things would go back to the way they were. I knew there was absolutely nothing to link me to Harry's death.'

'Only Denny,' I said quietly.

'You know, I often find myself wondering where he is. In the Baltic, perhaps, some faceless corpse. Those first few weeks, I kept checking the papers but there was no mention of him. There was just the one article in the *Express* saying he was missing, and if anyone knew of his whereabouts to contact the editor. I was lucky. There was an outside chance he'd downloaded his photographs before seeking me out.'

No, Denny wouldn't have done that. He wasn't the sharpest pencil in the box. His lack of sense would have landed him in all sorts of scrapes. What did he say about looking for trouble? *I don't need to. I know where it is.*

Liz's mouth twisted suddenly. 'For what it's worth, Mags, killing

Harry has brought me neither happiness nor peace. You saw how much he loved the twins.' Her voice broke on the word. 'And they really loved him. He was a fine man. In another life, I might have loved him too.' Her eyes were moist. 'And all those others I killed. I see them everywhere, on street corners, in shops, whenever I look at myself in the mirror. Even on the faces of my children. I wish I could turn the clock back, but I can't. If it weren't for the children, I'd go to the police. But I did it for them. I had no choice.'

'You had a choice, and you made it. And don't fool yourself by saying you did it for Annie and Lucy. You did it for revenge.' Hallengren's words came back to me: *Apart from greed, revenge is the strongest motive for murder.*

'I'm so sorry.' Her voice was a whisper. 'So terribly sorry. For everything,' she added, swallowing the word.

I gazed at her brimming eyes and distorted mouth. 'Whether you're sorry or not is immaterial,' I said. 'There's a special circle in hell reserved just for you.'

Her expression hardened. 'Then I'll meet you there.'

A pulse was beating in my temple. We'd come to the endgame.

Liz snatched up the syringe on the table. I tried to get up, but she crossed the floor and gripped my arm. Before I could react, she'd plunged the needle into my neck. Her lips moved but the words were strangely muted. Still talking, she released me and stroked my hair, an expression of pleading in her eyes. Terror swept through me, and I strained to make out what she was saying, but I could no longer hear. My limbs grew heavy, there was a sudden rush of blood to my ears, and I sank back into the sofa.

I fell sideways. My vision narrowed to a cone. And slowly faded into blackness.

CHAPTER 32

I slipped in and out of consciousness. My dreams were surreal. I was with Liz and the others, dancing in a circle, laughing raucously. No one seemed to have noticed the axe embedded in Harry's skull. I tried to speak, but they were making so much noise they couldn't hear me. Their laughter filled my head until it woke me. But waking was brief, and I drifted off again.

After what felt like days, I opened my eyes, struggling not to lose consciousness. It was too dark to see. My body ached, and there was a grinding pain in the back of my head that drilled into my neck and spine whenever I moved.

Then I remembered. Liz had shoved a syringe into my neck. I sat up sharply.

My forehead struck something hard and I fell back, stunned. I tried to stretch, twisting my body, but whenever I moved, a part of me hit a wall. Light was filtering through the cracks, but my vision was so blurred that all I could make out was the faint outline of the room.

My first thought was that Liz had locked me inside her coal bunker. I ran my fingers over the low ceiling, feeling for a latch or hinge. The surface was smooth and metallic. And too clean for coal.

The pain in my head was easing, and I was gradually becoming aware of the noise, recognising it as the raucous laughter of my dreams. It seemed to come from the walls, which were jolting me from side to side. My lower hip was pressing against something so hard that I was getting muscle cramps keeping my weight off it. I wriggled furiously, rocking back and forth, and managed to slip my hand underneath. It was a coiled piece of cable with metallic ends. I fingered them carefully. Crocodile clips. I'd been lying on a pair of jump leads.

This wasn't a coal shed. I was in the boot of a car. This could only be Liz's big Peugeot. My Ford was too small, and it had been rusting outside my flat for months.

I kept the panic in check and pushed against the door, but it wouldn't budge, not even when I delivered a couple of well-placed kicks.

My eyes had adapted to the gloom, and the interior of the boot was slowly taking shape. How long since Liz had drugged me? The quality of light suggested it was day, but I had no idea if it was the same day.

Fragments of our conversation crept into my thoughts. I pushed them away but they insisted on returning. Eventually, I surrendered myself to them, thinking through every detail, torturing myself by reliving it all. I was staggered by her duplicity, but what shocked me most was her patience, how she'd waited, befriending Harry, knowing that one day she would kill him. And how meticulously she'd planned his murder, positioning the chess pieces, her superb opening gambit of introducing Phenonal into Purple Kiss. I could almost taste her frustration as things began to go wrong.

It was growing stuffy in the boot. My eyelids started to droop but I made myself stay awake. Falling asleep now would be fatal:

with no advantage from inside a locked boot, I would need to be alert when Liz stopped the car.

After a while, the rocking became smoother and more rhythmical. Liz had turned on to a better road, a motorway, perhaps. Despite myself, the hypnotic movement lulled me to sleep. I lurched awake when we went over a bump. It was still light. I hadn't been dozing long.

I forced myself to think about what was going to happen. Liz couldn't let me live, not now that I knew everything. And what was one more murder, after all? But how would she do it? Drugs were out of the question. Too strong a connection with Wilson's death. Would she cave my head in as she had Harry's? Colonel Mustard did it with the ice axe in the conservatory. No, that was wrong: it would have to be lead piping since Liz no longer had an ice axe. Nor did she own a gun. She wouldn't even know how to use one.

And where in God's name were we going? Why didn't she murder me in my flat and make it look like aggravated burglary? She could wash the gore off herself in my shower. Ah, but she'd been clever wearing two snow-suits. And when she'd murdered Harry, both suits had been red. Had she planned that nauseating detail? Of course she had.

But she couldn't butcher me the way she had Harry. She would have to make it look like an accident, as with Denny. A terrifying possibility ballooned like a phantom: she'd push the car into the river Tay with me in the boot. I pictured the water level rising while I beat and kicked from inside. It would be difficult to explain, though, how I'd managed to lock myself into the boot before getting the Peugeot into the river. And, anyway, I'd drowned once before and Fate doesn't strike in the same way twice. But whatever Liz might try, I'd put up a fight – I still had pieces left on the board – because I was a survivor. That was what Hallengren had said and he'd been right about that, if nothing else.

I dozed fitfully. A while later, we cruised to a stop. The engine died, and the car juddered as Liz jerked the handbrake. I waited, my heart beating violently. There was the sudden scratching of a key in the lock. I resisted the compelling urge to struggle out fighting, and feigned unconsciousness, keeping my breathing slow and even.

The door of the boot was flung back and light streamed in. I smelt salt air and rotting seaweed. Gulls cried overhead. Were we on the north-east coast? Or had Liz driven south?

A large shape blotted out the light, and I smelt something warm and sensuous. Liz was wearing Paris. She wrapped her arms round my body and pulled hard. It was more of a roll than a pull, as even a strong man would find it difficult to lift someone out of the boot of a car. My body balanced on the lip, and then she released me. I fell face downwards, scratching my cheek on the metal clasp. As I rolled on to the ground, the sweet smell of wet grass filled my nostrils.

She manoeuvred me into a sitting position and propped me up against the boot. I kept my eyes closed, letting my head loll forward. Her face was close to mine and I could hear her laboured breathing as she waited for her strength to return. But she still had the advantage. I had little chance from a sitting position, even with Liz out of breath. She took a huge gulp of air, gripped my arms and, tugging them smartly, pulled me up and over her shoulder.

I opened my eyes and saw grass inches from my face. Liz was on her knees. With what must have been a superhuman effort, she staggered to her feet. Swaying dangerously, she stumbled forward, stopping briefly to shift my weight on her shoulder. I lifted my head to get my bearings. We were lurching towards the front of the car.

I was about to kick and punch when she stopped at the driver's door. She leant in and dropped me unceremoniously on to the front seat, letting my head bang against the doorframe. After a brief pause, she lifted my legs into the car and positioned them over the pedals. Something soft brushed my cheek and I smelt her fragrance again. I half opened my eyes, seeing the fur hood of her parka close to my face. With a rapid movement, she yanked the seatbelt across my body and snapped it shut. Then she released the handbrake, and sprang out of the car.

Nothing happened. She swore softly, and marched to the boot.

Panic swept through me as I realised I'd lost my best chance of escape. No longer caring if she saw me, I opened my eyes wide and looked around rapidly. Seagulls were wheeling and dipping across the expanse of grey sky, their sharp cries fracturing the silence.

We were on the edge of a cliff. She'd meant the car to go over, and me with it. It would look like an accident. She'd tell the police I'd taken her car without permission. Dr Langley would testify to my unbalanced state of mind. And Liz would get away with murder again.

I peered into the rear-view mirror, trying to see what she was doing, but she was behind the boot. She hadn't shut it after she'd rolled me on to the grass and she didn't bother to shut it now. I couldn't see her. And that meant she couldn't see me.

Suddenly, I felt the car sway. It inched forward. But Liz had made a fatal mistake – she'd left the driver's door open. With fumbling hands, I released the catch on the seatbelt and, gripping the doorframe, hurled myself out.

I fell and rolled heavily, coming to a stop several feet from the door. The Peugeot was moving briskly, gathering momentum.

The bonnet dipped sickeningly as the car balanced on the cliff edge, its back wheels spinning in the air. Then, with a sound like the splintering of bone, it tipped over and plunged towards the sea. Another second and I'd have gone with it. I didn't wait to see what Liz was doing – I scrambled to my feet and ran.

My heels skidded on the wet earth and I crashed to the ground. Before I could struggle to my feet, something heavy landed on my back, smashing me face downwards. My mouth filled with mud, and I gagged, trying desperately to pull my head clear. I kicked frantically, pushing against the ground, and somehow managed to twist my body round. Liz lay on top of me like a crazed lover, hands at my throat, her face so close I could hear the rasp of her breath.

It was then that I saw how close we were to the edge. I stopped writhing, terrified we would roll over, and clawed at her eyes. She threw her head back, arching her body to escape my fingers. Before I could push her away, she released her grip and started to bring her knees up. If she succeeded in straddling me, the game would be over. I bucked wildly, pounding my fists against her chest. As she perched on one knee and brought the other forward, I twisted my body and, with all the strength left in me, pushed her off. She overbalanced and rolled away with a cry. A second later, she was over the cliff.

I pulled myself on to my elbows, gasping convulsively, and dragged my body towards the edge.

The fall seemed endless. Liz bounced off the jagged slope, performing slow cartwheels like a grotesque acrobat, her agonised screaming stopping only when she hit the rocks far below. She lay in the obscene position that only a broken body can assume, her limbs splayed like a limp rag doll's, as the tide crept over her. The receding water left behind a dark stain, which grew slowly, only to be washed away with each wave. On the left were the burning remains of the Peugeot. I hadn't heard it crash, let alone explode.

I lay on the muddy grass, with the gulls screaming overhead, and watched the tide ebb and flow over Liz's body until they came and took me away.

CHAPTER 33

'My name's DI Gorska and this is DS Randall.'

I'd half expected this, an interview with detectives. The local Grampian police were more used to breaking up Friday-night fights than investigating deaths. Although they'd questioned me at the time, I was too numb with shock to tell them much, so it hadn't come as much of a surprise when, a few days later, I received a call from Dundee's West Bell Street police station, requesting I come in.

'We'd like to ask you a few questions about the accident,' the DI said. She had hazel eyes and thick blonde-brown hair. And a Polish accent.

'I told the local police everything I know,' I said.

'I understand that, Miss Stewart, but the preliminary reports have come in, and we'd like to go over your statement again.'

I nodded, keeping my expression neutral. I'd gone over my statement too, and was ready with the answers. The DI's sidekick, a skinny woman with messy dark hair, was watching me with an expression of challenge in her eyes. I was immediately reminded of Hallengren and Engqvist. Perhaps I was in for the good-cop-bad-cop routine again.

DI Gorska opened a folder. From where I was sitting, I could see a photo of the area near the cliff edge, with circles round the wheel marks and muddy footprints.

'Can you tell me what you were doing so far north of Dundee, Miss Stewart?' the inspector said, looking up.

This was a question I'd anticipated. 'Liz and I often go for drives to beauty spots,' I said, trying to keep my voice casual. 'And the cliffs up there are spectacular.'

'And you left from her house?'

'That's right.'

'But she didn't take her children.'

'No, she'd left them with a friend.' I tried a smile. 'Annie and Lucy aren't that keen on the great outdoors. Or sitting quietly in a car.'

Mention of the twins dragged me back to that day. After the local police had finished questioning me, a female officer had accompanied me to Liz's house so I could retrieve my handbag. It was lying in the hall where I'd dropped it, an oversight on Liz's part, but the only one. She'd cleaned up the vomit, and disposed of the newspaper cutting, syringes and drugs. Just as the officer and I were leaving, Siobhan rang Liz's landline because there was no answer from her mobile. She asked when she should bring the twins home.

'And neither you nor Miss Hallam were wearing seatbelts,' the DI was saying. 'Why is that?'

'We'd had them on for most of the trip. But we'd stopped earlier to look at the scenery.' I shrugged. 'We must have forgotten to clip them back on.'

'Strange that both of you forgot,' the skinny detective chipped in, sitting back and folding her arms.

I said nothing.

'And it was Miss Hallam who was behind the wheel, I take it, since she was wearing driving gloves,' DI Gorska said.

'That's right.'

'So what happened? Why did you go right up to the edge?'

'I think Liz simply didn't realise how close we were. It was muddy, she lost control of the car, and it started to go over the cliff.' I ran a hand over my face. 'I called out to her, and the next thing I know I'd opened the door and jumped clear. It must have been instinct. I only just got out in time.'

'If you were sitting in the passenger seat, how did you come to be lying on the ground on the driver's side?'

I was starting to wilt under the Polish detective's gaze. 'I must have been in shock. I couldn't get up. I remember crawling across the mud to the cliff edge.'

'Why do you think Miss Hallam didn't jump out?'

'I guess people's reactions are different.'

DI Gorska flicked through the report. 'Forensics corroborate that she'd been drinking. They found a high level of alcohol in her bloodstream.'

'I had no idea she'd been drinking,' I murmured.

'But no alcohol was found in your bloodstream.' The inspector glanced up. 'Only a trace of Phenonal.'

'I've been having trouble sleeping.'

She leant forward. 'What's been bothering us is that in your statement you say that Miss Hallam didn't jump out. But her body was found *outside* the car.' When I didn't reply, she added, 'It suggests she must have got the door open before the car went over. Did you see her do that?'

I gazed at her helplessly. 'I'm afraid I was too busy struggling out of the car myself.'

The DI glanced at the other officer. 'I did hear of a similar case. Witnesses saw the driver thrown out of a van that had gone over a cliff.'

'So what happens now?' I said, after a pause.

'There'll be a hearing. You'll be asked to testify.' She smiled. 'But I think we'll be looking for a verdict of death by misadventure.'

I was relieved nothing would be made of the seatbelt issue. Maybe they realised that not having to fumble for the catch had probably given me the extra precious seconds that had saved my life.

DI Gorska closed the folder. 'You're free go, Miss Stewart.' Her gaze bored into mine. 'Unless there's something you want to add?' she said slowly.

I shook my head, wondering what she was reading in my face.

If someone had asked me why I'd kept quiet about Liz and the murders at the Ice Hotel, I would have said it no longer mattered. I'd had the truth. And Harry had had his justice. Also, a part of me didn't want Annie and Lucy growing up knowing their mother was a murderer. It was bad enough that in time they would learn about their father. As for what became of them, I heard that a young married cousin of Liz's had offered to take them. Liz's parents, destroyed by their daughter's death, were unable to look after their grandchildren. Thanks to Harry's generosity – the bulk of his not inconsiderable estate was left to Liz's children in trust – the twins would be well provided for. They were taken to somewhere in Dorset, and the house in Abercromby Street put up for sale. I doubted I would ever see them again.

There was one piece of unfinished business. Yet I knew that it would expose Liz, her lies and plans, and ultimately ruin the lives of her children. I thought long and hard before making the decision. Someday, I might visit Kiruna and tell Hallengren everything. But until then, Denny Hinckley would have no memorial. He would remain a statistic, one more person on the missing list, his body slowly disintegrating in some northern sea.

I continued my visits to Dr Langley. We rarely spoke of Liz and the accident. She knew I was keeping something from her – there was little that could get past those watchful eyes – and she couldn't have failed to notice that my mental health improved rapidly after Liz's death. But she didn't question me, holding her wheesht, as they say here. Our sessions became easier and shorter until, one day, she pronounced me well enough to go it alone.

'So I'm cured?' I said, in surprise.

'You'll never be completely cured, Maggie. Few people are who've had your experiences.' She smiled her Julia Roberts smile. 'But you're the next best thing.'

I've been back at work for nearly a year, slowly picking up the threads and weaving them into a new life. It's not as neat and finely crafted as before but it's a garment that functions well enough. There is the odd flaw in the fabric – the dream visits me from time to time – but the material becomes less likely to unravel the more I wear it.

The dream when it does come is strangely different. I walk through the seemingly endless rooms of the dark house, no longer fearful of reaching the bathroom. When I find it and peer into the bath, the water is clear and sweet-smelling. The plug pulls easily and the water drains away, leaving behind tendrils of blonde hair.

Making new friends hasn't been easy, but Harry's colleagues still invite me to their parties. Keeping old friends has been more difficult. I found it hard to forget I once suspected Mike of killing Harry. I came to dread our chance encounters, the looking everywhere but at each other, the small-talk. We never took our friendship to the next level and, more to his regret than mine, grew apart. Although he accepted the official version of events surrounding Liz's death, he knew I was concealing something. But I've no intention of telling him the truth about Liz. That's my secret, the secret bequeathed to me by the Ice Hotel before it melted back into the river.

A month ago, I ran into him in the Overgate.

'Well, now, I'm glad I've seen you, Maggie,' he said slowly. 'I've been meaning to ring.'

I smiled. We both knew it was a lie.

'How have you been, Mike?'

'Never better.' He looked discreetly at his watch. 'I'd love to stay and talk but I need to crack on. There's packing to be done.'

'A holiday?'

'I'm moving to Stockholm for good. Looks as if Mane Drew's Swedish branch can't get it together without me.'

'You know you'll be leaving behind several broken hearts in Accounts Payable.'

He smiled his impish smile, the one that made him look like a boy.

Stockholm. Realisation moved slowly through my brain.

I gripped his sleeve, searching his eyes as if I could read the truth there. 'It's you, isn't it?' I brought my face closer to his. 'You can tell me, I won't do anything about it, I swear.'

'And tell you what, now?'

'The hotel killings. It's you, isn't it?'

'Is that what you really believe, Maggie?' he said sadly. He gazed at me for what seemed like an eternity. But his facial muscles betrayed him.

He walked away, leaving a silence, my last link to the past. I watched him go without regret.

As for Liz, in an inexplicable way I miss her, although what I miss is not the Liz lying in her winding sheet but the old Liz I'd known in another life.

And Harry? I miss him most of all – his sense of humour, his integrity and that funny way he had of peering over his glasses. I still have an old pair held together with sticking plaster, which he'd absent-mindedly left in my flat.

I visited Balgay Cemetery yesterday and tidied his grave, hunching my back against the scouring wind. The cemetery is untidy at this time of year, and the grass, which isn't cut until spring, had grown so thick and coarse over Harry's grave that it was no longer possible to tell where the coffin had been lowered into the ground. I replaced the dry flowers and got to my feet, turning quickly away from the simple black headstone watching in silent accusation. I'd once felt that I had a responsibility towards the dead. Not any more. I could rest in peace.

I removed a carnation from the vase and threaded it into my lapel. Without a backward glance, I left the cemetery, my feet crunching against the dark gravel.

The first snow of winter fell this morning, a light covering, veiling the garden in white.

I sat in the living room watching a solitary robin tug at a holly berry, red as carnations. As it came away, the branch shook, jolting the robin from his perch and sending a shower of snow into the air. He flew around the garden, then settled back on the branch, fluffing out his feathers in righteous indignation.

I watched for a while longer, then turned away.

Hallengren was right. I'd been through bad times. But I'd survived them. What I needed now was a change of scene. My gaze fell upon the travel brochures scattered across the floor. I would take a holiday.

Somewhere warm.

ACKNOWLEDGEMENTS

I owe a huge debt of gratitude to my agent, Jenny Brown, for her support, and for suggesting ways in which this novel could be improved. I am also deeply grateful to Hazel Orme for doing such a magnificent job of editing. Any errors in the text are mine and not hers. My thanks also go to the team at Little, Brown – especially Krystyna Green and Amanda Keats – for all their hard work in getting the novel to publication.